THEM AND US

BY PAUL RAND

the sequel to
JOE WITH AN E

To Janet
Best wishes
Paul

Beaten Track
www.beatentrackpublishing.com

Them and Us

First published 2024 by Beaten Track Publishing
Copyright © 2024 Paul Rand
Cover Art Copyright © 2024 Amelia Rand

All rights reserved.

No part of this publication may be reproduced, stored in a retrieval system, or transmitted, in any form or by any means, without the prior permission of the publisher, nor be otherwise circulated without the publisher's prior consent in any form of binding or cover other than that in which it is published and without a similar condition including this condition being imposed on the subsequent publisher.

The moral right of the author has been asserted.

Paperback: 978 1 78645 649 6
eBook: 978 1 78645 650 2

Beaten Track Publishing,
Burscough, Lancashire.
www.beatentrackpublishing.com

* * *

This novel includes scenes and themes which may be upsetting to some readers. A list of content warnings can be found at the back of the book (p. 395).

Author's Note

A little over halfway through *Joe with an E*, Joe, Nats and Cain leave their island sanctuary, off the west coast of Scotland, and begin their journey across Britain. They leave behind a collection of 'secondary characters' who inhabit the island.

The beginning of *Them and Us* takes us back to the island. Whilst I know all these other characters quite well, I realise that my readers do not, having left them behind to join Joe, Nats and Cain on their adventure.

For those who would like to know who's who in the island community, I hope the following will be helpful. If you'd rather just get on with the story, do skip straight to Chapter 1.

The undisputed leader of the island community is red-headed Sandra who is also the younger sister of Jay Taylor – the nurse who, in chapter 2 of *Joe with an E*, gives Georgy and Cris the news that their baby is a boy. At first, the island community was led by both Sandra and Tom. But things went sour between the pair after Sandra persuaded Tom to try to have a baby with her and he got the wrong end of the stick, thinking that Sandra was romantically attracted to him. In fact, the person she really loves is Eva. So Tom withdrew from the island community, finding himself a 'hovel' to live in on the other side of the island. Tom was also the one who caught Joe, Nats and Cain trying to leave the island and ended up helping to push their boat off.

At the same time as Sandra and Tom tried for a baby, Sandra encouraged Eva to do the same with Anthony. Both girls became pregnant and gave birth to the island's first babies Katie (born to Sandra) and Peter (born to Eva). Subsequently, Eva has another baby, Grace, whose father is also Anthony. Sandra and Eva live together as a couple, co-parenting Katie, Peter and Grace, and later adopting four-year-old Charlie who was the sole survivor of the boat wreck in chapter 18 of *Joe with an E*.

Anthony also became the father of various other babies with other girls on the island and stepped into Tom's shoes as co-leader of the island with Sandra.

There are four other named islanders in *Them and Us*:

Vicki, who runs the island café and was also the one who molested Joe in chapter 6 of *Joe with an E*.

Sally and her son Mikey. They got a brief mention in *Joe with an E* as Sally is pregnant with Mikey when Joe first arrives on the island.

Maisy, who was not mentioned by name in *Joe with an E* but is a slightly younger than some of the others – Sandra, Eva and Sally – and is spokesperson for a group which is beginning to question Sandra's leadership.

I hope you enjoy reading *Them and Us* as much as I enjoyed writing it. As with *Joe with an E*, we have chosen to use an accessible typeface – Atkinson Hyperlegible – and left-aligned rather than justified text, which is recognised as being helpful for those with dyslexia. Different is Good.

A key theme of this book is parenthood –
its joys and its challenges. So I dedicate it
to Martha and Amos, who are a joy.

Part 1

Chapter 1

Eva

Eva leapt to her feet and squinted out across the sparkling sea, searching for the source of the mechanical hum. The labouring ewe bleated with alarm, or was it just the next squeeze? Eva knew what that felt like and marvelled at how little fuss her woolly sisters made each spring, when it was their turn. She crouched back down and stroked the ewe's greasy coat.

'Sorry, old girl, did I startle you? I should be focusing on you. Not that you need my help really, do you? You're doing just fine.'

The ewe's bass-note reply, deeper than even Tom could manage, almost masked the other sound that had got Eva to her feet in the first place. Some sort of engine. But there was nothing out on the water today; no fishers to keep a watchful eye on, no nosy day-trippers to scare away. They'd long given up hope of Jay keeping their promise to bring one final boatload of children across.

The spring breeze, filled with promise of warmer days, now carried a constant purr. Definitely mechanical. Human-made, not natural, yet no boats in sight. Could a sound like that carry all the way from the mainland? But no, that didn't make sense. Today, the wind was in the west. No boat ever came from the west.

Eva straightened up again and turned to face into the wind, now gathering speed. Water leaked from the corners of her eyes and was blown towards her ears. She squinted and raised her hand to block out the white sun. A bee buzzed towards her. No, too big for a bee. Further away but thundering ever closer. A sort of flying car? Yes, there was sunlight glinting off what must be windows. Was this one of the machines from the stories her parents had told? Machines they had dreamed of putting back into the sky...before they'd left all that behind to move somewhere she wouldn't be discovered.

It hung right above the centre of the island now, radiating shock waves, pulling the sky downwards to stop itself from dropping like a stone. Katie and Charlie would love watch this. Peter and Grace, not so much. But of course, everyone, wherever they were on the island, would be witnessing this. Except even now, Sandra would be ushering everyone inside. Particularly the little ones.

Eva should have probably hidden herself, at least crouched back down beside the sheep and made herself less obvious to whatever eyes must be scouring the ground from those windows up there. Sandra would have every right to blame her if the machine settled and people streamed out of it to hunt them down.

The machine tilted forwards, circled back towards the endless western sea. A mix of relief and disappointment washed over her, as she fully expected the flying car to disappear back to wherever it had come from. Should she wave her arms at them – show the driver this was the right island, if this meant the world beyond had welcomed Nats, Cain, and Joe, and now searched for the rest of them? But what if whoever this was, wasn't a friend? What if the neuts had now created flying machines? Too late if that was the case; the air around her now shouted even louder as the machine began to descend. It was going to land right in the middle of the oat fields.

The machine dipped out of sight, its roar echoing off the hills. Then the sound of a distant memory invaded her – the slowing, lowering whine signalling the end of the washing machine cycle. The day before she'd left, her parents had insisted on washing every item of clothing she possessed, even though they all knew she'd fit less than half of them in the one rucksack they'd bought. Her parents would love to be here, marvelling at the fantastical flying machine with her. Or would they be pulling her away, shielding her eyes from the sight and even now packing bags ready to escape again?

The ewe's final push was celebrated with a congratulatory chorus from all her fellow mothers, then the first faltering bleat from tiny new lungs that would soon know exactly how they could be used to find their mother.

'Oh, well done, old girl. See, you didn't need my help at all, did you?'

Eva hurried the soggy newborn towards her mother. The sooner she could see the mother had accepted baby, the sooner she could go in search of the flying machine.

That was what she planned to do, wasn't it? Sandra would be furious – would want her back at the village, not striking out on her own to investigate. She and Anthony would already be arguing over how to deal with the mystery vehicle that had dropped out of the sky. But it would only take Eva ten minutes from here to get over to the oat fields. It made sense to go and look, and then report back to the village.

Eva's heart thumped almost as fast as the pulse of the flying machine before it went silent. What would

Sandra be planning? It wouldn't work to hide until the invaders left, not this time, and they had no boat to escape on. Even if they'd still had Joe's little boat, it could only have saved a few of them. Eva felt a sudden chill. Who would they choose to rescue? The children, probably, But who would go with them, and where would they go? And what about all the babies? She pulled on the thick woollen jumper that had been tied around her waist.

The ewe uttered a weary but healthy bleat, to which the lamb gave an enthusiastic reply. *Leave us alone now, we'll be fine.*

Yes, but what about the island's human residents?

Chapter 2

Nats

What now? What do I do if he doesn't come back? I've got to assume now that he won't. Not after four days. Or is it five? How do people even keep track of the days – whether it's Monday or Tuesday, Friday or Wednesday? Joe always seemed to know. What will I do without him? He knew when it was safe for us to walk during the day – when we wouldn't be stopped for not being in school. I wouldn't have a clue. How will I know it's safe to move again?

Ouch! Not today. Yesterday, I thought my ankle was fully better, but I must have slept on it funny. It was a non-school day when I first twisted it. I know that because he was so ratty with me that day, because we could have gone all day without stopping. But it wasn't my fault I tripped on a tree root. If anything, it was his fault because it was him who suggested pitching our tent on the edge of the golfing field. At least, I think it was his idea. There were some days when we'd reach the same conclusion at exactly the same moment. There were others when we didn't get each other at all – when even if I explained what I was thinking really, really carefully, he'd still have that blank look on his face. Or he'd say, *'Yes, I know, but...'* and then repeat back to me an argument that was almost exactly what I was saying but somehow still disagreeing with me. Is that why he didn't come back? Had he finally had enough of me?

I must have been horrible to be with, those last few days. I'm sorry, Joe. Please come back.

It must be only four days since you left, because last time you went shopping you bought two packs of bread rolls. I need you back, so you can show me again which coins are which. I don't mind choosing what to buy, but I get confused when it comes to paying. Our island tops are so much easier – all worth the same, no matter what colour or size they are.

So anyway, we started and finished the first pack of rolls just before you left. It was a bit greedy, but we were hungry. *'I can always pick up some more from the shop on my way back,'* you said.

He wouldn't have said that if he was planning to leave me, would he? He is a planner, but not a pretender. What I mean is, he wouldn't plan to leave me and then intentionally say something to pretend he wasn't.

Which means you can't come back. Either you're lying injured in a ditch somewhere, or you've been caught. Maybe you got onto the boat for a closer look at the controls while the fisher was off buying chips? But then the fisher came back. Would you have dared? I would have, but you're not me.

I could eat some chips now, I reckon – stuffed between the two halves of one of my remaining bread rolls. He promised to bring some back for us that night. My tummy must have been rumbling right up until I fell asleep. But I woke up and it was morning, and there were no chips and no Joe. So I opened the new packet of rolls and ate one of those instead, to keep me going until he got back. I've done the same each morning since, and now there are two left. So it's been four days. Or will it now be five because I'm about to eat another one, leaving one on its own in the packet? What will I eat the day after tomorrow?

I've still got the rest of the money, so I could go and find a shop. I've even got the book of maps, if I can work out how to read it. You'd said you didn't need it anymore – that you'd stick out less if you weren't carrying it. But what if it could have helped you escape? That's another reason you must have been planning to come back. You'd have taken at least some of the stuff with you. I probably wouldn't have noticed, even if you'd taken your blanket, though I've been glad to still have it while you've been gone –

What was that? I sit up and hold my breath. The stone we'd found to hold the barn door shut has just scraped across the concrete. Hidden behind the rusty old tractor, I can't actually see the door from here, but it's definitely now open a crack. There's a stripe of light down the wall to my right, and the smell of the manure heap wafts in.

'Joe, is that you?' Why did I do that? Stupid! Joe would be round here by now if it was him. Can't be him. I try to suck the words back out of the air. No sound. Maybe I was imagining it. Maybe it was only a strong gust of wind.

At first, I honestly thought it was Charlie, the little face peering at me from behind the enormous tractor wheel; so like the frightened but trusting face that I first met wrapped in blankets on that horrendous stormy night. Like then, I needed to act like everything was going to be fine.

'Hello, I'm Nats. What's your name? Don't worry about me. I'm just resting here for a while. No need for anyone else to know. You won't go and tell anyone else I'm here, will you?' OK, I'm starting to sound a bit nervous now. I roll up my trouser leg to expose my still-bruised ankle. It looked even more impressive a couple of days ago. The child probably can't even see the bruises in the dim light of this barn. 'I just need to stay a little bit longer for this to get better, see?'

I put on my most confident smile and look up, but the face has gone. The breeze wrapping itself around me tells me the barn door's still open, even wider than before. Crap! What now?

Right. I can't take Joe's bag with me as well as my own, but I should probably take as many of his clothes as I can carry – in case I find him, or in case I bleed all over my trousers again. I'm sure I must be due another bleed sometime soon. I shove all the clothes in, and my bag is already overflowing. I'd better take the book of maps too, but I could carry that in my hand and put the money in my pocket. Oh crap, I must be almost out of time already. How many minutes will it take for the kid to get to wherever there are adults? Will they come and find me straight away or will they take some persuading?

I'm going to be caught, I know it, and then I'll be put to sleep and given my operation to turn me into a neut. If they do put us to sleep. Anthony said sometimes they didn't. Joe and Cain have probably already had their operations. Mine would be different to theirs. Hani once told us about a girl who had died after her operation. *'Why do the neuts do it if it kills us?'* Vicki had asked. *'They didn't think we should exist anyway,'* was the reply. Oh crap, I don't want to die, and I don't want to be a neut!

I swing the bulging bag onto my shoulder and shove behind the tractor wheel what I'm leaving behind. What if Joe hasn't been captured? What if he's stuck somewhere, injured like me, or trapped like we were in the scrapyard? What if even now he's on his way here to find me again? Could I still hide here – tuck myself in behind the tractor wheel with all my stuff? Or should I leave everything and run? Come on, got to decide, one or the other.

Something thuds to the floor. What have I dropped? Is it something important? Not if I'm leaving everything here. A large, wrinkled apple rolls to a stop by my feet, showing me it's impressive bruises. *Thud!* And another. Where are these apples coming from? Joe hadn't bought any apples last time he shopped. I told him not to because they taste disgusting at this time of year. Apples are only good for eating raw in autumn and winter.

I spin around, perhaps a bit too fast because at that moment, the kid drops all the rest of the apples. I look past them, which isn't hard, given how little they are, searching for the adult who's surely followed them in.

'D'you like apples?'

I barely hear the question the first time it's asked. Satisfied that, for the moment, I'm not about to be wrestled to the floor by someone bigger than me, I dare to stare straight at the kid. Have you really come back alone?

'I got some apples. D'you like apples?' the kid repeats, quieter than before, but then I am concentrating on what they're saying this time.

'Thank you, yes, I like apples.' I can't be picky at the moment, can I?

The kid nods and is gone. I hope they've not gone to get more apples. The tumble of apples now littering the floor is more than enough, unless they come back with a jam pan and a stove.

The kid hasn't come back, either with more apples
or with the equipment needed to make jam, or with
a parent or police officer to take me away and turn
me into a neut. The apples are brown in the middle,
as well as on the outside, but together with the other
food I've got left, they'll keep me going for a few more
days of waiting for Joe to come back, so I won't be out
looking for more food when he comes, and I won't be
seen coming or going by whatever adult the kid belongs
to. Even if they come into the barn, I'll be out of sight
here – this tractor can't have been moved for years.

The door-stop-stone scrapes across the concrete some
more. I shuffle back behind the front of the tractor.

'D'you like sandwich?' a timid voice breathes.

I shuffle from my hiding place. Already the sandwich
is summoning my nose. Two doorsteps of something
not quite our island oatbread but a world away from the
bland fluffy rolls I've had to put up with recently. A pink
chunk of ham hangs precariously between the child's
greasy fingers. I can't let that fall to the ground. When
was the last time I had proper meat?

I lurch forward. The kid takes a startled step back.
'Sorry.' I grab the sandwich just as the kid is about
to let it fall apart on its way to the floor. 'Thank you,'
I remember to say before my mouth is too full to speak.
I feel rude as I edge back into the shadows. I should
try to befriend this kid in case they think I'm being
ungrateful and decide to betray me. I lick my fingers
and swallow the last bite as I try to work out what to say
and how to say it. But the kid is already gone.

Chapter 3

Eva

THE MACHINE PERCHED in the nest it had carved for itself amongst the unripe oats. If this was some sort of rescue, Sandra would still be livid about the oats. The machine's 'wings', if that's what you could call them, drooped towards the ground, now they were no longer spinning. How did such slim blades hold all that up in the air?

More oats had been trodden down into a path leading from the machine's nest to the edge of the field. There, two identically clad figures stood, hunched over something flat and black held by one of them – something about the size and shape of a large book. A few metres away in either direction, two others, guards, constantly circled, scanning their surroundings through masks that stretched from forehead to neck. In fact, yes, although the two in the centre had their backs to her, Eva could see that all four were similarly masked, as if the wonderful fresh island air would somehow poison them. Who were these people?

Eva gasped and ducked down into a crouch behind a bush not tall enough to hide her. One of the guards stopped, facing only a few degrees away from her and raised...yes, it had to be a gun held out in front of them. Had they seen someone? What if Vicki had told the children to go out and play for a bit and their games had led them away from the village, out to here? Eva couldn't breathe. The children wouldn't know what a gun was. She tried to pick out the same spot the stationary guard was staring at. Could she see movement? If only she had the watch binoculars.

She should move, draw their attention away, towards something that was definitely moving. Her pulse throbbed in her neck. If she stood up now, they wouldn't shoot, would they?

Eva pulled her knees under her, placed her hands flat on the grass and eased onto her feet, instinctively holding her hands up and out to show she held no weapon. A shout shot towards her, whistling past her ear without making any sense. She flinched but forced herself to stay on her feet. Her heart threatened to explode with the pressure, but she was still standing, not downed by a bullet. The two in the centre had turned. All four were now staring at her. She swallowed her fear, at least tried to, cleared her throat, but couldn't find any words to call back. More shouts, this time between the four companions, without any of them taking their eyes off her. The two sentries lowered their guns but not their guard.

The one holding the black book thing raised a hand in a wave and, no longer hunched, revealed their slim but curved figure. Eva gasped again. Female. Definitely female, under the hat, mask and clothes. So not neuts. Not sent by the government or police. Maybe from Anthony's 'world beyond'. Perhaps they'd been right when they speculated that Nats, Cain and Joe had selected themselves for Anthony's mission, without even telling him, and had gone in search of the world beyond. If so, was this evidence they had succeeded, that they'd made contact with other non-neut humans? Humans with technology far superior to anything anyone in the world Eva knew.

These people, whoever they were, were no picnicking day-trippers who could be scared off by a few ghostly hoots. And surely it was a good thing to be found, wasn't it? Many here had long dreamt of finding a bigger world of people like them; of no longer needing to hide; of no longer stressing over how to stay warm, dry and healthy through the next winter.

The female stepped forwards and called out again to Eva, but whatever it was she said was lost in the mask, or down the tube protruding from it. Eva didn't dare to move; those guns still looked ready to put a hole in her at a moment's notice. The female set out towards her. The guards didn't like that and called after her. The female stopped, turned, gabbled something to her companions, looked back towards Eva, dared to take a few more steps forwards, putting more distance between herself and the guards. She waved again, then beckoned, then shouted slow, purposeful syllables.

'Can...yoooo...*something*...slewly toovards...uz?' She beckoned again in such an over exaggerated way, which would have been comical had Eva been able to control her quivering limbs.

Keeping her aching arms outstretched, flitting her eyes from one guard to the other, Eva stepped her way down the hill. The female continued to beckon as if directing traffic until, when Eva was little more than three metres from her, she gave the firm signal to stop.

Although her accent was strange, Eva understood what the female said next perfectly well without the accompanying hand gestures, even through the muffling of the mask that tried to seal the words in, along with whatever air she was breathing in there.

'My name is Maggie. We're friends of Joe. What is your name?'

Chapter 4

Nats

Right, I've thought it all through logically, like you would, Joe, and here's why I've decided to stay here, for now.

I pick at the perished rubber of the old tractor tyre to help me concentrate. I need a pee but can't go until it's darker outside.

Firstly, if you've been caught, which I've convinced myself (almost) that you must have been - oh, please don't let it be true - then you can't have told them, yet, where I am. Are they hurting you to try to get you to talk? Please no. I can't bear to think of what they must have done to you. If you'd told them already, they'd have been here days ago, hauling me out of hiding. So you must still be holding out. Don't let them torture you Joe - tell them where I am. I don't care anymore. Maybe I should give myself up so they don't hurt you, but then what if you haven't been caught? Oh, I don't know.

Stop it! Think like Joe. Right. Secondly, they will be looking for me. Or still looking for us, if they haven't got you yet. They knew there were two of us, so if they have captured you round here somewhere, they'll definitely be on the lookout for me. I wonder how many people they've got searching for me. So anyway, if I go wandering off down to Dover or walk into some shop somewhere or even take a walk down the road, I'm putting myself in more danger than I'm in by staying here, even though Lottie knows I'm here.

Lottie's the name I've given to the kid, by the way. I don't know her actual name because she never stays long enough for me to ask. Yes, I know she's a neut, so I shouldn't really call her 'she', but to me, she's a girl. I've got this theory, Joe, that actually some neuts are really a 'him' or a 'her' inside; they just haven't got the right bits on the outside to show it. Does that make sense? At first, Lottie reminded me of Charlie, who is, of course, a boy, so because she's like Charlie but a girl, I thought maybe I could call her Charlotte.

A big chunk of rubber from the tyre comes off in my hand, and I start to break it into pieces.

Do you remember that game we used to play – you, Cain and me, when we were on the island? The one where we'd think up names for each other if we'd been a boy instead of a girl, or a girl instead of a boy? Cain hated it when we called him Caitie, and little Katie thought it was hilarious, which made it all the more fun. You were boring, insisting you'd just be Jo if you were a girl. If we called you Joanna, which is what Jo is usually short for anyway, you said that was silly because it was just two names stuck together – Jo and Anna – but it really was a name they used to give to girls. Why do lots of girls names end in an 'A'? Joanna, Victoria, Sandra, Eva, Matilda, Natasha. Urghh, I hate that last one. Even though I am a girl, I'd prefer Nathan or Nathaniel any day, if I can't just be Nats. At least then nobody could ever call me Tasha, which doesn't even start with the right letter.

Anyway, do you remember when Charlie started spending time with us and I said we needed to think of a girl name for him? Cain was so quick to say that

Charlie would be Charlotte. He almost buried us in books to find the one called *Jane Ayre*, written by a person called Charlotte, who Cain said was definitely female. And he said Charlotte and her two sisters were all famous book writers but at first, they pretended to be men because people then didn't believe women could write. People then must have been even more stupid than neuts are now.

That's another reason why I've decided that although Lottie is a neut, she must really be a girl inside. So, I've shortened Charlotte to Lottie. Yes, I know it doesn't start with the same letter, like Tasha doesn't either, but how else can you shorten Charlotte? Char doesn't work, and the only other option is Charlie, which just doesn't sound like a girl to me. Of course, Cain said Charlie was sort of short for Charles, which is stupid because it's exactly the same number of letters. He had lots of books by a man called Charles who wrote stories about people being poor and badly treated. But it always worked out well for the poor people in the end – do you remember? I wish we'd brought some of those books with us. Not *Jane Ayre*. That was too miserable. If you do come back, please don't be blind and injured like Mr Rochester was.

I really need to pee. Is it dark enough out there yet? I don't think so. Just give it a bit longer. A few more minutes, not that I have any idea how long a minute is, stuck in here.

I'm as miserable as Jane, here on my own. But I've decided to stay because firstly, they can't have found out from you where I am. And secondly, because they probably are looking for me, so it's best if I stay hidden, at least for a bit longer, so I'm not caught like Oliver Twist was, except it worked out all right for him in the end, because they found out he was related to the old rich man and it wasn't really his mum's fault he'd been left in the horrible workhouse. A bit like it's not our parents' fault they couldn't keep us. I wonder if my parents are still alive. Not that the farm was like the workhouse in *Oliver Twist*. It was actually more like Fagin's, except Hani was no Fagin because we were made to stay at the farm while Hani went out to get what we needed, whereas Fagin sent the children out to bring things back for him. *Get to the point, Nats!*

OK, sorry. Well, thirdly, I've decided to stay here because I don't know what else to do. At least here I'm being fed, even if it is only cold sandwiches and bruised, wrinkled apples, and I can stay warm under the extra blankets Lottie brought me yesterday. If I left, I'd have to decide where to go. Even if I did get as far as finding a boat in Dover without getting caught, would I be able to get it across the sea to France without falling in and drowning? What do I know about boats? I wouldn't be sorry if I never had to get on one again. But if I'm not going to France anymore, where should I go? If I could pluck up the courage to get on a train again, and didn't get caught, I could go back to Scotland. But how would I find the island? Even with your map book, you were never completely sure which bit of coast we'd landed the boat on.

So does that sound like the best thing, Joe – to stay put for now? I think you'd say that was best, wouldn't you? At least then, if you are still free, you'll know where to find me.

Right, I really do need to go outside and pee now.

Chapter 5

PEOPLE'S COURT OF CANTERBURY
Case No. 57-143
Date: 27-04-157 (Day 2)
JUDGE: The Hon. Just. Joh Samuels
DEFENDANT: Cn. Georgy Turner

(09:30)

JUST. SAMUELS: Citizen Turner, I see the seat beside you is empty. Where is your new legal representative?

CN. TURNER: Your Honour, I have not appointed a new representative.

JUST. SAMUELS: Citizen Turner, we adjourned this hearing yesterday after you dismissed your lawyer, and I instructed you to appoint new representation for the continuation of your case this morning, did I not?

CN. TURNER: You did, Your Honour. But –

JUST. SAMUELS: So, I assume the vacant seat beside you is an indication that you wish to be represented again by a court-appointed lawyer. Really, Citizen Turner, if we had been able to continue with your case yesterday afternoon, you might have been walking out of here a free citizen by teatime. I've never known someone so keen to be returned to their prison cell.

CN. TURNER: Your Honour, I have not appointed new representation because I intend to represent myself. According to the People's Constitution, Article 29.6, defendants have the right to –

JUST. SAMUELS: Yes, I am well acquainted with our constitution, thank you. I would usually counsel against such a decision, but since we are already almost at the end of your case, I am content to proceed. Citizen Kelly, can I ask you now to continue with the case for the prosecution?

CN. KELLY: Your Honour, we are calling no further witnesses and therefore conclude the case for the prosecution.

JUST. SAMUELS: Thank you. Now, Citizen Turner, I advise you to follow the example of the people's representative and keep your case for the defence as concise as possible. Do you have any witnesses to call, or shall we proceed directly to the summing up?

CN. TURNER: Your Honour, I would like to call Sergeant Stephenson as my first witness.

JUST. SAMUELS: Citizen Turner, Sergeant Stephenson has already given their evidence as a witness for the prosecution yesterday morning, and counsel for the defence had their opportunity to question the witness.

CN. TURNER: But as I am now representing myself, I would like to question the witness again, Your Honour. I'm afraid I can't remember the exact statute number, but I believe that when new representation for the defence is appointed, the new representative has the right to re-examine –

CN. KELLY: Objection. Your Honour, the defendant has not appointed new representation, therefore –

JUST. SAMUELS: Overruled. Citizen Turner, I sincerely hope you do not intend to cross-examine all of the prosecution witnesses we heard from yesterday. I recall Sergeant Stephenson to the witness stand.

[Pause]

JUST. SAMUELS: Sergeant Stephenson, thank you for returning to the stand. Do you understand that you remain under oath, following your testimony yesterday?

SGT. STEPHENSON: I do, Your Honour.

JUST. SAMUELS: Excellent. Your witness, Citizen Turner. Keep it brief, please.

SGT. FINCH STEPHENSON
Questions from CN. GEORGY TURNER

CN. TURNER: Thank you, Your Honour. Sergeant Stephenson, five and half weeks ago, on the morning of nineteenth March, you called me and arranged for a car to take me to a police station in Newcastle that same evening. Can you please tell the court the purpose of your call and my trip to Newcastle?

A. We wanted you to speak with a person being held by Newcastle police, whom we believed to be connected to your child.

Q. And what age was this person you wanted me to speak with?

A. I don't know. It's hard to say.

Q. Can you perhaps guess? Was this person an adult, over eighteen?

A. I can't be sure, but no, I don't think so.

Q. So you were holding a child in a police cell?

A. Yes, but –

Q. How long had you been holding the child when you called me?

A. I'm afraid I don't recall.

Q. I came up to Newcastle on the Friday. You told me at the time that the incident on the train had occurred on the Monday. Do you recall this now?

A. Er, yes, that sounds about right. Although I was not directly involved in the arrest of the person in question and was only made aware of the incident a day or two later so –

Q. So the child had already been in custody for four days. Is this normal, Sergeant, to hold a child in custody, in a police station, for over ninety-six hours, for the crime of pulling the emergency stop on a train?

A. It is not, but –

Q. What is the normal police procedure in such cases? What normally happens to children when they are arrested for a crime of this nature?

A. They would be returned to their parent, or parents, if possible and appropriate, or placed into temporary foster care if not.

Q. And can you tell the court where this child is currently – with their parents or with foster parents?

A. Um, neither.

Q. Neither with parents nor foster parents? So where are they?

A. They remain in our custody.

Q. In the same cold and stinky cell in which I met with them?

A. Er, no, we had them transferred to our custody in London.

Q. Ah, to more appropriate accommodation for a child perhaps?

[Pause]

Q. Why not into the care of foster parents or even the child's own parents?

A. I, er...no, the parents could not be located and a suitable foster placement could not be arranged.

Q. So, the poor child is still festering in a police cell. Am I correct?

[Pause]

Q. Has the child now spoken to you or any of your colleagues?

[Pause]

CN. KELLY: Your Honour, the witness was questioned comprehensively on the case in hand yesterday. Can you please ask the defence to move on to matters more relevant to this case or dismiss the witness?

CN. TURNER: Your Honour, when Sergeant Stephenson called me to Newcastle, it was because the police had been unable to get the child to speak. In my opinion, the child was in a state of severe trauma. If this is still the case, six weeks later, there should be serious questions raised about the mental state of this child being held in Sergeant Stephenson's custody. Surely, the court should be horrified to hear that a mentally disturbed child has been held in police custody for six weeks, against all protocols and in blatant contravention of the People's Constitution.

JUST. SAMUELS: Indeed. Citizen Kelly, I'm beginning to wonder just how comprehensive your questioning of this witness yesterday really was. Citizens Turner and Kelly, please both take a seat for a moment. I would like to ask the sergeant some questions of my own. Perhaps then we can move along more swiftly.

SGT. FINCH STEPHENSON
Questions from JUST. JOH SAMUELS

JUST. SAMUELS: Sergeant Stephenson, you lead a small unit of police officers from the London Police Force, am I correct?

A. That is correct, Your Honour.

Q. Excellent, and what is the brief of your unit, and to whom do you report?

A. Er, I'm afraid I can't divulge. This is state-sensitive information, Your Honour.

Q. Did you ask Citizen Turner to sign the Official Secrets Act before involving them with your investigations in Newcastle, Sergeant?

A. I did not, Your Honour.

Q. Then, I believe you can answer my question in open court, Sergeant.

A. I was leading investigations into a child trafficking gang, Your Honour.

Q. Yes, yes, but that was wrapped up months ago, was it not? It was in all the papers. Congratulations for your successful operation, but what is your unit investigating now?

A. Some of the children are still at large, Your Honour.

Q. At large? Surely, 'missing' would be a more appropriate term, would it not?

A. Er, yes, Your Honour, some of the children are still missing.

Q. So, when your officers attempted to apprehend Citizen Turner's child in Dover, this was simply to question them as a witness and then see them reunited with their parent. Correct?

A. Er, yes, Your Honour.

Q. And the child picked up in Newcastle. They remain under your care?

A. That is correct, Your Honour.

Q. Quite unusual for a serious organised crime unit to take on long term childcare, is it not? What's the story here? Why can the child not be placed with foster parents? There are procedures, are there not, for such situations?

A. There are, Your Honour, but this child is a little different. Difficult to place, Your Honour.

Q. Because they won't speak? An experienced, state-approved foster carer should be more than competent to deal with this.

A. There are other complications, Your Honour.

Q. Very well, please explain these 'other complications'.

[Pause]

CN. TURNER: Your Honour, it is not complicated at all really. The child in police custody is a boy. A male child. As is my sun, Joh.

JUST. SAMUELS: I beg your pardon – your what? No, don't answer that. Citizen Turner, I had asked you to sit down. At the moment, I am asking the questions, and Sergeant Stephenson, in the witness box here, is the one who should be answering them.

CN. TURNER: But this is ridiculous. The reason we are all here is because my child, Joh and his friend Cain are male children, like you get male and female lambs, or male and female chickens, or –

JUST. SAMUELS: Citizen Turner! You will sit down. May I remind you of the reason we are all here. You are accused of assaulting two police officers and conspiring in the theft of a fishing vessel.

[Pause]

JUST. SAMUELS: Thank you. Now, as to your suggestion that a human could be male or female, like an animal, I think we all find that notion more than a little distasteful when the subjects of these assertions are children. We will hear no more of this. The witness may stand down. Citizen Turner, do you have any more witnesses to call.

CN. TURNER: I do, Your Honour, but when I gave my list to the clerk this morning, they said they could only act on such a list if it was presented by my legal representative. I tried to explain I was representing myself, but –

JUST. SAMUELS: So you have no further witnesses to call.

CN. TURNER: No, I mean yes, I do have further witnesses to call, but they are not as yet in the courthouse, Your Honour.

JUST. SAMUELS: I see. Citizen Turner, let me be frank with you for a moment. It is, of course, your right to submit your list and call further witnesses, but your list will have to be examined by the prosecution as well as by this court, which will all take time, during which I must return you to custody. Or we could move directly to summing up, and I suggest to you that there is a, let's say, better than even chance you will walk from this courthouse today as a free citizen. Are you getting my drift, Citizen Turner?

CN. TURNER: I am, Your Honour, but I feel it is important for my witnesses to be heard.

JUST. TURNER: Very well. In that case, you will ensure the clerk has your list, and then you will be remanded in custody until such arrangements can be made.

Chapter 6

Eva

THE WOMAN CALLED Maggie strode along the road beside Eva. The other three kept a few paces behind, the eyes of the two guards ploughing grooves across Eva's back as they swept over the landscape. Half the oxygen she inhaled refused to be squeezed into her lungs. Was she their hostage now, or had she volunteered to lead them to the village? She could have led them away from the village instead, but they'd hovered over the island in their bird, and they weren't dumb neut day-trippers. They knew where to find the heart of the community. Besides, they came with convincing messages from Joe, and they weren't neuts. *These are people like us, for goodness' sake!* Sandra would still be suspicious, though. Sandra would have preferred to talk about it, make a plan before first contact with these invaders.

Where was everyone? Stupid question. It was normal to walk the length of the road and not see another soul. But the familiar sounds and smells of soil, air and sea all fled and hid themselves in their wake. Eva's ears rang with silence, aside from the grating rattle of the masked woman's breathing and the crunch of no-nonsense boots behind them.

The boots stopped. Eva took a few faltering steps onwards before halting herself, aware before looking up or back that she now stood as a solitary mediator between opposing sides.

'Eva?'

What was that look in Sandra's eyes? Confusion? Worry? Accusation? She could usually read Sandra's moods no trouble at all. That's what made them work so well together. Others didn't appreciate the burden Sandra carried for the community. Anthony carried nothing, except for a misguided sense of his own importance. The prize bull. Tom had a lot to answer for – dropping everything on Sandra's shoulders and excusing himself from community life. Selfish bastard. But here he was now, standing beside Sandra, worrying loose stones with his foot, refusing to look at Eva except for the usual injured, fleeting glances, ever puzzled over the relationship she had with Sandra. What was he doing here? Did he think Sandra suddenly needed his protection or something?

'Sandra, I...' She glanced over her shoulder. The woman, Maggie, was edging forward to join Eva. Arms by her sides, palms forward, trying her best to look friendly and harmless behind the mask that betrayed mistrust of even the air.

'So, I'm guessing they made it – Nats and the two boys. They're all safe with your people now, are they? Sorry, I'm Tom by the way.' Tom stepped forward, taking control, intentionally pushing Eva aside with his line of sight. 'I've thought about them every day since I pushed them off in their little boat, wondering whether we'd ever hear.'

'What? You helped them?' If it hadn't been for the presence of their invaders, Sandra would have swung around in an arc to face Tom down. But the road in front was too crowded for her, so she hung back, hurling rocks of accusation at his back. 'They were only kids. You should have stopped them! Why wasn't I told about this? Don't you think the rest of us have been wondering too? Why didn't you tell us, tell me, at least?'

Tom didn't look back, already trusting the new woman and looking to her for a steer, more than he ever had Sandra. But he threw words over his shoulder, nonetheless.

'And if I'd told you, what would you have done? What good would it have brought without knowing if they'd made it?' He paused. 'I didn't know anything about it until the night they left.' He was lying. 'I couldn't have stopped them.'

'Couldn't have stopped them? You told *her* you helped push their boat out!'

'Zandra, pleeze.'

Sandra's flaming eyes shot across to the woman in the mask, guttering into confused indignation at the use of her name by this uninvited alien presence.

'Eet ees Zandra, eesn't eet?'

Sandra nodded and edged up to stand beside Tom. Pulse beginning to settle, Eva sidled across to join them, reaching for Sandra's hand. Sandra allowed their fingers to intertwine, but Eva's squeeze was not reciprocated. The woman, Maggie, waited patiently for the three islanders to finish their shuffling. Even her weaponised companions relaxed their guard.

'I have news of your friends, but I think here on the road is not the place to share it with you. Is there somewhere more…comfortable, where we can talk?'

TOM'S HOVEL WASN'T what Eva would call comfortable. Why he'd chosen to live here was a mystery, when there were four much better built empty cottages too remote for anyone else to consider. Actually, it wasn't a mystery at all; it was one big sulking statement telling everyone how hurt and rejected he felt when Sandra dumped him. Except she hadn't dumped him because she had never seen him that way in the first place.

However much this hole might have suited Tom's bruised ego, it was hardly an appropriate venue for hosting their first guests from the world beyond. But it was Tom who correctly read Sandra's hesitancy and suggested his place might be best for a conference with the visitors, rather than marching with them into the village. It wasn't untidy exactly, nor was it dirty, but nothing was put away. A clean bowl, mug, spoon and fork, but no knife, sat neatly in the centre of the easy-wipe table, its faded green surface chipped around the edges long before its current careful owner. Next to the stove, a dented but pristine pan kept company with a well-sharpened knife - not the sort you'd want to eat with - on top of a home-crafted chopping block. A stack of neatly folded clothes towered out of an old crate perched at the end of the bed.

'Sorry, I'd offer you all a drink, but we'd have to take turns,' Tom quipped.

Idiot! Thought he was such a wit. Even if he had a full tea service, these visitors wouldn't accept any food or drink from him, and he knew that. They wouldn't even share the same air! And anyway, how would they drink anything with those masks on?

Maggie took the single chair Tom had to offer after a brief exchange - in words Eva couldn't decipher - with the other one, a male, who'd been introduced as Lewi. The two guards remained outside. There was barely enough room as it was. Tom, folding his knees up to his chin, perched on his low bed and shuffled across to offer Sandra the space beside him. Sandra chose instead to adopt a standing lean against the unlit stove.

Eva shifted from one foot to the other by the door, tilting her head this way and that to see past the bulk of Lewi, who seemed oblivious to the obstruction he was, or that there was a perfectly reasonable space he could have moved to next to Maggie's chair.

Eva almost coveted the masks still worn by the visitors, if they helped at all to make the stuffy air more breathable. Though if their breathing echoed around inside those masks as much it sounded like it did, she'd soon have to rip the mask off and escape this poky, suffocating room.

Maggie began to recount the details Eva had already heard from her: Joe in hospital, but with their people; Cain captured; Nats' last known location in a barn near to where Joe had set off across the sea, and she had an injured ankle.

Unable to see Maggie's face properly, and with her strange way of speaking, Eva only caught half her words. Perhaps she should make her excuses and escape back out to the hillside, see how the lamb and her mother were doing. Maybe she would have done, if it had been Sandra and Anthony. But Sandra and Tom? Not that Anthony was any better than Tom really. Eva always avoided being alone with Anthony, aside from those few occasions when it had been necessary. But that wouldn't be happening again now. She'd told Sandra she wasn't doing it again. The four kids between them, counting Charlie, was surely enough. She'd done her bit.

'So what are your plans for getting Nats out?' Tom had always had a soft spot for Nats. She was the one person he'd still talk to after his move out of the village.

'We would like to help to get her to safety, of course. But there are many risks to consider. We cannot simply fly in to such a populated area as we have done here, and there is a good chance she may by now have moved on or been discovered. Maybe a better way is through building relations with your government and then negotiations.'

'They're not *our* government. Nobody should be trying to build relations with them.' Sandra's eyes flamed again, outshining the dull light that pushed its way through the single, grimy window. 'And we don't want to build relations with you until Nats is safe, either back here with us or with Joe in France.'

Maggie didn't stop to translate Sandra's words for Lewi, launching instead into single combat with Sandra.

'But Zandra, you have children here, yes? And Joe tells us that many have died. Our first priority must be to bring all of you here to safety.'

'You think you're here to rescue us? We're doing fine here, thank you, and so are all our children. Joe was only here a few weeks – not long enough to properly integrate into our community – and he and Cain had no right to take Nats away on this –'

The bed creaked as Tom leaned forward. 'If you'd heard their arguing on the night they left, you'd know Nats was as determined as either of those boys to go. In fact –'

'If I'd been there that night, we'd not be having this conversation now because I'd have stopped them.'

'And you wonder why people keep secrets from you?'

What did Tom mean? Everyone trusted Sandra. They knew that everything she did was for the good of the community. OK, so maybe sometimes she had to make unpopular decisions. But they were always the right decisions, weren't they?

Maggie sat back, arms folded, a slight grin playing across her face, as if she enjoyed watching other people argue. Lewi was clearly agitated. His back shifting constantly, forcing Eva to also keep on updating her position to see past him. But Maggie looked like her pulse never rose above fifty-five and she was in no hurry. She would wait until Sandra and Tom's argument had burnt itself out.

'Don't you dare try to project your feelings onto anyone else. Or your guilt. I thought you cared about Nats, but it seems there's really only one person you care about, and we all know who that is.' Sandra took a breath and looked around at the others.

Taking his cue from Maggie, Tom was now almost horizontal on his bed. That was something Eva hated most about Tom – the way he could drop a few words in to make Sandra boil over without ever raising his voice.

The still moment Maggie had been waiting for had arrived. She chose her words carefully. Eva jealously admired how she already seemed to understand Sandra. It was like how Sally always was when Katie or Peter got a splinter and they wouldn't let Eva or Sandra anywhere near it but would sit still and quiet, with only the tiniest of winces, as Sally teased and broddled at their palm.

'I am sorry, but of course, you have built a wonderful community here. Do not underestimate how much of a wrench it was for Joe to leave. He has told us many impressive things about how your island works. I think my own community could learn a lot from your ways.'

Although she alternated her calm gaze from Sandra to Tom and even to Eva, like one well acquainted with public speaking, Maggie's words were crafted especially for Sandra.

'Of course, we will do what we can to secure the safety of Nats, and hopefully also the boy, Cain, but you understand this will take time and patience.' She paused, allowed the fog in her mask to clear. 'In the meantime, since we are here, with your permission, we would love to meet the rest of your community – particularly the children.' She beckoned Lewi forward, though really it was more a small step to the side. 'Lewi here is a doctor. He would like to...can...if you like, see your children and babies. Help with any medical issues. We have brought medicines in our helicopter.'

Helicopter. So that was what the machine was called. Eva allowed the word to do somersaults in her head, reliving the buzz of watching and feeling its thunderous descent. She could volunteer to accompany Maggie back to the helicopter to collect the medical supplies. Maybe she'd be allowed to see inside, examine the controls. Would they leave the helicopter there in the oat field or lift it off the ground again to bring it closer to the village? How much space did it need? In her mind, Eva was already hovering over the village, sitting beside Maggie in the driving seat, watching and learning about the science of flight.

'All our children are well, thank you. We have no need of a doctor. My sibling was...is...a nurse. I know how to keep everyone healthy. Nobody has died on this island for a long time.'

'Ah yes, your sibling is Jay Taylor, no?'

Eva landed with a bump. Sandra's head jerked up in surprise, but was that also a glimmer of hope in her eyes? Did Maggie know Jay? Was Jay alive and safe in the world beyond? Sandra hadn't knowingly spoken of Jay since the day after the storm, but Eva knew how Jay haunted Sandra's dreams.

'You know Jay?' Eva surprised herself, vocalising the question on Sandra's face.

'Only from what Joe has told us. Have you heard anything from Jay since Joe and his friends left? Joe told us about the storm and the many who died in the wreck. He said you hoped Jay would come himself – sorry, themself – with other children. Did he, sorry, they –'

'We are fine, and we don't need your interfering, thank you.' Sandra glared at Maggie as she spoke. 'We're glad for Joe that he reached you, but we never asked him to go. I knew it would be too dangerous, and so it proved to be, for Nats and Cain at least. Please, leave us and find Nats.'

Chapter 7

Nats

At the sudden burst of barking, I tumble off the top of the gate. I land on my bum – but as I push myself up, my ankle twinges for the first time in days. Crap! I should have opened the gate like any ordinary person. Why did I even try to set out for the shop? I can trust Lottie to keep feeding me, can't I?

I can't see the beast through the inky darkness, but its low growl through bared teeth rattles my bones. Can it see me, with its night vision? I shuffle away from the gate, into the prickly shelter of the dense hedgerow, but my movement triggers another volley of flesh-ripping barks. I pull the straps tight on my empty rucksack, give my ankle a reassuring rub, and place my palms flat on the damp earth, ready to push myself off and make a dash for it. The next bark bites my ear off, and my elbows buckle. The hedge quivers, soaking me in drips as the hound wrestles its way through, growling, barking, barking, growling.

'Oi, Nelly! Shurrup, you daft bitch!'

I gasp, catching more air than my body can hold. I can't force it down into my lungs and I daren't let it hiss back through my nose and mouth. A powerful beam blinks on and sweeps along the other side of the hedgerow, throwing up monstrous shadows that race towards me. It stops. It's found me. I duck my head, begging my grubby dark curls to blend in with the foliage. Flames of light dance across my front.

'Nelly! C'mere, leave it be, whatever it is you've found.'

I dare to glance up. Our eyes meet. Nelly is about half the size I expected with messy curls like mine. Her slobbery chops wobble with a half-hearted growl. I bare my teeth back at her, then whisper, 'Shoo, go-on, leave me be.' She doesn't budge.

The beam shifts as its owner takes a few steps towards us. I scuttled sideways, out of its range; squat with my back to the hedge, cursing myself for pointing my backpack with its stupid reflective stripes straight at the light. I push my palm into my hammering chest while crunching footsteps keep time with every second thump. The feet halt. I can't breathe. The dog gives a strangled cough and whines.

'Get here, you dumb bitch! Your mother was never this much trouble.'

I still can't breathe as Nelly is dragged back across the yard, her muted whines and half-barks promising *this isn't over*.

I wait until my feet prickle, and when I get up, my head swims. Stumbling forward to stop myself from toppling over, my ankle reminds me it might not carry me the however many miles it is to the all-night shop I might not be able to find, based on vague memories of Joe's descriptions of the route between here and Dover. I should have agreed to go with him, insisted on it, the very first day he decided to go to Dover. We might have had to go slowly, but my ankle would have managed. Probably.

I ease up the catch on the gate and wince at the whingeing hinges as I squeeze myself through the narrowest possible opening, pinging the pointless elasticated cords on my rucksack. I hobble back to the barn. Cain would tell me I was putting it on, because I wasn't hobbling like this a few minutes ago. Joe would have been sympathetic, though, if I'd hobbled a bit on our way to Dover. Is it better to hobble so you don't put too much weight on a slightly dodgy ankle, or does hobbling actually make it worse?

The stone scrapes across the concrete as I nudge the barn door open, the sound echoing around the yard. I squeeze in without pushing the door any further; although I know I could injure my back doing this, I bend down and heft the doorstop-stone back into its original position, then retreat to my corner behind the tractor.

A TRAIN IS growling its way into motion. Cain's voice calls out of the window of the retreating train, something like *don't leave me behind, you cowards!* I'm lying on my back. My trousers and underwear are round my ankles; a slobbering dog is tearing at the fabric. Joe is kneeling beside me, trying to spoon-feed me baked beans. Why isn't he getting that dog off me? Shouldn't we be running? The dog smells the beans and decides to go for those instead, just as they're coming close to my mouth. Its damp breath cascades over my face. I catch a whiff of ham. That's more like it! Cain must have bought it when he went shopping, before we got on the train. I part my lips, ready to accept a mouthful of tender ham, preferably sandwiched between some nice dense, island oatbread, but on its own will be fine too. A wet piece of ham slaps me round the face. Another belch of dog breath assaults me, seasoned with salty ham. My stomach churns. The ham hits my face again. I should open my eyes, take control of my own feeding.

I open my eyes. A pink tongue with a hint of ham flavour shoots out at me between pointy yellow teeth. A wet, black nose wipes itself across my cheek. I shriek. The dog bounds away from me. I throw myself back hard, into the corner, thrusting my arms and one leg out to fend off another attack.

Nelly spins around excitedly, stopping to face me again, tail wagging, panting with her ham tongue pulsing in and out. She shouts out a single, piercing bark, challenging me to respond.

'Shhh!' I instinctively reply, which on my second attempt becomes, 'Shhooo! Go on, get outta here!'

I stomp two steps towards her and bare my teeth, at which she does another twirl, all four feet apparently not touching the ground for the full three-sixty, then waits, grinning back at me, tail bouncing back and forth like a sapling in a hurricane.

I dare to turn my back for a moment, to grab an apple from the small pile I have left and hurl it at the dog. The apple bounces, falling short, and then jumps and rolls right under the dog's feet as she skids and springs around. Then she's on it, pouncing and chomping at it before bounding back towards me.

'Go away!' I growl at her.

I hop onto my right leg – thankfully the one with the good ankle – as a slimy lump of what was once a perfectly good apple drops and rolls towards my left shoe. Nelly springs back, does another three-sixty and then watches me expectantly.

'If you think I'm picking that up...' I kick it away, under the tractor. Nelly's under there like a shot, scrabbling, crunching, slobbering. For a few moments, I think she's got herself stuck under there, as various body parts bump and snag on the machine's rusty underbelly, but then a soggier, smaller chunk of apple is laid at my feet and another round is requested.

I have an idea. I bend over and pick up the slimeball with as little finger and thumb contact as possible. The dog dances around me impatiently as I walk toward the door, which has somehow been left open. I'm sure I pushed the stone hard up to it last night. The dog couldn't have shifted it, even if it threw itself against the door; it's a scrawny little thing really. I hurl what remains of the apple out of the barn as hard as I can and then flatten myself against the wall as Nelly barges past me. As soon as she's out, I slam the door shut and shove the stone firmly against it. The top of the door wobbles and clangs. Three barks echo around the yard.

'Nell-yy, here girl!' a child's voice sings out.

Lottie comes closer, is just the other side of the barn door. Thank goodness it's only her.

'What have you been up to, you naughty dog? Have you found my friend? Let's leave them alone now, shall we? Time for your breakfast.'

Now two have found me. How much longer can I really stay here? As Nelly is dragged away, I drag myself back to my spot behind the tractor, kicking a licked-clean plate across the floor as I go. My tummy rumbles. I groan. I must have slept later than normal. The door was open because Lottie had been in with my breakfast, and that wretched dog had eaten every last bit of it.

My stomach turns over, and not because I'm hungry. Leaving here means leaving you, Joe. Giving up on you, probably even trying to get back to the island, even though you told me how close France is and I should probably try to finish what we all set out to do. But I'm scared. I know I always act like I'm not afraid of anything, but all I want to do now is go back home.

Chapter 8

Eva

Eva hadn't realised how hungry she was until she and Sandra started their climb back over the hill. It was Eva's idea to go that way, check on the new lamb en route. It was only this morning, wasn't it, that she'd been up there with the ewe and her newborn lamb? So actually, breakfast had been many hours ago.

Sandra was starting to relax. They both loved it when they could get out onto the hill together – breathe in the fresh, carefree breeze. Eva wished she could let go, like Sandra did. Except she didn't want to let *them* go; she longed to learn more about these people and their technology, and it would be good to let their doctor, Lewi, take a look at the children, while he was here. Why had she followed Sandra as she stormed out? How long would it be before they felt and heard the helicopter lift off and fly away? Would Tom go with them? Sandra had made it pretty clear nobody else would. How would Anthony take it? Why hadn't he been there with Sandra?

'Where's Anthony this morning?' Eva asked, trying to sound casual.

'Throwing up, last time I heard. That's why Tom came with me.'

'Oh, do you think we should've got Lewi to take a look at him?'

'Don't be silly. It's Anthony. Probably self-inflicted.'

They walked on in silence.

'We could have asked them to look at Peter.'

No response. Eva wasn't sure Sandra had heard and was about to say it again.

'Why?' Sandra said eventually.

'You know, check his breathing. I told you. It really scared me that time when he couldn't take any breaths. And he's always struggled to keep up with Katie.'

'Katie's just fitter. Girls are stronger.'

'But Charlie doesn't have the same problems.'

'Charlie's older than them. You'd expect him to be stronger, even if he's not much bigger than Katie.' Sandra stopped walking and turned to face Eva. 'Look, all three of our children, and Charlie, are perfectly fine. OK?'

Sandra continued to the stile and clambered over it, waiting for Eva on the other side before striding on with both their walk and the conversation. 'I know you spend more time with them than I do, and you're probably more aware of all the little colds and bugs they get, but it's made you over-sensitive too. This island is a fantastic home for them and we're fantastic parents. That's all they need.'

Eva chased breathlessly after Sandra. She couldn't keep up their conversation at this pace. Had Peter inherited her own shortness of breath, while Katie enjoyed the benefits of Sandra's genes? 'But since they're here and Lewi's a doctor, it wouldn't hurt for him to take a look, would it?' Eva searched her memory for any weakness of Katie's that might benefit from a doctor's prognosis.

'Look, how many times did you get seen by a doctor when you were growing up?'

'Well, none, but we couldn't –'

'There you go. We don't need doctors.'

Eva stopped. Took a few deep breaths. 'But Sandra, these people are different. They're here to help us.'

Sandra stood several paces in front, shouting back through the swelling breeze. 'Eva, love, I can't stop and have this conversation now. I've got to get back. Got things to do. You go check on your lamb, not that it needs you to, and we'll talk later.'

Eva watched as Sandra strode off down the hill and decided against chasing after her. They'd make it up later, they always did. She glanced across at the rise behind which the helicopter had descended. No sign or sound of any movement there yet. How long would it take them to get back from Tom's and then ready themselves for leaving? Would they leave straightaway, or would they hang around, hoping for a change of heart? Or might they ignore Sandra's ruling and come to the village anyway? Maggie had implied they'd respect the islanders' decision, but would they come all this way and then leave again so suddenly on the say-so of one girl who wasn't much more than a child herself?

Sandra was right about one thing: the lamb didn't need checking on. It would be fine, as would its mother. But if the helicopter took to the sky again before she got there, Eva knew she'd regret it.

'Please, I'd like you to see my son, Peter. He struggles with his breathing sometimes.' Eva panted between every other word, having run all the way down the hill and over the rise. Would the doctor be able to diagnose Peter just from observing her own laboured breathing?

Lewi looked with concern at Eva and beckoned for her to sit down but showed no comprehension of anything she'd said. She considered trying again, now her breath was coming back, speaking slower perhaps. But Lewi had already turned to fetch Maggie from where she stood by the helicopter's tail, gabbling animatedly at one of the guards. The other guard sat in what looked like the driving seat, making their flying car ready to leave.

Lewi returned with Maggie, a friendly smile on her face, which was soon obscured by the fog clouding her mask whenever she spoke.

'Eva, what's up? Has Sandra changed her mind? We can still come to your village if you want us to.'

'No, well, I'm not sure.' Why did she still feel so breathless? 'But I'd like Lewi to see my son, Peter. He often struggles with his breathing, when he's playing with the other kids. He's probably fine, but...'

'Of course, yes, we'll come right away.' Maggie relayed Eva's message to Lewi, and he nodded in agreement and gave Eva a thumbs up.

'No, I will bring him here, if you can wait.' Eva didn't need to explain why. Maggie could tell that she had come back without Sandra's blessing. Even Lewi seemed to cotton on.

'Eva, our instructions are only to engage, even when it comes to children, if we have the permission of those who live here. You understand?' Maggie held Eva's gaze as Eva processed her meaning.

'Peter is my son, and I give you permission,' she replied. 'Will you wait, if I bring him to you here?'

'Of course.' Maggie smiled. 'We were not expecting to leave so soon, so we can wait for as long as you need. Unless your friends have plans to forcibly expel us from your island?'

Eva followed Maggie's glances towards the two armed guards. No-one needed to acknowledge who would have the upper hand in any confrontation, even though the islanders had the greater numbers.

Victoria was in her kitchen with the four kids. At least, Eva thought all four of them were there. It was hard to see past the pots, pans, bowls and mounds of partially prepared food littering every available surface. The older three enjoyed helping Victoria with her cooking and Eva trusted her, most of the time, to not let them handle the sharp knives. They were actually safer here than if she took them out somewhere to play. There'd been too many occasions when Victoria was supposed to be watching them but had wandered back to do something in her kitchen, certain they were fine. Charlie had only recently turned five, for goodness' sake, and he was the eldest! They might need to re-evaluate their decision to leave Grace with her, though, now she was crawling.

'Mummy!!' Peter and Katie cried out in tandem, rushing towards her with some sort of dough plastered over their hands and faces.

'Hello, my lovelies, but whoa! Those hands need a clean.' Normally, she didn't care. It was easier to scoop them all up and deal with the washing consequences later. But today, she and Peter needed to be presentable.

'Ah, Eva, you're a life saver! Thank you for coming early. I mean, I love your kids to bits – and Charlie,' Victoria gave Charlie a wink, 'but with the meeting tonight, there's so much I need to get ready. You know what it's like. Everyone wants feeding when it's meeting night.' Victoria did love to exaggerate, but her mass catering skills were rather admirable.

'There's a meeting tonight? I thought it wasn't till next week.'

Victoria stared with incredulity at Eva. 'Eva, babe, where have you been all day? Didn't you see the sky monster?'

'So Sandra's called a meeting already?'

'Well, no, not exactly, but there's bound to be one. She and Tom headed off to investigate several hours ago. Poor Anthony was devastated. He was desperate to go but was in no fit state. We were all outside the head house, arguing about where the monster might have come from and trying to hear what Sandra and Anthony were saying to each other inside. Sandra told us we should all wait in our houses, but none of us did.'

The children all stared wide-eyed and open-mouthed at Victoria, drinking in every word. Eva instinctively gathered up Grace, who'd been sitting there as still and quiet as the other three, clearly sensing there was some important news being shared.

'And poor Anthony kept dashing out of the house and running round the back to hurl his guts up. The gulls have had a right feast.'

Katie and Charlie giggled to each other whilst Peter turned slightly green around the edges.

'Anyway, then Tom turns up and bursts straight into the head house, and within a few minutes, he and Sandra are marching off up the road, leaving Anthony almost on his knees at the door.'

Victoria turned away and laid her hands on a towel, which she soaked in a bowl of water before attacking the children's paws and faces.

'So where's Sandra now? Is she back?' asked Eva.

'Oh yeah, she's back. Not sure where Tom is. But Sandra got back about an hour ago. Wouldn't answer anyone's questions – marched straight into the head house and slammed the door behind her.' They all jumped as Victoria slammed her hand down on the nearest bit of worktop to dramatise her account. 'Must have locked it too. I didn't even know there was a key. But Anthony had to hammer on the door for several minutes before she'd let him in. His tummy must have settled because neither of them have emerged since. So yes, there'll be a meeting tonight.'

Now what? Eva had hoped to somehow spirit Peter away, leaving the others with Victoria. She could get away with taking Grace easily enough, but if Sandra found out she'd taken Katie or even Charlie to see the doctor...

'Vicki, I don't suppose...'

Victoria looked up from the heap of potatoes she was vigorously scrubbing. Eva couldn't ask her. She'd have to risk it.

'No, it doesn't matter. Thanks for having them. Actually, though, can I grab some bits for a quick sandwich?' Her earlier hunger had vanished, but she ought to eat something.

Victoria threw together a sandwich for her. 'You can pay me later, at the meeting,' she said with a wink.

'Er, yes, at the meeting. Thanks.' She threw Victoria a smile, hoping it didn't look too false as she took the sandwich and herded her lambs out into the overcast afternoon.

'Right then, who'd like to go and see a very special bird I spotted this morning? Then, if you're all good, I'll take you to visit a new baby lamb.'

'Was there lots of blood?' asked Charlie, enjoying how much it made Peter squirm.

'Not a lot, and she'll be all clean and fluffy by now.'

GRACE WAS SOON asleep on Eva's back, head hanging to one side. Katie and Peter ran on ahead along the road, following a meandering route as they continued the game of tig, started outside Victoria's café. Was she worrying over nothing with Peter? Right now, he was a fit and healthy little boy, enjoying fresh air and friendship. Sure, he spent a little longer being 'it' than Katie, but that looked to be more down to Katie's devious nature than any physical deficiency in Peter. Charlie trotted along beside Eva, opting out of the game for now, lost in his own thoughts.

'Eva?' Charlie reached out for a hand.

'Yes, Charlie?' Eva gave it a squeeze. She loved his thoughtful moments.

'Are we going to see the flying machine?'

For a few moments, Eva tried to formulate some vague, noncommittal answer. But what was the point? He'd find out soon enough.

'Yes. Yes, we are, Charlie. Is that OK?'

Charlie didn't reply with words. Instead, he did a little happy skip then, letting go of Eva's hand, sprinted after Katie and Peter and tigged them both, much to the annoyance of Katie, who said he couldn't tig them because he wasn't 'it' yet.

It might have been better if Maggie hadn't come out onto the road to meet them as soon as she saw them coming. It was like the story of the Three Billy Goats Gruff come to life in front of them. Charlie always insisted he had to be Big Billy Goat Gruff since he was the oldest, leaving Peter and Katie to argue over the roles of the little and middle-sized goats. Nats had been the original troll and Eva or whoever else was looking after them was repeatedly told, *'No, that's not how Nats did it.'* Now there was a new troll casting its huge shadow across the road; a troll with big heavy boots, no messing hands on hips, and a strange mask obscuring its no doubt gruesome features and viciously sharp teeth. Three little billy goats came shrieking back towards Eva, almost bowling her off balance.

'It's OK, it's OK. This is who we've come to see, and she won't hurt you.'

'But that's not a big bird, that's a person,' observed Katie, after daring to take a quick peek.

'Yes, that's right, she's just a person. She's called Maggie, but she came here in the big bird I was going to show you. Except that isn't a bird either, it's a flying machine called a helicopter.'

'What's that on her face? Why is she wearing that?' Trusting Charlie now stood boldly observing, though still keeping a tight grip on Eva's hand.

Good question. Hadn't they worked out by now that the air was perfectly safe to breathe? What were they scared of? Or did everyone wear those masks all the time where they came from? Suddenly the world beyond seemed less enticing.

'I'm not sure, Charlie, but if we go a little closer, you'll be able to see her face properly, and you'll see she's a normal person underneath – just like you and me.'

Thankfully, the other three trolls stayed out of sight as Eva coaxed the children forward to take a closer look. Maggie got the message and helpfully got down on her knees, ready to greet them, at which point Charlie set an example for the other two, released Eva's hand and came straight out with the question Eva herself had been dying to ask.

'Can I see your flying machine?'

'I think we could arrange that. I'm Maggie. Are you Peter by any chance?'

'No, I'm Charlie. That's Peter.' Charlie twisted around and pointed at the little boy, who still clung to Eva's leg as Katie started to creep closer.

'Of course, silly me. And who's this coming to say hello now?'

'I'm Katie.' Katie got in before Charlie had a chance to steal her introduction. 'And that's our sister Grace on Mummy Eva's back. But she's asleep so you can't say hello to her.'

'That's OK.' Maggie smiled. 'Do you want to see our flying machine too, Katie?'

Katie nodded, and Maggie looked up at Eva for her consent before leading them all down to the helicopter, where it still sat amongst the flattened oats. Those kids were going to be full of it when they got back to the village. Sandra would be furious. Eva squeezed Peter's hand and got the little squeeze she wanted back. She'd deal with whatever flak she got from Sandra for Peter's sake.

By the time Maggie and one of the guards had shown the children every moving part and every control on their helicopter, and Maggie had patiently found out and relayed answers to every question they could think of, they were all best of friends. The masks had become invisible to the children, aside from the smeary fingerprints they'd managed to plant on them. They didn't even seem fazed by the many strange words that passed between Maggie and her companions.

When Lewi got out his stethoscope, at Katie's insistence, everyone had to have it pressed to their chest. Eva studied Lewi's face as he moved it over Peter's chest, but his expressions were as impossible to interpret as his words.

As the now weapon-free guards played peekaboo with the children, Maggie and Lewi took Eva aside.

'We cannot be certain, but Lewi thinks your son's heart is not quite as it should be,' Maggie relayed to her.

Eva's own heart thumped at the news. 'What do you mean, not as it should be? Is it serious?'

For a heart-stopping minute, Maggie and Lewi conferred. Were they arguing over how much to tell Eva? Sandra was right. Peter was fine. Why had she brought him here for Lewi to tell her he wasn't?

'If it is what Lewi thinks, it is a condition that is not uncommon. A hole between two parts of his heart. In France, it would normally be fixed when the child is a baby, and then they can live a normal life.'

'What do you mean, fixed? How do you fix a hole in a baby's heart?' And if fixing it gave children the chance of living a normal life, what sort of life did they have if it wasn't fixed? Peter had a normal life, didn't he? Well, as normal as they could make it here on the island. Better than normal, in fact.

'It is really a very simple procedure, but it has to be done in a hospital.'

'But Peter is fine. He is healthy. He doesn't need to go to a hospital. I shouldn't have bothered you about it.'

Lewi spoke in low tones to Maggie, though the whispering was hardly necessary. Eva would have no greater chance of picking up what he was saying if they shouted to each other through her ears.

'Of course, you have looked after Peter well and he is really very healthy. Some children whose hearts have very small holes never have them fixed and live a good life. But...' Maggie paused, glanced across at the cavorting taking place around the helicopter, smiled at the excited shrieks of the children. 'Although he cannot be certain, Lewi thinks the hole in Peter's heart might be quite big. It would be better for him if it could be fixed.'

'But how? That would mean...'

Maggie nodded. Eva didn't need her to complete the sentence. This was clearly what Maggie and Lewi had envisaged all along.

'Come with us back to France, Eva, with Peter. Only for a week or two. That's all it would take. Then, of course, we will bring you back here to your island.'

Chapter 9

PEOPLE'S COURT OF CANTERBURY
Case No. 57-143
Date: 03-05-157 (Day 3)
JUDGE: The Hon. Just. Joh Samuels
DEFENDANT: Cn. Georgy Turner

(09:30)

JUST. SAMUELS: Citizen Kelly, I trust that during the remainder of last week you had time to study the defendant's new wish list of witnesses. Does the prosecution need to petition for the court to bar any of these new witnesses?

CN. KELLY: Your Honour, the prosecution cannot see the pertinence of any of these witnesses to the case in hand and therefore we move that it is not in the people's interest to spend the court's time calling and cross-examining them.

CN. TURNER: But Your Honour, I have a right to –

JUST. SAMUELS: Citizen Turner, I will hear from you when I am ready. Citizen Kelly, I am inclined to agree with you.

CN. TURNER: Objection, Your Honour.

JUST. SAMUELS: Overruled. Citizen Turner. You will take your seat and not speak again until you are spoken to. Now, Citizen Kelly, whilst I am inclined to agree, regrettably, it is enshrined in our beloved laws that both counsels may call as a witness whosoever they believe can give substantive evidence in support of their case. The court may only move to bar a witness if there is credible evidence that the calling of said witness would cause excessive danger or harm to themselves or another citizen. Does the prosecution wish to offer any such petitions?

CN. KELLY: Er, yes, Your Honour. The State asserts that the child, named by the defendant as, er, Cain, would suffer excessive harm as a result of being made to take the stand. As we have already heard, there are concerns about the child's current mental and physical state. Furthermore, without establishing the identity of the child's parent or parents –

JUST. SAMUELS: Yes, yes, OK. I find the State's sudden concern for this child quite touching. You will submit your petition to the court in writing. Citizen Turner, whilst we could in theory organise a video link for later today, you will not call the child as a witness until I have had time to examine the prosecution's written petition. Citizen Kelly, any other petitions?

CN. KELLY: No, Your Honour.

JUST. SAMUELS: Then we shall proceed with the case for the defence. Citizen Turner, you may call your next witness.

CN. TURNER: Your Honour, I call Citizen Leslee King.

[Pause]

JUST. SAMUELS: Citizen King, please read the words on the card in front of you.

CN. KING: Yes, Your Honour. I do solemnly, sincerely and truly declare and affirm that the evidence I shall give shall be the truth the whole truth and nothing but the truth.

JUST. SAMUELS: Thank you. Citizen Turner, you may cross-examine your witness.

CN. LESLEE KING
Questions from CN. GEORGY TURNER

CN. TURNER: Thank you, Your Honour. Leslee, sorry, Citizen King, may I call you Leslee?

A. Yes, of course.

Q. Thank you. Leslee, please can you tell the court where you are currently living?

A. At Belmarsh Detention Facility. I am being held as a prisoner there.

CN. KELLY: Objection, Your Honour. This witness is being held in the same facility as the defendant. Their testimony cannot be trusted.

JUST. SAMUELS: Overruled. Citizen Kelly, the witness has given us their affirmation to tell the truth. We must allow counsel for the defence their right to question the witness and I will then allow you your right to discredit their testimony. Carry on, Citizen Turner.

CN. TURNER: Thank you, Your Honour. Leslee, can you tell the court what you have been convicted of, to be imprisoned at Belmarsh?

A. No, I cannot.

JUST. SAMUELS: Excuse me? Citizen King, you have given your affirmation that you will tell the whole truth. Please answer the question you have been asked.

A. I'm sorry, Your Honour, but I have answered the question. I cannot tell the court about my conviction because I have not been convicted of any crime, Your Honour.

JUST. SAMUELS: So you are on remand, awaiting trial. Very well. Citizen Turner, please phrase your questions such that the witness can give an informative answer.

CN. TURNER: I'm sorry, Your Honour, I believed that was what I was trying to do. May I continue?

JUST. SAMUELS: Please do.

CN. TURNER: Thank you. Leslee, we have established that you have not been convicted of any crime. Can you please tell the court how long you have been at the Belmarsh Detention Facility?

A. Er, yes, I was arrested in November last year and was transferred to Belmarsh two days after my arrest.

Q. So, six months in a high security prison without your case going to trial. Is that correct?

A. Er, yes, just under six months.

Q. Your Honour, I am no legal expert, as you know, but I believe that under the People's Constitution, a citizen may only be remanded in custody for a maximum of ninety days before their case is brought to trial, and yet –

JUST. SAMUELS: Citizen Turner, are you now acting as legal counsel for Citizen King here, as well as for yourself? Please confine your questioning and your comments to matters pertaining only to your own defence from now on. However, Citizen King, given that we must assume what you have told the court is true, I shall make personal inquiries into why your remand has been so extended.

CN. KING: Thank you, Your Honour.

CN. TURNER: Yes, thank you, Your Honour. Now, you may think my next question is not related to my own case, but I can assure you it is, and I would ask the court to bear with me a little longer.

JUST. SAMUELS: Very well.

CN. TURNER: Thank you. Leslee, can you tell the court why you were arrested in November last year?

A. I was arrested for suspected involvement in child trafficking.

Q. As part of Sergeant Stephenson's investigations?

A. Yes, as part of Sergeant Stephenson's investigations. I was one of eleven people arrested by Sergeant Stephenson and his colleagues, suspected of being in a child trafficking gang.

Q. Thank you, and were you involved in child trafficking?

A. No, we were rescuing children, not trafficking them.

Q. And can you tell the court what you were rescuing these children from?

A. We were rescuing them from being discovered.

Q. Being discovered by whom?

A. By the State. You see, these children are different, and the State does not like that they are different. If they were discovered, these children would be forced to undergo harmful and unnecessary surgery, in an attempt to make them like the rest of us, but all it does is hurt them. The surgery is completely unnecessary.

JUST. SAMUELS: And are you some sort of a paediatric expert, Citizen King?

CN. TURNER: That is a good question, Your Honour, thank you for asking it. Citizen King, can you tell Justice Samuels and the rest of the court, about your professional training.

A. Yes, I am a trained paediatric nurse and worked as a community health visitor.

Q. Thank you. And did you ever visit my child, Joh Turner?

A. Yes, I did.

Q. And in your professional opinion, is my child normal or different?

A. He is both different and normal. Being different does not make a child abnormal.

Q. And if Joh had been discovered by the State, would he have been made to have the unnecessary surgery you spoke of?

A. Yes, he would.

JUST. SAMUELS: I must interject here. Firstly, as I thought I had made clear last week, I will not hear of a child being referred to as 'he', as if they are an animal. You will use the correct human pronoun, 'they'. Secondly, whether or not the child would have undergone surgery is a matter of speculation, of which I have never heard any rumour before, let alone solid evidence. Therefore, if you wish to make such a claim, you will rephrase it as an opinion, not as fact.

Q. OK. Leslee, do you believe that my child, Joh, would have been forced to have surgery which you believe to be unnecessary?

A. Yes, I do.

Q. And do you therefore believe, in your professional opinion as a paediatric nurse, that it is in Joh's best interests to be beyond the reach of our state?

A. Yes, I do.

Q. Your Honour, it is enshrined in our constitution that the safety and protection of our nation's children is of utmost importance. Citizen King, do you believe that, in assisting with Joh's escape, I was acting to protect my child and keep them safe from harm?

A. Yes, without doubt. I would have done the same.

CN. TURNER: Thank you. I have no further questions for this witness, Your Honour.

JUST. SAMUELS: Hmm. Citizen Kelly, do you wish to cross-examine this witness?

CN. KELLY: I do, Your Honour.

CN. LESLEE KING
Questions from CN. AL KELLY

CN. KELLY: Nurse King, your testimony so far has been very enlightening. However, there are a couple of small details on which I hope you will be able to shed even more light. Tell me, prior to your arrest, by which health authority were you employed?

A. Um, most recently, I was employed by the, er, Staffordshire Health Trust.

Q. I see, thank you, and you were working for the, er, Staffordshire Health Trust right up until your arrest. Is that correct?

A. Um, no, actually.

Q. No. Actually, it has been six years, has it not, since you last worked for the Staffordshire Health Trust?

A. Er, yes, I suppose it has been about six years now, but I am still a qualified paediatric nurse and health visitor.

Q. Hmm, yes, and continuing to practise, it would seem, in a private capacity with these, er, different children, yes?

A. Well, I suppose you could say that, although I was never paid for my work with them, so I was not practising in any unauthorised way, only –

Q. No, indeed, I'm sure, though I do wonder, when there is currently such demand for people with your skills, why anyone with such expertise would not be offering their services for one of the many paid vacancies, and yet, prior to your arrest, you were claiming unemployment assistance. Why was that?

A. Um.

Q. Yes, um indeed. Your Honour, I have submitted a request to the Staffordshire Health Trust for Nurse King's employment files. However, since it is less than a week since we received notification of their inclusion as a witness for the defence, I hope you will excuse us for not quite having all the paperwork in order.

A. I left because I was ill.

Q. Ah, I see. Well, I am very sorry to hear that. Your Honour, perhaps the paperwork will not be needed after all. Citizen, sorry, Nurse King, thank you so much for enlightening us. However, you leave me a little confused. If you were unable to work because of illness for the five and a half years leading up to your arrest, why were you claiming unemployment assistance from the State, and not, for example, an infirmity pension from your insurance company?

A. My, er, condition was not covered by the insurance.

Q. No, quite, and I hope you don't mind me asking, but was your, er, condition related at all to your decision to call yourself by a different name?

[Pause]

JUST. SAMUELS: I'm sorry? Citizen Kelly, are you suggesting that the witness before the court is not actually called Leslee King?

CN. KELLY: Not at all, Your Honour. As far as I am aware, the legal name for this witness is Leslee King, but I have it on good authority that Citizen King here has, in recent years, chosen to tell some acquaintances that their name, or should I say her name, is Lily.

JUST. SAMUELS: What do you mean, *her* name?

CN. KELLY: Your Honour, if you would be willing for me to recall the defendant's former partner, Cris Turner, as a witness, they would testify that around this time last year, the person here before the court visited the Turners and during that visit, they informed Citizens Turner and Turner that they were choosing to be known not as Leslee, but Lily, and that this was because they had decided they were in fact a female human. Is this not correct, Leslee?

A. Well, er...yes. That is true.

JUST. SAMUELS: This is preposterous. Never in all my years of sitting at this bench have I heard of humans wanting to gender themselves like animals. Citizen King, I suggest you seek some professional help for your delusions. Citizen Kelly, can we now allow the witness to step down?

CN. KELLY: Thank you, Your Honour, yes. I have no further questions for them, or should I say, no further questions for her?

Chapter 10

Eva

Eva opened the café door to a cacophony of opinions. The only three not speaking were Victoria, Anthony and Sally. Victoria made up for her lack of speech with the clatter of dishes, busying herself with clearing the carnage of the meals she'd served up. Anthony slouched, sullen and green-tinted in the corner; what he clearly needed most was bed, but he wouldn't leave until every argument had burnt itself out. Sally sat quietly at Sandra's side, where Eva should have been. Tom was unsurprisingly absent, always the one to stir up the hornet's nest and then amble calmly away.

Eva ushered the three children into the crowded room. Before she could push the door shut behind her, Katie and Peter had squeezed between legs and under tables and were bouncing excitedly around Sandra. Eva took in a sharp breath. She should have spoken to them before they went in. She should have insisted they stay by her side. But the café was their domain as much as anyone else's, and during any gathering here, the kids belonged firmly to the community, not to any one parent. Grace squirmed, eager to be free of the fabric binding her tightly to Eva's back. Her fingers worked at the knots, but with her eyes she was imploring the children to look over in her direction, just for a moment. Would they understand a subtle shake of the head?

Please don't mention our trip to see the helicopter, not yet.

Thankfully, Sandra was caught up in debate. She loved their kids, but she could be remarkably impervious to their energetic presence when in the middle of an important conversation. Sandra would win the debate, she always did; but at the moment, a gaggle of the younger girls, led by Mouthy Maisy, were doing a pretty good job of fomenting a mutiny.

'What's the point in us staying here on this island when there aren't any boys? Did you ask them whether there were boys where they came from?'

'But we're doing fine here at the moment without boys. You have to think about what's best for the community, not just yourselves.'

'Ha, that's easy for you to say. Maybe we don't want you telling us what's best for the community anymore. And how can having no boys be best for the community?'

Eva glanced across at Anthony. His normal cocky demeanour had apparently emptied itself out of him along with the vomit. Maisy, meanwhile, was on a roll.

'When are you going to face up to it, Sandra? This is it. DiG is finished and nobody else is coming.'

'No, you don't know that. Didn't you hear what Jay said in the letter? There are others. Jay's going to gather them together and then bring them all over.'

Charlie shuffled closer to Eva and snuggled into her. Would he ever not be haunted by the memories of that night? How did he really feel about being the only survivor, the only one to successfully deliver Jay's letter? She hugged him into herself. He'd grown and filled out a lot in the last six months, in all sorts of ways, but he was still fragile.

'Are you crazy? That was six months ago! You can't seriously still believe that's going to happen. If Jay was still free, they'd have got here by now.'

'What, and risk another winter crossing? Do you think you know my sibling better than I do? Jay will have found somewhere safe to hide on the mainland until the weather improved.'

'Which it did, two months ago. Maybe you've been spending too long shut up in that head house of yours to notice it, but the sea's been pretty calm recently.'

'If we desert our island for this unknown France, who will be here to welcome them when they come? Or to be here for Nats when she finds her way back here?'

Sandra didn't like it when others implied she wasn't on top of everything. But she had a point too – what if, as they spoke, Nats was on her way back to the island?

'Fine, you stay here if you want to, but if the visitors are still here, I'm gonna go with them. You can't force the rest of us to wait with you.'

'Maybe Maisy's right,' Eva blurted out.

The café fell silent; all eyes turned to Eva. Had she really intended to say that out loud? Yes, she'd been thinking it, but she never actually spoke her thoughts in meetings. Often before a meeting, she and Sandra would mull over what contentions might arise. Sometimes afterwards, as they lay snuggled together, Eva would carefully question some of Sandra's assertions. But in the meetings themselves, she never spoke.

'Maybe some of us should go. See what France is like, visit Joe, see what help they can offer us here on the island, even see if we can persuade them to help us get Nats to safety. Surely, it's better if we work with them.' She'd said too much.

'And they could fix Peter's heart too,' Katie's little voice piped up.

Eva stared at the floor, tried to shrink into herself as her face flushed hot. She didn't dare look at Sandra. Sandra must have known Maggie and Lewi and the soldiers wouldn't leave on her command without meeting others from the community, without finding out what others thought or wanted. Maisy was right; all of them had the right to leave the island if they wanted to. But Eva had always stood by Sandra, before today.

Maisy was first to break the silence. 'Why does Peter need his heart fixing, Katie?'

'Fine, you can all go to France if you want to,' Sandra cut in before Katie could reply. 'I hope you're all happy there and find they can fix all your problems for you.'

Hoisting Katie onto her hip, Sandra marched out through the pathway that opened up between her and the door. As the door slammed shut, all eyes returned to Eva. Even Anthony looked at her with something approaching awe and respect rather than disdain. Everyone was waiting for her to speak.

'OK, look, so I was near where they landed their helicopter – that's what they call their flying machine – this morning, so I was the first to meet them, and then we met Sandra and Tom on the road.'

'And what did Katie mean about Peter's heart?' asked Maisy.

Peter sat, small and quiet, on the chair Sandra had vacated. She'd explained to the children a little bit of what Lewi and Maggie had told her, as they'd dawdled back along the road to the village. She hadn't wanted to, but Katie and Charlie had sort of wheedled it out of her. How had they worked out so quickly that she was considering taking Peter to France?

'I'll tell you all about it in the morning if you like. These kids need to go to bed, and I need to talk to Sandra.'

She beckoned to Peter, and he obediently wove his way back to her. She gathered him up with one arm whilst balancing Grace on the other. Charlie waited patiently by the door. As she put Peter down next to Charlie and guided them both out into the night, she turned back to the occupants of the still-silent café.

'I know I can't stop you, but please don't go out to see the visitors tonight. Some of them have guns. Let's all go and see them tomorrow, when it's light. They'll still be there, I promise.'

'I'M SORRY, I'D planned to only take Peter to see them, and maybe Grace, because I thought Vicki might prefer me to take Grace off her hands, but then she was so busy with getting things ready for the meeting...'

Eva perched on the corner of their bed, wondering whether to reach out a hand to run her fingers through that flame-red hair, which still flickered, even in the gloom of their bedroom.

'Oh, so it's Victoria's fault, is it? I know she's often to blame for things, but...'

It wasn't like Sandra, to not finish a sentence. Maybe she had, but her words were stolen by the pillow she was burrowing into.

'No, that's not what I meant. It's just...'

How could she put this? She knew it was risky, taking Katie. Peter wouldn't have blurted it out like Katie had in the middle of the meeting. She probably shouldn't have gone at all, after hearing there was to be a meeting. What did Sandra think when she and the children weren't there at the start? Maggie and Lewi would have waited until the morning. They wouldn't have flown away without seeing Peter, would they? Had Sandra fallen asleep now? Eva started unbuttoning her shirt, eased herself gently up off the bed, but still the old bedframe creaked and the mattress bounced, refusing to leave Sandra undisturbed.

Sandra turned onto her back and stared at the ceiling with puffy eyes. People thought Sandra lacked emotion; Eva knew the real Sandra, but even she rarely saw evidence of tears.

'It's just what? You thought it would be OK if you only took Peter and Grace because they're *your* children?'

Eva sat back down, soaked up Sandra's accusation, reached out a hand to tenderly stroke away the strands of hair still stuck across her lover's cheek. Hair that had left behind the imprint of a thousand swirls. Sandra pressed her head against Eva's hand, allowing her gentle caress, but stared past her at the ceiling with injured eyes.

'Is that how you see it? Katie's mine, Peter and Grace are yours?'

'No!'

Except actually, yes, sometimes at least, increasingly more so perhaps, as the children grew up, their characters defining themselves. Katie was so blatantly Sandra's child, and Tom's for that matter. She had Tom's dark curls and his tendency to go off in a huff when she didn't get her way. Peter was always more compliant. Sandra said he should stick up for himself a bit more, but he was happy enough and Eva loved his gentle nature.

'When I was growing up, Martey never treated Jay any differently to me. Jay was always just as much Martey's child as I was. I thought we'd agreed to do the same for ours, that we're both equally parents to all three of them – four if you count Charlie, which I do.' Sandra pulled herself up into a sitting position, shaking off any sign of sleep, ready to argue this out. The bed groaned again in protest.

Eva kicked off her shoes and shuffled back to sit beside Sandra, allowed an imperceptible sigh to expel itself through her nose. What was she supposed to say? She wouldn't apologise. OK, so she'd gone against... no, ignored Sandra's opinion. Sandra did it to her all the time – listened to her opinion and then completely ignored it and did what she'd always intended to do. And Eva had been right about Peter; she hadn't imagined a problem that wasn't there. She had nothing to apologise for. Sandra's hand came to rest on her thigh, gave it a squeeze. Eva pulled in a breath and held her words for a few seconds, still undecided how to start.

'I'm sorry.' Damn, that wasn't how needed to start. 'Actually, I'm not sorry. I did what I thought was best for Peter. I'd have done the same for Katie.' Would she?

Would she have dared to go against Sandra's wishes if it had been Katie's health she'd been worried about? Would she have been so aware of a little problem like Peter's with Katie? Except it wasn't a little problem, was it?

'Look. Come with us in the morning. Come and talk to Maggie and Lewi again. Have a listen to Peter's heart with their stethoscope.'

Eva waited. Not for a concession. She didn't expect for one minute that Sandra would concede. No, she waited for Sandra's self-assured declarations that Eva was wrong and she was right. She waited patiently for Sandra's persuasive assurances that staying here together on this island really was the best thing for them. She waited faithfully for Sandra's wonderful words of optimism that Jay would surely soon be here, with all their medical expertise and with more children to care for and nurture. But Sandra had nothing to say.

Sandra hmphed, slid back down the bed, curled back up into her cocoon, pulled the covers out from under Eva and up tightly around her own shoulders. Eva finished unbuttoning her shirt, shuffled out of her trousers, dropped her baggy pyjama T-shirt over her head and slipped under what was left of the covers to wait for the morning.

Chapter 11

PEOPLE'S COURT OF CANTERBURY
Case No. 57-143
Date: 03-05-157 (Day 3)
JUDGE: The Hon. Just. Joh Samuels
DEFENDANT: Cn. Georgy Turner

(11:40)

DR. NAZ KHAN
Questions from CN. GEORGY TURNER

CN. TURNER: Doctor Khan, sixteen years ago, you were working as lead consultant of the Wrexford Fertility Unit, is that correct?

A. Um, yes, that would be correct. I became lead consultant at Wrexford in June one-thirty-nine and was there until I moved to my current post in fifty-one.

Q. And you're still working in the area of human fertilisation and gestation, correct?

A. Yes, although my time is now divided mostly between teaching and research at the, erm, University of Nottingham.

Q. Thank you. So, you would consider yourself something of an expert on human fertilisation and gestation, yes?

A. Well, yes, I have been working in the field ever since I completed my medical training.

Q. Excellent, so could you please outline for the court the key stages in producing and gestating a human baby and how it differs from the fertilisation of animals. Sheep, for example.

A. Well, I am a doctor of human medicine, not a veterinarian, but er, for humans –

CN. KELLY: Objection.

JUST. SAMUELS: Yes, yes, agreed. Citizen Turner, I must insist that you move directly to questions of pertinence to your case and not ask your witness to give us a biology lesson.

CN. TURNER: But Your Honour –

JUST. SAMUELS: Move on please, Citizen Turner, or sit down and I shall question the witness myself.

CN. TURNER: No, Your Honour, I will move on. Doctor Khan, do you recall meeting me and my partner Cris, when we attended for our twenty-week scan on ninth September one-forty-one?

A. I'm sorry, I do not recall, though if indeed I did meet with you at your twenty-week scan appointment, I imagine there must have been some complication to discuss with you. The nurses handle all the routine cases and the twenty-week scan is almost always routine.

Q. We didn't get as far as a scan, Dr Khan. Instead, we were directed into your consulting room where you told us our pregnancy would be terminated.

A. Ah, well, it would have been advised, rather than told. I would have advised you that termination and re-fertilisation was the best course of action for your pregnancy.

Q. And why would this have been your, er, advice, Doctor Khan?

A. Well, as I say, I'm afraid I cannot recall your particular case, so I could not say for certain. There could have been one or more of a number of, er, complications with the foetus which would lead to a recommendation to terminate.

Q. Could you perhaps give the court some examples?

A. Well, um, there are many different, er –

Q. OK, would an abnormal growth on the foetus be a reason to terminate?

A. Yes, yes, if an abnormal growth is detected on the foetus, it would be investigated and, in most cases, the best course of action is to terminate. Nobody wants a deformed baby.

Q. And would you say that a penis is an abnormal growth, a deformity?

JUST. SAMUELS: I beg your pardon?

CN. TURNER: A penis, Your Honour. You know, the appendage common amongst the males in many animal species, through which they pass urine and fertilise females of their species. Have you forgotten your school biology lessons, Your Honour?

JUST. SAMUELS: I know very well what you are referring to, Citizen Turner, and if I hear any more impertinent remarks directed at me, I will hold you in contempt of court. We all know that humans do not have the appendage to which you refer.

CN. TURNER: Which is why we cannot reproduce in the way animals do but rely on the services of fertility units such as the one in which my partner and I met Dr Khan. However, am I not correct, Doctor Khan, in saying that occasionally a human foetus may develop what would appear to be a penis?

A. Well, er, we cannot be certain that the growths of this type on human foetuses are actually –

Q. Oh, come on, Doctor Khan, does it look like a penis?

A. Well, as I said, I am not a veterinarian, but we have no firm evidence to suggest that such a growth would function in the same way as an animal penis if such foetuses were allowed to develop to full term.

Q. Allowed to develop? I thought it was simply a recommendation to terminate in such cases.

A. Well, no, in that particular case, a termination would be the only possible course of action.

Q. Because?

A. Well, because [pause] because it is unnatural.

Q. Doctor Khan, I have worked in the actuarial industry, and I put it to you that in fact, any feature which is considered to be less than perfect in a human is weeded out through pregnancy terminations. That it suits our industry and yours to make humans who are uniform and predictable and in particular, that it would be a disaster for both our industries if humans were allowed to develop who might be able to reproduce without the assistance of your fertility units.

A. There is no evidence to suggest such reproduction would even be possible. It would also require the creation of, er, female humans, and it would be years before we found out. I would not even countenance supporting such a vile and inhumane experiment.

Q. So, all foetuses displaying such an abnormality would be terminated, correct?

A. Of course, without question.

Q. But if I told you that our foetus, which you wanted to terminate, was rescued by staff within the fertility unit that you led?

A. Impossible!

Q. And that foetus grew to be a perfectly healthy child, with a penis and testicles?

JUST. SAMUELS: Citizen Turner, that is enough! You will sit down. Citizen Kelly, do you have any questions for this witness?

CN. KELLY: I do not, Your Honour.

Chapter 12

Nats

'ALL RIGHT, HERE you go girl. Don't say I never give you anything.'

The slab of ham is caught and swallowed in one slick, slobbery motion, ensuring the compliance of my new friend. I can't have her making lots of noise around the barn – letting the adult know I'm here – so I have to let her in, and then, of course, she expects some sort of a treat. What'll I do when I'm feeling better and want the meat myself? Just thinking about it now brings bile to the back of my throat. I grab my bottle and glug down some water, but the acid holds fast, refusing to be washed down. I groan. How long is this illness going to last? For how long can I carry on throwing my guts up every morning at the slightest whiff of food? I can't leave when I'm feeling like this. I wouldn't get further than the end of the farm track without collapsing.

'It's your fault, this is!' I say to the dog as she sniffs the dust for traces of pig meat that surely can't exist. It must be the dog I caught it off, when she licked my face all over. I'm sure it wasn't anything I ate. Everything Lottie brings me smells good and fresh, even if I can't stand the smell of it now. OK, maybe my diet's been a bit apple-heavy, but apples can't make you sick, can they? Dirty dog licks can, though. Who knows what else that dirty dog has been wrapping its tongue round?

We had a dog at the farmhouse. I think his real name was Pluto, but we all called him Poo-dog after what we saw him licking out in the yard one morning. He was massive, and he'd pant his foul breath right into my face, wagging his tail as if I should be grateful for his company. Hani said he was useful for scaring off strangers. We could have done with him scaring off whoever set fire to our farmhouse, but when he was needed, he was curled up snoring in the warmth with everyone else, listening to Tom's spooky stories. So it fell to little me, shut out in the cold of the hallway, to realise we were under attack and warn the others. It wasn't till we got to the cave that someone remembered Pluto. Sandra said she was sure he'd have woken up and got out in time. I know it sounds awful, but I secretly hoped he hadn't.

'You're all right, though,' I say to my new friend, Nelly, 'even if you have made me sick. You're good company and you haven't given me away to anyone yet. Joe would be glad to know I've got some company.'

Nelly looks up from whatever scent she was chasing and comes bounding over to me.

'Oh no you don't! I'm saving the rest.' I seize the plate and lift it clear just in time, balancing it on top of the tractor's rusty wheel cover. Two miserable slices of bread, slightly ham scented. I couldn't eat them now. It would be a waste – they'd come straight back up, I know it. But if I wait till later and pinch my nose so I can't smell the greasy ham stains, I'll be able to keep them down long enough for my tummy to churn them up and pass them on down through my system instead of back up the way they came.

'Hey, you keep that tongue away from me. I've got to get better – strong for when Joe comes back. Yes, I know, he's probably not coming back, but...'

My empty tummy churns again. I am utterly hollowed out, in my heart as well as my stomach. I can't stay here forever being brought sandwiches by a little neut kid and their dog.

Chapter 13

PEOPLE'S COURT OF CANTERBURY
Case No. 57-143
Date: 03-05-157 (Day 3)
JUDGE: The Hon. Just. Joh Samuels
DEFENDANT: Cn. Georgy Turner

(14:45)

DR. WYN LEE
Questions from CN. GEORGY TURNER

CN. TURNER: Doctor Lee, can you begin by telling us what you are a doctor of?

A. I am a medical doctor, but my specialism is human fertilisation and gestation, although I am now retired.

Q. Ah, so you would perhaps be acquainted with our last witness, Doctor Naz Khan?

A. Yes, very much so. Doctor Khan worked under me when I was lead consultant at Bristol and I then recommended them for the lead position at Wrexford.

Q. Thank you. So, in your role as lead consultant of a fertility unit, did you ever come across foetuses that appeared to be developing features which might identify them as male or female, in the way that animals are male and female?

A. Er yes, occasionally a foetus would appear to develop male or female sexual organs, only ever in the case of dual-parent procreations, and rather rarely at that.

[Pause]

JUST. SAMUELS: Silence in court! Silence! We may not like what this witness is claiming, but I will not have them shouted down by those in the gallery.

CN. TURNER: Thank you, Your Honour. Doctor Lee, what happened to these foetuses? What action did you take, as lead consultant, at their discovery?

A. Well, the male foetuses were easy to spot and were terminated, at first, but –

JUST. SAMUELS: Silence! I will have people removed if necessary. Dr Lee, although I am disturbed by your assertions, please carry on.

DR. LEE: Yes, Your Honour. As I said, the male foetuses were easy to spot from about seventeen or eighteen weeks' gestation. The development of female sexual organs is harder to spot, so in the early days, some were not discovered until the moment of birth.

CN. TURNER: So you are telling us that some female human babies have been born and survived?

A. Yes, very much so. It greatly saddens and shames me to say that under the authority of the HRA, some were terminated at birth. Others were kept alive, usually at the insistence of the parents, but were operated on at a few days old to, er, repair them.

Q. I see, and did these babies go on to live normal lives?

A. No, they did not. In all the cases I am aware of, there were complications which led to infections and ultimately death within a few months. I believe the operation has been more successful, surgically and medically speaking, when carried out with slightly older children, but the cases have been few and far between because systems have now been developed for detecting the female organs at a similar stage to the males.

Q. Are you aware of any children who have survived without undergoing any surgical or medical interventions?

A. Yes.

Q. Thank you, Doctor Lee. Now, I know you are putting your professional reputation on the line in testifying today, and possibly risking a lot more...

A. I'm retired. I've cared for far too long about my professional reputation instead of the things that matter.

Q. Doctor Lee, I hope the court will appreciate that. So, can you tell the court what your involvement has been with these children.

[Pause]

JUST. SAMUELS: Doctor Lee?

A. I helped to hide and to keep safe some of the female and male foetuses. I worked with a colleague to acquire a disused fertility unit. Then, with the parents' consent, we moved the foetuses to our own facility and looked after them until birth.

[Pause]

JUST. SAMUELS: Silence! Citizens in the gallery, you will leave the courtroom or you will remain in your seats, keeping your opinions to yourselves.

CN. TURNER: And what happened to these babies, after their birth. Were they given surgery to 'repair' them?

A. No, they were not. There was no need. All the female babies I had delivered at my unit in Bristol appeared healthy. There was no medical need for any 'corrective surgery' and certainly no case for termination at birth. I also believed there should be no reason for male children not to be similarly healthy.

Q. So, what happened to the babies?

A. They were handed over to their parents, unharmed, with strong advice to keep their differences secret until we could find a way of getting society to accept them.

Q. And do you know where any of these children are now?

A. I do not. Well, except for one. I understand poor Cain is being held in a police cell somewhere, but the rest, no. Some I hope are still with their parents. Regrettably, some were discovered, operated on and then placed with foster parents. A few years ago, we decided to offer some the chance to live at a remote farmhouse, but I was never involved in that particular project and have no knowledge of where this farmhouse is. I think they had to move on from there anyway.

Q. And is your secret facility still in operation.

A. Sadly, no. It was raided by the police about six months ago. Everything was destroyed – all the equipment and every foetus.

Q. So, do you think it is now safe for those who have survived to live openly here in Britain?

A. Absolutely not. It should be, because they're as human as we are, perhaps more so. But society is not ready to accept them yet and that makes it too dangerous for them.

Q. Thank you, Doctor Lee. I have no further questions, Your Honour.

JUST. SAMUELS: Thank you. Now, before we hear whether Citizen Kelly has any questions for the witness, Doctor Lee, you have admitted today to actions which are at the very least gross misconduct for a member of the medical profession and, in all likelihood, will lead to a criminal prosecution. Therefore, after you have stepped down from the witness box today, you will be arrested and detained pending further investigation. Is that clear?

DR. LEE: Yes, Your Honour.

JUST. SAMUELS: Very well. Citizen Kelly, do you have any questions for Doctor Lee?

CN. KELLY: I do, Your Honour, just one or two quick questions. Doctor Lee, you mentioned that your secret fertility unit was raided by police. At that time, the police made a number of arrests. How did you avoid arrest?

A. I was not there when the unit was raided. I was always very careful.

Q. And yet every other member of your organisation, D-I-G, I believe you called yourselves, was arrested.

Well, all except one, a nurse who is still believed to be at large. Some were even arrested after other members of the organisation confessed and assisted the police with further names, and yet you appear to have escaped everyone's attention despite being at the heart of this secret operation. I wonder, could that have anything to do with the influence of an old school friend of yours, the Secretary of State for Health?

A. Absolutely not! They have never known of my involvement in all this. I am just a coward who has never dared to speak up until today.

Q. Well, perhaps we can judge the truth of that for ourselves when we see how things go for you after today. No further questions, Your Honour.

JUST. SAMUELS: Thank you, Citizen Kelly. Doctor Lee, you may stand down from the witness box. The constables will take you to the holding cell.

[Pause]

JUST. SAMUELS: Citizen Turner, I see we have reached the end of your witness list, so perhaps we can take a short break and then hear closing remarks and have this all wrapped up by the end of today. Yes?

CN. TURNER: Er, no, Your Honour. There is one witness on my list whom we have not yet heard from. The child, Cain.

JUST. SAMUELS: Ah. Well, Citizen Turner, you have represented yourself well and I believe we can reach a favourable verdict for you without putting young Cain through a grilling by Citizen Kelly here.

CN. TURNER: No, Your Honour, with respect, I believe that after all the court has heard, it is important that Cain is also given the opportunity to give his testimony.

JUST. SAMUELS: You mean 'their testimony'. We will use only the correct human pronouns in my court, thank you. From what I have heard, this child has refused to speak to anyone since their arrest and is therefore very unlikely to speak to this court.

CN. TURNER: But I would like to at least give him, sorry, them, the chance.

CN. KELLY: Your Honour, as the appointed representative for the people, I concur with your position and urge that this case now be brought to its conclusion. The child is not fit to be called as a witness.

JUST. SAMUELS: Indeed. Thank you, Citizen Kelly. I believe you have helped me to make up my mind. I have a few telephone calls to make. Court is adjourned until four-thirty.

(16:30)

JUST. SAMUELS: Citizen Turner, you wish to call the child known as Cain as a witness for the defence in this case and, indeed, under our laws, you have the right to do so.

CN. KELLY: But Your Honour, the prosecution –

JUST. SAMUELS: And as Citizen Kelly was about to remind us, the prosecution may petition the court with evidence that calling a particular witness would cause significant harm to the witness or another citizen. I have not yet received –

CN. KELLY: Your Honour, we will –

JUST. SAMUELS: I have not yet received that petition from the prosecution, but I have made my own inquiries concerning the child, and it is my conclusion that it will do no further significant harm to the child, or to any other citizen, for the child to be brought before the court as a witness. However, no purpose will be served by calling the child to the stand tomorrow.

Citizen Turner, you cannot claim that you did not assault two police officers in Dover on fourteenth April this year, but I do not believe you pose any ongoing threat, either to the police, any other individual, or to the general public. Therefore, I am overturning the previous ruling that you be remanded in custody until your case is concluded and release you on bail, pending the conclusion of your case.

I have also been impressed with the way in which you have represented yourself and questioned your witnesses. Therefore, I have asked for arrangements to be made for you to conduct a number of supervised interviews with the child, prior to the resumption of your case. If anyone can get the child to speak, I believe you can. Now, this all may take some time so –

CN. KELLY: Objection, Your Honour, this is highly irregular and without precedent.

JUST. SAMUELS: Objection noted but overruled. This case has already been somewhat irregular, and one role of this court is to establish new precedents. As I was saying, the process of organising and then conducting these interviews may take some time. Therefore, I now move that this case be adjourned for four months until the week beginning sixth September.

Chapter 14

Eva

'MUMMYYY...I NEED A carry.'

'Peter, I can't! Look, where would I put you?'

Peter flinched. Eva shouldn't have shouted. Grace let out a whimpering cough and sucked in a jagged breath, charging her lungs for a full-blown wail. She writhed against the bindings holding her tight to Eva's chest and kicked her little feet at the lumpy bag on Eva's back.

'I could carry the bag and you could carry me.'

Eva allowed herself a smile at her son's impeccable logic. Poor Peter. They'd gone twice the distance they normally would without a stop and at three times their normal ambling speed, and this was his first sign of complaint. Grace, meanwhile, had been whinging and wriggling in her cosy wrappings all the way.

Eva stopped and turned to face Peter. It shamed her to catch the momentary flicker of fear in his eyes before he could see she wasn't cross with him anymore. She dropped to a crouch and wobbled as the bag almost toppled her onto her back like an upturned beetle. She lowered herself onto her knees, ignoring for now the question of how she'd get up from this position, and pulled Peter into a Grace-squashing hug. Grace protested loudly, both with her lungs and with sharp knees against Eva's already battered ribs. But then she calmed at her brother's magical whispers in her ear.

'How do you do that?' she whispered in Peter's own ear. 'You'll have to teach me the magic sometime.'

'But magic has to stay a secret,' Peter replied. 'Otherwise it doesn't work anymore.'

Eva smiled. Those were Sandra's words; Peter would miss her and Katie terribly while they were gone. Would their family ever be the same again, or would what they were about to do tear a hole in their collective heart forever? Is that what it would cost to fix the tiny hole in Peter's heart? Perhaps they shouldn't go; he'd managed really well with being dragged along the road this morning. Maybe Sandra was right; if Maggie and Lewi hadn't come, if Nats and Cain and Joe had never left, they'd have none of them known any different and Peter would right now probably be enjoying a game of chase on the beach with Nats and Katie. And yes, maybe he'd have to stop and sit with thoughtful Charlie every now and then to catch his breath, but...

They should turn back and return to the village. Let Sandra persuade Maggie to leave them alone. She assumed that was where Sandra had gone this morning, her impression in the bed hardly visible by the time Eva opened her eyes. Would Maggie take Sandra's word for it and agree to leave without them? How long before Maisy and her gang marched along the road to stake their claims on a seat in the helicopter. How many people could the machine carry before it wouldn't be able to lift itself off the ground? Could this heavy bag on her back make the difference even? What if little Grace tipped the balance and she was told it had to be only her and Peter? Little Grace, whose steady breaths now pulsated against her chest. Maggie had only talked about taking Eva and Peter. She wasn't expecting them to leave Grace behind, was she?

Eva untangled from Peter and held him at arm's length, daring to experimentally ease herself back onto her feet without relying on her son to steady her.

'Do you think you can walk a bit further now? It's not far now, is it, to the oat fields, where the helicopter's made its nest? Or would you prefer to go the village?'

Peter gave a small but definite shake of his head. That was an unfair question for the little boy. Did he really understand the momentousness of the decision they were about to make, had already made, might decide not to go through with? If he did, would he choose to go to France or stay here with Katie and Sandra and Charlie and Vicki and Maisy? Perhaps she should have properly asked him what he wanted, but it was her job as a parent, wasn't it? To decide what was best for her children. You couldn't expect a three-year-old to know what was best. Anyway, he'd say yes just for the helicopter ride.

'Come on then. Let's see if we can get there before your sister wakes up again.' Eva tried not to groan too loudly at the aches and twinges as she straightened up and shook the blood back into her calves and feet. Then, taking Peter's hand, they set off down the road together, Eva taking care to match Peter's pace rather than him having to match hers.

'Look, there it is, exactly where it was yesterday. Do you think it's had a nice sleep?'

'Don't be silly, Mummy, it's a machine, and machines don't need to sleep.'

'No, you're right. Silly Mummy. Although, when I saw it land there yesterday morning, it felt then like it was a living creature.' Was that really only yesterday morning?

'And look! Mummy Sandra's talking to Maggie. Is she coming in the helpicopter too?' Peter bounced on his toes in excitement. 'And Katie? If Mummy Sandra's coming, can Katie and Charlie come too?'

'That would be lovely, wouldn't it?' Eva squeezed Peter's hand. 'But I don't know whether the helicopter can carry all of us, and anyway, Mummy Sandra needs to stay and look after things here while we're gone.'

Sandra certainly didn't look like she was requesting a place on the helicopter. Even from this distance, Eva recognised her lover's characteristic stance of defiance. Feet slightly further apart than looked natural, planted firmly on the ground; hands unmoving on her slender hips except when she needed her left hand to sweep the flaming hair off her face; head cocked slightly to one side in the pretence of listening to her opponent's every word.

Maggie, meanwhile, looked totally at ease, leaning against the dry-stone wall, propped up on her hands, lower than Sandra yet so clearly in control, nodding calmly at each of Sandra's objections. Yesterday's full-face breathing apparatus had been dispensed with, giving Eva a clearer impression of Maggie's square-jawed face, dark hair fastened back neatly in a plait which seemed to work backwards from the very front of her head. She still obviously felt the need for some form of protection from the local air, judging by the covering tightly masking her nose and mouth, but even without being able to see her mouth, Eva could tell she felt no need to interrupt Sandra's monologue anytime soon.

'...so you can tell Joe that we're very glad he's found a new home with you but that our home is here and we can look after ourselves, including our children, who are perfectly well and healthy and happy here, and –'

'Sandra, please.' Eva drew alongside her. 'Can you at least try listening to what Lewi has to say about Peter's heart. He is a doctor, you know.' She settled her free hand in the crook of Sandra's elbow and detected the drooping of her shoulders. How long had Maggie been letting her talk without interruption? Sandra was used to arguing, and winning, but not without a vocal opponent to spar with.

Sandra turned her head towards Eva, her eyes streaming with hurt and betrayal, a sleep-deprived night and one of those headaches that would be with her until bedtime. 'How can I listen to Lewi when he doesn't even speak the same words as us? How do we even know he's a doctor or that the words *she* tells us are his actual words? You see, we have no idea who these people are or what they want.'

'Please, Sandra, they want to help us. They might not speak our words, but can't you see? Apart from that, they are just like us. Women and men like us. Haven't we always dreamed of finding others like us?'

Sandra pulled away from Eva, feigning the need to sweep hair out of her eyes. 'I thought *we* were each other's dream. Am I not enough for you anymore, now you've seen what else is available?' She nodded towards Maggie, still listening on with patient self-assurance. 'That's it, isn't it? You're bored of me and you're hoping she'll sweep you off your feet in her flying machine. Well, I'm sorry I'm not exciting enough for you anymore.'

'Oh don't be so ridiculous!' Why was Sandra being so irrational? Was she really jealous of Maggie and her helicopter? Yes, seeing the machine had sparked in Eva a buzz she'd inherited from her engineer parents, and yes, Maggie was...magnetic, but... 'Of course I'm not bored of you. This is only about Peter and what's best for *him*.'

Had she squeezed his hand a bit too tightly when she said that? He slithered from her grasp like a slippery newborn lamb. Lewi was there in an instant, kneeling over her son as he lay on the stony track beside her.

'What happened? What's up with him? I didn't notice... He was fine just...'

But now his face was as grey as the sky hanging heavily over their bickering, and his unmoving lips were tinged with icy blue. Lewi straightened up to gabble something at Maggie and then, as Eva tore her eyes away from her son to hear Maggie's translation, Lewi gathered Peter up in his arms and started towards the helicopter, shouting instructions at the guards, who were already springing to action around the machine.

'Eva, don't worry, Peter is in very good hands.' Maggie reached out to gently guide Eva to follow Lewi and her son. 'But we must hurry now. There is no more time for debate, and you must come with us, yes?'

Eva nodded and stumbled towards the helicopter, accepting Maggie's steadying hand.

'Wait, let me look at him. I'm sure he will be fine,' Sandra called after them, but her feet remained rooted where they were. 'He's tired, worn out from the long walk. He's only three. He just needs to rest.'

Eva's mind threw her back to that night on the beach; twelve bodies hauled from the violent sea. Grey faces, blue lips. Sandra's mouth to theirs, inflating the lungs over and over, showing others how to pump the chests, refusing to admit defeat until long after everyone else had collapsed onto the pebbles in exhaustion. If anyone on this island could make Peter better, it was Sandra, but she hadn't been able to breathe life into any one of those twelve grey faces with blue lips. Eva ran towards the helicopter, not caring how many oats she trampled.

'Where is he? What have you done with him?' Eva's eyes hunted in every corner, every crevice of the helicopter's cabin. Lewi busied himself over some of the breathing apparatus they'd all been wearing yesterday. Was he worried there might be something poisonous in the air after all?

'It's OK, Lewi is just giving him oxygen.' Maggie led her over to where Lewi was kneeling, lifted the heavy bag off her back and Grace off her front. Lewi had obviously changed his mind about the breathing mask because he lifted his hand away from it to rest it on Eva's arm, guiding her down beside him. His eyes spoke both worry and reassurance.

'Where is he?' Where had they hidden him? Why couldn't she see him? She followed Lewi's earnest gaze down to the mask on the floor beside them. She spotted Peter's coat, discarded next to the mask, still far too big for him even though it had been a whole year since they'd first put him in it. Little fingers peaked out of one of the sleeves. Her eyes darted back to the mask. And there he was, sleeping beneath her reflection, pink seeping back into his lips, face still deathly white but not deadly grey. She hovered her hand over his chest and it rose up to meet her.

'Eva, we must go. You must sit.' Maggie tugged on Eva's other arm.

'No, I need to stay right here.'

'No, Eva, you must sit over here.' Maggie gestured towards a seat so far away it might as well have been across the sea.

'But I won't be able to reach him from there.'

'You can hold him soon, I promise, but we must make everyone safe for take-off.'

Eva allowed herself to be wrenched away from Peter and restrained by straps and buckles to the distant seat. Large, padded shells were clamped over her ears. The sound of motors and whirring blades shrank into the distance, and through it came the clear but incomprehensible gabble of urgent voices.

Her stomach fell through the floor. She reached out to steady herself, even though no other part of her body could go anywhere, so tightly was she held into the seat. She strained forward against the straps, desperate to see her son, but Lewi's bulk obscured her view.

Her seat tipped sideways. Her shoulder squashed into the seat edge, pushing against bony metal under the soft and springy flesh of the seat. The sky disappeared from the window as the ground pushed it up out of the way. Eva braced herself against the edge of her seat. Were they falling or rising? It was impossible to tell.

The ground twisted and turned beneath them and there was Sandra, hands still on her hips, staring up at them, red hair raging wildly across her face. Their waspish machine righted itself, leaned forward and then shot out across the choppy sea.

Where was Grace? Did Maggie still have her? She tried to twist around to look for Maggie behind her, but her face just met a headrest, dislodging the ear coverings. For a moment, the persistent gabbling was replaced by a deafening, roaring whine. She let her head drop back against the headrest and pulled the shells back over her ears. If she could hear them, could they also hear her?

'Maggie, do you still have Grace? Is she OK? Is Peter OK?'

But nobody answered.

Chapter 15

Nats

'No, YOU STAY there, you stupid mutt.'
I dash round to the side of the barn, but not as far round as I usually get, and vomit out the hamless sandwich I've just eaten. I groan. I thought I was getting better. Nelly's hot, hammy breath pants over my face and I retch again. There goes last night's cheese sandwich.

'Hey, no, get off! That's disgusting!'

In three licks, Nelly gulps down most of what I've brought up. My stomach churns, threatening to find more to force up and out, even though there surely can't be any more. I give Nelly a sharp kick. She yelps, leaps backwards, then stands at the corner of the barn, barking her head off.

'Shh, go on, go away!' I whisper while failing to waft her away. I cast around for something to throw for her. That stone should do; I won't aim it straight at her.

'Oi, Nelly, quiet! What's all the fuss about?' The voice I recognise as Lottie's parent, Nelly's keeper, advances across the yard. My stone thuds to the ground about halfway between Nelly and the voice. 'Hello, who's that?'

Shit! I turn and stagger further into the shadow of the barn. Nelly bounds after me. I recognise her bark now as playful rather than vicious, but that's not the point. I get to the heap of broken planks. Can I safely get over them? I feel so lightheaded.

'Urgh, what's this? Something's been sick round here. Is this yours, Nelly? Nelly, come back here!'

Nelly is at my feet again. She's stopped barking but is looking at me in excited expectation, forelegs low, tail wagging. Soon she won't be able to contain herself and will let out a barked reminder that we were in the middle of a game.

'No, not now, go away, Nelly.'

'Nelly? Where have you got to? What have you found?'

Nelly barks a cheerful reply. I try to ignore her, focus on the heap of wood, picture my foot slipping, a plank splintering, my ankle twisting. But if I don't...

I steady myself, eye up my first step. Nelly leaps past me, guessing my plan and pledging to accompany me. She flies effortlessly over the heap and then turns and barks encouragement from the other side. I've got to do this. Once I'm over, it looks like a clear run to the back of the barn and then over a low fence and I'm into open field. Would they chase after me? How far and fast can I run with no food in my belly? I can't not try. I put my good foot forward. The plank bounces slightly under my weight, I lean forward to take my next step.

A strong hand grabs my shoulder from behind. I gasp. My head swims and I feel the other hand catching me as I fall.

Part 2

Chapter 16

Nats

HEAVY SHEETS PIN me down, sinking me into a mattress that I find alternately cosy and suffocating. Everything below my thumping heart feels like it has been carved out. Have they operated already?

A CALLOUS HAND clamps the back of my head, hauls me up towards a sitting position. My insides protest but my outside is helpless to resist. Something warm and salty is poured down my throat. I cough and splutter. Bile clings to the back of my throat, refusing to be either swallowed down or coughed up.

I want to sink back down into the bed, but the hand won't let me go. A cold, hard glass is pushed to my lips. Icy cold water forces its way into me. I feel it chilling my heart as it rushes past. More of the salty broth follows. This time I surrender to it, but my stomach's not so sure, squirming with resistance.

SOMETHING WET AND scratchy attacks my hand. For a moment, I inhale the familiarity of Nelly but it's soon dragged away and an opened window flushes her memory away.

A SMALL HAND strokes mine. A small voice tells my ears stories that my mind only sort of hears. I've been caught now, haven't I? Like Oliver Twist. Except I didn't expect to be read stories. That's a twist. But it was all right in the end for Oliver Twist because they found out he was family. Would my family know it was me if they found me now?

THE WINDOW IS pulled shut. *No, please, open it again! I need fresh air. I need the smell of freedom, even if I have been captured. I need to smell the sea again.*

Chapter 17

Eva

THE HELICOPTER TILTS again and its nest of flattened oats comes back into view. Eva gasps. There in the centre of the nest lies Peter's prone form, pale and grey against the ripening green. Grace is sitting beside him, waving her little arms up and down, up and down, screaming her head off, except Eva can't hear any of it – all she can hear is the unintelligible gabbling of the helicopter crew, oblivious to her panicked protests that they must turn back, that they've somehow left their patient behind. And Grace too – why had she let go of Grace?

But it doesn't make sense because Peter was there, curled up on the floor of the helicopter under one of those masks they were wearing yesterday. Why did they throw him out again? Had they realised it was too late, that he was dead? Sandra will hear Grace's screams; she will dash back to them, rescue them, breathe life back into Peter. But no, Sandra's back is turned as she marches back to the village, arms crossed, flaming hair streaming behind her in defiance.

'EVA, EVA, HE'S opened his eyes.'

The gabbling of the helicopter crew morphs into the intense low tones of the impossible-to-read doctors. Eva straightens up in the slippery, squeaky armchair, eases her achy shoulders forward, no longer bound by the helicopter's restraints. She rubs her eyes and blinks them open. Joe's beaming face sharpens into focus, almost silhouetted against the bright white of the hospital room.

'Where's Grace?' Eva leaned further forward, searching past Joe for her daughter. She had been with them in the helicopter, hadn't she?

'Don't worry, Grace is fine. I've been playing with her over there while you slept.' Joe nodded towards the corner by the window, where Grace sat on the floor, violently waving her new favourite toy – a stuffed animal with an unlikely long neck, apparently called a jeeraff. Under the fabric and stuffing, there must be some sort of stiff spring forming its extended neck bone, and Grace has discovered that if she holds the poor creature's head in her fist, the body oscillates satisfyingly as she shakes it. 'She was getting a bit restless. When the doctors came in, I was worried her crying would wake you.'

Eva's brain caught up with what was happening. *He's opened his eyes*, Joe had said. Three figures in medical uniforms were clustered around Peter's bed. She was up out of her chair before her legs were awake, Joe catching her arm to steady her.

'Why didn't you wake me?'

'I just have, haven't I?' Joe said, a tinge of hurt in his voice, or perhaps guilt at having been the first to see Peter awake. 'Sorry, it all happened so fast. I looked over at him and he was looking back at me, and then as if the doctors knew what was happening, they all came bustling in, and that's when I came over to you. Anyway, he's fine. The doctors are pleased.'

'You can understand what they're saying?'

'No, well, one or two words perhaps, but it's mostly from the sound of their voices. You can tell when they're happy. They've been very pleased with how he's doing ever since the operation.'

'Can you? Have they?' Eva had thought they always looked worried, but perhaps they were simply mirroring her anxieties. And how could they have been pleased with his inert body in the bed for three whole days?

'Excuse me, can I see him?' Eva put her hand on the tall doctor's arm, gently trying to ease her sideways. She could have slotted in where there was space at the foot of the bed, but she had to get as close as possible, to look into her son's eyes, to let him see her face, not the faces of these solemn-eyed doctors and nurses with their masked mouths and strange words. She was his mother. He needed her. She pushed harder.

'Joe, can you find Barry? I want to know what these doctors are saying.' Eva watched for Joe's acknowledgement and then applied all her attention to squeezing herself between the doctor and the bedside table, no longer caring about being polite.

'Mummy,' Peter mouthed, smiling with his eyes, even though his mouth couldn't quite work out how to join in.

'Peter,' she managed before choking up. It was so good to see his little bright blue eyes again, even though they were also Anthony's eyes. She reached out for his hand, careful to avoid the cannula, which Barry had assured her was perfectly safe. 'How are you? Does anything hurt?'

Peter shook his head but then rubbed at his chest with his free hand and the shake became a little nod. The smaller, nicer doctor reached out and gently lifted the hand away and smoothed it down back by his side with a sympathetic shake of his head.

'Good boy,' he managed in their own language.

'Can you do something to stop it hurting?' Eva asked, looking from Peter's chest to the doctor's eyes.

'I'm sorry.' He shrugged, unclear whether he was apologising about the pain or about not having understood a word of Eva's question. Why did these people have different words for everything? It was so exhausting. Where was Barry? Where was Maggie, for that matter? Maggie, or Premier Stokes, as Barry called her, hadn't been seen since arriving and hurriedly introducing Eva to Barry.

To be fair to him, Barry had been incredibly attentive; verging on too attentive at times. He couldn't comprehend how there might be a limit to the amount of the flaky, stick-to-the-roof-of-your-mouth pastries a person could eat, and he loved playing with Grace far more than she was interested in playing with him.

Barry burst into the room as soon as the door swished out of his way; Joe limped in behind him. Grace's whine for attention turned into a giggle as Joe dropped down behind her and gave her a gentle tickle. Eva wondered, as she did every time she saw Barry, why nobody in this advanced civilisation had thought of making the papery masks they all wore in more than one size. Whenever Barry opened his mouth, his mask would slide off his large nose, unable to resist the friction of his bushy beard. She almost joined in with Grace's giggle.

Barry barked some words at the medical staff, listened to half of the tall doctor's reply before turning to Eva. Didn't he need to wait for the doctor to finish before launching into his translation? Apparently not.

'Doctor says she's sorry she hasn't been able to tell us much until now. She was confident Peter would make a full recovery but didn't want to get your hopes up until he woke up.'

'But he's OK, isn't he? He's doing well?'

Barry stopped speaking but stood there, flapping a hand as the tall doctor continued to talk.

'What is she saying now? Is Peter going to be OK?'

'Oh, she's saying again that Peter's condition should have been picked up sooner by your doctors, that it would have been a lot better for Peter –'

'But we couldn't... We had nobody we could...' Eva wobbled, felt Joe back at her side, his hand on her elbow, steadying her again. Grace made a whimpering demand for attention. Eva shifted her feet, planting them more firmly on the floor, like Sandra would. 'Is there still something wrong then? I thought she said she was confident of a full recovery.' Eva searched Barry's eyes and then turned to the muted doctor.

As if released from a spell, the doctor began to speak again.

'Doctor is sorry for your distress, understands how difficult this is. Under the circumstances, Peter is doing well.'

'But?' Eva braced herself.

'But his heart needs time to strengthen, and his lungs...his lungs may never fully recover. Only time will tell.'

'How much time? I should take him home – the air is good there.' The air here was so thick. Even outside, in the few moments Eva had dared to spend away from Peter's bed, the city sky had draped itself heavily over her; she'd attracted some peculiar looks when she'd tried to claw it out of the way, gasping for the real stuff.

'The air is good here too. The doctors will make sure he has the best air.'

Barry placed a heavy hand on Eva's left shoulder and gave it what was intended to be a comforting squeeze. The tall doctor nodded in agreement, pretending to comprehend Barry's words. Eva pulled what oxygen she could up through her nostrils, and her lungs yet again complained it was not enough.

'But we left in such a hurry. Peter will want to see his sister, Katie, and his mummy Sandra, and Charlie too.' Eva wanted Sandra and Katie and Charlie. 'Lewi could come back with us in the helicopter to look after him on the journey.' Eva trusted Lewi more than she did these doctors in the hospital. Was that because she'd grown up knowing hospitals were dangerous places and fearing the doctors who staffed them? Joe seemed to trust these doctors. 'We could even take some of your best air with us.' She still couldn't quite work out how more than a few minutes' worth of *best air* could be squeezed into those bottles they attached people to when they wheeled them around the hospital. 'If you could spare a few bottles.'

Barry was already shaking his head before she got to the bit about the bottles. 'Peter must stay here, under Doctor's care,' Did the doctor not have a name? 'But I think another trip to your island is planned soon.'

Why had nobody told Eva about this? Perhaps they had, but she hadn't heard amidst all the noise in her brain.

'The rest of your family could come back in the helicopter and join you here in France.'

Barry didn't know Sandra! But he had got one thing right. Sandra and Katie and Charlie were as much a part of her family as Peter and Grace. They needed to be together; why had she ever even considered taking Peter and Grace to France without them? Yes, in the end, there was no choice really, once Peter had collapsed, but if she hadn't marched him down the road to the helicopter...

Would Sandra leave the island, come with Maggie and Lewi to visit them here? Or would she insist she could look after Peter better than any hospital, and that nothing was better than island air?

'Please tell Doctor how very grateful we are for the good care they have given to Peter here, but now I will be taking him home. That the air on the island will be perfect for his recovery.'

Barry didn't even turn towards the doctor. He just shook his head some more. 'I'm sorry, Eva.' Why did he have to speak to her as if she were a child? 'We simply cannot send Peter back with you.'

'But I'm his mother!' Eva shouted, surprising even herself and definitely alarming Grace. 'It is my decision what happens to Peter.' Joe's hand tugged on her arm, holding her back. Whose side was he on?

'Under French law, doctors have the power to override the wishes of parents, to do what they believe is in the best interest of –'

'But I'm not French, and neither is Peter!'

'And neither am I, but as we are all guests of the French nation, we must live by their laws until it is safe for us to return to our homeland.'

But didn't they have their own government here – the community who called themselves British? Wasn't Maggie their leader, their president, or premier. That's what Joe had told her. Didn't the French let them govern themselves?

'I want to talk to Maggie,' she demanded as confidently as she could.

'Premier Stokes is very busy, but if she were here, she would tell you the same.'

Eva's ears popped and the noise of the corridor wafted in. Grace fell miraculously silent. And as if she'd heard Eva's call, Maggie Stokes stood in the open doorway.

'How's my little friend? I hear he's woken up.'

Chapter 18

Nats

'WHOA! DON'T PANIC, kid. I'm not gonna hurt you.'

I don't believe them! They're hurting me already, their vicious hands squeezing my shoulders. I snap at them with my teeth, remembering your story, Joe, of your journey to the island, when you freed yourself from the skipper by biting their arm. But my bite only finds the air and jangles my skull.

'Let go of me! I won't let you do it.'

'But if I let go, you're going to bite me, aren't you?'

Nevertheless, their grip loosens a bit, and I seize the opportunity to lunge forward. But the heavy sheets tangled around my legs hold me back, and my attacker dodges sideways. There's a crash and a smash and wisps of steam are rising from under a broken bowl on the bare floorboards. Wafts of cabbage and carrot and potato reach my nose, and for the first time in days, the smell of food doesn't make my guts churn. But then I go all light-headed as my stomach complains at how empty it is and I can't fight anymore. Sorry, Joe, I've got myself caught now too, so now nobody's going to make it to France.

Why didn't I make my move as soon as I woke up this morning? I could have positioned myself by that heavy white door with the big black keyhole. I could have waited, coiled like a spring as the key turned in the lock, and then rocketed out and down the stairs and away before they'd even realised I was there. I am upstairs, aren't I? The bit of sky I can see out of the window looks like upstairs sort of sky. How long have I been here now? The bedsheets are stale – no longer stiff and fresh like my first vague memories of them.

My captor has let go of me and backed away. I think they know I'm defeated. They're quite tall and heavy for a neut – like that Stomper at the car yard. They're muttering something, asking me a question.

'What did you mean? "I won't let you do it" – what is it you think I'm going to do to you?'

The sorrowful look in their eyes makes me almost ready to trust them. But they're a neut and you can't trust neuts. Well, except Hani and Jay and the other DiG neuts. And I'd like to think I could trust my parents, if I ever met them again and if I was sure it was definitely them. But oh, I'm sorry, Joe, we couldn't trust Cris, could we? And they're your parent. Can we ever really trust any neut?

DiG said the first thing the neuts would do if they caught us was cut us and make us like them. But it hasn't happened yet. I've checked and everything's still the same as it always has been down there. Were DiG telling us the truth or simply trying to scare us to keep us from straying too far from the farmhouse? What if they were the ones we shouldn't have trusted?

The heavy white door creaks open – a creak that's haunted my dreams for the last...however long I've been trapped in here. A familiar little human face peeks in a little below the level of the big black doorknob. The door blasts open and bashes against the ancient-looking wardrobe, as if there's a storm blowing through the house but without the wind, only a torrent of fur and wagging tail.

Nelly leaps straight onto my legs and then catapults off, back down to the floor where she finds the steaming heap of vegetably-ness under its broken bowl.

'Oi! Gerroff!' the neut shouts. 'Tris! I thought I told you to keep that bloody mutt outta here. What's she even doing upstairs?'

Lottie cowers by the door as Nelly is lifted clear off the floor, hurled back out through the door, and by the sound of it, halfway down some slippery wooden stairs.

'Now go put her outside!'

Lottie retreats and the angry neut slams the door shut again. The smell of cabbage, carrots and potatoes fills my nose and my tummy rumbles. The neut doesn't seem to notice as they stomp back and forth between the door and the window.

'I can't make any promises, mind,' they blurt out as if I already know what their not-promises are. 'But I know my Tris and our Nelly have gone and made a friend of you.' They stop still as my stomach lets out its loudest grumble yet. 'Sorry, I'll get you another bowl of stew in a minute. But first, let's get things straight.' They make me jump as they noisily clear their throat. But then they're speaking more quietly, trying their best to sound gentle. 'Look, I ain't gonna do anything to hurt you, and I ain't gonna hand you over to anyone else who might. That OK with you?'

Before my food-starved brain can even process what they've said, let alone say anything back, the big hands have scooped up the broken bowl and the biggest chunks of vegetables from the floor and the heavy boots have stomped out of the room.

I hear no key turning in the lock. Have I ever heard it? I could make a run for it now, get far away from here. That's probably what you'd do, Joe, isn't it? *But there's stew on its way,* my stomach protests. So I don't move. I'll eat first, and then go.

Chapter 19

To: j.samuels
From: i.jamieson
Date: 31-05-157
Subject: Protected Child Case No. 43092

Dear Justice Samuels,

Please find attached the transcript and observations from the first meeting between your representative and the protected child who we are currently referring to as Cain. I confess I was somewhat surprised to discover that your representative was in fact the defendant from your court case. However, they conducted themselves with professionalism, and I am content to facilitate further meetings, as requested.

My initial assessment has to be that the child's participation in the case, whether in person or by video link, would not be permitted since, in their current state of mind, they would be an exhibit rather than a witness.

Should the other meetings yield no further progress, I trust the attached may prove some use to you in the case.

Kind regards,

Indigo Jamieson

Child Psychologist, Central London Child Protection Services

CENTRAL LONDON CHILD PROTECTION SERVICES
MEETING WITH A PROTECTED CHILD – TRANSCRIPT

DATE: 31-05-157	CASE NO. 43092	
NAME OF CHILD Cain (unconfirmed)	DATE OF BIRTH Unknown	ID NO. Unknown
PARENT NAME(S) Unknown	REGISTERED ADDRESS Unknown	
CLIENT NAME People's Court of Canterbury	PRESENT AT MEETING Dr. Indigo Jamieson (for CLCPS) - **IJ** Cn. Georgy Turner (for Client) - **GT**	

IJ: OK, it's ten thirty-two on thirty-first of May one-fifty-seven. Present in the room are Doctor Indigo Jamieson, Child Psychologist for CLCPS, Citizen Georgy Turner for the client, the People's Court of Canterbury, and the child, identity unknown, currently under the wardship of the London Police Force. OK, Georgy, over to you. I will sit and observe, unless I feel there is a need to intervene.

GT: Right, thank you. Hello, Cain. It is Cain, isn't it? Do you remember me? We met before in a police station in Newcastle, a few days after your friends jumped off the train.

[Long pause]

GT: My child, my sun, Joh, was one of your friends, I think. I didn't know it when we met before, but then I found him again in a place called Dover, by the sea.

[Pause]

GT: I think you were all trying to get there, weren't you? I want to say thank you, Cain. Because I think whatever you did on that train helped Joh and Nats to escape, and then when I saw Joh in Dover, I had to help him escape in a boat across the sea.

[Pause]

GT: And I could see land on the other side of the sea. And I think Joh made it across to that land. So thank you, Cain. It is Cain, isn't it?

[Long pause]

GT: I'm hoping you can help me, Cain. And I hope I can help you too. You see, what I did to help Joh escape was to, er, hold up some police officers who would have stopped him. And so I got myself arrested and locked up in prison a bit like you. Well, not much like you, actually, because I was in a normal prison and I was able to talk to other inmates there, including some people from DiG who are in prison too. I think you might know some of them, from when you were still at home with your parents, or when you were travelling to the island. Some of them say they remember you. Maybe I deserved to be locked up, because I did intentionally attack a police officer with a bag of chips, whereas you didn't do anything wrong, did you, Cain? You shouldn't be locked up like this.

[Pause]

GT: And I'm trying to argue in court that I shouldn't be punished for what I did either. That I did it because I had to, because Joh was in real danger and I was trying to protect my child. I've told them the truth, Cain, about how you and Joh and the others are different from us. And it's not just me telling them that. I managed to get Lily to testify in court. And Doctor Lee too, who started the secret fertility unit. Doctor Lee bravely told the court the truth about what they had done to rescue so many babies, including Joh, and you, I guess.

[Pause]

GT: I'd really like it if you could come and speak to the court too, Cain? Could you tell them why you and Joh and Nats decided to leave the island? And what's happened to you since you were captured? Then, when the truth about everything is out in the open, we can help you find your parents, so they know you're safe. Maybe you can go back to live with them. Cain, what are you doing? What's the matter? Or if you'd prefer, we could get you back to the island, or even across the sea to be with Joh. Cain?

[Buzzer sound]

IJ: I'm sorry, Georgy, I think they've had enough for today. We can try again next week, although –

GT: Cain, please, I want to help you.

[Buzzer sound, door opening, door closing]

IJ: OK, child has left the room after getting up and pressing exit button. Time is ten fifty-three.

CENTRAL LONDON CHILD PROTECTION SERVICES
MEETING WITH A PROTECTED CHILD –
OBSERVATION NOTES

DATE: 31-05-157	CASE NO. 43092	
NAME OF CHILD Cain (unconfirmed)	DATE OF BIRTH Unknown	ID NO. Unknown
PARENT NAME(S) Unknown	REGISTERED ADDRESS Unknown	
CLIENT NAME People's Court of Canterbury	PRESENT AT MEETING Dr. Indigo Jamieson (for CLCPS) - **IJ** Cn. Georgy Turner (for Client) - **GT**	

The child appears well nourished but dirty and disorientated. They sat in a bent-over position and their attention appeared entirely focused on their fidgeting hands throughout the meeting. They would not make eye contact with either myself or GT.

GT left significant pauses between questions, hoping for a response from the child, but none was forthcoming.

When GT explained how their child, Joh, had evaded arrest in Dover and 'escaped' to the sea, the child possibly showed some reaction to this news, sitting up a little straighter for a while and showing signs of listening, though still no eye contact or verbal acknowledgement.

At mention of the child's parents, the child showed increased agitation and then stood up and moved toward the door, pressing the exit button twice. On the second press, the duty police officer opened the door and escorted the child from the room, at which point the meeting was terminated.

On the basis of this meeting, the child would not be fit to give evidence in court, either in person or via video link, and any form of cross-examination would likely cause significant mental and emotional stress for the child.

A further meeting is scheduled for the same time a fortnight from today.

I. Jamieson

31-05-157

Chapter 20

Eva

'I'M SO SORRY, Eva, I've been neglecting you all.' Maggie squeezed Eva's shoulders, probed Eva's face with a look of parental concern. 'The last few days have been such a worry for you, and Barry tells me you've barely left this room. That can't be good for someone who's used to so much fresh sea air.' The way Maggie said 'sea air' sounded more like one strange word, 'zeeaire'.

'And that's what Peter needs now too, but Barry's saying –' Eva began.

'Listen, first things first, let's get *you* out for some proper fresh air – clear your head a bit – and we'll get you something decent to eat while we're out too. Barry says you've barely eaten a thing.' As Maggie talked, she'd already pulled out her phone and was tickling its screen. 'Right, zat's all sorted, I've booked us a table for one o'clock in a great little restaurant. Before then, I'll take you on a little tour around the assembly buildings. We have quite a lot of green space there, for the centre of a city.'

'But I can't leave Peter here on his own. And what about Grace?' Eva backed away, unwilling to fall under Maggie's spell.

'But he won't be on his own. Joe will stay and keep Peter company, won't you, Joe? And Grace will come with us. She'll love it!'

Grace let them know she'd heard her name with her characteristic little shout that was neither grumbly nor cheerful. She was doing brilliantly but growing noticeably grizzlier as her confinement in this hospital room stretched into its third day. Joe, who'd been keeping Grace quietly entertained, turned and gave Eva an affirming nod. Peter's eyes were closed again, and his chest rose and fell peacefully. It would be good to get Grace out for a while, but...

'No, I need to stay here for Peter. Joe, how about you go with Maggie and take Grace with you? I'll just give her a quick feed before you go, to settle her a bit.'

'Nonsense. Joe's already seen the assembly buildings, and little Grace needs time with her mummy too, don't you, Gracie?'

Grace giggled and squirmed as Maggie bounced into a squat beside her and tickled her chin.

Eva bristled; Gracie was what Anthony called their daughter, on the few occasions he even acknowledged her as such. Not that Eva wanted Anthony to have any more to do with her children than the two rams she kept got involved in bringing up the lambs they sired. Joe, on the other hand, now he'd make a good dad; he'd want to be involved in the lives of whatever children he fathered, and she'd trusted him with Peter and Katie ever since she'd watched him join in their games with Nats days after he arrived on the island. Peter probably wouldn't be fazed one bit to wake up to Joe's face and not hers, but...

'Maybe we can all go later. Perhaps tomorrow. I'm sure Peter will be well enough to come with us tomorrow,' Eva said, trying to push aside all doubt. 'And if he's not well enough to walk far, we could take him in one of those chairs you wheel around.'

'What a lovely idea,' said Maggie with a hint of condescension, 'but you and your daughter need some fresh air today. Come on, Gracie.'

Hoisting Grace onto her hip, Maggie was heading for the door before Eva could protest. Grace protested, though, as the door began to swish shut behind them. It was the sort of whine that not even Vicki could quiet.

'Wait! You can't march off with her like that, and I said I was going to give her a feed!'

The door got out of the way again as Eva stepped forward, but Maggie was already halfway down the corridor and Grace's wail wasn't getting any quieter, despite the growing distance. Eva set off at a jog, the clump of her boots reverberating off the clean white walls. A trolley shot out from a door on her left that had opened without even the politest of warnings. She dodged to the right, scuffed the wall, and clipped the front wheel. 'Sorry!' she called back to the trolley's skeletal passenger, who stared back with uncomprehending eyes.

'Mademoiselle! Ne courez pas s'il vous plaît.'

'Sorry!' Eva called back again, this time to the much more solid-looking green-blue uniform driving the trolley. She turned away from the trolley and its driver, knowing that whatever the hospital porter had barked at her, to placate him she had to slow her jog to a fast walk and try to look where she was going.

Maggie and Grace disappeared through a door on the right.

'Maggie, wait! You can't –'

The double doors sealed themselves shut seconds before Eva bounded to a halt in front of them. Through the glass doors, the thick metal ropes were already carrying Maggie and Grace in their glass box, down to the lower floor. Eva stabbed at the button. *Come on, come on!* The ropes wobbled and hung unmoving for an age before reversing their direction. Eva peered through the glass, watching the slow ascent of the elevator's ceiling until it passed her eyes. Its floor slowed well before it could possibly need to and crept cautiously the rest of the way to being level with Eva's impatient feet. Even then, the doors teased her to be patient as she silently screamed at them to get a move on.

'Attendre!' shouted the hospital porter as their trolley interrupted whatever sensors stopped the doors from closing. Eva backed herself into the corner as the tattooed but clean hairy arms of the porter expertly swung the trolley into the elevator. With the doors closed, the elevator would barely be long enough to accommodate the trolley, so why was the porter fussing around with their feet to lock on the brakes? It couldn't exactly go anywhere. Eva huffed, the porter glared at her and shook his head as he shuffled round to stand beside the trolley, all the time holding it steady with one hand even though the brakes were now on.

The elevator was infuriatingly clever – waiting until everything and everyone was neatly tucked away inside before even considering closing its doors. Joe had teased Eva the first time he'd taken her down to get a drink from the cafeteria, letting the doors almost close before sticking his hand between their jaws. She'd yanked him out of the way just in time, so she thought, and he'd laughed at her terrified face as the doors clunked to a stop and reversed direction, coming nowhere near to crushing the space where his hand would have been.

The porter kicked at one of the trolley wheels to force it out of the way of the elevator's sensors, then stood back again so the elevator could make its final checks before sealing the doors. If Maggie wasn't waiting for her down in the entrance foyer, Eva would have no hope of finding them now. Should she return to the room and trust Maggie would return with Grace soon enough, when she got fed up with the wails? What if Peter had woken up again already? Eva's insides were left behind for a moment as the elevator began its descent. That was another thing she disliked about elevators.

As soon as the doors slid open again, the porter very considerately stepped out of the way and beckoned Eva out. Damn, she was hoping he'd hurry out with the trolley and then she'd stay in the box and push the button to return her to the first floor and to Peter. She stepped out, giving both of her fellow passengers a grateful nod.

The foyer buzzed with chatter and activity. A female voice boomed a message out of speakers concealed somewhere Eva hadn't yet managed to locate in the cavernous space with its unnaturally green foliage dotted around. Perhaps the speakers were actually hidden in the plant pots. What if the message was for Eva, telling her to rush back because Peter needed her? She spun around to return to the elevator, but already the doors were shut and the glass box was gone. How had the porter and his trolley evaporated so quickly? Perhaps they never intended to come to the ground floor and had actually stayed in the elevator to travel to some other unknown higher part of the hospital. But Maggie and Grace definitely had got off at the ground floor. Eva scanned around, in case Maggie hadn't marched straight out through those ever-revolving entrance doors that seemed to maintain an almost constant seal between the foyer and the outside air.

'Ma!' a little voice shouted at her from somewhere. They were still in here, somewhere.

'Ma!' Grace's voice called out to her again, and there they were, by a neatly trimmed, round-headed tree. Grace remained clamped to Maggie's hip despite the energetic flapping of both arms in an excited wave. Her jeeraff was miraculously still held tight in her little fist, its long legs repeatedly ruffling through the little round leaves of the plant, knocking plenty off as Maggie stood obliviously talking with Barry. She didn't even turn to acknowledge Eva as she wrestled Grace out of her grasp and stepped away from the beleaguered tree.

Eva wrapped her arms around Grace and turned back towards the elevator.

'Eva, wait, I'm sorry.'

Strong, slender fingers gripped her arm just above the elbow. Firmly, but also with some tenderness. Turning to face her, for a moment Eva expected to see the wild flames of Sandra's hair rather than Maggie's dark, neatly fastened back locks. Even the tone of voice contained something Sandra-like through that peculiar accent. The revolving doors puffed out a rare waft of outside air, which Eva hungrily inhaled before anyone could steal it from her.

'Listen, Eva, it's all arranged. Barry will go up and sit with Joe and Peter. As soon as Peter wakes up or if anything changes, Barry will call us. And um... Barry, go and stand over there for a moment, will you?'

Barry trotted off to stand by a vacant cafeteria table as Maggie took out her phone and tapped at it. 'There we go, look – we can even make a video call with Barry and you'll be able to see Peter as well as talk to him if he wakes up, and he'll be able to see you too.' Sure enough, Barry's face was chirping excitedly at them through Maggie's phone screen.

'I know how phones work, you know. One of my parents had one a bit like yours, only the network in Britain doesn't supports video calls anymore, and it didn't work as a phone anymore either. But we used it to make videos of each other.'

'Merveilleus. In that case, you take the phone so you can answer it as soon as anyone calls, and I'll take Gracie.'

Eva wrapped Grace in a tighter embrace, causing her to squirm and start to complain. 'But it won't be the same as being there in the room with him, and he'll wake up all confused about where he his and he'll want to know I'm there for him, with him, not somewhere else looking at him through a screen.'

'Eva, you've been there for him and with him all the time these last three days.'

'Well, no. I did come down here a couple of times.'

'Of course, but that doesn't really count, does it?' Maggie turned to Barry's face on her phone, still part of their conversation from across the foyer. 'Barry, you head up to Peter and Joe now, but stay on the call so Eva can see them both when you get there.'

Eva watched both on screen and in real life as Barry made his way towards the elevator but then disappeared through a door she'd not seen before, a door you actually had to pull on to open, and then the image on the phone bounced around as Barry panted his way up some stairs. Eva made a mental note to find the other end of those stairs later. They'd be much quicker than the elevator. The view on the phone swung up to the ceiling and under a doorframe and then Barry was on the corridor where she'd dodged past the trolley. She caught a glimpse of the scuff mark her boot had made on the otherwise clean white wall and then the sliding doors swished open, and Peter's face filled the screen.

'There we are, still fast asleep.' Barry's voice boomed through the phone's speaker.

'Shhh,' Eva scolded at the phone.

Joe's smiling face appeared half on the screen. 'He's fine, Eva. He's been fast asleep all the time you've been gone, and it doesn't look like he'll wake up anytime soon.'

'And when he does,' Barry's voice chipped in off-camera, 'if you're not back, we'll call you. OK?' The screen went blank before Eva could answer.

'So, we're good to go, yes?' Maggie slipped the phone into Eva's back pocket and reached out for Grace again.

Eva sighed. 'OK, but just for food, and then we come straight back.'

Chapter 21

Nats

Every time Lori mentions Tris, I have to remind myself they're talking about Lottie. Except she's not Lottie, she's Tris. Or rather, they're Tris. A couple times, I've slipped up and referred to Tris as *she* in front of Lori. The second time, Lori just frowned at me in a quizzical way, but the first time, well, I didn't even realise I'd done it. I was telling Lori how she (Tris) had brought me food every day in the barn, even though I knew Lori had already worked that out, and Lori looked at me as if I was doolally and said, 'It wasn't Nelly that brought your food, kid, it was Tris. And Tris is no bitch.' Bitch is the word for a female dog, like Nelly. And so I said, 'Yeah, I know that, and she...' and then I realised what I'd done, but it didn't stop me from making the same mistake again later.

It's weird. Why do I find it so hard to remember Tris is neut? I don't think of Lori as either he or she. Lori is definitely *they*. I guess all the kids I've ever known have been boys or girls. Mostly girls. Whereas all the adults have been neuts. Except I guess Lori's really not much older than Tom and Sandra and Eva. But I've never really seen them as proper adults, even when they looked down on me as the little kid. I'm pretty sure Lori knows that I'm a 'bitch', but they haven't said anything really to show that they know.

Halfway down the stairs, the longest I've been on my feet for about two weeks, probably isn't the best time to be thinking all this over. It's ridiculous, but my head is swimming and I need to put all my energy and concentration into staying upright and finding the next step with my feet. It doesn't help that each time I vacate a step, little Tris bounces down to fill it, sometimes wobbling against me to find their balance.

'Oi! Tris! Give Nats some space, will you? Otherwise, we'll all be tumbling down.' Lori extends a hand towards me, ready to catch me if I stumble. I'm now grateful that Lori insisted on slowly descending backwards in front of me.

Tris is not the only one excited by me coming downstairs at last; poor Nelly has had several kicks from Lori's boot as she's bounded up to meet us. Her claws scratch at the wooden steps as she tumbles down. She gives another excited bark and finds her feet again; spins round at the bottom of the stairs, making me even dizzier. Then she's on her way back up again, as if begging for another kick. This is just a fabulous game for her.

Of course, it would help if that banister rail was fixed to the wall as well, instead of taking up space down the edge of the steps. Lori catches me looking at it and reads my mind.

'Yeah, I know. Been meaning to fix that back on for months. Too much to do round here.'

'I could help,' I offer. 'Round the farm, I mean, or with whatever needs doing.' If I show I can be useful rather than an extra thing to worry about, maybe they'll let me stay here until I've worked out...whatever I need to work out next.

'Let's take one step at a time, shall we?' Lori chuckles. 'And I'm not just talking about getting down these stairs.'

I nod, attempt a smile, and shuffle down onto the next step. What is *my* next step? How long can I, should I, do I want to...stay here? Truth is, I want to stay until you come back safely, Joe. But how will you know I've moved into the house? I could leave a note for you in the barn, I suppose.

There's a cheer from behind and a cheer and multitudinous barks from in front as we reach the bottom and arrive in a kitchen where I immediately feel at home and homesick. There's a huge wooden table, exactly like the one we used to all cram ourselves around when Hani pulled out treats from their latest shopping trip...the table I last saw engulfed in flames. Vegetably steam rises from a pot, bubbling away on a stove, like the one I cooked on so many times in yours and Anthony's cottage. I bet that stove will be sitting cold and uncared for now – I never saw Anthony use it. I'll bet the ash from the fire that made our last meal there still sits in its tray behind the bottom door. And whilst the clutter covering every surface in this kitchen isn't books, the organised untidiness is so Cain-like, my tummy twinges and in my head, you and me are tumbling off a train, leaving Cain behind once again.

'Steady now, let's get you sat down, shall we?' A wooden chair with solid arms is pulled out from the table and I'm guided into it. 'Here, have some water. Dinner won't be long.' The water sloshes around in the glass now sitting on the table in front of me and I'm back on that boat, hidden under the nets, in the pitch-blackness, listening to the sea slapping against the boat as you and Cain try to push it off the sand. Maybe Cain was right; you and him would have been better off going without me.

We eat in silence. Nelly has been put outside for a bit with some dinner of her own. The old Nats would have filled the silence with chatter between mouthfuls, but having spent so long with only myself to talk to, I've no idea what to say to these real people. Every now and then, Lori grunts and I look up, thinking they're about to say something or ask something, but then they lift another spoonful to their mouth and whatever they were turning over in their head is clearly staying there for now. Lori doesn't say much and doesn't ask much, and apart from when they're barking orders at Nelly or Tris, their words are always well chewed over before being spoken out loud.

Lori hasn't asked where I came from or how I ended up in their barn. It's like they know it's not something I could give a straight answer to, so there's no point even asking. All I have been asked is how long I've been in the barn, how long I've been feeling unwell and was there anyone who should be told that I'm safe? Am I safe here? I think so. I haven't told them about you, Joe. I'll stay a while longer to get my strength up and put that note out in the barn, in case you come back. I still can't eat much first thing in the morning without bringing it straight back up again, but Lori's stews and soups hit the spot and stay where they're supposed to if I'm not too eager about them. That's another way in which I'm different from the old Nats – she would have finished this bowlful by now and would be eyeing up Tris's more-than-generous helping.

Tris has been a regular and more talkative visitor, but for Tris, words always have to go with pictures. I've lost count of how many pictures of me and Tris and Nelly I've nodded and smiled at. A cube of swede from Tris's spoon splats onto the table as their curious eyes stare at me instead of concentrating on their food. Lori grunts again, shakes their head, struggles and succeeds in picking up the slippery chunk of swede and drops it back into Tris's bowl.

Lori's spoon clatters into their empty bowl and, having carefully chewed and savoured a final mouthful, they say what they've been thinking. 'You could help getting Tris to school if you like.'

I look up. Is the horror self-evident on my face, or am I managing to hide it behind a more general sense of confusion and surprise? Doesn't Lori realise I can't let myself be seen by anyone else, let alone nosy schoolteachers? Wouldn't they start asking questions about who I was and why I wasn't going to school myself?

At least I now have an answer to one of the trivial questions I've occupied my brain with over the last few days. I got used to hearing the muffled shouts from Lori through the floor and would haul myself off the bed, wrap the blanket around me and shuffle over to the window in time to hear a door shut and then watch Lori, Tris and Nelly setting off up the track which I know leads to the road where I almost got mown down by a car – the track you virtually carried me down to find the barn. Ten minutes later, Nelly would be racing back down the track with Lori striding along behind her, but no Tris. The first time it happened, I stood for ages at the window, watching for Tris to amble back down the track. And I must have fallen asleep on the floor under the window because the next thing I knew, Lori was scooping me up off the floor and returning me to the bed and then mumbling something about having left some food over there when I was ready for it. Then later that day, I was woken again by a door slamming downstairs and seconds later, the bedroom door was creaking open and Tris was thrusting a picture in my face. A picture painted at school? Does school already know about the strange guest called Nats who'd been living in Tris's barn?

'If I didn't have Tris to get ready in the morning, if you could do that and see 'em onto the bus,' Lori continues, 'well, that'd be huge help to me in getting all my other jobs done round here.'

I gulp down another spoonful of stew too quickly and it threatens to come back up again. I sip at my water, trying to wash away the acid tang clinging to the back of my throat. Tris is bouncing with excitement at the prospect of me walking them to the bus.

'And Nats can be there when the bus brings me back too.' says Tris, and I can already see Tris's new drawings in my head, featuring all Tris's classmates and schoolteachers and the bus driver waving at me from lots of little square windows on a bus with wonky wheels.

'But people would see me,' I blurt out. I thought Lori understood that I mustn't be seen, mustn't be found.

'Well, it's gotta happen sooner or later, hasn't it? I mean, you can't hide yourself away forever. A kid like you should be in school yourself, doing your exams, not hidin' in a barn.'

A kid like me? Lori had seen me, hadn't they? It must have been them who'd stripped off my old smelly clothes, dressed me in freshly washed pyjamas. How could they even suggest sending me to school and have people examining me?

'But you said...' I didn't want to talk about this sort of thing in front of little Tris, but Lori had said they wouldn't hand me over to anyone who might hurt me. From all the stories I'd heard from others on the island, school was never a safe place for kids like us. 'Kids like me don't go to school. I've never been to school, and I don't need to.'

'Never been to school?' Lori shakes their head. Why do neuts think school is so important? Some of the neuts who came to visit us on the farm always used to go on about how we needed to keep up with our 'schooling' even though we couldn't go to proper school.

'I don't need school neither,' Tris chips in, grinning so much I think the stew juice around their mouth is at risk of dribble into their ears. It's impossible not to laugh.

'Oh yes you do, my little pup, and I need you at school too, otherwise I'll never get anything done round here.' Lori gets more serious again as they turn their eyes on me. 'And from next week, Nats'll be seeing you get on yer bus. If anyone asks, they're my cousin's kid, staying with us while the cousin gets used to their new baby.'

'But...' I begin to protest, but I kind of already know there's no point arguing with Lori. So I'll have to pack my bag and get going before anyone drags me onto that school bus.

Lori stacks our bowls, putting mine on top because I'm the only one who hasn't finished, but we both know I've lost my appetite. 'Don't worry, I can see you're not well enough to go to school yourself yet. It's nearly summer holidays anyway. I'll be glad of your help looking after Tris over the holidays, so don't you be thinking about leaving us. You can stay as long as you like, but I do think you need to think about getting yourself an education.'

'OK, thanks, I'll think about it.' I nod, not quite sure what I'm agreeing to. Have I got out of walking Tris to the school bus? How long do the summer holidays last? The sensible thing to do would be to pack up and leave today, whatever Lori says. But this solid wooden table already feels too homely to get up from, and while I'm staying here, building up my strength, maybe you'll come back, Joe.

Chapter 22

Eva

'Eva? Eva, the waiter is asking whether he can take your plate away.'

The man, dressed all in black, was waiting patiently beside their table. Eva had barely touched the piece of fish or the leafy, vinegar-coated salad that surrounded it. The plate did appear abandoned, pushed to the middle of the table, out of reach of Grace's grabbing hands, though Eva hadn't yet made a conscious decision not to eat any more. Anyone leaving that much on their plate at Vicki's café would have had Vicki standing over them until it was empty.

'I'll tell him you're still eating it, shall I? You've not really had a chance to yet, with Gracie not settling in the highchair. Or would you like to try something different? Sorry, I thought you'd like the fish.'

The little bit she'd tasted had been all right, though given the choice, she'd have preferred one of Joe and Cain's freshly caught fish, gently fried in butter, with a heap of sliced potato fried in the same butter. How far had this fish on her plate travelled from where it was caught? As far as she knew, they were nowhere near the sea. Still, she felt guilty leaving it.

Maggie spoke a few words to the waiter, who left them for a moment, returning with a copy of the unintelligible menu. Grace squirmed on Eva's lap and batted the menu shut as the waiter held it open in front of them. The woman in the flowery dress, sitting alone at the table next to theirs, frowned at them again. Eva threw some dark thoughts back at her, blaming her for the fact that Maggie had said she shouldn't breastfeed Grace here. It wasn't considered polite, apparently, particularly with a child of Grace's age. Maggie took control of the menu and cleared her throat, ready to once more talk Eva through the different choices.

'Actually, I think I'd rather get back now.' Eva straightened the cutlery on her plate and gestured to the waiter that it could be taken away.

'But you've had nothing to eat. How about some dessert? The gateaux here are wonderful. Gracie would love a bit of gateau, wouldn't you, Gracie?'

'Grace has eaten plenty, thank you.'

Maggie's phone made one of its pinging sounds and Eva pounced on it, making Grace giggle and shout again and the flowery woman frown some more. It was another message in words Eva couldn't decipher but that Maggie assured her was not from Barry, was nothing to do with Peter, and was boring work stuff.

'All right then, we shall ask the waiter to put some in a box for us. We'll get some for Joe and Peter too.'

The box of desserts took an age to arrive, and Eva wished she hadn't let the waiter take her plate away because now she could probably manage a few more mouthfuls, if only to give her something to do. Maggie had insisted on taking the increasingly restless Grace over to another table to be introduced to an acquaintance, to whom she was now gabbling incessantly whilst Grace squirmed in her arms. Eva sat on her hands, trying to ignore her hollow stomach as her eyes flitted between her daughter and the dormant phone in front of her on the table.

They stepped out of the restaurant and the ache in Eva's feet returned, reminding her of their long walk here along hard grey paths. Maggie had a strange idea of what *not far* meant. Eva could have walked from one end of their island and back again in the time it had taken to get from the hospital to the restaurant, and without any pain to her feet. While Sandra was quite content with their little island dominion, Eva had secretly yearned to be a smaller cog in a bigger machine, perhaps even a city, as her parents had been before her arrival had forced them to settle for a quieter, more isolated life. Right now, though, all she wanted was to be back with her children and Sandra on their lumpy, wild little island.

'Mummy! Mummy! Cain had to swim across a really wide sea, wider than this.' Peter stretched out his arms as wide as he could and winced as it strained his stitches. 'And he brought back a boat but with no oars, so then Joe made oars out of some old chairs and... Joe, can you tell Mummy what happened after that?'

'Maybe later, my love.' Eva smiled at her son through her fury, which she tried not to turn on Joe, certain he wasn't at fault. 'Where's Barry? I thought he was staying up here with you. You were supposed to call us as soon as Peter woke up.'

'I'm sure he won't be far away,' said Maggie as the door behind her sealed them in. 'I'll go and find him, right away.' The door obediently slid open again as she turned back towards it and then faltered as Maggie checked herself. 'I'd best leave this here, though. How would you like some excellent cake, Peter?'

The door slid shut and open and shut again and Maggie was gone. Eva found herself juggling with a box of cakes, feeling the cakes shift inside as she held the box out of the reach of little hands whilst lowering her daughter to the floor. If Maggie was a mother, then like Sandra, she had little hands-on experience.

'Here, let me take that.' Joe leapt up to rescue Eva from the cakes before they tumbled to the floor, which in her current mood, Grace would have no doubt found shriekingly hilarious. It was the food here that did it; whatever was in that pasta sauce still staining Grace's cheeks, it wasn't the plain vegetable diet she was used to. Cake was the last thing she needed right now.

'What sort of cake is it, Mummy?'

'I've no idea!' Eva snapped. 'Whatever sort of cake Maggie likes, I expect.'

'Why are you cross with us, Mummy?' Peter's voice trembled. All the excitement of his earlier greeting had gone, and he rubbed at his chest again.

'Sorry, it's my fault,' said Joe. 'I should have gone to find Barry as soon as Peter woke up again...or stopped him from leaving in the first place.'

Eva sighed and sat down on the bed, narrowly missing the box of stupid cakes. 'No, I'm not cross with you, Peter, and it's not your fault either, Joe. In fact, I'm glad you stayed here with Peter rather than chasing after Barry. I just don't understand these people.'

'That's cos they speak with funny words, Mummy.'

Eva laughed. 'Yes, it's partly that, although Maggie and Barry sort of use the same words as us, don't they?'

They sat quietly nodding to each other for a while. Even Grace was surprisingly reflective as she pushed Jeeraff around the slippery floor.

'So, Peter, tell me what happened after Joe made some oars out of old chairs. Wasn't that clever of him?' It wasn't really the question she wanted to ask Peter.

What she really wanted to know was how he was feeling. Did his scar hurt lots? Could he take big, full breaths of air without straining it? Could he feel his heart beating, and did it feel different from before? Did he feel strong enough to go home soon? It was so hard to tell, but as Peter recounted Joe's adventures, Eva saw that this amazing little boy still had the same adventurous heart, whatever the doctors had done to it. Hopefully now, the physical parts of it wouldn't let him down.

EVA DISENTANGLED HERSELF from her sleeping son, straightened her back with a quiet groan, padded over to scoop Grace up off the floor, and laid her down peacefully in her cot. The lights had gradually dimmed with the dusk outside and nobody had got up to override it. Neither Maggie nor Barry had reappeared. Food had been rolled in on a trolley, and Peter had eaten hungrily while the rest of them picked at it. The sugar-rich cakes had remained out of sight and forgotten. Eva stretched and yawned.

'Why don't you sit in the chair?' she offered to Joe.

Joe sat on the hard floor, his back against the wall, knees pulled up to his chest and making dents in his forehead. She was reminded of Cain, as he was before Joe managed to extract him from his shell. Joe's head wobbled from knee to knee.

'S'OK, you sit there. I'll head back to my room soon.'

Eva sank gratefully into the chair that had also been her bed for the last few nights. The chair sighed with her as it moulded itself to her familiar form. They'd offered her a bed in another room with Grace in a cot beside her, but she wouldn't have slept away from Peter.

'Thanks for looking after Peter.' She lifted her tired head off the back of the chair, opened her eyes again and looked over towards Joe, who still wasn't looking anywhere except down at the patch of floor beneath his knees. 'And I'm sorry. We've had three days together and I've not asked you anything about your journey here. Sounds like you had quite an adventure.'

Joe made a sound a bit like Eva's chair had when she'd sat on it, lifted his head off his knees and let it thud back into the wall. 'I shouldn't have told him all those stories. He thinks I'm some sort of hero now.'

'Well, you are a hero. You made it all the way across Britain and then across the sea to here. If you'd not done that, the helicopter would have never come to find us, and Peter might not be –' What would have happened if they hadn't been there when Peter had collapsed? She'd have lost him forever, wouldn't she?

'What sort of hero leaves two friends behind?' *Thump, thump, thump.* Joe bounced his head off the wall three more times. A tear trickled down his cheek.

'Hey, you can't think like that. From what I hear, it was that or be captured. If they could hear you now, they'd both tell you you'd done exactly the right thing.'

Joe didn't look convinced. He wiped at his cheeks with the back of his hand, but the stream hadn't yet dried up. Poor boy. Eva had been so wrapped up in her own worries over the last few days, she'd not stopped to wonder how Joe was. He'd been there for her, ready to do whatever needed doing, keeping Grace entertained, watching Peter, fetching drinks, and all this time he was carrying this burden.

'Let's have some cake. That'd be what Nats would do.' Eva dropped down onto her knees and shuffled forward to retrieve the box from under the bed. She slid over to sit beside Joe on the floor and folded back the lid. 'We can have two each. I won't tell the children if you don't. They wouldn't be good for them anyway.' Eva held the box out for Joe to choose first. He hesitated, was about to decline or insist Eva went first, but then she caught that glimpse of the kid in him – the child in need of consoling with cake – and he lifted the stickiest slab of sugariness out of the box. Maggie had been right about one thing at least: the cake was wonderful.

Joe quietly got up, found some paper napkins on the trolley of dirty plates that nobody had yet come to collect. He handed a couple to Eva, wiped his own fingers and face with a couple more, and edged towards the door.

'Thanks for the cake.'

'You're welcome.' Eva didn't want him to go yet. Her mind was awake again now; maybe it was the sugar. 'Joe, will you help us get back to the island?'

Joe turned back towards her, incredulity written all over his face. 'You mean escape here and take you back the way I came? I don't think –'

'No, I didn't mean that. At least, I don't think so.' Eva paused, lodged that idea as a possible plan B. 'No, I meant can you help me persuade Maggie to take us all back. Convince her that Peter's well enough. He seemed well enough to you today, didn't he?'

'Of course he's well enough. Well, I think so. But they won't let you go.' Joe started to pace, reminding Eva once again of Cain.

'But they can't keep us here as prisoners, can they? And you heard Barry this morning...' *Was that really only this morning?* 'They're planning another trip to the island soon. I need to be on that trip.'

Maggie had said more about the plans over lunch but wouldn't be steered into any conversation about taking Eva, Peter, and Grace back in the helicopter. If it hadn't been for Peter's sudden collapse, they'd have stayed longer on their first trip, to meet some of the other residents, whether Sandra liked it or not. Well, Maggie hadn't said that about Sandra, but it was more than clear from the way she spoke about the island, and its leader, that Maggie was not one to be dictated to by a girl twenty years her junior – practically a child – who led a community fewer in number than the staff in Maggie's office. Eva had tried to match Maggie's evasiveness when quizzed about the influence Sandra had over others on the island. She wondered how Mouthy Maisy and her gang had reacted when they saw the helicopter leaving without them. As soon as that helicopter was heard buzzing its way towards the island again, Maisy would, no doubt, be first on the scene.

Joe mumbled something about it being too soon – the planned trip back.

'What do you mean, too soon? Just now, you were certain Peter was already well enough.'

'Well no, I said I *thought* he was, but it's not about that, is it?' Joe stopped pacing and stared at Eva as if she surely knew what he was on about. 'Haven't you noticed how fascinated they all are with you?'

'With me?'

'Not just you, all three of you. You and Peter and Grace.' Joe sat back down on the floor. He tried to cross his legs but then remembered the injured one and settled for a half-cross-legged position, which didn't look comfortable. 'They don't want to keep you here because they're concerned about Peter. They want to find out, to make certain, that you're really a girl.'

'Well, of course I'm really a girl.'

'Yes, I know that, and I'm really a boy, but are we really male and female in the same way as they are, or are we still a bit neut? And what about Peter and Grace?' Joe hauled himself back onto his feet – maybe because sitting on the floor like that was too uncomfortable on his leg, or maybe because he was too excited about this bizarre nonsense he was now spouting. 'You and me, we're both children of neut parents, yes? And scientifically speaking, we shouldn't really exist. I mean, neut plus neut equals neut, not boy or girl. And until I turned up here, from what Barry says, most of them weren't even sure that any sort of humans existed in Britain anymore, let alone humans like us.

'And although their families have all been here in France for generations, there's still a dream among the British folk here that one day they'll be able to go back to Britain, except they're also dead scared about the virus. I think some of them are still worried they might somehow catch it from us, even though they know we're clear.'

Eva had heard bits and pieces about the virus that seemed to be the main subject of Cain's journal, which Anthony had got so excited about. But in support of Sandra, she'd never asked to read it herself. She'd always assumed whatever it was, it was ancient history, not something to be worried about now.

'Hang on, what do you mean, they know we're all clear? How do they know that?'

'Well, from tests, of course. Didn't you notice the suits and breathing gear they were all wearing when you arrived and how they locked you in here on the first day? They wouldn't even let me in to see you for a couple of hours. But now they're letting you out and even taking you to restaurants.'

'But they haven't done any tests on us, have they?' Eva thought back over the last few days. What did they need to test? Could they do it without her noticing? Had they tested her children without even asking?

'They took some of Peter's blood when they were operating. They did same with me when they were fixing my leg up. I think they must have decided that since Peter's was clear, yours and Grace's must be too.'

Grace whimpered and wriggled around a bit in her cot and Peter's sheets twitched. Eva held out a hand to silence Joe and got ready to push herself up off the floor if Grace made any more noise. She wanted Peter to get as much sleep as he could tonight, in case they were heading for the helicopter as soon as tomorrow. Except Joe was convinced that wasn't going to happen. Joe gave a silent wave, turned, and crept towards the door, which whooshed open with no regard to not disturbing the children.

'Joe, wait!' Eva hissed, getting up a little too quickly so that her head swam and she swayed like a drunk after Joe.

Joe halted just outside the door, stuck out his arm to stop it from closing between them.

'Do they really think we're not male and female like they are?' she whispered.

'Who knows?' he replied with a shrug. 'But that's why they're so interested in you. I'm just one boy, possibly a freak accident. But you're a family. And Peter and Grace are second generation – born naturally. You three are the miracle they never expected.'

Chapter 23

Eva

'Y‍OU'RE GOING TO love Dylan and Dominique's place.'

How many times had Maggie said that now? Her face shone with the morning light and Eva imagined her eyes were sparkling under those dark glasses hugging her face. The scepticism Eva had harboured over the last couple of days melted away as the sun warmed her face through the glass. The tension she'd felt as they sped through city streets had dissipated too as she relaxed into the whispered purr of the car's engine and resigned herself to this unnatural pace of movement. It was almost a decade since Eva's last car journey, and this was a different beast entirely from the battered old thing her parents had taken such pride in, with its dirty and noisy combustion engine.

They turned off the wide road and were soon racing along narrow lanes flanked by vast fields of wheat and barley. Maggie was right about one thing – it was hard to believe that this open countryside could be reached in such a short time from the heart of what had felt like a limitless metropolis. Eva didn't relish the thought of the numerous trips back to the hospital she'd consented to, but spending the in-between times out here might make tolerable their delayed return to the island. Though she hoped whoever was allocated the job of driving them for their regular trips back and forth might take the corners a little slower than Maggie was doing.

'Is anyone else awake?' Maggie asked, taking her eyes off the road to look at Eva for a lot longer than felt safe.

Eva twisted around to check on the three on the back seat. Grace's chubby little chin glistened with dribble that had also soaked one of the padded straps she'd fought so vehemently against less than an hour ago. Peter, who everyone had been most worried about making the trip, looked more relaxed in his special seat, with its winged headrest, than he had in all the deep sleep Eva had watched him through in that hospital bed. And yes, Joe was asleep too, head back, mouth open wide to accept any spiders that might dangle down from the ceiling – not that Eva imagined any such creatures really managed to make this sleek, spotlessly clean vehicle their home for very long.

'Yep, even Joe. Should I try to wake them?'

The smooth dark tarmac had been swapped for a crunchy gravel that bounced off the car's undercarriage and created a cloud of dust behind them, even though Maggie had slowed to little more than a crawl. Ideally, Eva would leave Grace and Peter be for a while, now they were asleep, but Maggie probably wouldn't have time to stop for long, even though she had insisted she had plenty of time today to drive them out there herself.

'Non, there's no rush.'

Eva concealed a smirk behind her hand and replaced it with what she hoped was a convincing looking yawn. She'd hate to be in a car with Maggie when she *was* in a rush.

They swept around a bend in the track and Eva shielded her eyes as the sun made the long white farm buildings glow bright white. Soon, they were pulling up in front of a squat cottage with a long, low-pitched roof made entirely from solar panels, save for the small square windows embedded in between, some tilted open to let fresh air into the rooms within.

Maggie was already out of the car, hugging and kissing the cheeks of the old couple who had emerged from the shadow of an open porch as soon as they'd come to a stop. His head was almost devoid of hair, save for a few white wisps picked out by the sun. Her hair, wrapped into a tidy bun, was also white and made even more striking by the healthy red-brown skin that came from spending most of your life outdoors. The car door opened and fresh, sun-drenched air wafted in.

'Eva, come, meet Dylan and Dominique.'

'But what about...' Eva gestured towards her children and Joe, still all fast asleep on the back seat.

'Oh, don't worry about them for now. Let them sleep if they want.'

Eva obeyed, unfastened her seat belt and untangled herself from it. Before she was even clear of the car, the woman had wrapped her in a lung-squeezing embrace, gabbling something unintelligible over her shoulder. She stepped back again and just as Eva thought the attack was over, she was being kissed on each of her cheeks, with more strange words between each kiss. The woman's face was soft and squishy, although when she stepped back to study Eva's face, Eva couldn't stop herself from noticing a few wiry white hairs sprouting from the woman's chin.

When the woman finally released her, the bald man stepped forward in her place, gripped Eva's shoulders and planted his own kisses on top of the woman's. His face was like the sandpaper she and her parents had used to scrub at the walls of their new home before making it their own with a fresh coat of paint.

'Eva, it is wonderful at last to meet you. I am called Dylan, and she is Dominique, my wife.' Maggie had said Dylan was British, like herself and Barry, but his words sounded more like that of the French hospital staff, as if he had to find them in the back of a cupboard and dust them off. Dominique, meanwhile, nodded and smiled.

Eva opened her mouth to speak, but what was there to say? *Hello, I'm Eva*? They already knew that. *Nice to meet you*? Eva had always thought that such a strange thing to say when meeting strangers about whom you knew almost nothing.

'Thank you,' she managed and then promptly realised she ought to qualify that with what she was thankful for. She was thankful to be out here in the fresh air, no longer cooped up in that hospital, but she didn't quite feel ready to say that yet. Right now, what she most felt ready for was a long walk, alone, to take in this new air.

She was saved from having to say anymore by her daughter's angry protests. She turned back toward the car in time to see Maggie wrestling a wriggling, red-faced Grace out of the car.

'Ahh, mignonne!' Dominique clasped her hands together and then started towards Maggie and Grace.

'Maggie, let me take her,' Eva said, cutting across Dominique's path and moving around the car towards them.

'No, no, Gracie is fine with me. You get Peter.'

What happened to leaving them to sleep? Grace wasn't behaving like she'd woken up of her own accord. Maybe Maggie was in a hurry after all. Dylan was now moving towards the still-closed door on Peter's side. Oh, well. Grace would have to stay with Maggie, she was robust enough to cope with a bit more parental neglect, but Peter needed his mum to help him out of the car, not some sandpapery stranger.

Grace reached out for Eva as she hurried past them, round the back of the car to Peter's door. Grace, instead, was swept into Dominique's embrace, who then delighted in 'peeping' her nose, to Grace's consternation. Eva reached Peter's door as Dylan swung it open, allowing Eva to duck inside before he could get there.

'Are we here, Mummy?' Peter gazed up at her, bleary-eyed. 'Can I meet the other children?'

'Yes, we're here my love, but I don't think Dylan and Dominique's grandchildren are here at the moment.' Eva gently freed Peter from his straps. 'Remember, Maggie said they don't actually live here, but they come and visit their grandparents lots and lots, so I'm sure we'll meet them soon.'

Joe busied himself with the contents of the bag he'd insisted on keeping on his lap for the journey, even though there was plenty of room for it in the boot. He shuffled in his seat, evidently dithering over whether to clamber out over Grace's bulky car seat or to wait until Peter and his seat were out of the way.

'Did you have a good sleep, Joe?' asked Eva, smiling across at him.

'Oh, I wasn't asleep.' His face flushed.

Eva nodded but gave Peter a little wink before lifting him carefully into her arms. 'Tell me if anything hurts, my love.'

'I'm OK,' Peter mumbled into her ear with his bravest voice, which told her it did hurt really.

'Who'd like a ride in this?' bellowed Dylan, who had somehow magicked up a wheelbarrow, which he was now wobbling side to side on its single wheel. 'Our little Claude loves his wheelbarra' rides.'

At Dylan's bellow, Peter had buried his face against Eva's neck, but now he gazed, wide-eyed, at the wheelbarrow and its driver. For the last couple of days, he'd loved being whizzed around by Joe in one of the hospital wheelchairs. But this was no wheelchair.

'Like being in a wheelchair at the hospital,' said Dylan, reading Eva's mind. "Cept more fun.'

'Can I, Mummy?' Peter whispered.

'I don't think...' Eva began to say, more to Dylan than Peter.

'How about if I push it for him?' said Joe, in her other ear, having finally managed to extract himself from the car around Peter's car seat. 'Don't worry, I'll go carefully.'

'Yes, Mummy, Joe can drive me. He'll be careful.' Peter pushed himself with his hands against her chest so he could look at her with his beautiful bright blue eyes, betraying no discomfort now.

Of course, as soon as Peter was installed, hands tightly gripping the sides, Grace was dangling herself head first out of Dominique's arms, determined to join her big brother, and before Eva could protest, a delighted little girl was perched between her brother's knees. Maggie and Dominique laughed, pointed, and gabbled at each other as the procession set off.

'It really would be easier if you weren't holding on too.' said Joe, addressing his complaint at Eva but intending it for Dylan too. But there was no way Eva was deserting her position on the right flank, even if Dylan gave up his on the left. So they all awkwardly shuffled the few metres to cottage door, Joe at the rear, on both handles, Eva steadying the boat from the right and

Dylan from the left, and Grace doing her best to capsize it with her bouncing in the bow.

It really would have been easier without the wheelbarrow at all, and Eva wouldn't then be trapped between the blasted thing and the house as her children were scooped up by strangers and bundled inside. But what brought on the tears in the end wasn't any of that, but the simple smell of the wood burning on the stove, blended with something healthy and good bubbling away, filling the room with a homely kitchen fug.

As the steam puffed its way out from under the heavy pan lid, so Eva's tears could no longer be held back behind her eyelids or blinked away. She should really be checking whether both her children were still in one piece and not touching anything they shouldn't. But now Dominique was coming towards her, wrapping around her, gently, comfortingly, nothing like the lung-crushing greeting she'd given outside, and Eva let herself sink into her.

Chapter 24

To: j.samuels
From: i.jamieson
Date: 28-06-157
Subject: Protected Child Case No. 43092

Dear Justice Samuels,

You will see from the attached transcript and notes that today's meeting was rather different from the previous two. However, I remain extremely doubtful about the child's fitness to appear as a witness in Cn. Turner's case.

As I am on leave for two weeks from 12th July, I have not been able to schedule another meeting for Cn. Turner until 26th July. I should warn you that Cn. Turner was not very happy about this and threatened to bring this matter to your attention. However, I believe the longer break between sessions may be beneficial for the child, for whom they are clearly an ordeal. You will also see that I am taking some additional actions based on matters which have come to light and have made space in my diary to meet with the child myself before I go away.

Kind regards,

Indigo Jamieson

Child Psychologist, Central London Child Protection Services

CENTRAL LONDON CHILD PROTECTION SERVICES
MEETING WITH A PROTECTED CHILD – TRANSCRIPT

DATE: 28-06-157	CASE NO. 43092	
NAME OF CHILD Cain (unconfirmed)	DATE OF BIRTH Unknown	ID NO. Unknown
PARENT NAME(S) Unknown	REGISTERED ADDRESS Unknown	
CLIENT NAME People's Court of Canterbury	PRESENT AT MEETING Dr. Indigo Jamieson (for CLCPS) - **IJ** Cn. Georgy Turner (for Client) - **GT**	

IJ: Meeting commencing at ten thirty-eight on twenty-eighth of June one-fifty-seven. Present in the room: Doctor Indigo Jamieson, Child Psychologist for CLCPS, Citizen Georgy Turner for the client, the People's Court of Canterbury and the child, identity unknown, currently under the wardship of the London Police Force. Good morning again, Georgy, and er...Cain. Now, Cain, Georgy's come to try to talk with you again and my job is to make sure you are safe. If you feel distressed by things Georgy says to you or asks you, you know you can leave this room at any time. OK?

[Pause]

IJ: OK Georgy, over to you.

GT: Hello again, Cain, I hope –

Child: Where's Nats?

GT: Well, I, um –

Child: You said you found Joh in Dover and that you helped Joh escape on a boat, but you left out Nats. Nats should have been there too, with Joh. Why wasn't Nats with Joh?

GT: Thank you for talking to me, Cain. It's good to hear you speaking. Your voice, it reminds me of how Joh sounded when I found him in Dover. His voice had changed since –

Child: You didn't answer my question. What happened to Nats? Something must have happened to her if she wasn't with Joh. Joh wouldn't leave her behind.

GT: Cain, I'm sorry, Joh had no choice. The police would have caught him otherwise.

Child: So Nats was caught by the police but Joh escaped. You helped Joh escape but not Nats.

GT: No, that's not what happened, Cain. You were right, Nats wasn't there.

Child: But why wasn't Nats there with Joh? Joh wouldn't leave her behind. Why was he in Dover without Nats? Had Nats already been caught by the police before they got to Dover? Yes, that's what must have happened. Joh wouldn't leave her behind.

GT: No, Nats wasn't caught by the police. She still hasn't been caught, as far as I know. Joh told me...

she hurt herself, her ankle I think, but she was in a safe place.

Child: Did she hurt herself jumping off the train? She wasn't well. That's why we got on the train. But Joh wouldn't leave her behind there. Joh would have waited for her to get better.

GT: Yes, that's right, Joh didn't leave Nats behind. They carried on with the journey you all started together. They came through Leeds and came to our flat, except I wasn't there when they came because... Well, it's not important where I was, but they carried on and they made it. They got all the way to Dover.

Child: But Nats didn't. You said Nats wasn't with Joh in Dover.

GT: No, but Nats was... Nats was safe, I know that, and I know that Joh didn't want to leave her behind. I think Nats is good at hiding because I think she still hasn't been found. And maybe if you can help me convince the court that you, and Joh and Nats are really no different from any other children, then –

Child: But we are different. And different is bad.

GT: No, Cain, different isn't bad. Different is good.

[Pause]

GT: So, will you help me, Cain?

[Pause]

IJ: Cain?

GT: Cain, we can do this. At first, Judge Samuels wouldn't hear any talk of there being boys and girls like you and Joh and Nats, but I think they're starting to believe us. And it was their idea I should come and speak with you.

[Pause]

IJ: Cain, you've done really well today. Is there anything else you'd like to say?

[Pause]

GT: OK, Georgy, I think we need to leave it there for today. Maybe Cain will have more to say to you next time. Meeting ending at ten forty-nine.

CENTRAL LONDON CHILD PROTECTION SERVICES
MEETING WITH A PROTECTED CHILD –
OBSERVATION NOTES

DATE: 28-06-157	CASE NO. 43092	
NAME OF CHILD Cain (unconfirmed)	DATE OF BIRTH Unknown	ID NO. unknown
PARENT NAME(S) Unknown	REGISTERED ADDRESS Unknown	
CLIENT NAME People's Court of Canterbury	PRESENT AT MEETING Dr. Indigo Jamieson (for CLCPS) - **IJ** Cn. Georgy Turner (for Client) - **GT**	

The child entered the room and sat down without any need for guidance, but during my introduction gave no indication of being any more ready to communicate than in the previous two sessions. However, as soon as GT started to speak, the child interrupted to ask a question about the whereabouts of Nats – the other companion who was travelling with the child and Joh. From the pronouns being used, it would seem both GT and the child understand Nats to be 'female', whilst the child and Joh (child of GT) are both given a 'male' identity.

The state of the child's voice was shocking. It was deep in pitch, like that of some elderly adults whose jobs have involved working in fumy environments. At first, I thought it was a symptom of the child's long period of muteness, but then GT commented on the child's voice, saying it reminded them of how Joh's voice sounded when they met in Dover. I am concerned about what both might have been exposed to, causing such vocal damage, and have filed a request for the child to be seen by an ENT specialist.

The meeting continued for some eight minutes with the child asking most of the questions – focused on concern for the whereabouts and safety of the child Nats, who is known to have travelled with Joh at least as far as Leeds.

At various points when trying to answer the child's questions about Nats and reassure them of Nats' safety, GT appeared hesitant, as if about to give more concrete details. This may suggest that GT knows where Nats is, or at least where they were at the time of meeting Joh in Dover, or knows more about Nats' fate than they feel able to divulge to the child. I tried to question GT further on this after the child had left, but GT was as evasive with me as they were with the child. I cautioned GT about their legal duties if they have information about a missing child. Transcript and notes from this meeting will be shared with Kent Child Protection Services, since the missing child's last reported location is somewhere in the vicinity of Dover.

Although the child appeared very communicative today, in stark contrast to our previous meetings and all attempted police interviews, there was a clear trigger that caused the child to shut down. It would appear that whilst GT is seeking to establish before the court that this child, their own child Joh, and the missing child Nats are 'really no different from any other children', it is clear that the child themself is all too aware of their abnormalities and views these abnormalities as undesirable. Now the silence has been broken, I have scheduled further meetings between myself and the child, in which I hope to again try to identify details about child's parent(s) and to broach the subject of corrective surgery.

Whilst it has now been established that the child is not completely mute, they are not yet ready to talk about their abnormalities and their mention clearly causes significant distress. Therefore, appearing as a court witness on such a subject remains out of the question.

A further meeting with Cn. Turner is scheduled for 26th July, conditional on the child's consent.

I. Jamieson

28-06-157

Chapter 25

Nats

Tris's little hand tugs on my arm as I stall by the farm gate.

'Come on, Nats, we need to wait over there.' Tris points to a spot right out in the open, on the opposite side of the road, where vehicles have carved out a dusty curve in which to pull slightly off the main roadway.

'We're all right here, aren't we? We'll see the bus coming from here.' A trickle of sweat dribbles out of my armpit and down my side. I'm sure my 'udders' have doubled in bulginess in the last few weeks, just as the weather's getting too warm for this coat that hides my curves. Even so, I hunch my shoulders forward. I wipe my hand across the back of my neck and it comes back wet.

'But that's where we need to wait or the bus won't stop.' Tris pulls on my arm with both hands. The inside of the coat sleeve sticks against my bare skin.

'OK, well, how about you go and wait over there, and I'll watch from here until the bus comes.'

'But Lori said I have to stay close to you.'

A car comes careening around the corner, throwing dust at us as it passes. I leap back and lose Tris's hand. My memory throws me back to the car that almost ran me and you down at this very spot what, two months ago? It could even be the same car, its low growl swearing at us as it zooms off into the distance. I reach for Tris's hand again and brace myself to cross the road.

'All right then, let's go.'

But now Tris is holding me back as I try to lead us across.

'What is it now?'

Tris doesn't need to reply as another car rumbles past, much slower than the first but still lethal if we'd stepped out in front of it. When it's gone, Tris leads us back to the edge of the road and I watch as they look right and then left and then right again before allowing us to go any further. A welcome breeze momentarily chills my damp forehead and I blink as the saltiness of the sweat stings my eyes.

I stand exposed and shiver as the perspiration under my coat cools in the shade that still stretches across this side of the road. I pull Tris tighter into me, but I'm too big to hide behind them. They wriggle and try to pull away. Am I holding on too tight?

'Hey, I thought Lori told you to stay close.'

They don't seem to hear; still try to tug us closer to the road's edge.

'No, Tris! We need to stay back. Listen! There's another car coming.'

'That's not a car, that's the bus, silly!'

Tris starts waving frantically as soon as the bus comes into view. I release my grip and take a step back; dig my hands into my pockets, study the gritty stones with both my eyes and my feet. The bus pulls tight into the edge of the road, imprisoning me between it and the steep verge. Its engine rumbles menacingly. A hiss and a clunk tell me the door is open. Don't look up, it'll be gone soon. Why's it not going yet? I dare to half look up.

'Morning, Tris, morning, er...' The driver is peering out at us, wondering who this stranger is with little Tris. This stranger wearing a heavy coat in the heat of a summer morning. The heat rises up my face and the sweat pools around my neck again. What's the hold-up? Are they taking a long, hard look at me? Memorising my face so they can give a detailed description to the police later?

'Well, go on then, on you get!'

Tris is still there, facing me, arms outstretched. 'Need a bye-bye hug first.'

There's no chance to object. Tris wraps their arms around my stiff body, pins my arms to my side, and gives me a tight squeeze. I feel the driver's eyes boring into me, spotting the shape of my strange curvy chest as Tris burrows their head under it. I extract my arms to offer a proper hug back, to at least look a bit more normal, but Tris is already skipping up the steps and onto the bus. The bus is gone. The silence should be peaceful, but my heart is thumping and my head is screaming at me. *Run, now!* But which way and where to?

I dash back across the road, remembering too late that I should have looked first. Good job there was nothing coming, but the faint twinge in my ankle, which feels like it will never completely go, reminds me I need to take more care. I set off at a jog down the farm track; it would be stupid to run away without any of my stuff. If Lori's out in the fields, I might even see what food I can find in the kitchen, although the thought of stealing from them plants guilt in the pit of my stomach.

I stop to catch my breath, look back towards the road and ahead towards the house. Have I really only run that pathetically short distance? I'll have to walk for a bit while I get my breath back. With any luck, Lori will be out all morning. It's usually well past one before they come back for something quick to eat before heading straight back out to do a bit more before it's time to fetch Tris. I'm getting better at reading the time off a clock, Joe. You'd be proud of me. Sometimes, the short hand is even a bit past the two before I hear the scratch at the kitchen door and Nelly comes bounding in, followed by Lori, looking weary from whatever hard work they've been doing. I've felt useless over the last week, sitting around in the house while Lori does everything, insisting I need to take it easy until I get my strength back.

I thought I *had* got my strength back, but now I'm not so sure. That little bit of running has done me in. Or is it the heat? I stop again and bend forwards, hands on my thighs. Sweat dribbles down my arms and my 'udders'. A weird thought crosses my mind. *What if* – No, we only did it once. But maybe one day, these udders will fill with milk for a little one, if I ever meet a boy again. I straighten up and my head protests, my vision blurring. Need to sit down.

'You OK, Nats?' Something is interrupting the sun. I can't feel its warmth on my face and the world behind my eyelids has gone darker. 'You've chosen a strange place for sunbathing, and aren't you a bit warm in that big coat of yours?'

I blink my eyes open and see the silhouette of Lori against a bright blue sky. I had for a moment imagined I was sunbathing, next to you, Joe, in the corner of a field, waiting for that time of day when we can set off again without the danger of anyone questioning why we're not in school. How can Lori imagine I could go to school now? Where I am now is gradually returning. I feel the stony track digging into my back. I'm on my way back from taking Tris to the bus, except I think that was a while ago now. I stopped for a sit-down.

'You're looking a bit peaky, actually. Shall we get you back to the house?'

Lori walks patiently alongside me, casting concerned glances in my direction.

'Don't worry, I can fetch Tris later. Looks like it might have been too soon for you after all.'

'Yes, maybe.' But if it's too soon for me to manage a walk down the track to the road, how can I even consider setting out on my own to...well, to where? To Dover and on to France? Back to the island? No, that would be way too far. But then everywhere feels too far away right now. Why does the world have to be so big?

'BUT I WANT Nats to take me!'

Tris's protest shoots up through the floorboards from the kitchen below. I feel bad, staying in bed, pretending to be asleep until after they've gone. I feel bad that Lori hasn't managed to hand this little job over to me. I can't hear all of Lori's vexed words but I can fill in the gaps. *I'd like Nats to take you too, but Nats needs their rest. I know they look well, but they were sick for quite a long time. If we let them rest now, they'll be well enough to play with you after school.* I don't need all that much rest really. In fact, I get restless having to stay up here for so long after the sun's come up.

The morning before yesterday, when I saw that the sun was behind some dark clouds and I could feel the cool, damp breeze and hear it rattling the open window and I knew it was legitimately a coat-wearing day, I did pluck up the courage to get dressed, go downstairs, and announce that I was feeling a lot better and perhaps I could take Tris to the bus again. Lori gave me a doubtful look and suggested maybe we could all go before turning back to the task of making Tris's packed lunch. Tris stomped a foot and said, 'No, just Nats take me!' Lori swung round, knife in hand, almost tripping over Nelly as they stepped backwards to avoid me, standing in the middle of the kitchen being useless, getting in the way. Poor Nelly yelped and then Lori shouted, and Tris burst into tears, and I muttered apologies and said maybe it wasn't such a good idea after all and retreated back upstairs to consider whether today could be the day I packed up my things and got myself permanently out of their way.

When they got back from taking Tris, Lori stomped upstairs and I quickly shoved my half-packed bag under the bed, though why I felt the need to hide my plans to leave, I'm not quite sure.

'Don't worry, I get it,' Lori said. 'And don't you go thinking about leaving us. Tris likes having you around.'

I felt with the back of my foot for my bag and kicked it a bit further out of sight under the bed.

'We'll find somat else for you to do to help round here, but mebbe for the next few days it's best if you stay up here till I've got Tris off to school, yeah?'

Tris bursts in as I'm shutting the oven door. The kitchen is a mess still, but Lori never seems to mind and will usually clear things up later whilst I bath Tris. Poor Lori. Tris insists I do the bathing every night now.

'Mmm, something smells good,' Lori says, standing in the doorway, obviously not planning to stay for long. 'But I've got quite a lot to do yet, so it might be a bit early for whatever it is to go in the oven.'

'That's OK,' I say. 'What I've made us tonight will be even nicer if it has a good long time to cook.'

'What is it? What is it?' squeals Tris, bouncing on the end of my arms. Lori warned me Tris would be even more excited to come home than usual today.

'It's a special surprise for the last day of school. That's why I made sure to get it in the oven before you got back, and so I could spend more time with my favourite little friend when they got back from school.'

Lori raises an eyebrow and chuckles. 'Hope you still think that way at the end of the summer, when your favourite little friend hasn't given you a moment's peace in weeks.'

'I'm not little anymore, I'm a big one now,' Tris shouts, stomping a foot.

Tris has been telling me all week about how some little children have been visiting the school – children who will be starting school properly in September, so Tris is a big one now. Does Lori still think I should start going to school after the summer? Nothing's been said about it again since that first day I came downstairs, and Lori's accepted that I won't go anywhere too far from the house, and certainly nowhere off the farm. Still, now I am feeling so much better, I should really think about venturing out, perhaps at least go and look at Dover and the land you said you could see across the sea.

'So, if you're such a big kid now, you won't want to make gingerbread people with me anymore, cos those are just for little kids.'

'I do, I do! Can we make some right now?'

'No wonder you two are both getting so big,' says Lori with a smile, still standing in the doorway.

'What do you mean by that?' I blush. 'Tris is getting bigger, but I'm not still growing.'

'Mebbe not upwards like Tris, but you're piling on the kilos now you're eating properly. S'good to see. You're looking healthy.'

Lori turns, gives a little wave, and heads back out to do some more work before I have the chance to reply. I put a hand on my stomach. They're right, of course. I am piling on the kilos, and I'm always hungry, but I feel good.

'Pleeease can we make them now?'

'All right, let's make some gingerbread people.'

Chapter 26

Eva

THE LAST OF the lambs bolted through to join his cousins and Eva swung the gate quickly shut. Some of the lambs bleated for their abandoned mothers and the mothers moaned back. Eva sensed this was just the start of a call and response between the ewes and their young that would crescendo and go on for some time. How much did the older ewes, the ones who weren't first-time mothers, still remember last year's separation, and the year before?

Dylan pulled up on the quad. 'Good job, you're a natural with them.'

'Thanks.'

The compliment felt good on more than one level. After the interminable days trapped in the hospital, when Dylan had suggested she joined him for his daily jobs on the farm, Eva hadn't hesitated for long. At first, the way the farm operated here felt worlds apart from the loose and haphazard approaches they'd adopted on the island, but at the end of the day, the sheep were still sheep. On a deeper level altogether, Dylan's words said that he accepted her as a fellow *natural* human. All right, what he'd said was that she was a natural *with the sheep* and she'd learnt quickly with Dylan that he said what he saw. But in the way he'd spoken, there was again a reassurance that to him and Dominique, Eva, her children, and Joe were now part of the family, no matter what the doctors and scientists might discover.

Sheep might be the same the world over, but were humans? Would the scans and DNA tests expose them to be weird mutants who belonged no more here than they did among the neuts they'd been created from? The days of tests had been far from enjoyable, and she always breathed a huge sigh of relief when they got out of the car, back at the farm. She hated watching her sedated children lying as if dead as they were sucked into the scanner, but all that paled into insignificance compared to the doubt now plaguing her. How would they be treated if the scientists concluded that they were something other than human?

At first, all Eva had wanted was for her and Peter and Grace to be on that helicopter when it left four weeks ago. She'd smiled for the video Maggie had insisted on recording of them all, to show their friends on the island how lovely it was here. The letter she'd written for Maggie to deliver had urged Sandra to come with Katie and Charlie, so they could all be together again until Peter was well enough to travel. But all the while she'd wished it was them, not just their messages Maggie was taking back with her.

Now, as Eva felt the warm French sun on her face, as she heard the children's happy voices carrying across the breeze, as her stomach started to look forward to the crusty bread, soft cheese, and sweet tomatoes they'd all enjoy sitting outside for lunch, she wondered when exactly the homesickness had stopped.

How long would it take for these ewes and their lambs to calm down; for the pain of their separation to subside? There were no pauses in the racket now through which to hear the children. But there was one sound that did begin to cut through. Some sort of engine with a mechanical purr, like a giant bee buzzing, beating at the air with its wings. It flew across the sun and then circled right above Eva's head before hovering over the farm buildings and dropping down until the spinning blades looked like they were fixed to the roof of the house instead of the helicopter that had disappeared behind it.

The helicopter was back! Eva's heart thumped in her chest. *Please let Sandra be here now.* She looked towards Dylan, seeking his permission to go and see, even though he always said plainly it was up to her how much help she gave him and how much time she spent with the children.

'S'all right, I'll finish up here,' said Dylan, clambering off the quad, 'and you can take this if you like.' He patted the seat of the quad. 'Tell Domi I won't be long.'

Even with the quad's speed, the helicopter's passengers had all disembarked by the time Eva rounded the corner of the house. It was a bigger machine than the one that had carried her and the children off the island – one designed to carry a dozen or more people in addition to the crew. Bile lodged itself in the back of her throat as the first islander she saw was Anthony, being introduced to Dominique by Maggie. He towered over lovely little Dominique, which didn't stop her from tousling his mop of fair hair. Eva couldn't help smiling. How would Anthony cope with Dominique and her kisses? Then Eva's smile turned to a frown. How would *she* cope with having Anthony around without Sandra to regulate him? She halted that thought – why was she already assuming Sandra hadn't come?

Vicki was there too. She'd cope with the kisses, although her attention was currently being taken up by Grace, of whom she had already taken possession, blowing raspberries and zooming her around above her head as if re-enacting the flight of the helicopter. Where was Peter? Peter was on Maisy's hip. Would she know to be careful with him? Eva had never felt easy about leaving the children with Maisy when it was her turn to look after them, but Peter and Katie both seemed to like her. Dominique and Dylan's grandchildren gazed up in awe at Maisy, hanging on her every word, although Eva was never quite sure how much English they understood.

Eva searched the gaggle of disorientated girls who still hovered near the helicopter, but she already knew she wasn't among them. Sandra was by far the tallest of the island girls, and her flame-red hair made it impossible to for her to hide, even in a crowd. And if she were here, would Maggie really be introducing Anthony first? Already, Eva resented him and Maisy, and even Vicki for invading her new home and not bringing Sandra, Katie, and Charlie with them. Her new home – was that what this place was now? She strode forward, refusing to yet accept that Sandra wasn't here. She ignored the cheerful greetings cast in her direction but couldn't help noticing the absence of all the older girls, and therefore also their children.

Anthony stepped into her path. 'Hi, Eva, this is from Sandra.'

He thrust a crumpled envelope at her; the same envelope in which her own letter had been delivered but with Sandra's name neatly crossed out and her own name written below. She took the envelope, turned it over in her hands, toyed with lifting the flap and taking out its contents but then thought better of it and shoved it deep into her pocket.

'Um thanks. So, Sandra's not come then?' She tried her best to seem unbothered.

'No, sorry.'

'Did you think she would?' piped up Mouthy Maisy. 'Anyway, it probably wouldn't be safe, given her condition.'

'What do you mean, *her condition*? What's wrong with her.' Eva's heart raced. What if all this time, Sandra had been suffering from some terrible illness?

'Oh, nothing's wrong with her, unless you count mating with Tom again and getting herself pregnant.'

'Maisy, we don't know that's what Tom and Sandra have been doing,' said Anthony.

Maisy laughed. 'Well, *you* might not be able to see the signs, Anthony, but it's clear as day to all of us girls.'

'You're a liar Maisy!' Eva bit her tongue.

Peter gazed, aghast at his mother's words. Eva flushed with shame; she never made accusations like that, even if she often thought them, and she made a point of never arguing in front of the children. What had come over her?

Nobody spoke. The distant complaints of lambs and ewes blew across the stunned gathering. Eva spun back towards the quad, leapt onto it, and zoomed away.

It was Dylan who found her. 'Mind if I borrow the quad?'

Eva managed a smile and shook her head. Did 'borrow' have a different meaning here? Dylan didn't need to ask to borrow something belonging to him, particularly not when it was something she'd as good as stolen. When the engine didn't start, she looked up. Dylan's concerned face looked down at her.

'I thought you had to rush off somewhere with the quad,' she said with a rudeness Dylan didn't deserve. 'Sorry.'

Dylan came closer and she shuffled along the felled tree trunk to make room for him. Dylan always stopped to make time for anyone – adult or child – even when he had a million things to do.

'It's nothing that won't wait.' Dylan perched beside her at a considerate distance. 'Dominique tells me your...friend hasn't come.' He paused, but not the sort of pause that required an answer. 'And she told me what that Maisy said to you.'

'Dominique understands English?'

'Enough. She just won't speak it.'

Heat flooded Eva's face and neck as she once again replayed Maisy's words, and her own, and then thought of all the other things she'd said to the children or to Joe over the last few weeks within earshot of Dominique, assuming she wouldn't understand.

'And she understands too what it's like, being a mother. She thinks a lot of you, you know. And she understands how much you care for this Sandra too.'

Eva smiled again after licking away the salty tear that had dribbled its way down the valley between her cheek and nose and settled on her lip. Dylan and Dominique were awesome. She hadn't once actually confided in either of them about Sandra, and neither of them had probed into things she didn't want to talk about. Well, Dominique hadn't probed into anything because she'd kept it secret that she even understood their language. But they'd quietly listened to things said, and unsaid. They nodded with interest at all Peter's stories about things he, Katie, and Charlie had got up to, and they put the pieces together and understood. Did they understand that Sandra was to her like they were to each other? Did they understand that two girls could love each other in the same way as they so clearly loved each other?

'Is that your letter from her?' Dylan nodded towards the crumpled, tear-smudged piece of paper in her hand.

Eva nodded.

'And does it tell you the same as what that Maisy told you?'

Eva shook her head, then shrugged. The letter said nothing about Tom. It had no hints about any possible pregnancy. But if that is what had happened, would she put it in a letter? The letter said how Sandra missed them all, wanted them back. Would she write that if she was now welcoming Tom into her bed? The letter expressed hurt that she and the children hadn't returned, contained no concessions that this might not have been possible, that Peter might not have been well enough. Might still not be well enough.

'Maggie's going back out there in a couple of weeks. You should go with her. Go see Sandra for yourself instead of expecting some letter to tell you what's what.'

'But what if Peter's not well enough to go home yet? What if he needs a doctor again? Or what if Grace gets ill and needs a doctor.' These questions had been dogging Eva more and more. They'd been so lucky – none of their kids getting seriously ill over the last few years, until Peter collapsed, just when Lewi was there to diagnose what was wrong and they had a helicopter to fly them straight to hospital.

'He's strong as an ox, your lad, and little Grace too.'

Eva wondered what an ox was. Was it a French word or an old English one? She reckoned she'd learnt more old English words than French ones since coming here...and let many more pass without asking what they meant.

'But if that's gonna worry you, they'd be fine here with us, you know.' Dylan started to push himself up off the log. 'I mean, I know you'd prob'ly rather take them with you, but it might be easier, having those conversations with Sandra, if you don't have them to worry about.' He pushed his hands into the small of his back and let it crack. 'And it'd give you an excuse to come straight back, if you needed one.' He lifted his leg over the quad, reached for the handlebars and sat down. 'It's an option for you to think on, anyway.' He rode away, leaving Eva to her thoughts.

Could she leave the kids here and go back to see Sandra alone? Even two weeks ago, she wouldn't have imagined any answer but a straight no. But Peter and Grace loved it here. They loved Dylan and Dominique; they loved their grandchildren and somehow managed to play all sorts of imaginative games together, despite having so few words in common. They were safe here – of that Eva had no doubts.

The lambs' bleating was already getting less frequent, though their mothers still called for them. Eva got up and wandered back to the house, to see what her own children were up to and to try to look pleased to see the new arrivals.

Chapter 27

To: j.samuels
From: i.jamieson
Date: 26-07-157
Subject: Protected Child Case No. 43092

Dear Justice Samuels,

I regret to inform you that the scheduled meeting between Cn. Turner and the child did not take place today. Cn. Turner arrived as arranged, but the child refused to see them. Cn. Turner was understandably frustrated by this turn of events. My diary is very full over the next few weeks, but I have nevertheless offered to try again next Friday (6th August). However, I think we must now conclude that the child will not be fit to testify in the trial.

With reference to your other question, I am sorry but for reasons of patient confidentiality, I am unable to share with you the notes from my individual consultations with the child.

Kind regards,

Indigo Jamieson

Child Psychologist, Central London Child Protection Services

Chapter 28

CENTRAL FAMILY COURT & COURT OF PROTECTION
Case No. 57-2043
JUDGE: The Hon. Just. Dafyn Williams
Date: 03-08-157

(11:00)

JUST. WILLIAMS: Good morning. We now hear case number 57-2043. Application by Central London Child Protection Services to assume the wardship of found child, reference CL57001. I must stress that this is a preliminary hearing, and as such, no firm decisions will be made today. Can we begin by going around the table to record those present?

DR. JAMIESON: Doctor Indigo Jamieson, Child Psychologist for Central London Child Protection Services.

SGT. STEPHENSON: Sergeant Finch Stephenson, London Police Force.

CN. PARKER: Citizen Pat Parker, legal counsel for the London Police Force.

CN. GROVES: Citizen Ol Groves, Court Recorder.

JUST. WILLIAMS: Thank you, and I'm Justice Dafyn Williams, family court judge. For the record, the child is not present today, which I can accept when we are only setting out the basic facts of the application. However, I will expect to meet the child before making my judgement, and except in the case of very young children, I do expect them to be present when that judgement is made. Would anyone at this stage like to raise any issues or concerns about that?

DR. JAMIESON: Your Honour, I accept that normally a child of this age would be present, even for today's hearing, but I should warn you, the child in question suffers from severe selective mutism and other signs of anxiety, particularly when discussions are centred on their family and identity.

JUST. WILLIAMS: All right, thank you, Doctor, and speaking of family, I assume all avenues have been explored in terms of identifying and locating the child's parent or parents, or any other family member?

DR. JAMIESON: They have, Your Honour. Both I and Sergeant Stephenson's team have tried to engage the child on this matter, but we have not even been able to establish what part of the country the child is from. Although they were picked up in the northeast, from the small amounts of speech I have heard, I would not say –

JUST. WILLIAMS: All right, thank you, I am familiar with your findings through your written reports, Doctor. Sergeant Stephenson, I assume the usual checks have been carried out against the police's missing child database.

SGT. STEPHENSON: They have, Your Honour. There are no records on the database matching the description or apparent age of this child.

JUST. WILLIAMS: Thank you, Sergeant, and can I assume a Found Child report has been issued and published on the government's Found Child hubsite?

[Pause]

JUST. WILLIAMS: Well?

SGT. STEPHENSON: Er, no, Your Honour. When we took the child into our custody, it was part of an ongoing investigation and –

JUST. WILLIAMS: Sergeant Stephenson, please forgive me for telling you your job, but if a child is taken into police custody, the first step is always to identify and locate the parent or legal guardian, and if those facts cannot be established directly from the child or the missing child database, the next step must be to issue and publish a Found Child report. Am I right?

SGT. STEPHENSON: You are, Your Honour, but –

JUST. WILLIAMS: Thank you. So, before we can go any further with discussing any application for permanent wardship, I will require that Found Child report to be sorted please, Sergeant.

SGT. STEPHENSON: Yes, Your Honour.

JUST. WILLIAMS: And of course, that needs to be in the public domain for a minimum of twenty-eight days before any change of wardship can be granted. Therefore, assuming it is done first thing tomorrow, we're looking at a date of thirty-first

August, earliest to conclude this case. I suggest a date is set by the court in the week beginning sixth September. Please could you both ensure you are available to be called back to court during that week, and, whilst I will endeavour to meet the child before then, I would like them to also be present at the hearing or for Doctor Jamieson to submit a written statement at least seven days ahead of the hearing, detailing the reasons why the child should not be present. All right?

[Pause]

JUST. WILLIAMS: All right, so given the child is clearly not currently resident with a natural parent, can we turn to the question of their current care arrangements? Doctor Jamieson, your reports were not quite clear on this matter. The child has been placed with a foster carer, have they not?

DR. JAMIESON: They have not, Your Honour. The child remains in the care of the London Police Force. This is one of the reasons why I –

JUST. WILLIAMS: In the care of, or in the custody of? This is most unusual. Is the child a danger to society, that they are being kept in police custody rather than with a foster carer?

DR. JAMIESON: No, Your Honour, I do not believe so, which is one of the reasons we are bringing this application.

JUST. WILLIAMS: Doctor Jamieson, you do not need to go through a permanent wardship application to transfer a found child into foster care. You do know that, don't you?

DR. JAMIESON: Yes, Your Honour. However, the child is in need of some surgical procedures before we can place them, and –

JUST. WILLIAMS: I see, but again, urgent medical or surgical procedures can all carried out under a temporary wardship order, which your own department can issue without any ruling from me.

DR. JAMIESON: Not this medical procedure, Your Honour. I have consulted with the appropriate surgeons and they will not carry out the procedure without the written consent of a parent or permanent legal guardian, but there is no temporary foster care placement into which we could put the child before the procedure is carried out. It would not be safe for the child, nor fair to the foster carers.

JUST. WILLIAMS: Doctor Jamieson, you shall have to enlighten me. What non-urgent surgical procedure does this child need which makes it safer for them to live in a police cell rather than with one of your foster carers?

DR. JAMIESON: Your Honour, the condition is so rare that there does not appear to be an agreed medical term for it, but in essence, the child has the urinary and apparent reproductive organs of a male mammal.

JUST. WILLIAMS: I beg your pardon?

DR. JAMIESON: I have found one or two articles about such a deformity being discovered in foetuses pre-birth, around twenty weeks' gestation, but such foetuses are always terminated, as are the female equivalents, though I have also read that around twenty-five years ago, a few babies were born with the female derivative of this condition and were treated with surgery. Not only did this child somehow evade termination as a foetus, but they have survived to near adulthood with their condition. This has clearly put severe strain on them both physically and emotionally, and I am convinced this is the root of their current mental state, which is exacerbated when they are made aware of their abnormality, such as would happen in any foster placement. The only remedy is to arrange the surgery, albeit unproven and experimental. But for that, we first need permanent wardship.

SGT. STEPHENSON: Er, shouldn't all this wait until after the Turner case is concluded?

JUST. WILLIAMS: Turner case?

DR. JAMIESON: Sorry, Your Honour, I should have mentioned. I first became aware of the child because of a case currently being heard in Canterbury. It's an assault case in which the defendant claims they were protecting their child, who they say suffers from the same deformity as our found child. In fact, they claim the two children knew one another. But I have spoken with the judge in that case, and the child is not going to be called as a witness, and it is surely in their best interests to –

JUST. WILLIAMS: To get them placed into proper foster care. Except you're trying to tell me that of all the foster carers you have on your books, none can be relied upon to take on the child before they've had this procedure?

DR. JAMIESON: Your Honour, most foster carers are reluctant to take on children over the age of five, let alone –

JUST. WILLIAMS: And what do you usually do in cases where no suitable foster carer can be found?

DR. JAMIESON: Well, as you know, that never happens. We are always able to reach some mutually agreeable settlement, but the cost of such a settlement in this case –

JUST. WILLIAMS: Ah yes, of course, it all comes down to money and budgets. Well, I'm sorry, but that's not good enough. As you well know, Doctor Jamieson, in our law, nothing comes above the welfare of a child. Therefore, you will find, and fund, a suitable foster placement for this child whilst your application for permanent wardship is being considered. Am I making myself clear?

DR. JAMIESON: Yes, but –

JUST. WILLIAMS: Good, then I shall visit the child in their foster home, week beginning twenty-third August. You may accompany me on that visit, Doctor Jamieson, if your budget will stretch to it. Sergeant Stephenson, Citizen Parker, thank you for your time. This session is now concluded.

Chapter 29

Eva

THE EMPTY JAR, thrust into her line of sight, snapped Eva away from her latest round of rehearsing what she might say to Sandra. Her eyes wandered up the tanned arm covered in sun-bleached hairs holding the jar out to her. Yes, she was sitting and he was standing, but Joe had definitely grown in the last three months. He was no longer the bewildered little lad who'd washed up on their island in his boat last summer. Was that really a year ago? How grown up would little Nats be now? If she was still out there, somewhere. Eva rubbed her arms to stop the involuntary shiver coursing through her despite the hot sun. She really ought to move into the shade if she didn't want to look like a beetroot when she saw Sandra tomorrow.

'Sorry, silly idea, don't worry about it.' Joe put the jar on the table, beside the glass of cloudy water that had once been ice cubes in the bottom of Eva's apple juice.

'What's a silly idea? Sorry, Joe, I was miles away then. What's the jar for?'

'It doesn't matter. Like I said, it was a silly idea.' Joe half turned away, back towards the house. 'Only, it was one of the first places she showed me on the island. It was her special place, and I thought she'd like it if at least something of her made it here in the end.'

'I'm sorry, Joe, I've still no idea what you were asking me to do. But whatever it was, it doesn't sound like it was a silly idea.'

As soon as the others had arrived, poor Joe had been bombarded with questions about his journey with Nats and Cain and how he'd ended up making it here when neither of them had. So, whenever it was just the two of them together, which, now she came to think about it, had been quite a lot over the last week or so, she carefully avoided any mention of Nats or Cain. Had Joe been looking for comfort from her – for someone sympathetic to talk to? Had she been too absorbed in her own woes over Sandra and Tom to notice what Joe was going through? She picked up the jar, unscrewed the lid and caught the faint whiff of Dominique's sweet strawberry *confiture*, which the newly expanded group of guests had devoured within hours of their arrival.

'So tell me, what am I collecting for you in this jar? Some poo from Nats' chickens?'

Joe chuckled. It was good to see a smile on the face that was often far too serious, except when he was playing with the children.

'Eva, That's gross!' The smile all but disappeared. 'But I thought you might bring back some of those tiny shells from the shell beach. Although you'll probably be too busy sorting things out with Sandra and spending time with Katie and Charlie, and it would mean going right past Tom's hovel, which you won't want to go anywhere near. So don't worry about it. Like I say, it was a silly idea, and it won't bring her here.'

Eva reached out for one of Joe's big male hands. 'It's not a silly idea at all, and of course I can get you some shells. I'll take Katie and Charlie with me, to help, and to keep me safe from Tom.' Eva smiled now. She had always felt happier passing Tom's hovel if she had the kids with her. 'And no, it won't bring Nats here, but it will be a nice present for her when she does get here.' Eva swallowed past the growing lump in her throat and blinked back the tears threatening to emerge any second. 'As soon as I get back, you and I are going to make a plan to find Nats and get her over here. In fact, I'll work on Maggie when we're in the helicopter – while she can't escape.'

Joe's face brightened and a sort of smile returned. 'Thank you, Eva.' He slid his hand out of hers and took a step away before turning once again. 'Oh, and one more thing. I left my old watch on the table beside the bed there. Do you think it might still be there?'

'I guess so. I can have a look for you anyway.'

'It's probably pointless. I stopped wearing it on the island and then the battery ran out, or perhaps it was killed by the sea water from when I jumped off the trawler, although it was still working at least two weeks after. But I thought maybe Dylan might look at it with me. See if we can make it work again with a new battery, except they probably won't have any that will fit, but –'

'It's OK, I understand. I'll get your watch for you as well, if it's still there. But I'm sure if you asked Maggie or Dylan, they'd get you a new one.'

Eva could tell straight away that Joe didn't want a new watch, he wanted his old one – whether he could get it working again or not. Something else he needed as a memory of times passed and people left behind.

'No, I don't really need a watch. I've never really taken to wearing one, but Georgy and Cris bought this one for me. Made sure I was wearing it the day I left for the island. I should have packed it when we left the island, but it didn't seem so important then. It's not really important now actually. Like I say, I've never really been bothered for wearing a watch, so don't worry if it's not there.' He turned again, drifted further away.

'Of course, you could come with me, you know.'

Eva had rather counted on Joe staying to keep an eye on Peter for her – selfish really – and she hadn't imagined Joe might have anything he wanted to return to the island for. But why shouldn't he come with her? Both her children would be fine here with Dominique and Dylan, and Vicki was assuming her old childcaring roles too. Eva trusted Joe with them more, and Peter still needed a bit of gentleness, but it was unfair to assume Joe would be there for her children whenever she couldn't be. He wasn't their father. Not that Eva had any desire for Anthony to take any greater interest in them. She was more than happy with Anthony's lack of interest in any of his many children.

'No, I couldn't.' Joe said, after a moment's hesitation. 'You want me here for Peter, and that's fine. Anyway, whatever grief I've had from the others these last couple of weeks about landing Nats and Cain in trouble would be nothing compared to the lashing I'd get from Sandra.'

'Oh, Joe, nobody here really blames you for what happened to Nats and Cain, and I'm sure Sandra doesn't either.' Of course, Sandra *did* blame Joe, and Eva was sure Sandra would lay blame at her door too now – probably not for the disappearance of Nats and Cain, but for the desertion of the island by so many others. Would she stand up to Sandra when it came to it tomorrow?

Chapter 30

Eva

Eva clung on to Grace for twice as long as Grace was willing to tolerate and then Peter clung on to Eva for twice as long as she felt she could cope with, without losing all her resolve to go. But then she was being bustled into the helicopter, and before long, the farewell party were all scurrying about below them like ants, getting on with whatever they needed or wanted to do next. Peter had been dragged off to play football with the French grandchildren. Joe was patiently walking Grace around the garden. Only last week, she'd managed her first few steps unaided, but although now she expected to go everywhere on her own two feet, she still needed a hand to cling to most of the time. Dylan and Dominique still stood where she'd left them, side by side, arm in arm, still looking up into the sky and waving, as if to say, *Don't worry, we'll all still be here for you when you come back.*

The helicopter swung around to face the sea – so far away when you were down on the ground and yet now racing towards them. Eva drew in a long, deep breath through her nose, hoping to catch the salty scent, but all she got was the oily and sweaty aroma of the helicopter cabin to go with the unintelligible French gabble assaulting her ears through the headphones they'd insisted she wear.

Before long, all she could see below them was sea. Maggie had explained they'd be keeping well clear of the large island of mainland Britain, skirting around to the south and then up the western side, beyond the slightly smaller island called Ireland, until they came level with their tiny little island, when they had no choice but to head in towards land. Eva had asked how they hoped to evade the detection of the British authorities who might be watching from the Scottish coast. Maggie had dismissed her concerns. As far as they could deduce, the population in that part of Scotland was pretty small and isolated, and it was a risk they had to take. Anyway, she'd concluded, soon they would be airlifting all the island's remaining inhabitants and bringing them to safety in France such that all the British authorities might find was whatever the islanders left behind.

'But what if some don't want to leave?' Eva had asked. Was Maggie expecting Eva to convince Sandra to desert her beloved island when so far, she'd shown nothing but resistance? Or did Maggie not care if those who chose to stay behind were discovered by the neuts? 'What if we're too late already? What if the neuts have already found the island?'

'They haven't.'

'But how do you know?'

'Because we have planted monitoring devices around your island, which send their signals all the way back to France. We will know if anyone else approaches the island.' Maggie had crossed her arms, as calm and in control as ever.

'And what if one of those signals tells you the island has been found when you are nowhere near?'

Maggie had shrugged. 'We would do our best to get there in time.'

Did Sandra know about the monitoring devices? If so, would she leave them be, grateful for the extra security they offered, or would she try to disable them? Eva didn't need to ask Maggie to be sure the devices hadn't been planted with Sandra's consent and therefore they had also probably been put there without her knowledge.

Maybe Sandra was right – that they were better off looking after themselves. It would have been better if the French had never come, if Joe, Nats, and Cain had never set out to find help. The community had been working well. Surviving at least. Mostly. But then Peter's heart would never have been repaired. Peter would probably be dead now, and how many others had died because they hadn't had the medicine or the skills on the island to save them? No, it was good the French had come. They had saved Peter and might save many more. But only if everybody was rescued before the neuts found them. Eva had to make Sandra see sense. She closed her eyes, tried to block out the French gabble to practise in her head what she would say to Sandra.

'EVA, WE'RE COMING into land.'

Maggie's voice cut into a dream in which Eva was somehow pregnant with Sandra's baby and Sandra was insisting that as soon as it was born, she would take it away to a remote island in the middle of the ocean, far away from any other people. Eva had asked how they would get there and Sandra replied they would fly, but not in a helicopter.

The *chop-chop-chop* of the helicopter blades changed, perhaps slowed slightly, and Eva's stomach rose into her chest. She opened her eyes. The oats flailed in the storm being created by the helicopter. They looked ready for harvesting any day.

'No, wait! Can't we land it somewhere else?'

Too late. A flurry of oat kernels wafted around the windows. Eva estimated they must have flattened nearly a tenth of the crop. But then what did it matter, if everyone left here would soon be evacuated?

The *chop-chop-chop* had somehow become a whine, which pierced even through the headphones until it descended in pitch and then became a *swipe-swipe-swipe*. Maggie had already removed her headset, unbuckled, and was bundling things into a backpack. One of the two pilots in the cockpit pressed a button, and the huge side door clunked outwards and slid open. A waft of oats blew in and settled along the edge of the floor. Gulls screeched their welcome. The sea air rinsed through the cabin. Eva closed her eyes again and inhaled deeply.

'Are you coming then, Eva, or do you plan to stay there all the time until we are ready to fly back? You want to see Sandra, yes?'

Eva fumbled with the mechanism into which the various straps around her body were fastened. When she'd got into the helicopter, someone else had strapped her in and made sure everything was secure. Nobody had bothered to show her how to release herself. Just as she was about to give up and call out for help, something popped, and everything went slack and came apart. She wrestled the remaining straps off her shoulders and propelled herself up and towards the open door. Her stiff legs still weren't working quite right when she reached the edge, but not wishing to look helpless, she went for it and half leapt, half fell out of the door, flattening a bit more of the oat crop as she landed with an ungraceful roll.

If Maggie or any of the others saw her awkward landing, none of them thought it necessary to come and check if she was hurt or to help her up. When she located them, they were stood in a huddle, apparently receiving instructions from Maggie.

'Ah, here you are. So, we think it's best if you go on ahead of us and find Sandra. Meanwhile, we'll be setting up camp here and then we have a few checks we can be doing on the monitoring equipment. OK?'

What had she expected? A welcoming committee waiting to greet them as the helicopter came into land? Sandra and Katie bounding towards her with joy as she set off towards the village? Maggie and the helicopter pilots marching on the village with her? The image of how things would be was blurring now as Eva pushed alone against the wind, which blew straight through her thin T-shirt. She'd been softened by the reliably temperate French summer. How had she forgotten that the island's weather was an unpredictable beast with no regard for the season? She turned around and retraced her steps back to the helicopter to fetch the jacket she almost hadn't bothered to pack. Although no longer against her, the wind was no more friendly, gusting her back towards the invading flying machine, whispering in her ear all the way *you don't belong here anymore*.

The helicopter doors were all locked. Probably the only doors on the island that were. Maggie and the two pilots were nowhere to be seen. By edge of the oat field, two domes of olive-green canvas now stood firm, deforming only slightly against the stronger gusts of buffeting wind. But they too were deserted, with little padlocks securing the bottom of each zip. She called out for Maggie, wished she'd learnt the names of the other two, and resigned herself to the fact that nobody was near enough to hear her in this wind. It hadn't taken them long to get those tents up. How long would they take checking the monitoring devices? Where even were these monitoring devices? Had she lost any head start they'd given her, returning for the jacket she couldn't even get at?

By the time she passed Sally's house, Eva's throat was dry and sore from the gasping breaths she'd taken as she alternated between jogging and striding into the wind, never sure which was gaining her more ground. Chilled rivulets of sweat dribbled down her sides from under her arms. Even here in the village, she felt like the only soul left on the island, other than the ghosts of those buried up on the hill. What time of day was it now? Having fallen asleep on the helicopter, she wasn't even sure how long they'd been in the air, and the thick grey clouds gave away no hint of where the sun was hiding.

Her tummy rumbled, reminding her that too much time had passed since the early breakfast she'd forced down before rousing her sleepy kids to say her goodbyes. Was that really only this morning? She could nip in to get something from the food store before seeking out Sandra, but she didn't have any tops to pay for anything and wasn't sure she still had the right to claim the free stuff. Vicki would be able to rustle up a quick snack for her. But Vicki's door was shut and no smoke rose from her chimney. Of course, Vicki was back in France, probably right now helping Dominique to rustle up lunch for the hungry hordes.

The pebbles on the beach rattled as the sea tossed them against each other. Eva remembered those first few nights here, unable to sleep because of that constant noise, wondering about moving to one of the cottages further from the sea. But on the fourth morning, she'd realised it wasn't bothering her anymore and from then on, only occasionally, when she woke in the middle of the night and lay there worrying about something or someone, did she really hear them again.

One door was open, though not really in an inviting way. The door to the head house creaked back and forth in the wind, as if whoever came through it last had forgotten to push it or pull it shut behind them. What if everyone had gone – deserted the island? But how would they, without a boat to carry them all, and where would they have gone to? Unless they hadn't chosen to leave but had been taken. Eva pushed the door open wide enough to creep through and, out of the wind, was relieved to hear voices from behind the door to the room Sandra used as an office.

The catch clacked as she twisted the doorknob. She stepped forward and peered around the door, feeling like an invader in what had once been part of her own home. Sandra stopped talking mid-sentence, looked up and frowned in annoyance at the intrusion. Her eyebrows remained frozen in position, unsure what to do next as her mouth widened a little. Tom and Sally were sitting across from Sandra with their backs to the door. They twisted around to follow Sandra's gaze. Tom barely met Eva's eyes before choosing instead to stare at a patch of floor in the space between him and Sally. Sally wrestled her mouth into a smile.

'Hi, Eva. How nice, we didn't know you were back.'

Chapter 31

Eva

'RIGHT, WELL, I'D better go and rescue Mikey from Charlie and Katie. See what mischief the three of them have been getting up to.' Sally caught her chair before it toppled backwards from her sudden decision to vacate it. She turned to Tom, whose eyes were still glued to the floor. 'Come on, Tom. I reckon Katie deserves some time with her dad, don't you?'

'But I had her for the whole day yesterday, and we haven't finished here, have we? We were in the middle of...'

Sally looked at Eva, grinned, and rolled her eyes. 'I think we've covered all we need to for now. Come on.'

Tom harumphed, got to his feet, and followed Sally to the door. Eva stepped into the room, to get out of their path. Her mind spun with questions. What had the three of them been plotting? Was Tom now a fully-fledged member of the community again? Were he and Sally now running the island, with Sandra?

'Wait, you've got Katie and Charlie looking after babies for you now? Aren't they a bit young?' Eva wasn't sure she'd meant to ask those questions out loud.

'Well, we've not exactly got many other options left, have we?' Sally's previous warmth towards Eva was sucked out of the room as a gust of wind came in through the window and out through the door. Sally ushered Tom past her and then slammed the door shut behind them. Although perhaps she didn't mean to. Maybe it was the wind that made it slam.

'So, you're back,' was all Sandra said after a long, awkward silence, during which Eva continued to hover by the door, waiting for what? For Sandra to give her permission to come in properly and sit down? For her to step out from behind the desk and wrap her in a warm embrace? Eva shivered, even though the air in the room was now still, and her face flushed hot with the heat that always comes when you stop moving but your heart's still pumping hard.

Eva tried to dredge up one of the opening lines she'd considered, but none of them now fitted. She took a step forward, hoping Sandra might at least invite her to sit down. But why wait for an invitation? She never used to need Sandra's permission to take a seat in her own house. She crossed the floor and sank, exhausted, onto the chair that had been Sally's, but before that had always been the one she herself sat in. She remembered those times when she used to wander in and sit down opposite Sandra, when Sandra was deep in thought and minutes would pass with Sandra not even noticing she was there. Minutes when she could trace every hair on her beloved's head with her eyes, take a journey down over her forehead, along the fine ridge of her nose, tiptoeing over her slightly parted lips, and then follow her jawline back up to catch sight of her ear as she swept her hair back behind it. Eventually, she'd look up, catch sight of Eva and smile. *'How long have you been watching me?'* she'd ask, and Eva would simply reply, *'A while.'*

'Where are Peter and Grace? You have brought them home, haven't you?'

Eva cleared her throat. 'Sandra, I've only come back for a few days, this time, so it didn't make sense to –'

'You're not seriously telling me you've left them over there with a load of strangers?' Sandra shook her head and laughed a cold laugh. 'And you accuse us of not looking after our children properly?'

This wasn't going well. But what had Eva expected – for Sandra to fall into her arms, sobbing, pleading for forgiveness for not believing her when she told her about Peter's heart, and his need for an operation, and then confessing whatever she needed to about whatever had gone on after they'd left? Or even better, setting her mind at rest that nothing had happened, that Maisy was a nasty lying stirrer whose words were pure fantasy? But then, when she'd grilled Vicki about Maisy's claims about Sandra and Tom, she'd been evasive and although she hadn't exactly confirmed what Maisy said, she hadn't refuted it either.

'And only here for a few days? I thought you were only planning to be *there* for a few days – just to get Peter's heart fixed – not three months!'

Their eyes met. Sandra's glistened with hurt. Eva couldn't blink back the tears from her own. She leaned forward and reached out a hand across the desk, but it remained there, unmet by Sandra's, until she retracted it and slumped back into the chair.

'They're not with strangers. They're with loads of people they know over there now. Vicki's looking after them a lot of the time, like she used to. And there's Joe – he's wonderful with them. You know how much they used to love spending time with him and Nats and Cain. And Dominique and Dylan love looking after them too. They were in the video Maggie brought with her last time she came. You saw that, didn't you?'

'Sounds like you love your life over there.'

Eva paused. What to say? The truth. 'Yes, I do now. I didn't at first, not when we were in the hospital and all I wanted was to be back here with you as soon as possible. But now, at Dylan and Dominque's, I feel welcome – we all do – and I feel like I belong.'

'You belonged here.'

Belonged, not belong. Was that intentional or a slip of the tongue? Did Sandra want her back, or was her life with Tom now?

'You'd be welcome there too, Sandra, and then you wouldn't need to be constantly worrying anymore about how much food we have or about keeping watch or people getting sick.'

'But I'm sure they wouldn't really welcome people like us, if they knew.'

'If they knew what?'

'You know, two girls. Surely, it's all girls with boys and women with men over there – like your Domineek and Dylan.'

Eva's heart leapt. If Sandra was talking like this, surely, there was still hope for them. Anything Maisy had said about Sandra and Tom must have been the vivid imagination of a silly girl. Sandra wanted to be with Eva. She just didn't think a couple like them – two girls – would be understood or accepted in France, where they'd never had anything other than male and female.

'Oh, Sandra, if that's what you're worried about, there's no need. Dominique and Dylan know about us and it doesn't bother them.' Eva became breathless with excitement. If this was all that was stopping Sandra from coming to France, this should be easy. 'I don't know because I've not met many people there yet. It's quiet and peaceful and out of the way at Dylan and

Dominique's farm, but I think – no, I'm sure, there are others in France who are just like us.'

Sandra pushed her chair back and got up, circled around the end of the desk. Eva got up and stepped towards her, ready for a hug. Her lips tingled in anticipation of soon joining with Sandra's. She thought she'd forgotten what it felt like. But Sandra brushed past her and headed for the door.

'Where are you going?' Eva said in a small voice.

'Sorry, Eva, I'd love to stop and hear about how wonderful your new life is, but I've got watch duty. We're all having to do extra now.'

The room darkened as Sandra pulled the door shut behind her. Eva stood, rooted to the floor. Inside her, her heart descended as the helicopter had earlier, with its own set of rotor blades too, thrashing at whatever it passed as it dropped.

Chapter 32

Eva

THE BEDROOM DOOR creaked. The rattling of the pebbles on the beach got louder. Eva opened one eye and swivelled it towards the door. Katie bounded over and leapt onto the bed, her growing frame slamming into Eva's shoulder. The springs protested in their usual way and the mattress flapped up and down.

'Katie! You know Mummy Sandra doesn't let you do that!' Charlie stood in the doorway, apparently unsure whether it was OK to come in. He didn't used to be that shy about coming into their bedroom. At least, not since the first month or so after he arrived, when he was a scared little boy who'd been dragged from the sea and who missed his own parents terribly.

'But Mummy Eva doesn't mind, do you, Mummy Eva?' Katie had now climbed on top of her and was bouncing on her bulging bladder.

'Mummy Eva still can't get over how big you've got, little Katie,' Eva replied, pleased to find the threat of a tickle was still enough to make Katie retreat to the edge of the bed, giggling but scared to come any closer. 'Where's Mummy Sandra anyway?' Eva tried to say this in as carefree a way as possible.

'At the watch station, prob'ly,' Katie replied with a big sigh.

'Again? But she was on duty yesterday afternoon.'

'She seems to spend most of her time up there now,' said Charlie, who'd left his position at the door and was perching on the edge of the bed beside Katie. 'She says somebody needs to keep watch in case anyone new arrives. But I don't think anyone new will arrive now, will they?'

Eva didn't really want to answer that question. She doubted even Sandra now believed anyone from DiG was still out there, finding and rescuing children like them. Even if they were, would those children really be safer being brought to the island than they were with their own parents?

'Well, I arrived, didn't I?' Eva chose to say.

'Yes, but you're not new, silly!' said Katie.

'Who's calling their Mummy Eva silly?' Eva advanced across the bed towards a giggling Katie, tickling fingers at the ready.

Did Sandra really spend so much time up at the watch station, or was this a cover for her being elsewhere? Was Charlie knowingly trying to protect her feelings when Sandra had in fact spent the night with Tom? Did Katie know her mum and dad were close again?

Eva HADN'T SEEN Sandra again after she'd left for the watch station yesterday. She'd almost raced out after her, followed her up hill, but as she'd opened the front door, the rain had come down in sheets, and then she'd seen three drenched figures – two small and one large one – hurtling towards her through the downpour. Before she knew it, a sodden Katie was wrapped around her middle, Charlie was beaming up at her, and Tom had darted back out into the rain without anything more than a grunted acknowledgement of Eva's presence.

So then all attention had turned to getting warm and dry. Charlie had fetched towels while Eva threw more logs than Sandra would approve of into the stove. Of course, Katie demanded to know where her brother and sister were, and Eva spun the lie that Peter wasn't quite well enough yet to make the journey but they were hoping Katie and Charlie and Mummy Sandra would all be able to come over to France to see Peter and Grace there.

'But Mummy says this is our home and we're never going to France, even if everyone else does,' was Katie's immediate reply. How long had she been calling Sandra just Mummy instead of Mummy Sandra?

'I'm sure she didn't mean you wouldn't ever visit France. You'd like to go in the helicopter, wouldn't you?'

Katie's head had bobbed up and down with enthusiasm at that suggestion, but inside that head, Eva knew a battle was raging between her unstoppable spirit of adventure and her fierce loyalty to Mummy Sandra. Until Grace came along, they'd never talked about how Peter had also grown in Mummy Eva's tummy but Katie had come out of Mummy Sandra. Both babies had sucked from both their breasts. It made sense – two nipples for two mouths – and gave each of them the freedom to keep up their respective roles in the life of their island. But from the day Katie learnt that Sandra was her tummy mummy – a term she herself coined – she began to give Sandra's words greater credence, even as Eva took on the greater share of the childcare – a decision that made sense at the time, since she was the one with the milk for Grace.

When Eva's tummy had rumbled and she'd not been able to convince them it was actually thunder from outside, all talk of going to France or staying here was set aside in favour of addressing the more urgent issue of their hunger. Charlie jumped to, announcing he now knew how to make scrambled eggs and that he could also cook up some fried tomatoes to go with them because they had lots of tomatoes at the moment but he'd do the tomatoes separately because Katie didn't like them.

'You liked them when we had them last summer,' Eva tried to remind her.

'Yuck, no! Tomatoes are horrid!' she'd replied.

It had almost felt like old times when Eva finally tucked Katie and Charlie into their respective beds, except the other two beds in the room remained empty, unslept in for months, and Eva suddenly couldn't believe she'd left her babies behind, far away beyond the other end of Britain. She'd retreated straight to her own bed, sobbing, as the northern summer sun finally sank below the sea.

INSTEAD OF TICKLING her, Eva pulled Katie into a big squeeze and then pulled Charlie in too, and they wobbled there, locked together for a few seconds until the saggy old mattress defeated her sense of balance and she toppled backwards, pulling both the children down with her.

'Can you play with us all day today, Mummy Eva?' Katie whispered in her ear once the giggles had subsided.

'Well, I'd like to, but first I need a wee,' said Eva as Katie bounced on her bladder again, 'and then I really do need to see if I can find Mummy Sandra to have a chat with her. But after that –'

'But that'll take ages!' Katie's bottom lip pouted out further than Eva thought physically possible.

Poor Katie was probably right, at least, Eva hoped she was because she didn't want whatever conversation she planned to have with Sandra this morning to be a short one. She wanted to walk somewhere with her where they could be alone. To hear Sandra say that of course there wasn't anything going on between her and Tom and then for them to start making plans for Sandra and Katie and Charlie to come back to France with her.

'I promise I'll be back in time to make lunch for us all, with Mummy Sandra too, hopefully. Then, this afternoon, I need your help to pick out some special shells from the shell beach to take back to Joe, and maybe we should find some nice things to take back for Peter and Grace too.' Of course, what Eva really hoped to take back for Peter and Grace was Katie and Charlie themselves, but that depended on how things went this morning.

WITH RELUCTANCE, SALLY agreed to keep an eye on Charlie and Katie at her place for an hour, two at the most.

'Although they're perfectly OK looking after themselves now, Eva, you know. They've had to be, and I was planning to go and look at the damage that machine's done to the oats this morning. I was all set to start harvesting them yesterday before that thing came and sat on top of them again.'

Eva thought about saying that she did try to suggest the helicopter landed somewhere else, but it wouldn't really be true because she was asleep at the crucial moment.

'I'm sure Katie and Charlie could come with you to look at the oats. They've been begging to go and see the helicopter anyway.' That was stretching it a bit too, although they had both looked excited when she'd suggested going to see it.

'Ha! You think I'd dare to take Sandra's children anywhere near those people and their machine? She'd never forgive me.'

Sandra's children? Is that how people saw things now – that Katie *and* Charlie were Sandra's children? By the sound of it, Sandra didn't spend much time with them. She never had done really, at least not since Grace came along. Would she even miss them if Eva put them on the helicopter now and took them back to France with her?

'I'm sure Sandra won't mind them having a look, and it's not like Maggie and the others are planning to kidnap them or anything.'

'Just go and do what you need to do and come back as soon as you can,' Sally said, walking away into her house, leaving the door open so Eva could peer in and see Charlie and Katie already settled on the floor, playing peek-a-boo with little Mikey.

The climb to the watch station was steeper than Eva remembered, and by the time she reached the top, both the jumper and the coat she'd brought were tied around her waist. Her thumping heart punctuated her gasps for breath.

At first, she thought it had been a wasted trip because Sandra didn't appear to be up here after all. Perhaps she had spent the night somewhere with Tom. Or maybe she'd returned to the house at the end of a long night shift up here while Eva was dropping the children at Sally's. Eva cursed herself for not going back into the house to check. The outer door was firmly shut, like Eva had left it, and when Sandra was home, she always left it slightly ajar, unless it was blowing a gale, which certainly wasn't the case today – even up here. Nevertheless, when she finally spotted her, the hunched figure was huddled up in the watch poncho with her hood drawn tight around her head. Had it not been for the wisps of coppery hair plastered over the top of the hood, Eva would have guessed it was someone else. Sandra never hunched and never slouched.

What should she do? Go and sit beside her? No, she was far too close to the cliff edge for Eva's liking – that was like Sandra, at least. She didn't want to startle her either; sitting that close, and with her arms and legs all tucked under that thick blanket, she could easily go toppling over the edge before she had the chance to steady herself.

'Hello, my love. I've missed you. I missed you last night too.'

Had she heard? Eva cleared her throat, was about to repeat herself, but louder this time, when the hooded head turned, looked at her with empty eyes, and then turned back to stare out to sea.

'Can I come and join you? If you don't mind, I'd rather not sit so close to the edge.'

Booted feet emerged from the front edge of the poncho as Sandra shuffled two bottoms back further from the edge, but her face remained locked on the horizon. Eva settled herself alongside though a little behind Sandra because she really was still too close to the edge. Eva hesitated, then reached out to place a hand on Sandra's shoulder.

'I have missed you, you know.'

A slight breeze caught a few strands of Sandra's hair and wafted them over Eva's hand, and the intimacy of it almost made Eva pull her hand away and apologise for the uninvited touch.

'Missed you too.' Sandra still didn't look round.

Eva dared to shunt forward, far enough to rest her head on Sandra's shoulder. The poncho was damp and smelled musty. Had she been out here all night? No, the poncho would still be more drenched than this from last night's rain.

'You haven't been out here all night, have you?' Eva asked anyway, feeling sure the answer was no. 'I missed you last night. I'd hoped you'd come back to the house.'

'I didn't want to disturb you.'

'I wouldn't have minded. Anyway, it's not right – me coming back and turfing you out of your own bed.' There had been plenty of times when one of them was out on watch and the other had been woken in the middle of the night by a frozen body slipping under the covers beside them. There'd be groans of complaint, of course, from the one who'd been warm and cosy, but that was all part of being in love – sharing warmth, tolerating someone else's cold feet.

Sandra remained silent and stiff. Eva squeezed her shoulder but she didn't relax. How could she find out whether what Maisy had said was true? Could she ask her straight up? That's what Sandra would do if it were the other way around. Eva shuddered at the thought of her and Tom, or her and any boy for that matter. The few times with Anthony had been more than enough.

'You all right?' Sandra had obviously felt the shudder, and Eva now felt her chin on the top of her head.

'I think so.' She lifted her head off Sandra's shoulder, took a deep breath, held it in, let it out and took in another. 'Maisy's been spreading the stupidest rumour over in France, you know. She says you're pregnant with Tom's child.'

Sandra's head moved, but away from Eva, not towards her. She said nothing for far too long.

'Why would that be stupid?'

Now it was Eva's turn to stare out at the sea in stunned silence for far longer than was comfortable. Was Sandra saying it was true, or only that it wasn't as far-fetched as Eva had made out? If it was true, was there anything in it other than Sandra deciding the island needed more inhabitants and that she had a duty to make her contribution? Eva almost felt sorry for Tom if that was the case, because that wouldn't be what he'd read into their renewed intimacies. Eva swallowed past the growing lump in her throat and asked the question whilst she could still breathe and talk at the same time.

'So is it true then? Are you pregnant?'

'I think I might be.'

Eva's hand was still on Sandra's shoulder, only now it felt heavy and awkward to keep it there. She let it drop, leant back on her hands and watched the clouds amble past. If Sandra wasn't sure yet, it couldn't have happened that long ago. She could just be a bit late with her bleeding. But even so, there was only one way she could be pregnant, and if the way Maisy spoke about it was anywhere near the truth, Sandra and Tom hadn't tried very hard to hide what they were up to. Unless it was all planned and Sandra had actually wanted others to know – to show she was willing to play her part in keeping their community viable.

'So you and Tom have...how many times?' Was that a fair thing to ask? If Sandra was determined to get pregnant, she'd mate as many times as possible when she thought the chances were highest. Her answer wouldn't tell Eva anything really. 'I mean, how many times have you missed your bleeding?'

'The last three, probably, although they can vary, can't they?'

Not Sandra's; she was as predictable as the moon. Three months? Eva had barely been gone three months. 'Hang on, this happened after I left, didn't it?'

'Of course it did. I wouldn't have...if...'

So that confirmed it. This wasn't a planned strategy because Sandra thought they needed more babies. She'd probably run to Tom as soon as Eva was in the air, and Tom had no doubt been only too happy to comfort her.

'If what? If I hadn't decided to do what was needed to save our son's life? You can't pin this on me when I was sat at Peter's bedside day and night, not sure whether he was going to live or die, while you were cosying up in Tom's bed.'

'We didn't do it at his place. I have got some standards, you know.' Sandra shuffled away from Eva and pushed herself up onto her feet. 'And Peter was never going to die. He just got a bit out of breath from you rushing him along the road, that's all.'

'Oh, is that right?' Eva got onto her feet as well, stepped closer to Sandra. 'You're certain of that, are you? Like you're certain Jay's still out there somewhere, gathering up more boys and girls to bring over to us, and that we can all carry on living here on this island until we die of old age without anyone ever getting sick and needing a doctor.'

Sandra pulled down her hood and turned to face Eva for the first time since she'd got up here. She swept her hair out of her face, tucked it behind her ear. Her face was pale, her eyes puffy. She put a finger to her lips. 'Shhh!'

'Don't shush me! And don't you dare try and tell me I'm getting hysterical over nothing. I've let you tell me what to think and what to do too many times, and I'm not going to –'

'No, shhh! I can hear boats.' Sandra crouched down, wrestled the binoculars out from under the poncho, put them to her eyes and scanned the sea.

She was right. The sound of engines, but definitely boats rather than the buzz of a helicopter. Eva crouched beside Sandra and followed the direction of her now steady binoculars. She didn't need any binoculars to make out the three distinct black dots in the water and the trails of white foam spreading out behind them. There was also no doubt about their course – they were heading straight for the island.

'They're coming here. They must have seen the helicopter.' Eva tugged on Sandra's elbow. 'I'm sorry, Sandra, but we need to go now. The helicopter will carry us all, I'm sure of it. We can't stay hidden here anymore.'

'Don't be silly. Of course we can stay here, and I'm not going anywhere in that machine. Those boats'll turn around in a minute, you'll see. It'll be some neuts having a race out on the water.' Sandra let the binoculars drop and swing around her neck. She wrestled her elbow out of Eva's tightening grasp. 'But if you want to go and get everyone worked up over nothing, don't let me stop you.' She crawled forward, almost to the edge of the cliff and lay on her front, propped up on her elbows, binoculars back on her eyes. She glanced round at Eva for a moment. 'Well, go on then, if that's what you want to do. I'll stay here and keep watch. And if it turns out they are coming here, I'll be down before anyone sets foot on land, I promise.'

Chapter 33

Eva

'Eva, there you are. Now, I don't want you to panic, but you need to go to the helicopter right away. We must leave as soon as possible.'

Eva had spotted Maggie jogging along the road towards the village as she was herself stumbling down the path from the watch station. They met where the path intersected with the road, Eva panting, Maggie apparently totally calm.

'There are boats coming... Three of them... I think we've been found.'

'Yes, we know. We picked them up about half an hour ago on our monitoring equipment. One is now docked at the jetty, the other two are circling the island. So we must hurry.' Maggie took Eva's arm and guided her down the road, away from the village.

Eva pulled her arm free, stopped still in the middle of the road. 'But wait, we need to warn everyone, get them all to the helicopter. It's big enough for everyone, isn't it?'

'Yes, yes.' Maggie grabbed her arm again. 'Everybody else is already on their way there.'

'You have the children?'

'Yes, we have the children. Sally and Tom have been making sure we miss nobody. We have all the babies, all the children, all the girls.'

'But you don't have Sandra.'

'No, it was just you and Sandra who were missing. Now we have you, and Tom has gone to find Sandra.'

'But I've just been with Sandra. She's up at the watch station. She said she'd come down as soon as the boats reached land. I'll go and make sure she's coming.' Eva shook herself free again and turned back towards the watch station path.

'Then she'll be on her way,' Maggie called after her, 'and if not, Tom will bring her. So, you can come to the helicopter with me.'

'No, I have to get Sandra.' Eva shed the coat and jumper tied around her waist, let them drop to the ground and launched herself up the path, ignoring Maggie's calls for her to stay.

The nearer she got to the top, the more futile it felt. Surely, Sandra should be on her way down by now. What if she had taken the other path, the one that came down nearer to the helicopter and further from the jetty? That would be the sensible thing to do. Well, if the watch station was deserted, she would take that path down too and they would all meet at the helicopter, unless the neuts cut them off before they got there. How many neuts did each boat carry? They would be outnumbered, for sure, and if they were police, the neuts would all be armed. Could they stop the helicopter from taking off... or shoot it out of the air?

The watch station wasn't deserted. Sandra was still there, and so was Tom. The two stood facing each other, arguing. Sandra stood rooted to the ground, feet apart, hands on hips. Tom looked like he was trying to push his hands through the bottoms of his pockets and was shaking his head, growling something Eva couldn't make out.

'Sandra, Tom, we need to go now. The helicopter is only waiting for us.'

'Don't you think I've been telling her that?' Tom barked. 'She won't listen to me, and I don't suppose she'll listen to you either.'

'Then why are either of you bothering?' Sandra shouted back into the space between them.

'Because we love you,' they both said at the same time.

'In that case, stay here with me. We know this island better than anyone. We'll hide out from the neuts until they think we've all left in the machine, and then –'

'And then what? We have a nice happy time just the three of us? That'd work!' Tom laughed.

'But the helicopter won't leave without us,' Eva shouted, infuriated at Tom's laughter and Sandra's intransigence.

'Are you sure about that?' Tom shouted back.

It took a moment for Eva to register that this time, Tom wasn't joking and to hear the unmistakable thrum of the helicopter blades. As one, they turned and watched as the machine emerged from behind the rise that was between them and the oat field.

'No!' was all Eva could say. Would they ever come back for them? Would she see her children again? Could the three of them hide from the neuts until the helicopter returned? *If* it returned.

'I'm sorry, Eva. I know you wanted to make a home for us there, but you must have known I would never leave here. Sally and others will see that the children are looked after.'

'But they're *our* children. How could you, Sandra?' Eva rushed at Sandra and beat at her chest. Sandra didn't move, didn't try to stop her.

'Wait, it's coming this way,' said Tom. 'I think they might be coming to pick us up.' He started to wave his arms at the helicopter, as if they didn't know and wouldn't be able to see where the three of them were.

Eva couldn't see how it would land when it got here – there wasn't anywhere big and flat enough. Even so, it started to descend, right above their heads. The three of them backed away clutching at their clothing in the growing tornado that the helicopter brought down with it. The door opened as the helicopter hovered just off the ground. Maggie jumped down and ran towards them.

'Come on! We can't stay here for long.'

Eva stepped past Maggie, towards the open door with so many anxious faces peering out of it, but stopped and turned as she heard Tom's shout.

'Sandra! What are you doing? Where did you get that?'

Sandra stood, feet apart, hair blowing wildly, hands not on her hips but stretched out together in front of her, wielding a gun pointed directly at Maggie.

'You have ruined my home, and I won't let you get away with it.'

'I'm sorry, Sandra, but we can offer you a new home in France.' Maggie held out a hand towards her, apparently unperturbed by the gun pointed straight at her. 'And I am also sorry to tell you that the gun will not work for you. We realised we were missing a gun after our last trip here, but our guns only work if you are wearing one of these.' Maggie pointed at what looked like a watch around her right wrist.

Eva remembered she hadn't looked for Joe's watch or got any shells for him.

Obstinate as ever, Sandra tried the trigger, one, two, three, four, five times and then threw the gun to the ground and staggered back away from them all. 'Go then, see if I care.'

'Sandra, stop!' Tom shouted.

'Come away from the edge!' Eva cried out.

They all stepped towards her but too late to do anything, as she teetered, glanced behind her, and then toppled backwards off the cliff edge.

'No!' Eva screamed.

She lurched forward towards the spot where Sandra had been. But Tom grabbed her, wrapped his massive arms around her, and pulled her back.

'We can't have the helicopter blowing you off as well.'

Is that what had happened? Had she been blown off by the wind from the helicopter? Or had she gone over deliberately?

Maggie was at the edge now, on her knees, peering over. Then she was backing away again, then tramping against the wind, grim-faced towards them.

'I'm sorry, but we must go now.'

Eva shook her head. 'We can't! We have to go down and get her, take her to the hospital!'

'I'm sorry. Even if we could, it would be no use. We have to go now.'

Eva was helpless against Tom's strength as he dragged her back towards the helicopter. But even so, she writhed and fought him with every muscle in her body.

'Eva, I'm going to do something to help us all now,' she heard Maggie say.

There was a sharp pain in her arm, and she looked around to see Maggie pushing something against it, just below her shoulder. Fog filled her brain. Her arms stopped obeying her instructions, and then her legs. She felt herself being lifted, dragged, and rolled onto a throbbing hard metal floor and then everything was black.

Chapter 34

Georgy

'Hello.'

'Georgy?'

'Who is this?'

I'd hoped it would be Indigo Jamieson, the psychologist. I'd spend most of the past three days trying and failing to actually speak to them after receiving their perfunctory hubmail message informing me that, due to unforeseen circumstances, they could no longer accommodate my meeting with Cain on 6th August and would be in touch soon to reschedule. At least they'd not had the audacity this time to claim that Cain was refusing to see me. Less than a month now till I had to be back in court and I was certain Jamieson was doing all in their power to stop Cain from testifying.

'It's Stephenson. Sergeant Finch Stephenson. Can we meet?'

'What about? Has someone at the police station put in a complaint about me? Look, I know I shouldn't have come to try and see Cain without an appointment yesterday, but –'

'No, no complaint, as far as I know. I can't say anymore on the phone – I've probably said too much already. Can you meet me tomorrow, first thing?'

'OK, I guess.' This didn't make sense. Stephenson was the enemy but was acting like a conspirator. 'What time's first thing for you? I could be at the police station around eight.' Whatever this was about, I might as well try my luck. 'And then will you let me see Cain after? I was promised access to him by the court, and we were making progress until Doctor Jamieson started fobbing me off.'

'No, we're not meeting at the station. There's a café called Jule's, about twenty minutes' walk from where you're staying. Do you know it?'

I'd not told anyone where I was staying. As long as I went and showed my face at a police station twice a week and didn't do too much shouting the place down when they wouldn't let me see Cain, I could stay where I liked and nobody needed to know my whereabouts... except they obviously did.

'Jule's. No, but I can look it up.'

'About eight-fifteen then. If you're there first, go for a table away from the window, and don't sit too close to anyone else.'

'OK, but why the...' The buzzing tone told me they'd gone already.

IT WAS NO surprise I hadn't stumbled across Jule's in any of my many walks through the streets of London. The area around my dive of a bedsit was hardly salubrious, but in comparison to the dingy backstreet, well, I hoped Stephenson was there already.

The smattering of other customers all looked towards the door as the bell above it warned of my arrival. Stephenson had chosen a table right in the back corner. If Jule's was ever full to capacity, based on the sheer number of chairs and tables they'd crammed in, I had no idea how the staff would get to most of them, unless they could hover above them like bees. Perhaps they'd pass plates of food along a chain of greasy-fingered customers at different tables until they reached whatever table had ordered them.

I reached Stephenson's table and sat down, scanning the table for a napkin or something with which to wipe the grime off my fingers.

'You need to order at the counter if you want anything.'

I took a moment to survey the route from here to the counter and also to evaluate the plateful of flaccid sausages and watery scrambled eggs that Stephenson was already tucking into.

'I'm fine thanks.' I waited for them to finish their mouthful and wash it down with a swig of tea from a chipped mug. 'So, what's this all about?'

'The kid. Have you got anywhere you could hide them...sorry, him?'

'What do you mean?'

'We need to get them out. Tonight if we can.'

'Sorry, are we talking about Cain here? The child you've kept locked in a cell for the last five months without any regard for his welfare?'

Stephenson still hadn't made eye contact with me, except for that briefest of moments when I was scanning the café after coming through the door. What was I even doing here, having an apparently clandestine meeting with the police officer who'd led the operation to close down DiG and hunt down our children?

They stabbed a sausage with their fork but then set the fork down on the plate.

'Yeah, look, I know you see me as the enemy, and you've every reason to, but from what I've heard you say in court, and from what I've seen of the kid, well, they're just an ordinary kid when it comes down to it, aren't they...sorry, he? There's no need to keep them locked up.'

I had to give the officer some credit for at least trying to say 'he' instead of 'they'. 'OK, but why now? You said tonight, if possible. Has something happened?'

'Not yet, but any day now. They're planning to move th...him, and...'

'Who's they, and move him where?'

'Jamieson, the psychologist.' They picked the fork up again, waved the floppy sausage around in the air. I hid a smirk behind my hand, as the sausage reminded me of Joe's strange appendage, which I'd got so used to tucking into his nappy when he was little. 'They're planning to operate, do what they call "corrective surgery", to make er...him like a normal kid.'

'No! When?' My heart raced. DiG had always warned that this could be forced on us, on Joe, if his differences were ever discovered.

'Well, I think if it had been down to Jamieson, it would've be done already, but thing is, for surgery like that, the doctors are saying you have to get parental consent.'

Interesting. I wondered what choice Cris and I would have had in giving our consent if it had been Joe. Cris would have probably signed without even questioning it. No, perhaps that's unfair. Cris did love our son, but would it need to be both parents consenting, or would they accept just one?

'And so, because we don't know where the kid's parents are, or even who they are, Jamieson's put in an application for Child Protection Services to get permanent wardship, so they can sign off the consent, but the judge has said –'

'Judge? What, Judge Samuels? When did all this happen, and why don't I know anything about it?'

'No, a family court judge, Judge Williams, and the first hearing was last Tuesday.'

'As in a week ago today?' All other conversations in the café stopped. I felt my face redden. 'Sorry, I'll try to keep my voice down,' I whispered, 'only, I can't quite work out what... Is this a trap or something?'

'No! You can trust me. I'm sorry for not calling sooner – it's not been easy for me to –'

'Not been easy for you?' I hissed. 'What do you think it's been like for Cain these last few months, or for all those DiG members you've locked up, or all the other kids and their parents who've had to keep everything hidden all these years?'

Stephenson held out a hand over the table. 'All right, all right, look, I was only doing my job, but as I say, what you've said in court, and what I've seen of the kid, it's made me think, and an operation is the last thing that kid needs. They just need people to accept...him for what he is.' Stephenson paused and took a deep breath, still with a hand held out, as if moving it would release another torrent of abuse from me. 'So, if I can get him out, tonight, can you find somewhere to hide him?'

I surveyed the café. Was anyone else watching, listening? Stephenson knew where I was living at the moment, which presumably meant others did too. I couldn't risk taking Cain back there, not before the end of my trial at least, and that was still almost four weeks away. And if we were going to break Cain out, kidnap him, hide him, he wasn't going to be testifying for me anymore. What did that mean for my case? I shook my head.

'I don't know. I couldn't take him, you must recognise that, not that I wouldn't love to. But I don't know anyone else on the outside.' I ran my fingers through my hair. It desperately needed a cut, certainly before I appeared before the court again. 'I suppose there's Doctor Lee. They'd keep Cain safe, and they've retired to Scotland. It would be good to get him as far away from London as possible. They might even be able to help him get back to the island.'

'Hmm, I shouldn't be telling you this, but their island's been deserted.' Stephenson cut a corner off the toast now visible under the pile of scrambled egg and shovelled it in.

'What, when? What's happened to all the other kids?' I now had an image of dozens of kids locked in individual cells like Cain, then an even darker thought of them all lying unconscious in a sterile white hospital ward, maimed by 'corrective' surgery.

'I don't know exactly. It wasn't actually our operation. We weren't allowed to be involved. Security Service people swept in and took over after the first sightings of the flying machine, just as we were making progress on –'

'Flying machine?' Oops, that was a bit loud again. I looked around at the other occupied tables. One had now been vacated. At another, the two occupants both had earphones in and seemed barely aware of each other, let alone anyone else. At the third, the person in the apron who I presumed to be Jule stood chatting with their customers. Nobody seemed to be taking any notice of us. 'What do you mean, a flying machine?' I repeated, in a lower voice.

'I dunno. Some sort of bus that can fly, I think. I haven't seen the pictures. Anyway, whoever it was in the machine must have been evacuating the island. No-one there now, they say, except...' Stephenson shoved another mouthful in, mid-sentence.

'Except what?'

'There was a body, on the rocks at the foot of a cliff. One of the older ones, they reckon. Hadn't been dead long when they were found. But they've done a thorough search and apart from that one, there was no-one else, but there obviously had been quite a few of them.'

'And this flying machine. Where do they reckon it came from?'

'I don't think anybody knows. Rumour is we used to have machines like it once, but it's a very well-kept secret if we have anything like that these days. And why would the Security Service be investigating it if it was part of some secret government project?'

'So from over the other side then – the other side of the sea.'

I was certain then that Joe must have made it across, that my boy had found others like him over there and they'd drawn up plans to evacuate the island, to bring all the children somewhere they would be welcome and well looked after. Just in time, by the sound of it, and all thanks to my Joe. I felt sad for the one who'd fallen off the cliff. Or perhaps they'd jumped. Why would they do that, though, when they were being rescued? Whatever had happened, it was too late for them now, but it wasn't too late for Cain.

'I think we should try to get Cain across the sea to join the rest of them, not to Scotland,' I said. 'And we should try to find the other one they were travelling with too. Joh tol...'

I stopped myself before I said it – *Joe told me where she was hiding.* Stephenson was still the police, still the one responsible for tracking down all of DiG, for almost stopping Joe from getting away, for keeping Cain captive all this time. Could I really trust them? This story of theirs could all still be some elaborate trap. Perhaps they knew exactly what I'd do once I had Cain – lead them to Nats as well, if she was still there.

'But maybe we should find somewhere to hide him over here first, at least until after my trial.' I needed to play it safe if I was going to get them both to safety.

We sat in silence. I racked my brain. Stephenson scooped up the remains of the watery egg on a soggy scrap of toast.

'What about Cris?'

'What do you mean, what about Cris? No, you're not suggesting we hide Cain at my ex-partner's – the one who was happy to betray their own son to you lot when he turned up at my flat on his way to Dover? The one who was a witness for the prosecution in their case against me?'

Stephenson finished their mouthful, set their cutlery down neatly on their empty plate, shook their head. 'I'm serious. Cris would do anything now to get back in your good books, if there was a chance of you two getting back together.'

'There isn't.'

'I'm not suggesting there is, but if we drop hints, it could help matters... The reason Cris called us when Joh turned up at your flat was because I'd suggested we could help you all be a family again. At the end of the day, that's what Cris most wants. But if we're careful, and if we plant the right seeds in people's minds, Cris's place would be the last place anyone would search for the kid.'

Was that true? Did Cris really think the police would let us have Joe back, unharmed. I suppose I'd been willing to believe that might be possible when I thought Joe could have been the one they had locked up in Newcastle. Didn't that show how Stephenson was devious, with no scruples, spinning whatever story suited the police's purposes? And if that was the case, I could be getting myself tangled in one of their webs right now. I started to stand up, pushed my chair back until it collided with the thankfully empty chair behind me.

'I'm sorry, but I don't trust you. I'll fight for Cain's freedom and mine through the courts.'

'There's no time for that, I'm afraid. Please, sit down. I'm telling you the truth. If we don't do anything about it, Cain is going to be placed with foster parent somewhere in a matter of the next few days. It could happen tomorrow even.'

'Good. About time he was with someone who can look after him properly.' I sat back down but didn't pull my chair back in.

'No, not good.' Stephenson waggled a finger at me. 'Whatever foster parent they've found will only be doing it because they're being paid handsomely for it. That was what Jamieson was trying to avoid, but the judge insisted the kid had to be placed in some sort of foster care as soon as possible, even if they had to pay a premium for it. And once Cain's there, you can be sure you'll be getting no more access to th...him. Jamieson will keep on coming up with excuses until the permanent wardship's come through and then Cain will be fast-tracked straight into surgery.'

It was a game of probability with a high chance of no winners except the state – though what they really had to gain in all this was beyond me – but as I calculated the odds, they tipped slightly in favour of trusting Stephenson, even if it also had to involve Cris in the equation. 'All right, so what do we do now?'

'You call Cris, talk them into taking the kid. But not on your phone. Here, best use this.' Stephenson held out a tatty-looking phone, not the standard-issue sleek police device. 'It's one I keep for calls I don't want tracing back to me.'

I pulled my chair back in. Before making this call, I needed to get everything worked out. How was it going to work? What might go wrong? How were we going to avoid falling into any of those pits?

'How about we just turn up with him on Cris's doorstep – no phone call, no warning, and I stay up there with Cain?'

'But you'll need to be back in London, to keep on reporting in to the police station twice a week.'

'There are police stations up there too. There's nothing in the terms saying it has to be a London police station.'

'And that's not going to look suspicious – you showing up in the Midlands after the kid's gone missing? No, you need to act as if everything's normal and you're also still expecting more meetings with Jamieson and the kid at the police station.'

I sighed at my lack of options. All Stephenson could do, or was willing to do, was sneak Cain out of the police station. After that, we were on our own, and as I didn't have a car to whisk Cain away, I needed someone else who did. Cris was my only option.

Chapter 35

Georgy

'I'M SORRY, GEORGY, I can't do this.'

I could see the white of Cris's knuckles reflecting the light of the streetlamp as they clung to the steering wheel even though we were no longer going anywhere. I closed my eyes and tipped my head back against the headrest. For a moment, we weren't parked in a dimly lit side street two blocks down from the police station. I was fifteen and a half years back in time, waiting at one of the many traffic lights we'd had to stop at on the way to picking up our baby boy, wondering whether Cris was still OK with what we were about to do.

'You wanted to say that fifteen and a half years ago, didn't you? I could tell even then you weren't as sure as me about accepting Joe, taking him home with us. But –'

'No, that's not true, I loved Joh every day he was with us, and I love him and miss him still now.'

I reached out and gripped Cris's knee – an instinct I'd not felt in a long while. 'Cris, I wasn't saying you didn't love Joe. I know you did. But you also had your doubts about whether you could do what we needed to do, and it's the same now.'

'Except it's not, is it? Then we were picking up a baby who was our own flesh and blood. Now we're waiting to kidnap a kid who's bigger than I am, with serious mental health problems and who's been locked up in a cell for months. It's not the same at all. And you're asking me to look after him on my own.'

Cris reached for the ignition key. My hand was off their knee in an instant and leaning across to stay their arm. 'OK, I understand it's completely different, but it's only for a few weeks this time, and then, once my trial's done, I can take him off your hands. Or...' I took a deep breath. Could I say this convincingly enough? 'Or I could come and live with you until we think it's safe enough to go in search of Nats and find a way of getting them both across the sea to join Joe.'

'I still can't see why I have to be involved in this. Isn't there someone else? What about the kid's own parents – where are they?'

'Cris, we've been through all this. Nobody knows who or where Cain's parents are, and he's not saying. I'm no psychologist, but I reckon his relationship with his parents might not have been all that good before he left them.' I closed my eyes again. We may have fallen out with each other because of Joe, but neither of us ever wavered in our love for him. 'And remember, at the end of the day, we're doing this for Joe. Because this is Joe's friend we're rescuing here. I saw it in Joe's eyes, that night in Dover. It really cut him up that he'd left Cain on that train. He'll be so pleased when he sees Cain again, safe and well, and hears that we were the ones who rescued him.'

Cris was jangling the keys hanging from the ignition, still clearly contemplating firing up the engine and driving away. If that's what happened, what would I do? Get out of the car, let Cris go, and wait alone, without a getaway vehicle, for Cain to be brought out? What would I do with him then? Where would I take him? Would Stephenson leave me with him and retreat back into the police station, or would they take pity on us both and drive us somewhere safe? I pressed the button on the dashboard that lit up the digital clock display: 23:16. They were more than fifteen minutes late. How long should we wait before assuming something had wrong and getting out of there?

'They can't have made it out,' Cris said. 'Someone must have worked out what Stephenson was up to, caught them in the act. We should go. They might start patrolling the area, searching for accomplices.'

'Give it ten more minutes, please. Then, if there's no sign of them, I promise we can go.' Would I go? If we didn't have Cain with us, there was no point in me going back with Cris. 'Or you could go. I think I'd stay and wait a bit longer, just in case, and then walk back to my place.'

Cris peered out into the gloom. 'I couldn't leave you here in this dodgy back street. Who knows who or what might be lurking around here?'

I smiled, turning my face towards the window so Cris wouldn't see. What would they make of the dodgy back street I now called home?

Eight of our remaining ten minutes passed. Cris fired up the engine.

'Hang on, it's not been ten minutes yet, and I thought you said you weren't going to leave me here.' I opened the door a crack, ready to leap out as soon as Cris put the car in gear. I forgot that opening the door also switched the internal lights on.

'Shut that door!' Cris hissed at me.

I pulled my door shut. Cris reached for the gearstick. I reached again for the door handle. The back door behind me swung open and a dazed Cain was bundled in.

'Sorry we're late,' Stephenson's voice whispered through. 'Had some drunken lowlife brought into custody just before shift changeover so the desk sergeant who was due to go off duty at eleven didn't go until quarter past. Right, gotta go. Good luck.'

Stephenson slammed the door shut, Cris revved the engine, and we sped away. I'd have pulled away slowly if I was at the wheel – much less suspicious looking, but then Cris always was the more impulsive one. As soon as I felt it was safe to do so, I slackened my seat belt so I could twist around to talk to Cain.

'Hello, Cain, you're safe now. It's Georgy and Cris – Joe's parents. We're going to take you home with us and keep you safe.'

'But we need to go and find Nats,' Cain's deep and urgent voice replied.

Chapter 36

Nats

I TIPTOE DOWNSTAIRS, CAREFUL to plant my foot in exactly the right spot on the sixth step down to avoid the creak. I grip the banister rail tight in my right hand, hoping the screws I tightened while Lori held the whole thing in place will be secure enough to hold me if my socks slip against the bare wood. At least Nelly isn't going to bound up to meet me halfway down. I took care of that. A pang of guilt strikes at my chest. But she'll only be shut outside for one night, unless Lori somehow manages to blame her for my escape.

Poor thing, she gave me such an injured look as Lori kicked her out, and I admit it, she had every right to feel unjustly punished. I made sure to move the plate of defrosting lamb chops right to the edge of the worktop. I even arranged it so one of the chops was temptingly visible from Nelly's eye level. Then I busied myself in the kitchen, always keeping one eye on the dog and the other out the window until I spotted Lori strolling back up the track with Tris. Tris let go of Lori's hand and raced towards the house, no doubt eager to tell me all about their first day back at school.

I had intended to leave before this, Joe. Before any further suggestions of signing me up to start school or before Lori decided I was fit enough now to at least walk Tris to the bus again. But with a little person clinging to me like a limpet throughout their summer holidays, I had no chance to plan and prepare, other than in my head. As yet, there's been no more mentions of school for me, and this morning Lori walked Tris to the bus, just as they had before the holidays. As Lori and I ate our lunch in a Tris-less silence, and Lori glanced repeatedly at their watch, I wondered whether I ought to offer to fetch Tris from the bus, but that would have scuppered my plans.

When Tris's feet crunched the gravel outside in the yard, I retreated to the toilet, shoved the door shut, and listened.

Smash! The plate hit the floor before a gust of air wafting under the toilet door told me that Tris had burst into the kitchen.

'Guess what I did at school today, Nats? Oh...Nelly! Bad Nelly! Nats, where are you? Lori, come and see what Nelly's doing.'

'Oi, gerroff those, you greedy bitch!'

I flushed the unused loo, ran the tap in the sink, and returned to the kitchen. 'Hi, Tris, hi, Lori – oh dear, what's happened here?'

I emerged in time to see Lori drag Nelly by the collar away from the two remaining lamb chops half covered by pieces of plate – in time to catch Nelly's doleful look as she was booted out.

The coldness of the tiles seeping through my sock confirms I've counted right and have reached the bottom. I daren't turn on the light. Even if the click of the switch didn't wake up light-sleeping Lori, Nelly's barks from outside on seeing the light come on certainly would. So I edge my way around the table in the dark, feeling for each chair back one by one and then for the worktop. I crouch down, ease my backpack off and round in front of me, unfasten the top. Opening cupboard door number one, I feel for the tins I pulled to the front, intentionally separated from the ones at the back. Unless someone's messed around in the cupboard since, it should be three tins of beans, which I transfer to my bag. I'm still not entirely convinced by your claim, Joe, that they make a perfectly balanced meal all on their own, but I do quite like them now – even when they're cold. I shut the door of cupboard number one gently against my finger so as not to let it shut with a bang.

Cupboard number two is vegetables. I open the door to the earthy smell of freshly harvested carrots, potatoes, and onions. Could it waft all the way upstairs and stir Lori from their dreams? I bundle what I've set aside into my bag and shut the door as quickly as I dare. I'm still not sure taking uncooked vegetables is really wise. Where and how will I cook them, or will I have to gnaw on them raw when the beans and bread have both run out? I like vegetables, though, especially the ones Lori grows.

The whole loaf of bread is the thing I feel most guilty about taking because there's barely any of the old loaf left for Tris's packed lunch in the morning. I did try suggesting Lori got an extra one when they went into town yesterday, saying Tris might need extra sandwiches for school now they're not so little, but Lori chuckled and said it sounded more like I just wanted more to snack on myself. It is true, I have been helping myself to an extra slice or two between meals from time to time. I have got good at cutting very thin slices, so you can hardly tell the loaf is any smaller, and then I carefully sweep up all the crumbs and wipe the knife clean. Only thing is, the slices are so thin, I want another one straight away.

I shuffle round to the fridge. Do I dare open it, or do I go without the block of cheese, the bag of just-ripe tomatoes, and the foil-wrapped hunk of ham I've kept hidden at the back for the last few days, hoping Lori forgets its existence? The fridge light isn't all that bright, but it will give the added bonus of showing me my escape route for a few seconds. The fridge will buzz after I've opened it, to cool itself back down, but it does sometimes buzz for quite a long time even when it hasn't been opened.

Opening the fridge enough to get my arm in seems to flood the room with a chill light. The loudest fridge-buzz ever starts up immediately, rattling through my brain. As I fumble around for the cheese, my hand catches a jar of pickles, which topples forward out of the fridge, smashing and leaking out its pungent contents onto the tiles. The cold vinegar soaks through the knee of my trousers. 'Shit!'

'Feeling peckish, are we?' says Lori's voice from the direction of the armchair in the corner.

Chapter 37

Nats

I SPRING BACK AWAY from the still-open fridge. In its cold light, all I can see of Lori are their long legs stretched out, with their slippered feet resting on the wooden crate that doubles up as a vegetable-collecting box and a footstool.

'I... What are you doing down here, Lori?'

The fridge door swings wide open and the rest of Lori emerges from the gloom of their armchair corner. They don't move, except for crossing one leg over the other.

'I think that's a question I should be asking you. Me? I just fall asleep down here every now and then if I've had a tiring day. Obviously not on a night when you've come down to raid the fridge before.'

'No, I've not done it before, I'm sorry. It's just...' What excuse can I come up with for why I'm down here rifling through the cupboards and fridge in the dark, after midnight?

'Oh, I don't mind if you want to raid the fridge in the middle of the night. And by the way, don't think I haven't noticed how quickly we've been getting through a loaf of bread recently. Do you want to shut that fridge? Best not let all the cold out into the room.'

Lori reaches to flick on the lamp that stands beside the chair as I push the fridge shut and the room begins to warm, except I'm still standing there shivering.

'Sorry, I'll clear this mess up.' I reach down to pick up the bits of broken jar.

'Leave it for now. Sit yerself down. We need to have a chat.'

'Do we?'

'Well, yes, cos that bag o' yours looks like it has more than just food from my kitchen in it.' Lori nods at my bag. 'Though I already had my suspicions you were getting ready to leave us. Mebbe that's why I decided to sleep down here tonight.'

So they hadn't fallen asleep down here by accident. How did they know what I was planning? I step in front of my bag, as if I can hide the evidence Lori's already seen. But the bag conspires against me, toppling over and belching out the bread, some potatoes, and an onion, which roles under the kitchen table. I lunge for the onion.

'Leave it!' Lori barks at me, like they often bark at Nelly and sometimes at Tris, but never before at me. 'Sit yerself down.'

I scrape a chair out from the table but stand there, pulling at the damp knee of my trousers, my eyes flitting between the spilled contents of my bag and the spilled contents of the fridge, wishing I could wind back the last couple of minutes. Had Lori really been sleeping before I smashed the jar? If I'd been more careful, could I have snuck out without waking them? There's a scratch at the door and a whine from Nelly.

'Should I have shut you outside tonight instead of her?' Lori nods towards the door.

Or had I given myself away when I tried to insist I should be the one to go without a lamb chop? Had I looked too guilty? Was that when Lori started to suspect and decided to sit up and watch what I might do in the night?

'I'm sorry. I should have thought more carefully about where I left those chops.'

'Ah, but you did think carefully about it, didn't you?'

'What do you mean?' I thought I'd planned it so well.

'Let's just say Nelly confessed all, but I wasn't convinced by her confession, and neither of you are particularly good liars.' Lori lifted their feet off the crate, nudged it to one side and sat forward on the chair. 'What do you want to leave for anyway? I thought you liked living here with us, and me and Tris and Nelly – we like having you.'

'I know, but I can't stay hidden here forever.'

'Yes, I've been thinking that too. A young'un like you shouldn't be cooped up here, too scared to show yourself to anyone. But where'll you go? And what'll you do if you're on your own when your time comes? It can't be that long off now.'

Something in my tummy did a flip. 'When what time comes? What do you mean? What can't be that long off?'

'The time for your pups to arrive, of course. You do know you're having pups?'

'What?'

Lori frowned and rubbed at their forehead. 'Thought mebbe that was why you'd decided to leave us – find somewhere quiet to have 'em. That's what Jess did when she had her pups.'

'Jess? Who's Jess?'

'Nelly's mother. It was instinct, I s'pose, but it would've been much better if she'd stayed here. So it's best you stay, at least until after yer pups are born.'

I start to piece things together. Lori thinks I'm... No, surely not. It's impossible. Well, almost impossible.

'By the time we found her, Jess that is, most of the pups were already goners. We only managed to save Nelly and one other.' Lori rubs their eyes with the back of their hand. Are they crying?

'And you think I'm having pups? Like, babies...a baby?' They definitely said *pups*, not *a pup*. Is it possible for a girl to have more than one at a time? I know sheep do, and there was that one time when one of the cows was found licking two newborn calves clean, except one of them was dead already and the other one didn't live long. But none of the girls have ever had more than one baby at a time.

They blow their nose in a big hanky before answering. 'Well, I can't really say I know if it works the same with you natural humans like it does with dogs and bitches, but all the same signs are there.'

'What signs?' No, it's a nonsense thought. I can't be. Tell them, Joe. Tell Lori it can't be true, because we only did it once. I'd have done it again, but I couldn't persuade you, could I? *'What if someone found us while we were doing it?'* you said. But you knew we weren't ready to be parents, and you were right. You are right. I can't be pregnant, especially not without you.

Something inside me flutters like a butterfly caught in some curtains. It's not the first time I've had that feeling. I remember asking Eva once what it was like having a baby inside you, and could you feel it moving around in there? She told me the first time she felt sure she was pregnant with Grace was when she felt those little tickles inside her again, just as she remembered with Peter. Except with Peter, she didn't work out what it was until the movement was a lot bigger, even though she and Sandra had both done what they thought they needed to with Anthony and Tom to make a baby inside each of them. My legs quiver and prickle and I sink down onto the chair before they refuse to hold me up anymore. Lori kicks the footstool crate out of the way, plants their feet on the floor, and leans forward, as if ready to get up and catch me if I topple forward. Do I look that weak all of a sudden?

'I think you might be right.' My heart thumps in my chest, or is that the baby too, trying to punch its way out through my ribs? 'Yes, I'm going to have a baby, a pup. I don't think it'll be more than one, though.' There, I've said it. I even manage a little laugh. My heart, or whatever it is pummelling me, slows and calms down. 'We didn't... I hadn't thought it... How did you know?'

Lori relaxes back into their chair, content for now that I'm not about to keel over. 'We've had bitches ever since I can remember. Never dogs, only ever bitches, and I've seen more than a few of them go through having pups to spot how they behave when their time's coming. We never got any of them neutered, see. My parent said it wasn't natural, wasn't right to neuter 'em. I always wondered why it was us humans didn't come in two sorts like dogs do, and if we did, whether we'd be able to have young'uns grow inside us like they do in bitches.'

Lori pulls the crate back into place with their feet, to use it again as a footstool. 'Now, I don't know where you've come from or how you even exist, and I daren't ask how you've... But whatever, it's plain as day to me that you've got pups coming. Or maybe only one, if that's how it is with humans. I wouldn't know. I s'pose it would make sense of why they only ever do one at a time for us at the pregnancy units.' They run out of words and we just sit.

The sky at the window is starting to glow pink. It will be morning soon and I'm still here. If I am having a baby, I don't want to be on my own when she or he comes. I want you with me, Joe. Sandra would try to tell you to keep right out of the way, but I'd tell her no, you had to stay. But Sandra's not here to make the rules, and you're not here either.

Lori's still watching me, not waiting for any response, just watching to make sure I'm OK, and to make sure I know I'm still safe here. I glance up, wondering how to say thank you, and yes please, I would prefer to stay. But then the stairs creak and we both turn to see Tris, mouth wide open, mid-yawn, descending into the kitchen.

'Can Nats take me to the bus today?'

'I think I'd like to take my kid to the bus, if that's all right,' Lori replies, saving me from needing to make up any excuse. 'But you need to go back to bed first. It's very early still – a long time till school time.'

Tris ignores Lori's instruction and plods on down the stairs.

'Whoa, hang on there a moment, my lovely,' Lori says with a rare show of parental tenderness as they push themself up off their chair and amble over to the jar of pickles I broke, picking out the bigger bits of glass.

'Let me do that, Lori.' I stand and refuse to give in to the fuzziness swimming around in my head. I feel the baby swimming around lower down as well.

'You're OK, I've got this, but you could put those other bits of food back where you found them, assuming you're staying?'

Part 3

Chapter 38

Eva

THE BEDROOM CURTAINS were flung open. A grey light flooded in. Eva pulled the covers up over her head and curled into a tight ball. Now she was that tiny baby, curled up inside Sandra's broken body. Had it died instantly the moment her body smashed against the unyielding rocks? Or had it huddled in the cooling darkness for hours, days even, wondering why the world around it had stopped moving?

'*La vie doit continuer.* Life must go on.' Dominique's hand pulled the covers back enough to stroke the top of Eva's head. And then, when Eva didn't move, she left, easing the door shut behind her. Eva caught the whiff of warm, fresh bread left in the room by Dominique.

For three days, Eva had been allowed to wallow in darkness. Almost everyone had wandered in to see her at some point or other. Maggie, apologetic but matter of fact; Tom, pronouncing that he understood because he was grieving too, but the kids needed her to pull herself out of it; Dylan, telling her what was happening on the farm, how much the lambs had fetched at auction, what his plans were for the day, what he'd love to have her help with, when she felt up to it; Peter, lying beside her on the bed, wrapping his little arm around her, stroking her hand, her face; Vicki bringing Grace in to climb all over her; Charlie, thrusting some sort of card towards her, taking her back in a flash to the night of that storm when poor Charlie had been the only living carrier of the dreadful message from Jay.

She reached across to grab Charlie's card again from the bedside table. There were some lovely pictures of sheep and trees, and even a helicopter on the front, but the real marvel was inside. As she eased the card open with her thumb, the video inside played once again. A smiling Peter, with Grace standing on his knees, swaying back and forth, and then Charlie, coming into shot from behind the camera, whispering a *one-two-three* and then both the boys saying together *We love you, Mummy Eva*.

Eva closed the card and tucked it under her pillow as Dominique bustled in, no doubt hoping to take away an empty breakfast plate, but instead stood their shaking her head and tutting at the untouched food. 'Eat and then get up today, oui?'

'OK, in a bit, maybe.' Eva rolled over onto her back and made it look like she was about to pull herself into a sitting position but slumped back down as soon as Dominique had left the room.

Joe was the only one she hadn't felt pestered by. He'd sit there, exuding a calm that lingered in the room long after he left. She'd started a mumbled apology to him about not having retrieved his watch or filled his jar with shells, and most of all, not having spoken to Maggie yet about searching for Nats. But then she'd realised, on opening her eyes, that he was no longer there and she'd been speaking to an empty chair. Poor Joe, who was surely mourning Nats as much as she was Sandra. Except he still clung on to hope.

Today, it was darker than usual, but everything was noisy. Rain hurtled past the open window, cascaded off the edges of the low roof, outside the bedroom, *drip-*

drip-dripped from something onto something else. Eva hadn't realised it could rain like this in France. Was it raining there now too, on their abandoned island? Was Sandra still lying there, exposed to whatever the sky might throw at her, unable to run for shelter anymore? Or had the neut invaders taken her body away to probe at and dissect? Eva shuddered and screwed up her eyes against another torrent of tears.

But each time Eva closed her eyes, she was on the doorstep of the head house again as three figures dashed towards her out of the rain – Katie, Charlie, and not Tom, but Sandra. Eva was there, with Sandra's favourite, biggest towel, ready to throw it around her and pull her into a warm embrace as soon as she reached the threshold. Except she never got there. Eva's stupid mind couldn't hold on to her image long enough, couldn't reach out and grab her, to clasp her wet face, look into her deep-brown eyes to say, *'I love you, and I'm never going to leave you ever again.'* Instead, Sandra would somehow dissolve as she splashed through a turbulent puddle, morph into thousands of tiny water droplets to be gusted down the road, out towards the sea. What if Eva had gone out in the rain, raced on up the watch hill to find her? Might they have then had long enough to talk things through? Would Sandra have still been up there the following morning, too near to the cliff edge?

It wasn't only the rain wearing Eva down, refusing to be blocked out, however much she buried her head under the covers. The grizzles and stomps of crotchety children echoed around the house, replacing the usual joyful shrieks that had wafted in on the summer breeze from somewhere outside. Why couldn't someone do something with them? Why was it always up to her to keep the children occupied when it was too wild and wet to be outside? Couldn't Sandra... She caught herself before she finished the thought, sucked in a lungful of air, and held it captive. The children only had one mum now, and that was her. The breath she'd been holding stuttered out of her between a renewed round of sobs. But this time, she was crying not for herself, but for Katie and Charlie and Peter and Grace, and for all the other children who'd been wrenched away from a parent when they were far too young.

It took a few seconds for the bickering and whining to stop after Eva stepped into the kitchen. Peter was the first to notice her and break away from the wooden brick balancing game they were playing, much to Katie's disgust because it was his go next. He skirted around the carefully constructed tower before heading straight for Eva. Grace, now fully confident on her feet, squealed in delight and toddled towards them, straight through the middle of the game, scattering bricks far and wide.

'No! Grace, that's naughty! I'm telling Mummy Sandr...' And that's when Katie fell silent too, looked around to see what or who everyone else had gravitated towards.

Everything froze. Nobody breathed. Then life started again as Katie turned and fled out of the other door. Joe and Vicki both leapt to their feet at the same time.

'I'll go,' Vicki said first, breaking the silence as she headed after Katie.

Joe nodded, turned towards Eva and put on a smile. 'Hi, Eva, it's good to see you.'

Chapter 39

Georgy

I DESCENDED THE STAIRS into the large hallway with its polished wood floor. I still couldn't get over the size of this place that Cris lived in, all on their own. Or at least, they had done, until we'd moved Cain in three weeks ago. And it was all so clean too – no black mould or peeling wallpaper. Yes, a fine layer of dust now coated all the smooth surfaces and the smell of furniture polish was not as pungent as it had been when I stepped through the front door behind a dazed Cain in the early hours of that Thursday morning. I wondered what story the cleaner had been given when Cris told them not to come for a few weeks. Could I have stayed up here with them both? Not to do the cleaning, but to help look after Cain. I think I could have coped with being around Cris, given how much time they spent out at work and the amount of space the house had.

Of course, to avoid raising any suspicions, it had probably been right to stay on in my skanky bedsit in London, making my twice-weekly trips to show my face at the same grey police station, keeping up with badgering Indigo Jamieson for more sessions with Cain before the looming deadline set by Judge Samuels. I hadn't actually ever managed to speak to Doctor Jamieson. My messages on their phone went unanswered and I'd had just one curt reply to my hubmail messages, simply stating that it was 'not possible to arrange any further meetings' and that 'Judge Samuels was fully appraised of the situation'.

I'd have loved to have been a fly on the wall in whatever meetings or phone conversations Jamieson had managed to have with Stephenson's team over Cain's disappearance. I assume the psychologist knew that Cain was no longer in police custody, hadn't been there when arrangements had been made for his transfer to foster parents. What explanations had been given to the family court judge, or had everything been swept under the carpet, erased from the files, as if Cain had never existed? I had been hauled in by Stephenson and a colleague to give account for my movements on the evening of 11th August, but Stephenson had pulled the strings so well that nobody could prove I'd not been in my bedsit all evening, let alone that I'd actually travelled up to Birmingham and spent the night there before returning to London on an early train the following morning. Could I have stopped a bit longer, spent more time settling Cain in?

It took a while to realise he was watching me. Strange, I'd got so used to the feeling of being watched, wherever I went, that perhaps I'd become desensitised to it. That could have been dangerous. What if I actually had been followed to the station yesterday morning and watched as I boarded the Midlands-bound train? What if I'd been followed onto the train, or if some local officer had been tipped off to watch for me stepping off the train and follow me here? Had I trusted Stephenson too much when they'd promised to ensure only a light watch was kept on me for these final weeks? Cain's eyes followed my progress down the stairs.

'Please, Cain, it would be safer if you stayed in your room – just for a couple more days. Then we can –'

'I'm coming with you.' Cain stood between me and the front door. Was he intentionally blocking my path or simply unaware of the space he took up?

'What? No, you can't. You need to stay here, just for a couple more days.'

'But when you came to see me, you said you needed me to speak to the judge, to show that I'm a boy, like Joe, and tell them what the police have done to me.' His hands fidgeted with each other. I could see he was nervous. How much did he really know about the danger he was in - the real reasons we'd had to get him out of there so suddenly?

'Cain, you know we broke the law when we took you from the police station and brought you here?'

'But you didn't take me from the police station.'

'No, you're right, Sergeant Stephenson did. But we planned it together, and we'd all be in a lot of trouble if anyone knew it was us who helped you escape.' *Who got the blame?* I wondered. Had the custody sergeant been disciplined or even dismissed? Did anyone there suspect Stephenson?

'But you're in trouble anyway. That's why you're going to court today and why you need me to speak to them, so you don't get sent to prison.'

'OK, yes, I am in a bit of trouble still. But that's me - not the rest of you - and after today, that will all be over and I can come back up here and we can plan together how we can get you across the sea to join Joe.'

'And Nats. We need to find Nats and take her too.'

I took a deep breath. Could I keep on promising that we'd find Nats? Surely, she'd moved on by now. Was she really still going to be hiding out in the same barn Joe had left her in nearly five months ago? 'Yes, we'll find Nats on the way and get you both on a boat, somehow.'

'But what if they send you to prison today?'

'They won't.' I did my best to sound as sure as I could be. 'They've already heard plenty of evidence for why Joe was in danger, and I did the right thing when I helped him escape. The way the judge was speaking in the end, they probably would have cleared me anyway, without hearing anything from you.' I moved closer to Cain, trying to catch his darting eyes. 'I'm sorry, Cain, perhaps I shouldn't have even tried to get you to come and be a witness, but I wanted to get the court to see you, to understand and accept how you and Joe and all your other friends are different from us, but how you're also just harmless kids – not animals or monsters. I wanted you and Joe and Nats and all the others to be free to live here in Britain with us if you wanted to, without having to hide who you are – without having to go and live on some secret island or escape across the sea.'

Cain's shoulders slumped a little. I stepped forward, reached out a tentative hand to touch his arm. I fought the urge to pull him into a hug as I would have done with Joe, aware of how little I knew this tall boy standing before me and the traumas he'd been through, and not only in the last few months.

'I'll be back here tomorrow. I promise. But please, go back to your room now, where nobody will see you until Cris comes back.'

I thought for a few long moments that he wasn't going to budge. I had to go soon or I'd miss my train and then be late for the hearing, and that wouldn't bode well for me. If I skirted around him and opened the door, would he do as he was told and stay in the house? He was bigger and stronger than me. If he got hold of the open door, I'd not be able to pull it shut and lock him safely in.

'Cain, please...'

Cain stepped aside and slunk down the corridor towards the back of the house where Cris had set him up in a room next to the kitchen, only visible from the large rear garden.

'I'll see you tomorrow,' I promised again before slipping out of the door and double locking it behind me.

Chapter 40

PEOPLE'S COURT OF CANTERBURY
Case No. 57-143
Date: 06-09-157 (Day 4)
JUDGE: The Hon. Just. Joh Samuels
DEFENDANT: Cn. Georgy Turner

(09:30)

JUST. SAMUELS: Citizen Kelly, Citizen Turner, good morning. I trust we have all read the new documents distributed to you by the clerk of the court last week concerning the child who the defence had asked to call as their final witness. For the record, documents E1 through to E4 are transcripts and reports from the meetings carried out with the child, by the defendant under the supervision of Doctor Indigo Jamieson from Central London Child Protection Services. Document E5 is then Doctor Jamieson's summary report, which concludes it would not be in the child's interests to be called as a witness for this case.

Document F1, which I read with some alarm, is a letter from the assistant chief constable of the London Police Force advising us that the child in question is no longer under their care and is in fact missing, the circumstances surrounding which are the subject of an ongoing police investigation.

I must stress that no details of that ongoing investigation may be discussed here today. However, I have been assured nobody connected with this case is considered an ongoing person of interest in the investigation. Since, in any case, the child would not have been called as a witness, we must proceed on the basis of the documents provided, and it is my firm intention to conclude this case without further delay. At my request, Doctor Jamieson has kindly agreed to take the stand today, if either of you has any questions for them, having read the very comprehensive documents they have provided. Citizen Kelly, does the prosecution wish to call Doctor Jamieson as a witness?

CN. KELLY: We do not, Your Honour.

JUST. SAMUELS: Thank you. And Citizen Turner, do you have any questions you wish to put to Doctor Jamieson in pursuance of your defence? Although you do have the right to question any witness you wish to, I would strongly advise we wrap things up quickly now and move straight to closing statements. I'm sure Doctor Jamieson won't mind if we choose not to call them as a witness.

CN. TURNER: Er, no, Your Honour. Since Doctor Jamieson was only able to facilitate three meetings between me and Cain and has been increasingly evasive towards me in recent weeks, I would like to ask them a few questions here today.

JUST. SAMUELS: And you believe this will benefit your case for the defence?

CN. TURNER: I hope so, Your Honour.

JUST. SAMUELS: Very well. Please call Doctor Jamieson into the courtroom.

DR. INDIGO JAMIESON
Questions from CN. GEORGY TURNER

CN. TURNER: Doctor Jamieson, you observed my two meetings with Cain, and I understand from your report contained in document E4 that you also had further meetings with Cain after that. Is that correct?

A. Yes, that is correct.

Q. Thank you. In my first meeting with Cain, he didn't speak. However –

JUST. SAMUELS: Citizen Turner, whilst I understand your assertion that the child is somehow like a male animal, I must insist that in my courtroom, you refer to them using human they/them pronouns.

CN. TURNER: Yes, Your Honour, may I continue?

JUST. SAMUELS: Yes please.

CN. TURNER: Thank you. As I was saying, we couldn't get Cain to speak in my first meeting with him, sorry, them. However, in the second meeting, as can be seen in document E3, they said quite a lot. Did they speak further to you when you met them for your meetings without me?

A. Your Honour, as you will be aware, I am not required to divulge the content or details of confidential meetings I have with vulnerable children in my role with Child Protection Services, so I decline to answer that question.

CN. TURNER: What? But you've just promised to tell the whole truth.

JUST. SAMUELS: Citizen Turner, again this demonstrates why, competent as you have shown yourself to be, you really should have delegated your defence to a legally trained professional. Doctor Jamieson is correct. Therefore, I must ask you to limit your questions to those which relate to the meetings you had with the child, under Doctor Jamieson's supervision. Do you have any further questions for Doctor Jamieson?

CN. TURNER: But that's... OK, I understand. Please, give me a moment.

[Pause]

CN. TURNER: Doctor Jamieson, in document E4, you note the use of male and female pronouns in relation to Cain as well as my child, Joh, and the other child, Nats - pronouns which we are forbidden from using today in this court. Would you agree, based on your observations of Cain during our meetings, that they could in fact be a male human, and not neutral like you or I?

A. No, I did not observe anything in those meetings that would lead me to such a conclusion. What I recorded was simply my observation of how you and the child referred to them and the other two children.

Q. OK, but you noted that there was something shocking and different about Cain's voice, and you also noted my comment that it was similar to how Joh's voice sounded when I saw them in Dover. So, you accept that Cain and Joh are in some way biologically different from other children who you have met.

A. No, I'm afraid you are drawing conclusions from my notes that are simply not there. Firstly, I can only take your word for your claims about changes in your own child's voice, and as I understand it, your meeting with them in Dover was extremely brief and no doubt emotional. With regard to the child Cain's voice, as I set out in my notes, there could be any number of reasons for its condition, ranging from simple lack of use over the last few months to some damage to the vocal cords from exposure to some sort of fumes. However, I am a psychologist, not a medical doctor, and I am afraid the child went missing before we were able to get them seen by the ENT specialist.

Q. I see. And did you arrange for them to be seen by or have you discussed the child with any other medical professional?

JUST. SAMUELS: Citizen Turner, your questioning is again straying into areas about which Doctor Jamieson is under no obligation to give answers. In order to avoid this, please stick to questions that are directly related to the documents Doctor Jamieson has provided, based on your meetings with the child.

CN. TURNER: But Your Honour, I have reason to believe... OK, I will do as you ask. Doctor Jamieson, also in document E4, you write 'it is clear that the child themself is all too aware of their abnormalities and views these abnormalities as undesirable'. And you go on to say that you plan to broach the subject of 'medical assessments and interventions'. To what sort of abnormalities were you referring, and what clinical assessments and interventions did you have in mind?

A. Well, as you know, the child is a selective mute and displays various unusual physical ticks and mannerisms. Now these could all be attributed to the trauma they have clearly experienced following their arrest and prolonged incarceration. However, such symptoms are also common in children with a now rare condition known as autism. Indeed, I would postulate that what we have seen in the child could well be autistic traits exacerbated by recent events.

Q. But I put it to you that the interventions you were planning to broach were in fact of a surgical kind. The court will recall Doctor Lee's testimony in which they described the unnecessary and harmful surgical procedures performed on some of the female children born in their fertility unit. 'Corrective surgery' was what Doctor Lee called it – surgery that was completely unnecessary and in some cases fatal. Doctor Jamieson, amongst the interventions you were considering for Cain, was 'corrective surgery' one of them.

A. Citizen Turner, Your Honour, I am not, and do not claim to be, a medical practitioner. I am a psychologist employed by Central London Child Protection Services to assess and advise on the psychological state of children in their care and other children of concern within their jurisdiction. As such, whilst I might refer those children for assessment by medical experts, I would never presume to make any medical diagnosis or recommend any medical or surgical procedure.

Q. And did any of the medical practitioners you consulted discuss 'corrective surgery' with you?

A. The child was not seen by any of the medical practitioners with whom I consulted.

Q. But you don't deny that you did consult with medical practitioners, including surgeons?

JUST. SAMUELS: Citizen Turner, Doctor Jamieson has said all they need to say on this matter. More, in fact. We must respect their right to maintain professional confidentiality. I understand your frustration that you only had one fruitful meeting with the child before their disappearance, and I am disappointed by the apparent dereliction of duty on the part of the London Police Force, particularly when we're talking about a clearly vulnerable and damaged child. However, I think we must assume Doctor Jamieson was doing their professional duty to protect and help the child and, had they remained under their care, would have worked only in the child's interests, and the child would not have come to any harm. So, can we now please allow Doctor Jamieson to step down from the witness stand?

CN. TURNER: But... Yes, Your Honour, I can think of no further questions that you will allow me to ask.

JUST. SAMUELS: Good. Then we will take a short recess now, prior to hearing the closing statements. Court will adjourn until eleven a.m.

Chapter 41

PEOPLE'S COURT OF CANTERBURY
Case No. 57-143
Date: 06-09-157 (Day 4)
JUDGE: The Hon. Just. Joh Samuels
DEFENDANT: Cn. Georgy Turner

(11:00)

JUST. SAMUELS: Citizens, we will move now to closing statements. Citizen Turner, when it is your turn, please remember to stick to the facts and testimonies that have been presented to us during the case. This is not a time for introducing new arguments. We will hear from the prosecution first.

CN. KELLY: Your Honour, I would like to begin by congratulating the defendant. Questioning witnesses and presenting arguments in court is something for which I have been trained and had many years of experience. I thought this case would be an easy one to prosecute, but I have met my match in this defendant turned defence lawyer. Citizen Turner, when you have served your sentence, if the actuarial profession will not have you back, or if you consider your old career a tad boring compared to your exploits of the last few months, I believe you could easily carve out a new career for yourself in law.

However, first you must serve your sentence.

Your Honour, as a parent, I love my two children dearly, and I say that I would do anything to protect them, anything to keep them safe. Would I be willing to break the law to protect them? Quite possibly, if I felt it was the only way to keep them safe. However, I would be doing so knowing that actions have consequences, that the law must be upheld and that I would need to be punished for my illegal actions. The defendant is a professionally trained actuary. They know all about calculating risks. They knew what the risks were of turning on and attacking the police and they knew the probability of being arrested and tried for their crimes was one hundred per cent.

The defendant has never denied the facts – that they assaulted police officers, and according to our laws, that is illegal, and a good thing too. Otherwise, every criminal or suspect being apprehended would lash out without any fear of punishment for their actions, and no sane person would consider a career in the police force. Then where would we be?

The defendant has presented convincing evidence to us that some children have been born different and perhaps our society has not done the best we can for those children. This is certainly something that should be looked into further, and perhaps it will be concluded that changes are needed. There are many ways in which our society is not perfect. I sometimes feel our society has not done the best for my own children – they've had to put up with a teacher who doesn't know how to control a class, or they've been bullied by other children.

But neither violence nor trying to circumvent proper procedure is the solution.

And I confess to being a little confused about what the defendant wants for their child. On the one hand, they have been trying to build their defence on the basis that their child is different and therefore worthy of special consideration. But then in document E3, I read about them telling the child Cain that they wanted to convince the court that these three children about which we've heard so much were, and I quote, 'really no different from any other children'. Are they different or are they not? And either way, does it make any difference to how the law is upheld?

Your Honour, you have the sacred duty of upholding the law as it stands. By all means, call for an inquiry into the treatment of these children whom the defendant claims are different, or not different, from other children. If you like, seek a change in the law that allows us all to use our takeaway meals as weapons against police officers. But since the law as it stands tells us that assaulting police officers is a crime, the defendant must be held accountable for their actions and sentenced accordingly.

JUST. SAMUELS: Thank you, Citizen Kelly. Citizen Turner, you may now present your closing statement.

CN. TURNER: Thank you, Your Honour. I am sorry to hear from Citizen Kelly about the hardships their own children have had to endure and I am pleased to hear they would probably be willing to break the law if necessary to protect their children from harm.

You have heard from three different medical professionals about the harm children like my Joh have endured because of their differences. Some have been destroyed before they were even born and many who were born were operated on as tiny babies and subsequently died, without any consideration of what might happen if they were allowed to grow and thrive as they were. Thanks to the bravery of Doctor Lee and others, we now know these children can grow and thrive. In this respect, they are no different from any other children. But at the same time, they are different, and those of us fortunate enough to be parents of these children have had to keep their differences hidden and teach them to do the same because our society has not yet accepted that different is good. Our society wants everyone to be basically the same and punishes those who try to change things.

I admit it. I broke the law when I assaulted those police officers, and maybe, Your Honour, you feel you have no choice but to pass sentence and have me punished. But is it also possible for police officers – the agents of the state – to break the law, or are they immune from the law? Because our laws as they stand declare that we must, as a society, protect our children from harm and do nothing we believe would risk harming a child. I'm not a lawyer, so I can't point you to the exact statute numbers, but I know it to be true because I had to sign statements declaring my commitment to upholding these laws before my genetic material could be used to make a baby.

Before I found Joh in Dover, I had seen the conditions in which Cain was being held by the police and the harm it was doing to him. I wish I had been bold enough to do something about it there and then, and I am sorry that I did not. I therefore maintain that I was upholding the law, not breaking it, or perhaps both, when I acted to protect my child from the harm the police would have done to him – the harm they had already done to poor Cain.

JUST. SAMUELS: Thank you, Citizen Turner, as Citizen Kelly has suggested, you really should consider a career in law. Your arguments are most compelling. However, as Citizen Kelly reminded us, our present law states that assaulting a police officer is a crime, and since the consequences of making any ruling that would weaken that law could lead to chaos, I must uphold it.

Therefore, Georgy Turner, of the crime of assaulting police officers, I find you guilty, and the sentence for that crime must be a custodial one. I sentence you to one hundred days in prison. However, I calculate that you have already spent nineteen days on remand prior to the start of this trial and before I released you on bail on third of May. Therefore, you will be required to serve a further eighty-one days to complete your sentence.

Take them down.

Chapter 42

Eva

'Are you coming then?' asked Joe, peeking around the door.

Eva sat up on the bed. 'Yes, sorry, give me a moment.' Why did every day have to feel so exhausting? She'd only come in here to fetch a cardigan for Grace but since they weren't in any hurry, she'd lain on the bed for a couple of minutes, just to calm herself before this meeting. She must have dozed off and now the others would all be waiting for her.

'I'm sure people would understand if you decided not to come.'

Eva swung her legs round and over the edge of the bed and pushed up onto her feet. 'No, I'm coming. This is our chance to corner Maggie about Nats.' However good Joe was being about it, Maggie's visits were rare, and Eva hadn't forgotten her promise to Joe. If she didn't manage to speak to Maggie about Nats today, who knew when she'd next have a chance?

'No, it's OK. I've already done it.' Joe wouldn't meet Eva's eyes, was trying to be brave, holding back the tears. 'Spoken to Maggie, I mean.'

'When?'

'When you were... A couple of days after you came back from the island, when she came to see how you were doing.'

'And...? Are they sending someone over to look for her?'

'No. She said they can't. That it would be too risky, and too late.' Joe turned and fled from the room.

'Joe, no! They can't say that,' Eva called after him, grabbing Grace's cardigan before marching out after him.

SHE VERY NEARLY turned around and walked straight back out again. How could people transform a place so completely? She'd been in here this morning – helped Dylan and Joe to arrange the hay bales to be makeshift seats. She wasn't expecting to step into the barn and feel like she'd stepped through some sort of magic portal, straight into the island café. All the girls sat in their usual cliques, chattering as if nothing had changed. Toddlers shrieked with delight as they chased each other around the hay bales, some wielding fistfuls of hay.

If Dylan minded the decimation, he didn't show it – watching them all with the sort of smile Eva imagined a proud grandparent might have, though she'd never been introduced to her own. Anthony hovered at the front, evidently wanting to look like he was still in charge. Tom skulked in a corner at the back, apparently as reluctant to be there as Eva was. He glanced up from his feet just at the moment when Eva's eyes were passing over him, as if he could tell she was looking at him, except she really wasn't. He gave her a nod. What was that supposed to mean? She never could tell with Tom. Joe and Anthony were so much easier to read, though in very different ways. Even Vicki was playing her part – circulating with a plate heaped with home-baked biscuits, which she and Dominque had almost come to blows over earlier as each tried to show Peter and Katie how to make them.

'Eva! Wonderful to see you looking so well.'

Eva turned and almost collided with Maggie as she lunged towards her, grabbing both shoulders and pecking her on each cheek in a rare display of affection. A retinue of three underlings, none of whom Eva recognised, hovered behind Maggie, each clutching one of their tablette devices, looking so out of place amongst the hay and fresh air.

'Hello, Maggie, I need to talk to you about something.'

'Of course. My ears are always open for you, Eva. We will speak after, yes? I must start this meeting now, I think, before we are choking on the hay dust.' Maggie waved a hand in front of her face and scanned the barn. 'But isn't this lovely – all the children here too? I'm glad their parents felt able to bring them.'

Eva frowned. Why would you not have children at a community meeting? Not having them there would mean excluding whoever you asked to look after them. And then at what age would you invite those children to be part of the meetings? Maggie was already on her way to the front, ruffling heads of little ones as she went. Anthony stepped forward to welcome her, but unintentionally or not, Maggie ignored him and turned to face her audience.

'Friends, welcome to France.'

The barn fell silent. Even the toddlers stopped and gawped at the tall woman calling the meeting to order, who wasn't red-haired Sandra.

'I know you've all been here for a month already, and some of you a lot longer. I'm sorry it has taken me so long to come and greet you all.' Maggie paused and let her eyes rest for a few moments on each cluster of islanders and an equal time for each person who stood apart from the rest – Tom, Anthony, Joe, Eva. 'I trust you have all settled in well with your hosts. Do speak with me or one of my colleagues here,' she gestured towards the three underlings who stood sentry against the wall behind her, tablettes still tucked under their arms, 'if anything is not to your satisfaction. Our host families are all very excited to have you and keen to make you feel at home.

'I hope, in time, we will be able to help each of you to find a more permanent place within the British community here in France and in the wider society of the French nation. As Premier of the British Assembly, it is my privilege to serve all who identify as British, and I will make it a top personal priority over the coming months to ensure each of you is given opportunities that are right for you – in education, training, or employment – and, for those who need it, the best medical attention and counselling to make you strong and happy citizens.'

Maggie stopped speaking and, without needing to say anything, somehow gave permission for people to speak amongst themselves, to digest the offers being presented to them, to imagine a future living openly in a proper grown-up and modern community with real jobs, the chance to go back to school, to train in careers they'd only ever been able to dream of. A smile spread across Maggie's face as wide-eyed girls chattered and dreamed.

Eva wondered what conversations she might have with Maggie when it was her turn to discuss her future. It hadn't occurred to her before now that they were truly here to stay, but that wouldn't be forever staying with Dominique and Dylan. Of course it wouldn't – they would want their home back at some point. Eva should want to settle into a home of her own with the children, and... Well, perhaps it would be just that - her and the children. That was the normal way of things for normal families in Britain. Why would it be any different here, now she was one of the normal people?

A lump caught in her throat. What would her family consist of? Her and four children? Would Charlie even want to stay on as part of the family? Would Maggie have her own conversations with him - give him other options? Would the authorities here even recognise Katie as one of Eva's children, or would she go to live with Tom? Would Tom want that? What would Katie want? Where did Joe fit into all of this, or others with no children - like Vicki? Of course, most of them were still children themselves in the eyes of people here. Would they be expected to go to school? Would they be adopted into families and given the chance to return to some sort of childhood?

'You all have a lot to think about, I can see that, and please be assured, there will be no hurry to make any decisions. All of your host families - every single one - have said you are welcome in their homes for as long as you wish to stay.'

Eva noticed a hint of relief on the faces of a few, and her own heart lifted a little. Dylan and Dominique had treated her children like their own grandchildren over the last few months, and she herself almost felt adopted as an extra daughter by them. Could it stay like that if she wanted? Could she carry on working the farm with Dylan and Dominique; maybe one day continue to run it for them as they grew older? Neither of their own children seemed to take any interest in the day-to-day running of the farm - both had their own jobs, their own lives, their own families. Dylan had never said as much, but she sensed a sadness in him that both his children had chosen paths that led them away from the farm and an unexpected joy that Eva had taken so much interest in it. But was she simply holding on too tightly to what she knew? As a child, she'd dreamed of being an engineer, like both her parents. Was it too late to learn the skills she needed to be an engineer here in France?

'And continuing on the theme of welcome, I am inviting you all to attend a special welcoming ceremony for you all, at our assembly buildings next Friday.' Maggie paused, expecting a cheer perhaps? Instead, a sea of mostly nervous faces stared back at her. 'Don't worry, we don't bite! But the other assembly members are very keen to meet you and extend their own welcome, and some members of the French government will also be present to welcome you formally to France. But I promise, it will be fun – not really formal at all.' Maggie smiled again but then transformed her face into a more sombre picture.

'Of course, whilst we hope this will be an occasion of great joy, we will also be unveiling a special memorial to those we were not able to rescue and those who were lost to you in the years you spent on your island and before. All of their names, those that are known, will be engraved on the memorial, and spaces too for those I know you recovered from the sea whose names we shall never know. But we want to name as many as we can, because nobody deserves to be forgotten. So, I must leave you now. I look forward to welcoming you all to our assembly buildings next Friday, but my three colleagues will remain here with you a while to record the names of all who we need to remember, as well as to find out whether any of you have any special dietary requirements or other special requests for the party. Thank you, it has been lovely to meet you all.'

The three colleagues took an awkward step forward, forcing smiles onto faces that wished they could follow Maggie as she made a beeline for the exit, rather than engaging in conversations with this gaggle of adolescent girls with their unruly children.

Eva stepped into Maggie's path, bringing her to an abrupt stop. 'You said we would speak after.'

'Ah, Eva, yes. I'm sorry, I really do have to dash. Can we perhaps talk when you come to the assembly buildings? It is only a little more than a week away.'

Eva kept pace with Maggie as she strode out of the barn and on to her car, hurriedly parked in front of another sleek, black vehicle, which would presumably carry the three underlings home later.

'I want to talk with you about Nats, now everyone else from the island is safe. And the longer we leave it, the lower the chance we have... But we can't just say it's too late...so...'

Maggie reached out for the car door but turned to face Eva at the same time. 'Eva, I'm sorry, but Joe and I have already had this conversation.' She raised the sunglasses she'd donned as soon as she'd left the barn and offered sad eyes to Eva. 'Of course we would have loved to save Nats too. I know she was very special to Joe, to lots of you. But the chances of finding her now are so very small, and the risks of sending a team to mainland Britain so very large. The French would never give their permission.'

'Then give one of us a boat, and we'll go back to find her.' Eva surprised herself with that suggestion. Would she be brave enough to set off on her own, back across the sea, in search of Nats?

'Again, Joe has already asked me this, but he is only a child and we could not countenance sending a child on their own, even if I could persuade the French to lend us a boat. I know it is hard, but we must rejoice over those we have been able to save and –'

'But in there you said, "Nobody deserves to be forgotten." Those were your very words.' Tears now streamed down Eva's cheeks. 'How can you say that one minute and then stand here the next minute, telling me Nats isn't worth saving?'

Maggie pulled open her car door and tossed her tablette onto the passenger seat. Was that it? Was the conversation over? Perhaps Eva should have waited for a time when Maggie was in less of a hurry, when she could have perhaps sat across from her in her office, with Joe and others to back her up.

'I'll go,' came a deep voice from behind Eva. 'Nobody could claim I'm still a child, and I'm well used to taking care of myself. You lot don't know Nats. If you did know her, we wouldn't be having this conversation – you'd already be over there looking for her. But I get it. She's only a number to you, on the list of those you couldn't rescue. She's more than that to me, to us – a lot more – so I'll take the risk that you won't. Give me a boat and I'll go and find her. And if nobody'll let me have a boat, point me towards the sea and I'll find a way to get across, even if I have to swim.'

Had Tom followed her out intentionally or just stumbled across Eva's confrontation with Maggie, making his usual quick getaway from any meeting? Either way, he was now standing a few paces behind her, promising to find Nats, no matter what. Of course he'd support any mission to find Nats – he'd always had a soft spot for her and was happy to see her, even when he shunned everyone else on the island.

At that moment, Joe emerged from the barn with a small child hanging from each arm. He stopped dead and looked from Tom, to Eva, to Maggie. Hope filled his eyes. Eva turned back to Maggie too, making it three of them pinning their eyes and their hopes on her. No, four actually, because there was Vicki, standing off to the side but very much a part of this campaign, her arms folded in a *won't take no for an answer* sort of a way.

Even though her sunglasses had slipped back over her eyes, Maggie's smile was undoubtedly genuine and warm, with a hint of pride as if she'd been in some way responsible for the mature adults they'd all become.

'All right, I'll see what can be arranged. But I'm making no promises. The French aren't going to like it, and if they say no, it isn't happening, no matter how much jumping up and down we all do. OK?'

'So when will you let us know?' Eva asked before Tom could take over the negotiations completely.

'We'll talk about it more when you come up for the party next Friday. I won't be able to do anything sooner than that, so don't even ask.' Maggie waggled her finger. 'And don't think that means you'll be heading across La Manche next Saturday. These things take planning, and if the French are going to give it their stamp of approval, they'll want to see all your plans and contingency plans and risk assessments et cetera.'

Eva nodded, not that she really knew what the French might expect to see in a contingency plan or a risk assessment or whatever miscellaneous *et ceteras* they might place as obstacles in their path.

'So that's something you lot can get your heads together on between now and next Friday,' Maggie continued. 'Get Joe to explain exactly how to find this barn they were hiding out in. Because one thing's for certain – Joe won't be going himself. I've made that clear, and I'm not budging on that. No under-eighteens. So whoever's going will need to upload every detail from Joe's memory before they go. Who do you think should go? Just Tom, or is someone else going to volunteer to go with him? Or is it too much of a risk sending Tom at all, given he'd never pass as a neut if spotted? Make a list of the provisions and equipment you think you'll need, but don't be too demanding, and no weapons.'

'Yes, thank you, Maggie, we'll put together a plan,' said Eva. Tom might be the one who ended up going, but she would lead on the planning – make sure Joe was listened to.

'Right, can I go now?'

Maggie didn't wait for an answer before ducking into her car, crunching its wheels through the gravel and speeding away.

Chapter 43

Georgy

THE FIVE-MINUTE TIMER started counting down as soon as I keyed in the number – one of the many small ways in which they let us know in here that we deserved no favours. *Come on, Cris, pick up*. If Cris didn't pick up, I'd have to wait another week before I could try again.

'Your lover not wanting to speak to you again?' someone jeered from the queue behind me. 'Come on then, let someone else have it.'

The phone ringing sound stopped. I didn't have time to wait for Cris to say the first hello.

'Cris?'

No reply. It connected, didn't it? Or had the prison phone system ended the call automatically after so many rings? I was sure it rang for longer last week before I gave up. I pulled the phone away from my ear to studied the display. No, it was definitely connected, and the timer on the phone display was counting up the seconds, as well as the big display on the wall above, already at 4:06, counting them down.

'Hello...who is this?' said the tinny voice inside the phone.

I thrust the phone back to my ear.

'Cris, it's me. Why weren't you picking up?'

'Why wasn't I picking up? Why haven't you called till now? Georgy, it's been three weeks nearly.'

'Yeah, I know. I wasn't allowed any calls in the first week, and then I tried you last week, but you didn't pick up.'

'Well, you obviously didn't try very hard. I don't remember getting lots of missed calls.'

'I only get one attempt a week. That's all. And if nobody picks up, I don't get it back. So please, save this number on your phone and then make sure you pick up whenever I call.'

I glanced up at the countdown timer.

2:53 ...52 ...51 ...49

The person at the front of the queue stepped forward, misreading my silence as a cue that I was done. I shook my head at them, which only made them invade my space even more. I moved away from the wall, trying to inhabit the space a bit more, claim it as mine, at least for the next two and a half minutes.

'All right, just a moment, I'll do that now.'

'No, don't do it now! Do it after we've finished. We've only got a couple of minutes and then my time's up.'

'What? But that's ridiculous. You should complain.'

'Yes, thank you, Cris. Maybe I will.' It was a good job they couldn't see my look of exasperation or they'd have wasted even more of our precious time on pointless indignation. 'Anyway, how have you been? How are things?'

'What do you think? It's a nightmare, Georgy, and if I'd known this was going to happen, I'd never have agreed to –'

'Yeah, OK,' I cut in before they said anything incriminating, 'I get the picture. How about you ask how I am?'

'What, but you just asked... Don't you want to know how he's –'

'Cris, I'm sorry,' I cut in again. 'I know you must be finding it hard. I know you were only supposed to be looking after my hamster for a few days, until I moved back into somewhere more permanent...'

'Hamster, what hamster? What are you on about, Georgy?'

0:59

I considered hanging up, before Cris actually mentions Cain by name, but didn't.

'Look, I've got to go now, and I might not get the chance to call again.'

'But you told me to save the number.'

'Yeah, I know, well, just in case. But what I wanted to say is, please can you take care of the hamster for a few more weeks. Make sure you feed him, and don't let him escape. Just for the next sixty-two days. Less than nine weeks. Then I'll take him of your hands, I promise.'

'But Georgy, I don't und –'

0:00

I wanted to sink down onto the ground with my back to the wall for a few minutes, but the phone was already being wrenched out of my hand and I was shoved aside. Was someone, somewhere already analysing our brief conversation, doing background checks on whether I really did have a hamster? If I called again next week, would Cris get that I was really talking about Cain? I probably couldn't risk ringing again. I hoped they were both all right.

Chapter 44

Nats

'Wᴉʟʟ ᴛʜᴇ ʙᴀʙʏ come today?'

'No, Tris, it needs to get a bit bigger first,' says Lori. 'Come on, you need to get your shoes on now, or we'll miss the bus.'

'But will it come when I'm at school, or –'

'No, we've already said. It's not coming today, so you don't need to worry about –'

'No, I know it's not coming today. But when it does come, will it be when I'm at school?'

Lori sighs, kneels down to do up Tris's shoes. I could have been doing that while Lori was packing Tris's bag, except I'm finding it harder to crouch down without feeling like I'm squashing the baby, even though I'm not really bulging yet – not like I remember some of the girls getting. I once got Peter and Katie to ask Sally if we could borrow her ball. She didn't get it at first, and then she didn't think it was funny.

'Ow, you've done them too tight!'

'Well, you should have done them yourself then, shouldn't you. You're a big kid now, and when Nats' baby comes, you'll have to try and do a lot more things for yourself.' Lori holds out a hand as Tris tugs at the edges of their shoes. 'Come on, we'd better run down that track today. Who's going to get there first?'

'Me, me, me!' squeals Tris, dashing out the door.

Normally at this point, Nelly would be racing round in circles, making herself giddy with excitement before racing after Tris and then looping around and racing back to the door to check that Lori was coming too. But today, Nelly's nowhere to be seen.

'Lori, where's Nelly?' I ask, without realising that Lori's already out of earshot, striding after Tris. 'Nelly! Where are you?'

I should probably clear up the breakfast things, but there's no rush. It will only make the rest of the long morning drag on. I want to do something, but not the clearing up and tidying. I want to be with other people again. I guess before long, I will be with another person all the time – a very little, very demanding person. But what will I do when you won't stop crying, eh? If I was on the island, there'd always be someone else I could leave you with for a bit. But Lori won't have time to stop working and look after you. It'll all be down to me.

What will I do when you're a bit older and want to run around? I can't keep you hidden inside all day. And when you're old enough for school, will Lori insist on sending you? I haven't thought this through right. I should have set out for the island as soon as I knew about you. Lori might have paid for a train ticket if I'd asked. But now I'm too big and bulgy to be seen, and anyway, I've promised I'll stay.

I wipe the wetness off my eyes and dry my hands on my jumper, for which I get a little kick. So you're awake again, are you? I wish you'd sleep at the same time as me, little Joey. I do like to feel you move now, but why do you always have to do a somersault inside me just as I start to drift off? And you make me get up in the night to go for a wee. I need to remember to drink less in the evening. Except Lori probably won't let me get away with that They're always telling me I don't drink enough – that I need to make sure you don't dry out. What would they know about it? They've never had a baby. Well, not in the way that I'm having a baby. They just went to a fertility unit somewhere, gave a bit of their blood or something to make Tris out of, and then went back to get Tris when they were a fully grown baby. They say that in all the pictures they've seen, babies are always 'swimming around' in lots of water, and that when pups are born, they're all very wet until the mother licks them dry. I hope they don't expect me to lick you dry when you come out, little Joey.

I've decided you're probably a boy, little Joey. I know I can't really decide that. I don't really mind which you are. I'll still call you Joey, either way. Sandra would probably say Joey wasn't girlish enough – that I should go with Joanna or something. But Joanna doesn't sound enough like Joe, and Joey will always remind me of the first time I met your dad and he told me he was Joe with an E, cos he was a boy. Of course, if you want to be Joanna when you're older, that's up to you. Except it might sound a bit odd if you're a boy. Probably. It's weird really – why are some names definitely girls' names and others are definitely boys' names? The neuts don't have boys' names and girls' names. Of course they don't.

I suppose I should get up and clear up these breakfast things before the cereal Tris has left in their bowl gets all dry and difficult to scrub off. Tris is so excited about you, little Joey. Every day, they ask in the morning whether you're going to come today, and even though we say no, well, probably not, they still come dashing in after school and the first question on their lips is, 'Has the baby come yet?' They do know they mustn't say anything about you to anyone at school.

We weren't going to tell them about you at all, until we realised they'd heard too much from the top of the stairs that morning when Lori caught me packing my bag with food and trying to sneak away. How did Lori know before I did that you were growing inside me? Maybe I still should have gone anyway, not agreed to stay.

At least Tris knows we both have to be kept a secret, and I know they're good at keeping secrets because they kept me secret from Lori for all that time when I was hiding in the barn. I didn't think Tris would believe us when we said you were actually growing inside me, but they accepted it like it was natural, which of course it is, except not for neuts. I guess they know that Nelly grew inside her mum, Jess, and they don't have any younger siblings to know much about fertility units. And they've felt you kicking now too. I love seeing the grin on their face when they've waited patiently for a long time and then *whoomph*, you give them a great big kick, right where their little hand is.

Tris has left quite a lot of cereal today, so I scrape it out into Nelly's bowl and give her a whistle. The whistle is never needed really. As soon as that dog hears scraping, she knows what it means and comes skidding across the kitchen tiles to her bowl. But not today. I look around towards the door – maybe it's blown shut and she's stuck outside. But then she'd have even heard it from outside, through the closed door, and would be scratching at it and whining even now. Anyway, the door's still wide open from when Lori and Tris left. I like to keep it open because it gets me the fresh air without actually going outside. Where has the bitch got to? Maybe that's why I'm feeling so alone today.

I stand at the open door and give her another whistle, holding the tea towel out in front of me at belly height to hide my bump, in case anyone happens to walk past. I know I probably could venture outside, but we do sometimes get walkers coming almost right past the house. Lori says it's a public footpath but not one that's used very much anymore. I do sometimes go for an evening walk around the farm with Lori, Tris, and Nelly, after it's starting to get dark. I hope you come before it gets too cold to have the door and windows open during the day.

I wish I'd paid more attention to how long Sally and Eva and others were pregnant for before their babies arrived. Funny thing is, Lori seems to have a better sense of it than I do. I even think Nelly somehow understands I've got a pup inside me, the way she likes to come and squeeze herself in between me and Tris when Tris is feeling for your kicks.

'Ah, here you are.'

Nelly pads through the door, her shaggy coat looking even more dishevelled than usual.

'Where have you been, girl? There's some leftovers in your bowl.'

She takes a look in her bowl and slurps it up, though as if it's a duty rather than a treat, then squeezes herself between me and the cupboard and sniffs at my belly as I start to wash up the breakfast things. The smell of damp fur wafts up to me.

'What you been up to then? Would you tell me if you could?'

I shake the water off my hands and crouch down as best I can to give her a scratch. Her fur is damp, like she's been out all night. I'm not quick enough to move away and get a lick right on the lips.

'Yuck! Gerroff! Don't you go making me sick again.'
Although I know now that my weeks of sickness were

probably nothing to do with Nelly. 'Do bitches get sick when they get pregnant? I suppose you wouldn't know. You haven't had any pups, have you? Do you even know any boy dogs? I wonder whether I'll ever meet another boy human. What should I do, eh, Nelly? What should I do once this little one's born?'

Chapter 45

Eva

'So, CAN EITHER of you two ride a motorbike?' asked Maggie, pressing her forefingers together to her lips and leaning back in her chair, which seemed to tilt without effort or sound in whichever direction she chose.

'Sorry, which two of us did you mean?' said Eva.

Five of them were arranged in an arc on the opposite side of the desk – Tom, Eva, Joe, Vicki, and Anthony, who wasn't involved from the outset but worked out they were plotting something and demanded to be included in whatever plan was being hatched. Joe had reasoned it might do more harm to keep it from him, so Anthony had been included in all their subsequent meetings but largely ignored.

'You and Tom,' replied Maggie. 'Correct me if I'm wrong, but Vicki here is not much older than Joe, so is ruled out on age and, sorry Anthony, but it's plain as day to me you don't have the stomach for it...'

'That's not true.' Anthony flushed red but wouldn't meet Maggie's probing stare.

'It's OK, nobody's asking you to volunteer. I'm sure your skillset is better suited to other things. In fact, I have a few other things in mind already.'

'Really? Well in that case, yes, it's probably best if I stand aside and allow someone else to take my place.' Anthony straightened himself up and smiled, visibly pleased someone as influential as Maggie was recognising his talents and thinking of ways they could be usefully employed. He didn't spot the smirk playing across Maggie's face, which transmitted itself to Tom, forcing him to hide behind one of his enormous hands for at least a minute.

'And you've been saying "we" and "us" as you've talked through your plans, so I had assumed two of you would be going, which can only mean that you, Eva, plan to accompany Tom.'

'Well, I...er, we hadn't firmly settled on who would be going with Tom, but yes, we think it's best if it's not just him going on his own.'

Had the others assumed it would be her? Surely not. Everyone knew she and Tom didn't get on and that she'd want to stay here for the children. But then she had left them here when she went back to the island; perhaps that made the others think she'd be up for it again. But deserting the children to go on a dangerous clandestine mission to Britain? They'd already lost one mum in the last few weeks, and Katie was fragile enough as it was without any more trauma. Having said that, the way Katie had been with her since they got back to France, she probably wouldn't mind if Eva just disappeared. Maybe Tom should be staying for Katie. He was her actual dad. But then who would go in his place?

'Well, if you think it should perhaps be somebody else, don't you think they should be with us in this meeting?' said Maggie.

'You ride Dominique and Dylan's quad around the farm, don't you, Eva?' Joe said, pulling them back to Maggie's original question. 'That's like a motorbike.'

'What? Oh, yes, but we haven't asked for motorbikes. We'll be on foot once we get to the other side. It's not far and we'll be less noticeable on foot.'

'There you go again – "we this, we that",' said Maggie. 'This is your mission, Eva, as much as it is Tom's. N'est pas?'

'Sorry? Well, yes, but it's also Joe's mission, and Vicki's. We've all been part of the planning, and I was just meaning "we" as in whichever of us is actually going.'

'I'll go on my own if I have to. But like Eva said, I'll be fine on foot.' said Tom, speaking his first words since they'd come into Maggie's office. In fact, probably his first since they'd boarded the coach this morning and Tom had taken an aisle seat at the front. Others had wittered on about how he could have sat further back so they didn't all need to push past his massive knee sticking out into the aisle, and what gave him the right to effectively claim a double seat all to himself anyway? If Tom had heard the complaints, he'd paid no attention. He would probably prefer to go on his own. He certainly wouldn't consider Eva as the ideal companion. But why shouldn't she be? She was as capable as him, and a quicker thinker.

Maggie leaned forward and again studied the lists and maps arrayed on the desk before her. It was never easy to tell what she thought, but she looked impressed.

'You've put a lot of thought into this, and yes, you're right, you don't want to be sailing straight back into the middle of Dover. You'd be picked up straight away. But we need to choose carefully where you do aim to land. Did you know that along the coast here is mostly high cliffs? There are a few bays, but I think the best one to aim for is here, Sandwich Bay. Yes, I know, funny to name a place after something you eat. But here, there is a long stretch of quiet beach and also this area is less populated than the other bays nearer to Dover.'

'How do you know all this? Have you been there?' Eva asked. She could see how someone more expert than her at reading the maps might be able to tell where there were cliffs, but how would they know about where people lived?

'No, of course not. But for a long time, we have studied the satellite images of the coastline closest to us here in France.'

'What's a satellite image?' asked Vicki.

'Photos taken from a satellite.' Maggie scanned their blank faces. 'Ah, sorry, of course, you probably have no idea about satellites. All the ones Britain once used were decommissioned long before even I was born. Um, let me see, a satellite is a spacecraft that flies above and around the Earth all the time, very high up, above the Earth's atmosphere. There are thousands of them up there, and we can use them to take photos, and to triangulate exactly where we are anywhere on the planet, and lots of other things. We used satellite images to first work out which island we thought you people were on.'

'You could watch all of us on the island with these satellite images?' said a wide-eyed Vicki.

'Well, no, not exactly. For example, we can't see faces from the satellites – remember they are a long way up above us. But yes, we could see some elements of the life you were leading there – that you were farming the island and had both animals and crops, that no boats travelled to or from the island, and even that there were small children living amongst you.'

'Wow, and you can look at everywhere in Britain like that?'

'Yes. Everywhere in the world, in fact. But –'

'Look, this is all very interesting,' said Eva, 'but don't we need to stop soon for the ceremony, and we've not even worked out how we get across the sea yet.'

'Of course, you are right, Eva. We must return to your plans.' Maggie returned her eyes to the map and pointed again with her pen to Sandwich Bay. 'So, as I was saying, this area has nobody living nearby so would be a good place to land. But it is much further to here,' Maggie moved her pen to the spot they'd already marked with a cross, as the location of the barn where Joe had left Nats. 'That is a long way to walk in one night. And then you need to get back again also in the same night, possibly with Nats, if she is still there.'

Why did Maggie have to be so pessimistic? They all knew not to get their hopes up, especially Joe. But before even looking at any of their plans, Maggie had talked for a whole ten minutes about preparing themselves for the likelihood that Nats was no longer there, and that they would find no clues about where she might have gone. Of course, she was right, but it didn't mean they shouldn't try. They had to at least try.

'Yes, but we walked all the time on the island, and Joe, Nats, and Cain walked a lot further than that on their travels,' Tom replied, bringing Eva's head back into the room.

'C'est vrai. But is it not also true that the reason Nats is not with us now is precisely because she was injured and couldn't walk with Joe to Dover? What if she is still not able to walk?'

Joe blew his nose and took a sip from the glass of water in front of him. Eva swallowed in sympathy.

Poor Joe, still wondering every day what would have happened if he hadn't jumped on that boat or hadn't stepped out of the shadows when his parent called him or hadn't ever gone to Dover without Nats.

'But Joe has given me an even better idea than motorbikes.' Maggie picked up her tablette and tapped on the screen. 'Joe said you ride a quad, Eva. Well, these are like quads, except look...'

The five of them crowded in to watch the video on the tablette screen. Music blared from the device as a man and a woman rode quads down onto a beach and towards the sea. When they reached the sea, they kept going and the quads floated and became like little boats, speeding out across the water. Eva's heart raced, imagining the rush of excitement from doing that – riding out on a quad, out onto the sea, and then feeling the spray all around you and the salted air rushing past.

'You think we could ride one of those all the way across?' Tom asked, looking doubtful. 'I saw some big waves when we flew over here in the helicopter.'

Maggie tapped her screen again to stop the video. 'Non. These are only really OK for a calm sea and shallow waters near the coast. But with these, perhaps we can do as you have asked and provide someone to pilot the boat across La Manche for you, at least most of the way. The French will be happier if the boat does not need to go all the way to the British coast and it can wait somewhere out at sea for your return.'

'And if we are spotted and the police come after us, we can just drive straight into the sea, which they won't expect!' Eva added.

'Oui, exactement.'

Eva heard none of the words from any of the many speakers during the ceremony. Not only because Grace wriggled on her lap and tried to stick her fingers up Eva's nose and tugged at her shirt to try and get a feed, even though Eva had put a stop to the last bit of breastfeeding weeks ago, before her return to the island. No, the British and French words blurred together into a meaningless soup as Eva kept dragging her mind back from visions of racing along dark lanes, pursued by blaring police cars and then splashing into the water and skating out across the sea, the flashing lights of the police cars shrinking away into the distance behind her. When they stood in silence, to remember all those who had died, she couldn't bring Sandra's face to mind, only Nats - as a little girl on one of the many occasions when she fell and scraped her knee - bawling her eyes out until somebody noticed, but then moments later, giggling and running around as if nothing bad had happened.

She would have liked to have the brain space to marvel at the enormous arches and domes, made almost entirely of glass, as others around her had been doing ever since they stepped off the coach beside the spurting and cascading water feature. Near the centre of this was now what Eva recognised to be a scaled-down replica of their island, including all their homes, and surrounded by bubbling water. Etched all over the island were the familiar names of those they had lost. Many blank spaces had clearly been left - perhaps for those whose names had never been known - but was one reserved for Nats, expecting their mission would fail? And what about poor Cain? Would his name one day also be scratched into the model, even though they would probably never know what had become of him - whether he still lived or had died?

As the mingling began, Eva just about remembered bearded Barry's name when he came bounding towards her with a big smile and scratchy kisses on both cheeks. She smiled and nodded and expressed thanks as a steady flow of other miscellaneous faces greeted her and asked how her son was doing. Couldn't they see the healthy boy who constantly darted between her and the table of food?

Could she leave Peter and Grace again and go with Tom to search for Nats? If she felt she could ask them, Peter would say yes straight away. He loved Nats and missed her almost as much as Joe did. Grace had always had a big smile for her too, not that she would remember her now. Eva would only be gone for a couple of days, at most, if all went to plan. But what if it didn't?

Chapter 46

Eva

THE BLUSTERY AIR was filled with a sticky sea mist, even though they were a good twenty paces from the crashing waves. Eva pulled her hood back up, tucked as much as she could of her hair in, and tightened the cord around the hood's edges. Gusts of sand needled at her cheeks and even with her hood pulled tight around her face, she knew she'd be brushing sand out of her hair later. But it was exhilarating to see and smell the sea again. The kids were enjoying it too. Peter, Charlie, and Katie were already racing towards the waves, Grace toddling after them as fast as her little legs could carry her in the waterproof all-in-one that Dylan and Dominique's daughter had kindly found amongst her own children's old clothes. It looked like it had been barely worn, as did all the other 'old clothes' they'd been gifted. Grace tumbled face first into the sand and Eva started towards her, anticipating the wail that would soon reach her on the wind. But she was already back on her feet, chasing with even more vigour after the others. Eva stopped, turned back to the others standing by the quadskis, torn between going after the children and hearing the instructions for which she was here.

'That's far enough, you three!' Eva shouted after the older ones. 'Don't get close to the water, and watch your sister!' If they heard her through the noise of the wind and waves, they took no notice. A hand snagged her shoulder as she set off again towards the children. She turned to see Joe holding her back.

'I'll go. You need to stay here.'

'No, it's OK, you don't have to.'

He also ignored her shouts and marched off into the wind, head down, hands deep in his pockets. Eva turned back to Maggie, Tom, and the French boy who'd been introduced to them as Etienne. He looked no older than her and Tom but was apparently their quadski teacher for the week. Maggie and Etienne still had their heads together in conversation as the sand drifted deeper and deeper against the three quadskis that were at least twice the size of the quad back on the farm. Finally, Maggie turned towards Tom and Eva.

'D'accord, so, Etienne says today the sea is far too rough, but you can practise driving the quadskis on the beach. Tomorrow it is supposed to be calmer for trying them on the sea, if he thinks you're ready.'

'And what if it's as wild as this when we're doing it for real?' asked Tom. 'I mean, when we're out there getting Nats.'

'Well, that is why you are here this week to learn. But also, we will choose a time when we know the weather will be better.'

'Like next summer?' Tom shouted back. 'I'm not waiting that long to go and get Nats.'

'No, of course not,' replied Maggie, although Eva knew she'd have preferred them to wait until a better time of year, or even cancel their plan altogether. 'In two or three weeks, the weather is set to be much calmer. So then you will be able to go.'

How they knew with such certainty what the weather would be like two or three weeks from now, Eva still couldn't fathom. It was something to do with these satellites flying around miles above their heads. Sally had been quite good at predicting the weather when they were on the island, but even she got caught out sometimes – announcing that the weather would be good for a few days yet so they didn't need to finish harvesting the oats today, only to find them flattened by an overnight storm.

Tom was already astride one of the quadski beasts and Etienne was pointing out the different controls with Maggie then relaying his instructions. Eva mounted the one Etienne had already indicated would be hers. Apart from a few extra buttons in the middle, which she guessed were something to do with switching it from land-mode to sea-mode, it all looked simple enough and similar enough to the farm quad. She probably should wait for Etienne's induction but then again, she didn't want Tom to be zooming out across the beach first.

She looked across at the other three, heads together, paying her no heed. There was no key to turn, just a button to press, which would start the engine as long as she was wearing the device already strapped to her wrist. That much had been explained as they'd donned the bulging lifejackets and inflexible gloves. Her fingers didn't quite fill the gloves, so she had to keep on pressing even after the glove finger made contact with the button. But then she felt the vibration of the otherwise silent engine beneath her. She pulled her hood down and, as quickly as she could, replaced it with the helmet that was balanced behind her seat. She eased off the brake and immediately she was off.

'Non, non, non! Attendez!' Etienne waved a hand up and down.

'Eva, wait!'

Eva deftly steered the machine away from Maggie, who had foolishly tried to stop her by stepping into her path, and then accelerated away. The beast underneath her handled even more smoothly than in her dreams. A slight turn of the handlebars and she was guiding it round and down onto the wetter, flatter sand. She inched up her speed as she cruised the long stretch of smooth beach, parallel to the sea.

The third quadski, not the one Tom had been on, was now drawing up alongside her. She expected Etienne to overtake her, pull in in front of her, forcing her to slow down and stop. Instead, he kept pace with her. She dared to glance for a moment in his direction. She couldn't see his face behind the helmet visor, but one hand was off the handlebars, giving her a thumbs up. At least hand gestures were the same here in France. Now he was pointing left, back up the beach. She eased off her speed and, in sync with Etienne, arced around and back towards the distant dot that was Maggie. A long way behind, Tom was also now looping back.

'Mummy, why has Tom come on holiday with us?'

Eva loosened her seat belt and swivelled around to face her son on the back seat. Joe, sat beside him, raised an eyebrow. None of the children yet knew the real reason for their trip out to the coast. To them, it was a holiday before the weather got too bad – ironic – and before Peter, Katie, and Charlie started at school in two weeks' time. Dylan had assured her there were plenty of other British kids there who'd not learnt a word of French before starting at the fully French-speaking school. She found that hard to believe.

Peter gave her a quizzical look. What was the question he'd just asked her? Joe helped her out, mouthing the word Tom behind his hand. Tom was travelling in Etienne's car, together with Katie and Charlie. She wondered for a moment what conversations, if any, would be taking place in their car.

'We thought it would be nice for Katie to spend a bit of time with her dad before she starts at school. That's OK, isn't it?'

'Then why didn't we invite Anthony to come with us too. He's mine and Grace's dad, isn't he?'

'Well yes, but... Sorry, love, would you have liked Anthony to come too?'

Should she and Sandra have made more of an effort to give their children time with their dads? Was it her fault that Anthony took no notice of any of his many children, having set the trend with Peter? Her own parents had always shared the role of bringing her up, as she and Sandra had done with Peter and Katie at first, though without the breastfeeding, of course. And you didn't have to be female or neut to be an active parent. Look at Joe, not that he was a parent yet, but he'd not leave it all to his children's mother when the time came. And Dylan and Dominique's son – he didn't live with his children's mother but they still shared the child-caring equally. They even lived half the time with him and half with their mother. Then last week, she'd been introduced to two men, who were a couple like she and Sandra had been a couple, and they had a baby, though surely there must have been a mother involved somewhere. She didn't think the French ever grew babies in pregnancy pods like the British neuts did. She'd done her best on several occasions to answer questions about how the neuts made babies.

'Sorry, love, I missed that. Tell me again.'

'No, it's OK.'

Was that a *no, it's OK* that Anthony hadn't come or that Peter didn't feel he'd said anything worth repeating? He was giving her a contented smile anyway, so she smiled back and then turned to look out of the windscreen again as Maggie steered them into the car park behind the apartment block.

Etienne's car was already parked, and Tom was carrying a sleepy Katie across to the building, her head snuggling into his neck. To be fair to Tom, he'd really taken to parenting in the last few weeks, and he and Katie were getting closer by the day. Who would Katie live with, if they gave her the choice?

Chapter 47

Nats

'Go on then, girl, out you go.'

I stand holding the door open. Nelly reverses back into the middle of the room and shivers as the diagonal rain drives into the kitchen, bouncing off the floor tiles, forming rivers that run even further in, down the crevices between the tiles. She retreats under the table. I can see she shares my indecision – desperate to go outside but reluctant to be pummelled by quite such heavy rain. Lori would have given her a boot up the backside by now and slammed the door behind her. I only feel able to coax her with words.

This is the third time in the last hour we've done this. She'll have to go out soon or there'll be other puddles on the kitchen floor, not just rainwater. I hook my fingers under her collar and give her a gentle tug.

'Come on, let's do this together.'

Without letting go of her, I slip my feet into the boots Lori picked up for me from a market the other day. For some reason, my feet are swollen and aren't comfortable in the only pair of shoes I can call my own. Not that I wear shoes much at the moment. Even when I venture outside to pick some herbs, I'll usually put up with the spike of the stones on my bare feet.

I can't be bothered with a coat. I'd need something that covered my body from head to toe to avoid getting wet in this rain, and my coat won't even do up around me anymore. Lori offered to get me a new coat too, but I told them not to bother. I don't think they have much money to spare and they're giving me enough just letting me live here with them and eat their food. Once Joey's out, which can't be far off now, the coat will fit again.

Nelly tries to dig her claws into the hard, slippery tiles – scratches and skids as I drag her out into the downpour. Can you still call it a downpour if the rain is closer to horizontal than vertical? My already sodden T-shirt clings around my bulging tummy. Cold trickles tickle the underneath of my bump, defying gravity as they crawl towards the top of my trousers – the one part of my clothing that, sheltered by Joey, has so far managed to remain dry. I wonder how this feels to him. Is he also being tickled by the cold trickles? Can he feel the stabbing rain, getting him back for all the times he's stabbed at me? As if our thoughts are connected, I get a double punch.

Nelly slips from my grasp as she gives herself a shake. If I wasn't already drenched, I would be now. I lunge for the door and pull it shut before Nelly can slink back inside.

'Come on. Now you're wet, we may as well do what we came out here for.'

I know why Nelly needed to come out here, but what did I come out for, other than to drag Nelly out? I did need to get out – breathe some fresh air, even if I was at risk of drowning in the process. I've been drowning in a different way stuck inside. I step further out from the house, stand in the middle of the yard and point my face up at the sky – let the rain drive into me. Out of the corner of my eye, I see Nelly slinking off round the side of the house, keeping close to the wall. That would have been the sensible thing to do, but I've never been one to go for the sensible, safe option. Perhaps I should have taken the risk months ago of striking out from here on my own. But not now. Not until Joey's out. How much longer are you going to be, Joey?

A tall figure bounds towards me out of the rain.

'What are you doing out here, Nats?' Lori shouts. 'Come on, let's get you back inside. We need to take care of that baby.'

Yes, I know we do. But since when has a baby still inside its mother been harmed by a bit of rain? I don't want to sound ungrateful, but I wouldn't mind if Lori was a bit less protective of me. I let them guide me back towards the door, stand obediently in the doorway as they dash around to grab and throw towels in my direction. Encased in towels and boots removed, I plod up the stairs to get into some dry clothes.

'Make sure you hold on to that banister rail all the way up. Those wet feet could easily slip from under you, and we can't have you tumbling down, can we?'

No, Lori, of course we can't. I don't blame them really. They're scared – knowing they can't go calling a doctor or rush me to hospital if I injure myself. And when the time does come, there'll be nobody other than them here to help Joey into the world. I'd be scared too, if I let myself think about it.

Chapter 48

Georgy

TWENTY-SIXTH OF OCTOBER. One month to go. The bit of sky I could see out of the little, high-up square of window was almost black, and large droplets of water told me it was raining outside again. I guess it was typical October weather, but tensions were running high in here; they wouldn't let us out in the exercise yard if there was more than a dribble of rain. What did they think the rain would do to us? Surely, it couldn't be worse than the effect of not letting us go outside for a whole week.

I felt bad that another whole week had passed without calling Cris. I knew all calls were monitored, so I couldn't risk it, even if we did pretend it was a hamster they were looking after. I wondered how they were getting on - Cris and Cain. I would have heard about it, somehow, wouldn't I, if they'd been discovered? Someone would have come to the prison to rub my nose in it, wouldn't they? Questioned me about my involvement. Cris would have dobbed me in anyway - maybe even tried to make out they didn't know about the strange kid hiding out in their backroom. So I'd know about it, wouldn't I?

Thirty-one more days, Cris. That's all you need to hold out for. Please keep him safe until then, for Joe's sake if not for his or mine.

Chapter 49

Eva

Eva jabbed at the screen on the phone to end the call, except Maggie had already done that at her end. She thrust the phone back at Dylan, who'd brought it to her moments ago. Dominique paused midway through reaching to hang up Tom's coat and turned to give Eva one of her looks and a *tut-tut-tut*.

'Cancelled again?' said Tom with too much calm acceptance, dropping his neatly packed bag by the door. Had he unpacked and repacked it each time? Or did he just sling it down in the corner of a room at Sylvie's house, ready to pick up and go whenever they next got the call? Eva had been surprised at first when Tom was placed with Sylvie and not a man, but they'd slotted together perfectly from day one, and by the sound of it, the old lady had Tom doing all sorts of odd jobs she'd not been able to do since her partner had died. Tom was only too happy to help out.

'Don't be so bloody calm about it, Tom. What happened to your "I'm not waiting till next summer to go and get Nats"? Or were those just words to impress Maggie?'

Dominique ushered the children out of the room. Dylan followed her out and pulled the door shut behind him.

'No, of course not. We really do need to go as soon as we can.' Tom pulled out one of the dining chairs and sat on it, if you could call it sitting, the way he positioned himself diagonally, almost lying across the chair, legs stretched out in front of him, hands clasped around the back of his neck, elbows out. 'But we all agreed on the risk assessment, didn't we? We don't go until the sea is calm enough and until their satellites tell us it will be fine for the next three days.'

'Well excuse me if I don't trust their satellites anymore. Look out the window – the trees are barely moving. How can it be like that here but "*trop mauvais* to even take the boat out" at the coast? I mean, I'd understand it if was blowing a gale here too, or if we were further from the sea, but –'

'Eva, stop and listen to yourself a moment. You know as well as I do, even on the island, it could sometimes be raining at one end and bright and sunny at the other. I'm sure we'll get to go soon, but there's no point getting ourselves all worked up about it.'

Eva sighed, turned her back on Tom, and marched over to the door, pulling it open to look out on the perfect autumn day. She stifled a shiver as a chilly breeze wafted in. On the island, she'd still be walking round in a T-shirt and shorts if it was this warm.

'What if they're lying to us? We know they don't really want us to go. We should head back to the coast anyway and see for ourselves. We could go and speak to Etienne. He'd be straight with us. I reckon I could drive one of his quadskis all the way across. Maybe we don't even need a boat to take us. We just need to persuade Etienne to –'

'Eva, shut the door and come and sit down, will you? There's a right draught blowing in past you.'

Eva pulled the door shut and marched out and around the side of the house to where Dylan always parked the quad. She retrieved the key from underneath the seat, climbed on, started the engine. The gravel flew out in all directions behind her as she accelerated away at full speed.

She slowed to a stop as she reached the junction with the road. In the strengthening breeze, the gate that was never shut rattled back and forth between the stone holding it open and the fence post. A few spots of rain landed on her bare arm. She spun the quad around to face back towards the farm. She wasn't turning back because of the change in the weather. She'd not really intended to keep on going when she reached the road, had she? She could have done. She felt angry enough with Tom and Maggie, and even Dylan and Dominique for some reason, to drive the quad all the way to the coast, break into Etienne's shed, swap the quad for a quadski and jet off across the sea. But if she was going to do that, which she wasn't, she needed to say a proper goodbye to the children first.

'W̲h̲a̲t̲'s̲ g̲o̲i̲n̲g̲ o̲n̲?'

Katie was dancing her favourite teddy around the bedroom as Tom stood over her bed, stuffing a bag with Katie's clothes, folding and rolling each garment into a perfect cylinder before finding its perfect position within the bag. Eva moved to face Tom across the bed, took custody of the bag and closed the flap, then rested her hands on top before Tom could add anything else.

'I thought we agreed,' she said between gritted teeth. 'Katie stays here with us, with her brothers and sister.'

'What are you talking about?' Tom frowned. Did he think she was stupid, or blind?

'What do you mean, what am I talking about? Maybe the fact that you're packing a bag with Katie's clothes, like you're getting ready to take her back to Sylvie's with you, and not just for lunch.' Eva moved the bag to one side so it was no longer between them, though the bed still was and Eva had no desire to get any closer to Tom, but it felt like the thing to do, to put the immediate issue to one side. 'Look, you're welcome to spend as much time with Katie as you like, and you know I don't mind you taking her over to Sylvie's, and I know how much she loves Sylvie, but can we please hold off talking about anything more than that until after our little trip?'

Tom shook his head and smiled.

'What's there to smile about?'

'Haven't you heard?'

'Heard what?'

Dylan and Dominique had both had their backs to her, engaged in some sort of mega sandwich-making operation as she wandered back into the house via the kitchen. She'd heard the excited voices of the children, though evidently not Katie's, coming from the boys' room but, hoping for a lie down, had headed straight for the room she shared with Katie and Grace.

'Our little trip is exactly what we're packing for. We're all heading to the coast, if that's OK with you.' Tom reached for the bag and shuffled its contents back into position before reaching for the small pile of paired socks – all of which appeared to have been unpaired and re-paired with precision. 'It was Dylan's idea. He thought you might be happier if we were actually there to see the weather for ourselves and to be ready to go as soon as we're told we can. Katie's really excited about it, aren't you, Katie? She loved it when we went before, and I think she really misses the sea air.'

'But the kids have only just started going to school,' Eva said in a low voice that she hoped Katie wouldn't bother listening to as she continued to prance around the room. 'Won't it be unsettling for them to take them away again, just when they're getting used to the new routine?'

'And you think they'll feel settled when we disappear off and maybe don't come back?'

'Shhh, keep your voice down. We can't even think those thoughts around the children.' Eva sucked a big shaky breath in through her nose as if she could drag the sea air all the way here, including through the fastened windows and drawn curtains. It would be good to be back at the coast, seeing for themselves when the weather calmed down. They might even be allowed to get more practice in on the quadskis, and Tom was right; the kids had loved being near the sea again. It was where they belonged. 'But I suppose if they don't mind missing a bit more school, it won't do them any harm, will it?'

'Is that OK then? Can I carry on packing, or do you want to take over?'

'I can if you like, but I think I might need to pull everything out and put it back in again less neatly. So, perhaps I'll go check on the boys instead.' Eva backed away towards the door. 'Thank you, Tom, and...' She didn't feel ready to finish her sentence, so left it hanging in the air for Tom to catch if he could see it. *We really can talk about Katie coming to live with you after we get back, if that's what you both want.*

Chapter 50

Eva

Tᴏᴍ'ꜱ ᴍᴀꜱꜱɪᴠᴇ ʙᴏᴀᴛ-ʟɪᴋᴇ shoes crunched down the shingle beach until he stood towering over, blocking out the rare bit of sunshine Eva had been enjoying. She pulled herself up into a sitting position and opened her eyes to see what he wanted. She looked past him, out beyond the gentle waves, to the sparkly horizon.

'You coming then? The kids'll want to say goodbye before we go.'

'I do know that. I'll be there in a minute.'

She should have been spending more time with everyone else, but the apartment was far too cramped for all of them, and with the weather they'd been having, the children had resisted spending too much time outdoors. They'd grown too soft these last three months. A few raindrops and a bit of a breeze on the island would never have driven them inside. They probably should have waited back at Dylan and Dominique's and let the children carry on with school.

Whenever Etienne would allow it, Eva had been out on the quadski. The machine understood her mood better than anyone else here. *'Haven't you got the hang of those controls yet?'* Tom had repeatedly jibed, like he was the expert! She'd even had, *'What, again?'* from Joe a couple of times on announcing she was going out on the quad. She wasn't spending much less time with the kids than she did back on the farm, was she?

Besides, when she was with them in the apartment, they all looked at her like there were clouds above her head, darker than those hanging in the sky outside.

The satellites had been right, at least. The clouds overhead had lightened, and for the first time in weeks, there'd been no rain. It would have been an ideal day to get out on the water, but Etienne had said there was no time for that, insisting on running some final checks before they were loaded onto the boat. So Eva had come out to sit on the beach for a while instead, to stare out at the sea she'd rather be skating across. She squinted at the horizon again. Was the dark smudge she could see actually land? Was that Britain she was seeing, or just a slightly darker ridge of cloud that the sun hadn't quite managed to chase away?

Tom was still standing over her, like he didn't believe she'd move if he turned and walked away. Eva sighed and held out a hand for Tom to pull her up. It took a while for him to grasp it. To be fair, they made skin contact even more rarely than they did eye contact. Why would they? They didn't even like each other.

'Are you nervous?' Tom asked as they set off back up the beach.

'Are you?'

'Well, it's only natural, isn't it?'

Typical Tom, not willing to actually admit his own feelings. If Eva later tried to suggest he'd confessed to nerves, he'd claim he never had. Anyway, who could really say what was *only natural*? Everybody was different, and different was good, wasn't it?

'Why don't you stay here? I don't mind going on my own.' said Tom.

Eva stopped. Tom walked on.

'Why would I do that?' she called after him.

Tom turned, retraced his steps back to her, almost met her eyes with his. 'Because, well, you've got people who would mind if you didn't make it back, and you've got the kids to consider.'

'I reckon Sylvie would mind if you didn't come back. Who would do all her jobs for her?' Was that a smile on Tom's face? 'And more importantly, you've got Katie. She'd miss you. In fact, maybe I should go and you stay, because it wouldn't be fair on Katie to lose her dad as well as her mum.'

'Nah.' Tom dug a hole in the shingle with his foot. 'You're more of a parent to Katie than I'll ever be, or than Sandra ever was, if you don't mind me saying that.'

Eva shook her head, not because she didn't mind. She did mind. She shook her head to dull the scream inside. How had she been able to talk about Katie losing her mum without a second thought, but then whenever Tom mentioned Sandra, her head immediately started throbbing?

'Let's stop talking about this. We're not going to *not* come back, and the best chance we've got of finding Nats and bringing all three of us back is if we both go.'

A GAGGLE OF gabbling French and French-Brits huddled at the dockside. Dylan, who'd been dispatched from the apartment to reassure everyone that Eva and Tom were on their way, was now apparently bearing the brunt of Maggie's impatience. Etienne, meanwhile, appeared to be once again going over instructions concerning the quadskis with two yawning, black-uniformed boat crew. Doctor Lewi, whose name Eva had recently learnt was spelt *Louis*, stood on his own, a bulging medical pack slung over his shoulder. He was the first to acknowledge their approach with a grin and a reassuring wave.

Peter's tight grip on Eva's hand loosened a little as he waved back at his doctor friend. Eva was glad that the doctor who'd filled her with hope and confidence for Peter, despite the language barrier, was now accompanying them across on the boat and would be the first to examine Nats, if they found her.

'Will Nats need to stay in the hospital when she gets here?' Peter asked. 'Or will she come to live with us at the farm, like Vicki and the others did at first?'

'I think that will be up to our friend Doctor Louis,' Eva replied, 'but as we've talked about before, we can't all stay with Dominique and Dylan forever. They've been very kind to us, letting us stay for so long, but you and Katie and Charlie are all getting so much bigger, and Grace too. Soon we'll have to think about finding a home of our own. That's OK, isn't it?'

Peter nodded and squeezed her hand. Did he still have unwavering faith in their plans, that they really could find Nats and bring her back safely? She was glad the children now knew what she and Tom were planning to do. She could have killed Vicki when she let the cat out of the bag in front of them and then had the gall to claim she thought the children already knew! But the look of pride in Peter's eyes whenever they talked about the plans, and the therapy it had been for Katie to chatter about all the things she would do with Nats when she arrived, made Vicki's faux pas forgivable. And Vicki was right; they'd have had to tell them sooner or later.

But now everything was happening too soon and too quickly. Louis and the boat crew were already aboard. The engine had spluttered into life and settled into a gentle purr. Katie was giggling as Tom spun her around and then deposited her in front of Joe, who clamped a hand on each of her shoulders to stop her climbing aboard after Tom. She'd come like a shot if she was allowed. *Thank you, Joe, for explaining to her that even you aren't allowed because you aren't old enough.*

'Go on then, Mummy, or they'll leave you behind!' Peter let go of her hand and gave her a gentle push towards the boat.

She turned back to her son, crouched down, and wrapped her arms around him once again. He squirmed.

'Sorry, was that too tight? Did I hurt you?'

Peter shook his head and smiled as she held him at arm's length, searching his eyes for signs of residual pain from the operation or breathlessness from it not having worked properly. *Don't be silly, he's fine*, Sandra's voice chided in her head. Last time she'd left him, he'd hoped she'd bring Mummy Sandra back, as well as Katie and Charlie. Did he know how much smaller their chances of success were this time?

'Eva, you need to go now, or I might call the whole thing off!' Maggie scooped Peter into her arms and gave her a shove much stronger than Peter's.

'OK, I'm going.' She stumbled towards the boat and hands reached out to pull her aboard. 'Wait, hang on, I've not said goodbye to Katie or Charlie or Joe.' *Or Grace either*, she thought. Why had she agreed that Grace should stay with Dominique?

'You did all that back at the apartment, remember?' Tom stood beside her, waving at the small crowd, already separated from them by a widening gulf of water. 'And if you'd wanted more time with them, you should have thought of that earlier.'

'Shut up, Tom. Don't you dare lecture me about spending time with others.'

The boat picked up speed and lurched over a wave. Eva's stomach churned. Did she really think they could find Nats and bring her safely back? What if the neuts spotted them and intercepted before they even made landfall? Why was she doing this? And why did it have to be with Tom?

Chapter 51

Nats

'So, is there anything else you want me to buy while I'm out? Anything we've forgotten?'

'Lots and lots of toys!'

'I wasn't asking you, Tris.'

Tris bursts into fits of giggles as Lori puts the pen down and reaches out to tickle them under the table. I take a sharp breath in sympathy, except then I can't let it out again. I wince as my tummy holds my breath captive.

'You've got more than enough toys, little pup, and before you say it, the baby doesn't need any. Little babies don't play with toys, and when they're not so little, we've got that big box of your old toys, remember?' Lori picks up the pen and studies their shopping list again. 'I haven't forgotten anything, have I, Nats?' They look up at me. 'Nats? You OK? You're looking a bit peaky.'

My body releases me, and I breathe out. 'I'm fine, it's nothing.'

'It doesn't look like nothing. This is it, isn't it? The baby's coming.'

'No... Well, maybe. I don't know.' The ache in my back ripples away, Joey gives me a good old punch, and my body feels normal again. Or normal in as much as I've got used to being a big round tight ball that gets punched and kicked from inside and has to go and take a leak every five minutes. I push my chair back and stand up.

'What is it? What do you need?' Lori stands up and moves around the table towards me. 'Stay there. I'll get whatever you need.'

'You can get me a bucket if you like, but I'd rather wee in the toilet if it's all the same to you.'

Lori smiles, breathes a sigh of relief, and moves out of my path. They know that when I need to go, I need to go, even if I'm halfway through dishing up the tea, or how I might have only just been in the downstairs loo but by the time I've got up the stairs, I'm heading straight for the one up there.

'All right. I'll wait until you come out, in case you think of something else we need while you're in there.'

'I'm sure I won't,' I call out before shutting myself in and pulling my trousers down. Oh, I seem to have leaked something. Not wee, though. It's jelly-like and pinkish. I lift the lid and lower myself onto the seat, then grab a bit of toilet roll to clean up my underwear.

I gasp. Here it comes again. A band constricts around the top of my tummy and then seems to work its way downwards. Joey wriggles in protest. I screw up my eyes. My left hand presses against the cold tiled wall while my right clutches the toilet seat. Don't come out here, please, Joey, I don't want to drop you down the toilet.

'You all right in there?' Lori's muffled voice calls through the wood of the door. 'It is coming, isn't it? What can I be getting ready for you?'

How should I know? I've never done this before, and I've never seen anyone else do it. Sandra and Eva never let anyone else get involved when somebody's time came, and after the first time I heard the shrieks coming through closed windows, I didn't ask again. Lori probably has a better idea than I do of what's going to happen next, if pups come out anything like babies do.

'I'm OK. Just do whatever you'd do if it was Nelly having pups.'

As the back pain subsides again and Joey stops his wriggling, my bladder reminds me why I came in here and I let it out with a sigh. I'm drinking nothing else until this is over, although Lori will have something to say about that.

Lori and Tris are both waiting there as I open the door. Lori holds out a hand to steady me, like I'm about to collapse out into the hallway. Tris looks deadly serious, fingers fiddling with one of Lori's belt loops.

'Where do you want to be? We should have thought about this. Do you want to be up in yer room or down here? Can you make it up the stairs? I've drawn the kitchen curtains already and put some extra logs on the stove. But looking at the sweat on you, it might be too warm in there now.'

I don't think I've heard Lori ask so many questions, or even say so much, all in one go. My heart pounds. What do I want? A grin spreads over my face. What would Lori think if I said I wanted to have Joey born in the barn, round the back of the old tractor?

'What? Have I said somethin' funny?'

'No, it was just a silly thought I had.' I pull the toilet door closed behind me. 'I think I'll head upstairs. Then I'll be out of your way. I think this might go on for a few hours yet. It went on for more than a night and a day with some of the girls. You could still go shopping if you wanted to.'

'I'm going nowhere now 'til this baby is safely out. The shopping'll have to wait.' Lori puts a hand under my elbow. I let it stay there. 'You sure you don't want a sit-down first?'

HEADING UP THE stairs is like that first unsteady time I came down them, but in reverse, and with the added benefit of a functioning handrail. Lori brings up the rear, arms out ready to catch me. Tris is bum shuffling up the steps in front of me, studying me with shy curiosity. But where's Nelly? Nelly should be leaping up and down the wooden steps below us.

'Where's Nelly?'

'Oh, I let her out a while ago. She's probably scratchin' at the door right now.' Lori turns their head to listen for a moment. 'She can take care of herself. Tris'll go and let her in in a minute, won't you, Tris?'

I get to the top of the stairs, step over Tris and straight into my room, slamming the door behind me, a little bit harder than intended. 'Whoops, sorry,' I say, not sure whether I'm apologising to the door or to my adopted family who I've shut out. I sink down with my back to the door as the biggest squeeze yet makes me yelp like Nelly.

'Nats, can I come in?' Lori's voice again worries from the other side of a door. Then quieter, 'Tris, go and let Nelly in, will you, but keep her downstairs.'

'She's not there, I can't see her,' Tris's little voice calls as her footsteps race back up the stairs.

'OK, go get yerself into your pyjamas and I'll go look for her in a minute.'

'But I want to see the baby.'

"Course you do, but as Nats says, it'll prob'ly morning before baby's born and yer not stayin' up all night. You need yer sleep, little pup.'

I could do with a sleep now too. I feel exhausted already, and one thing I did pick up from the other girls was it only gets worse as the hours go by. Of course, they might have all been kidding me – making out it was worse than it really was, getting me scared for when it was finally my turn. But Sandra was always very serious about everything to do with having babies. She wouldn't have joked about it. I wish I had Sandra and Eva with me now.

'Nats, you still OK in there? You need to let me in.'

I can feel the pain building again. I take a deep, pre-emptive breath, clench my teeth, and scrunch up my eyes. 'I'm all right. Sorry, I think I just need to rest right now.' That's all I trust myself to say in a normal voice before the squeeze takes control and the best I can do is keep myself from growling.

'Well, I guess you know best.' Lori's worried, uncertain, and trying not to be grumpy.

Do I know best? I suppose I could let them come in. If Joe was here, I'd want him to be with me, I think. No, I would, definitely. Oh, Joe, where are you? I guess you'll never know that you're a dad, nearly. I don't want anyone worrying and fussing over me, though, like Lori was doing downstairs. That'll make me worry and fuss too. If I relax and go to sleep, maybe my body will stop trying to tear me in half and maybe Joey will calm down too and we can all stay as we are. I crawl to the bed, pull myself up onto it and curl up on my side.

Something heavy is being dragged along the landing, coming to a stop outside my door. Lori's chair from their bedroom probably. Are they going to spend the night out there? I draw a tentative breath to tell them they can come in if they like, but I'm too sleepy already. My head is pulled back into the present by the door handle turning, bringing back memories of those days when I was sick, after they first brought me in from the barn. I hear Lori's whispered protest – 'No, Tris, leave Nats be!' – but I'm glad when Tris makes it past the guard outside my door to come and whisper at Joey through my tummy button, 'Don't come out while I'm asleep, little Joey.' I breathe steadily, pretending to be properly asleep.

As Tris creeps away, another squeeze creeps up on me. I let it come, put a hand on my tummy to feel as it tightens, and this time it's not so bad. Maybe the girls were kidding me and as long as I stay calm, the pain will get less, not more. I think that's the sort of thing Eva would say if she was here. She's great at calming the sheep mothers.

Chapter 52

Eva

'Eva? Tom? What can you see?'

Maggie's loud clear voice in Eva's ear made her jump. Neither she nor Tom had spoken since they'd left the quads hidden behind a hedge, under a tatty old tarpaulin they'd brought with them especially for the task.

Everything had gone so perfectly, so exactly as they'd planned. No police boats had raced out to meet them as they zoomed towards the coast. No spotlights had picked them out as their wheels hit the wide deserted beach. They'd only had to pull off the road and switch out their lights twice when Maggie, following their progress on the satellites, warned them of an approaching car, and each time her information had been spot on and the car had sped past them without incident. Eva couldn't accept it had all been for nothing.

'She's not here. Nothing in the barn except a sick-looking dog.'

Eva stopped holding her breath and let out a sigh, wishing Tom could have said something else, something less definitive.

'And you're sure it's the right barn?'

'Yup. It's all exactly as Joe described it. There's still an old tractor in there, and a big heavy stone by the door. The dog was round the back of the tractor, probably right in the spot where Joe and Nats were hiding when they were here.'

At least Tom hadn't mentioned the upstairs light that was on in the nearby solitary house. Maggie would be commanding them to get out of there quick sharp if she knew about that. But it was only a light. It had probably just been left on by accident. Even so, they'd retreated round to the moonlit-only darkness of the far side of the barn, just in case. Of course, Maggie would still expect them to turn around and head back now. In and out in one night had always been the deal – whether or not Nats was found.

'I am truly sorry, Eva, Tom. But we always said it was unlikely.' The line went silent again. Was Maggie still there? She'd probably just switched off her microphone to share the disappointing news with others. Was Joe with her, as he'd asked to be, or would he not be told the news until they were all back in France, as Maggie had told Eva would be best? There was a click and Maggie was back. 'So you have, I think, four hours until sunrise, so plenty of time to get back to the coast. But please, you should depart without delay. Our monitoring has shown that those roads start to get busy well before dawn.'

Busy? Eva had seen the satellite video pictures and the data collected over the last few weeks, and OK, they might have to stop six times instead of only two if they left it a couple more hours, but it could hardly be called busy. Her parents would have laughed out loud at Maggie calling those little country roads busy at five in the morning. But Eva wasn't thinking of only delaying for an hour or two. She signalled to Tom to switch off his comms unit and she did the same to hers.

'What if we've missed something?' Eva began as Tom moved close enough that she could feel his warm breath wafting around her head. 'Nats would have left some sort of message for Joe if she could – something to tell him where she'd moved on to.'

There was a break in the mist of Tom's breath. He was thinking and holding his breath, and then it all came out again in a tidal wave as he exhaled. 'I dunno. She was never one to think that far ahead, but...'

'But if we go now, we'll never know,' Eva finished off for him as he held another breath for longer than she was willing to wait. 'We're bound to have missed all sorts with just our torches and with that dog in there. We need to have a proper look in the light, when hopefully the dog has moved too.'

Tom was nodding. Eva could barely see him, but she could feel the nod.

'If Joe was able to come back and forth to the barn multiple times without being spotted when he was here, we should be OK hiding out back here till it's light.' Eva flicked on her torch and shone it down the side of the barn, picking out the heap of broken planks with weeds growing up all around and between them. 'Doesn't look like anyone's been round here for a while, and we can move to the other side of that lot if we want to be a bit more hidden. Of course, once it does get light, we'll have to stay till it gets dark again, so we probably need to find somewhere good to hide for a few hours. But we could wait it out under the tarp with the quadskis if we had to.'

Tom said nothing.

'Tom?'

'Yeah, it's OK, I agree. I was just waiting till you stopped talking.'

Eva rolled her eyes. It was a good job Tom couldn't see that, as he'd have probably gone off on one. 'OK, good. So, what do we say to Maggie?'

'Do we have to say anything? We could leave the comms off until we're ready to head back. She's not gonna like it, but she won't like what we're planning either.'

'Yeah, but what if she assumes we've been caught or something and calls the boat back, gives up on us?'

'But she's still watching us, though, isn't she – on the satellites? She'll see we're on our own and aren't going anywhere.'

Eva stared up at the sky. A few stars poked through the clouds. Or were some of them actually Maggie's satellites? She imagined Maggie looking down on them, berating them for switching off their comms and not already being back on the quads. She imagined Maggie calling Louis and the crew on the boat and commanding they return to France, to teach her and Tom a lesson. Although who was really in charge here? The boat was provided by the French. They were doing Maggie a favour really. Maybe it would be them telling Maggie that they needed to recall the boat, that it was never part of the deal for it to sit out there in the middle of the *La Manche* for more than the one night. She switched her comms unit back on.

'Hi, Maggie?'

'Hello, Eva? What happened? Why did you switch us off?'

'Look, Maggie,' Eva swallowed, quietly cleared her throat. 'Tom and I have decided to wait here 'til morning.'

'Eva, that wasn't the deal.'

'It's so dark here, we might have missed something – some message Nats left that might tell us where she's gone to – and with the dog in there as well, we couldn't really look properly, so we're going to –'

'Eva, no, that wasn't in the plan. Look, even if I call the French now and ask them to stay out there with the boat, they probably won't agree to it, and if they return to France, they probably won't come back out to meet you when you're ready. And what if later we find out where Cain is, or indeed where Nats is, and we want to go and get them but the French won't let us?'

Tom gave a big sigh beside her. Was he sighing at Maggie, or at her for deciding to switch the comms back on? Eva clenched her fist.

'Those are all risks we'll have to take. We'll come all the way back on the quadskis if we have to.'

'Don't tell her that,' Tom cut in, though thankfully his comms unit was still switched off. 'The quads are only designed for shallow waters.'

'What was that Tom said?'

'He agrees with me.' Eva cut the comms.

Tom sighed again.

'What? You think we should have just left her wondering what we're doing?'

'No, probably not, but –'

'You don't think we can get back on the quads. Well, OK, you might find it a bit of a challenge, but I know I could!'

'Shhh! Keep it down!'

'Sorry,' she whispered. 'Look, you're welcome to head back now if you're worried about it, but I'm staying.'

'All right.'

'All right what?'

'All right, I'm staying too. I never said I wouldn't. But I'd have preferred it if you hadn't told Maggie she could recall the boat back to France.'

'I didn't tell her that, I – Oh, never mind.' Eva stood up and turned away from Tom.

'What are you doing now?'

'Going to find somewhere private for a wee. If that's OK with you.'

'I'M SORRY ABOUT Sandra.'

Eva opened her heavy eyelids, pulled her hood down, and eased her left leg around under her right to take some weight off her numb bum. How much time had passed since she'd returned from her toilet trip was hard to say. Knowing Tom, he'd probably spent the whole time formulating those four words and contemplating how to say them.

'Sorry for what? That she died or that you were mating her?'

Tom shuffled but didn't say anything more until Eva began to wonder whether he'd fallen asleep. Maybe he'd even been talking in his sleep.

'I didn't think Sandra would tell you about that.' Another long pause. 'Anyway, it's not like it meant anything. Not to Sandra, anyway.'

Relief washed over Eva. So it had always been about having another baby. Sandra hadn't wanted Tom. She hadn't gone to him for comfort, just for his seeds. Probably. 'So she was only doing it for the baby then?'

'What baby?'

'She didn't tell you?'

'Tell me what?'

Tom could be dumb sometimes. Did she need to spell it out?

'Sandra was pregnant. With your baby. Didn't you know?'

'I didn't, no.'

'Sorry.'

Neither of them said any more, but with the thought of babies firmly in her head, Eva's heart plummeted into her belly. Across the sea, Peter, Grace, and Katie would be waking up in the next couple of hours, expecting her and Tom to be back with them. That's what they'd promised. Why did people make promises they weren't sure they could keep? How many times had she and Sandra told a pregnant girl *everything will be fine* when her pains started? She gasped. The cry of a girl in her birthing pains rattled her memory. It was almost as if she could really hear it. But that was crazy.

'Tom? Did you hear that?'

Tom only answered with slow, heavy breaths. Eva pulled her hood back up and tightened the cords. She turned her back on Tom, pulled her knees up to her chest, and hugged herself for warmth. If he was sleeping, she'd better keep watch for dawn and make sure nobody found them.

Chapter 53

Nats

THE TRAIN HURTLES towards me. I stand, trapped between the rails. I could step over them, except I can't – my feet won't move. Joe and Cain – no, it's Lori and Tris this time – bellow at me from the edge of the bridge. It's too late, I can't get to them in time, even if I can unstick my feet. The buzz of the train singing along the tracks courses up my spine and out like fast-growing branches, wrapping themselves around me, squeezing, contracting, rooting me to the spot even more firmly. The train hits. I scream. The door bangs open.

'Nats, settle down! You're OK, you can do this.'

A damp cloth presses against my forehead. I shiver – my clothes are drenched. I shuffle myself back onto my side as the pain levels out and pull my legs up as much as I can against my still-taut tummy. My underwear is sopping wet; my whole bottom half is. I must have wet myself, except my bladder still feels full, even though I've drunk nothing since I last went. How long ago was that? I open my eyes. Clear moonlight threads its way through the curtains, which Lori must have drawn while I was sleeping. Have I really been asleep?

'What time is it?'

'I'm not sure, three or four perhaps. You got some sleep then?'

'I think so.' I was dreaming, so I must have been sleeping, though apart from that, my memory is filled with endless waves of pain and breathlessness, but there must have been times of calm in between, like this.

Lori can tell I'm in a calm spot for now so strides back towards the door.

'You can stay...if you want to.'

'All right, I will do,' Lori says over their shoulder whilst hauling their chair through the doorway. The chair sticks out its 'wings' against either side of the doorframe. It's not going to fit through, is it? Lori grabs it by its legs to pull it through. I wince and feel sudden sympathy for the doorframe.

As Lori's still wrestling with the chair, I have a feel between my legs. It's like I'm touching the secret bits of some other creature that's not me. I wish I could see what's going on down there. Or actually, maybe not. It's all wet. Is it blood? I retrieve my fingers and they're wet but clean-ish. No blood anyway. I put my fingers to my nose. It's not wee either. It doesn't smell. I should probably get out of my wet trousers and underwear. They'll have to come off at some point to let Joey out, though I'm still not sure how he's going to fit. I glance back towards the door as Lori manages to get the last part of the chair through with some sort of twisting action.

'Arrghh!' The next squeeze is on me without warning.

Lori bounds over to the bed, leaving the chair where it is, blocking the door. What if I need a wee now? I'd have to climb over it. Actually, I feel more like a need a poo. I want to push everything out. I start tugging at my trousers.

'Here, let me help you.'

'No, don't! I'm sorry, they're all wet.'

'I can see that. But that means you'll not get them off without help.'

'Arrrrghh!'

'OK, it's OK, I'll leave it.'

'No, that was just another squeeze. You can help take them off now if you like.'

'Are you sure?'

'Yes! Take them off. Now, please!'

Lori wrestles with my trousers like they wrestled with the chair. They're not usually this clumsy. But then it is the middle of the night and they've probably not slept. I kick my legs to help shake them out of the wet trousers.

I plant my feet on the bed as another squeeze grabs me. This one's not as mean as the last one. I clench my teeth, screw up my eyes, determined not to yell, but the pain doesn't stop growing. 'Nnnnyaaaarghh!'

'Try taking some breaths now.'

'What?!'

'I don't know. Just don't forget to breathe.'

'All right. Whatever!' I suck some air in and puff it out again, but I don't think it reached my lungs. The next breath does, and I feel myself relaxing again, though I know it won't be for long. 'Can you take a look?'

'What?'

I tug my underwear down off my bottom. Lori doesn't make any move to help me. I've got them past my knees, but now I need to brace myself for the next wave of pain. I can't do this. 'I can't do this! Gnnaarrrrrghh!'

'Nats, I think you nearly have!'

'What?'

'Well, I think I might be able to see a bit of head.'

I reach to feel. Lori's hand takes mine. This should feel too weird, but I let them do it and they guide my fingers until they're touching something firm and a bit hairy that's definitely not part of me but is definitely mostly still inside me. Every part of me around that bit of not-me is as tight as it will go. I really can't do this, unless you expect me to split in two to let you out Joeyyyyyy – 'Yyyyaaaaarrrrghhhhhh!'

'Can you stand up, do you think, if I help to hold you?'

Lori grips my hand as if to pull me up off the bed. I shake myself free but then grab their hand back and squeeze hard as the pain refuses to let go of me. Lori takes it as agreement and starts to pull me up.

'Hang on, what are you doing?' I say as soon as I can speak again.

'I think it'll come out easier if you're standing. You'll have gravity to help you.'

'But then he'll fall out and break his head on the floor.'

'No, because I'll be there to catch 'em.'

'Not if you're holding me up you won't.'

'All right, sorry, it was just a thought.'

'Yeah, well, thanks but... gnnaaaaaooowww! Owwwww! It's stinging. He's going to rip me apart.' I roll over onto all fours, but my arms can't hold me up and my head collapses down onto the bed as I shuffle my knees towards the edge.

'What are you doing? Shouldn't you stay still now?'

'No, I want to stand up, like you said.'

'But you said you didn't want to –'

'I think I can hold myself up against the bed, sort of. You just make sure you catch himmmm – aaarghhowwwwwaaarghhh!'

My feet are on the floor now. It does feel a bit better. I push my elbows against the mattress and lift my head to speak. 'Let go of me and get ready to catch!'

Lori's solid hands don't leave my waist. 'It's OK, the head's not out yet. I reckon I'll see when I need to let go and catch.'

OK, so if Lori let go now, I know I'd crumple into a heap on the floor. Maybe I should get back up onto the bed, but my knees are like those massive pebbles on the beach you only have a hope of shifting if you wrap your whole body around them, and then you end up with an achy back for days afterwards. Every part of me, inside and out, is going to ache for weeks after this is done. I crank my head round, try to see if I can see what's going on, but the bed and the rest of my body is in the way and then I'm biting into the covers. 'Nnggggggggg! Grrrrrraaaarghh!' I so need to poo.

One of Lori's hands moves. 'OK, here it comes. Just keep doing whatever you're doing.'

'Mmmnnngggggggnnnnaaaaaa! But I'll poo on the floor.'

'No you won't – well, I don't know, but whatever you're doing, it's working. Keep going. This is amazing!' Lori's let go of me with both hands now.

I grab fistfuls of bedclothes with both hands, not that they're much good for holding me up. I wobble. 'Lori? You need to hold me again.'

'I can't now. This is it. Next time you growl, it'll all be done, I reckon. Just take you ti –'

'Grrrrrnnnnnnnngggaaaaaahhhhhh!'

'OK, now's fine. That's it! Keep going!'

I feel him slither out of me and I sink to the floor. There's a mess of blood and water and bits of white stuff, like the scum the sea sometimes washes up onto the beach, and Lori's kneeling in front of me, holding something out to me that's also covered in blood and the scummy stuff and has something dangling down off it that goes all the way back to between my legs.

'Here, you take them, and I'll get a blanket to put around you both.'

Lori holds the messy lump closer to me. There's little leg sticking out, and an arm, and then it starts up a gasping squawk, a bit like the cry of a new baby. And then I realise it is a new baby. It's my new baby. My Joey.

'It's a boy, isn't it?'

Chapter 54

Nats

'I DON'T UNDERSTAND. IT can't be.'

I push away the blanket that Lori is draping around me. I need to have another look. The bloody tube that still joins the baby to me hangs down between its legs. I need to get it out of the way so I can have a proper look, but the baby keeps kicking its legs as I try to untangle it and I don't want to risk pulling the thing off altogether. I know it comes off eventually but...

'Can't be what? What's wrong, Nats?' Lori tries to tuck the blanket round me again. 'Come on, you're shivering and the pup must be cold too. We need to keep you both warm.'

'OK, in a minute, but let me have a proper look first. I need to see what it is.' I know already what it was, but it can't be. I manage to disentangle the tube from its legs and then have a gentle feel with my hands to confirm what my eyes can see. Or rather can't see. No tonker, but not right for a girl either. I've seen newborn baby girls before. I taste the salt as the tears drizzle down my face. I don't understand. 'Why have I got a neut baby?'

'A what baby?'

There must be some mistake. The pressure builds inside me, and I burst into full-blown raging tears. 'It's a bloody neut, like you and Tris. It's come out all wrong. It should be a boy. I was sure he was a boy. OK, I didn't know for sure, it could have been a girl, but not a neut! That's just wrong!'

'Oh, I see, but why? Why is it wrong?' Lori reaches out and gently wipes the hair out of my eyes. 'As you say, Tris is a *neut* and there's nothing wrong with that. Here, let me take them for a moment. Let me wrap them up nice and warm, and then I can pass them back to you.'

I let Lori lift the baby away from me. There's no weight to the little thing, but without it I'm suddenly aware of my throbbing, aching, scooped-out body. I double over and howl at my bloodied legs.

I OPEN MY eyes. I think I've been awake for a while, but not owning up to being awake meant I could sort of not admit to how everything's different now, although the ache in my stomach and below betrays my attempts at denial. The light has been switched off and the grey glow from the window as the curtains billow tells me the sun's not up yet, but it will be soon. I'm tucked up in my bed, but I know that under these covers, the mess and smell still lingers undisturbed. I'm glad Lori has opened a window. I can't make out whether or not Lori's eyes are open. Their head is either bowed in sleep or gazing down at the bundle in their arms. The baby. My baby. But how can it be my baby?

'Can I see...them?'

Lori lifts their head with a start and grunts. I guess they were asleep then.

'Sorry, didn't mean to disturb you.' I stick a hand out from under the covers and motion for Lori to stay put. 'It's OK, don't bother. The two of you look quite comfortable there.'

'No, you should have a look, and a cuddle.' Lori eases up off the chair, their eyes all the time on the baby. 'Tris'll be up soon and wanting breakfast, and to see the baby. I'd better try to clean things up, if you think we can shift you off the bed for a bit. No, no, you don't need to move yerself right now.'

'No, sorry, I'm just sitting up so I can hold the baby.' Though as soon as I shuffle myself up the bed, I can feel that I'm not going to be comfortable sitting up for very long. 'Could you spare a bag of frozen peas or something?'

Lori frowns.

'To put down here.' I lift the blanket a little and point towards my sore bottom.

'Oh, yeah, sure. Here, are you ready to take the little one? That's it, you know what yer doing, don't you. Right, I'll go fetch the peas. And how about somat to eat. For you, I mean?'

Of course, the baby will need feeding soon too. Should I have done that straight away? The bundle in my arms is still and quiet. Is it too still, too quiet? Is it OK? Babies have to feed every couple of hours or so to start with. How many hours has it been so far? What if I've left it too long already? My udders are hard and bulgy – I touch a finger to my nipple through my T-shirt. It's wet, and instinctively, I take a sniff and I'm reminded of all the little babies I've taken off their mothers as they tuck themselves back into their clothes after a feed.

'How about I make you a piece of toast? What would you like on it?'

My tummy rumbles. The baby twitches at the disturbance. I breathe a sigh of relief – it's still alive.

'Yes, thanks, toast would be good. I should feed the baby too.'

''Course, yes. The baby needs feeding too. But we've not got any milk for the baby yet. I knew there were somat else I meant to put on that shopping list. Been meaning to pick some up. I'll have to go to the shop to get some.'

The wet patches on my T-shirt are growing. 'No, it's OK. I think I've got my own milk.' I pull out my T-shirt at the bottom.

Lori's eyes widen. 'I s'pose you have. I'd not, I mean, I know bitches feed their own pups, but I hadn't thought about how you might. Well, I'll leave you to it for a bit then and go put some toast on.'

'Tris! Just back off, will you? You can see the baby properly later,' I shout.

Shit, now Tris is bawling too.

'I'm sorry, Tris, I know you're excited and you want to meet the baby. It's just I've been trying to feed it and I was almost there, but then you came in and...'

And now Lori appears at the door. 'What's going on? Oh, sorry, Nats, I didn't realise Tris had woken up.' Lori scoops a wriggling Tris into their arms. 'Come on, come and have some breakfast. I won't even make you get dressed first.'

'But I want to see the baby!' Tris wails.

'And you will do, soon. But let's give Nats a few more minutes with the baby first. It is her baby.'

Lori pulls the door shut behind them and one set of wailing is dulled by the wood and grows more distant as it is carried down the stairs. But the angry rasps of the little creature in front of me only get louder.

'All right, shhh, let's give this another go.' I hold my breath, hold the baby's sticky, milk-spattered head, and guide it in again towards my nipple. As soon as it touches, it goes wild again and I lose my grip and the head swipes back and forth across my already sore nipple, which hasn't even been sucked on yet.

'Ow! Keep your head still! You won't get any in your mouth if you keep thrashing around.' I thought this was meant to come naturally. It all looked so easy when Sally or Eva did it. Maybe neut babies just don't know how to do it. But surely everything a baby does has to be taught, doesn't it? Although they don't have to be taught how to cry. Maybe their mouths are different somehow too and don't work with nipples. I've never looked that carefully at a neut mouth, but I don't think it's any different. So it's probably me. I'm not doing it right. I should have looked more closely at how the other girls did it. Eva, I wish you were here now to show me, like you did with the other girls. And Joe too. You wouldn't know what to do any better than me, but you'd make me feel better about it. Did I ever tell you how you always made me feel better about myself? I wish you were here now, to help with the baby. Our baby. I can't do this on my own.

I put the baby down on the bed, between my knees, cover my ears and shut my eyes. The wailing fades too quickly to nothing. What have I done? Has it died already? Have I starved it to death? I dare to open one eye. No, phew! Its tiny chest is still rising and falling, rising and falling. How can it be sleeping yet breathing so fast? I sit, more frozen than the peas between my legs, hands still over my ears, watching the up down, up down of my baby's breaths, unsure right now whether I'll be more relieved if they stop or carry on. How can I be thinking this? I love babies, don't I?

The door creaks open. Two faces appear. Cheeks stained with tears, Tris hovers in the doorway, holding out a plate of toast. Lori reaches down and steadies the plate before it tilts far enough for the toast to slide off onto the floor. Lori gives Tris a nudge forwards with their knee so they can both come in and shut the door.

'Still not managed then? I thought the sudden silence might mean you'd got them feeding at last.' Lori watches my face. 'But don't worry. Babies are like that. Tris was, anyway – screaming their head off one minute, fast asleep the next and never knowing what they really want.'

'I can't do it. It's not going to work.' I try to wipe the tears off my cheeks with the bedsheet, but they won't stop.

'Ok, so I go out and get some baby milk from the shop. You can always try them on your milk again later.'

I can't say it to Lori, but I wasn't just talking about the milk and the feeding. I was talking about everything. How can I have a baby? I'm too young for a start. Joe and I should never have done it. Maybe that's why it's a neut, because I wasn't old enough to have a baby. I can't go back to the island now, not with a neut baby, and I'm glad Joe's not here to see it. Maybe I can just leave it here with Lori. They'll make sure it's looked after, and Tris will love it for me. Yes, as soon as I'm not too sore, that's what I'll do. It will be better for everyone.

Chapter 55

Georgy

K EYS WERE TURNED and then the door was being held open for me. Out there, a door being held open is a sign of politeness. Inside, it's just a necessity. No prison officer is ever polite to a prisoner. The duty front gate officer – a posh title for someone who's there to unlock and open a door – dismissed me with nothing more than a quick tilt of the head, telling me to get out of here. No directions for how to get from here to the nearest train station. No *have you got somewhere to stay tonight?* Not even a *good luck and keep out of trouble*.

'Thank you, boss,' I said as I stepped over the raised threshold, and then the door slammed shut behind me.

The night sky still lingered overhead. Why they'd had to get me up so early and kick me out before it was even properly light, I had no idea. I guessed because anything else would be too civilised. I sucked in a lungful of air through my nose and almost choked as the chill of it stung my nose and throat. Clouds of steam billowed out of my mouth.

'Georgy! Hi!'

'Cris, what are you doing here?'

'I've come to pick you up, of course.' Their nervous smiling face appeared out of the foggy breath between us.

'You didn't have to. What time did you have to set off?' I looked again at the sky, already several shades lighter than my first glimpse of it but not yet what could be called daylight.

'Well, someone needed to be here to meet you.'

'Thanks.' I would have been calling Cris, sorting out where and how to hand over Cain at some point today, so it might as well be now. 'How's...?' I stopped before saying his name, still cautious about who might be watching or listening to my every word and move.

'The hamster? He's fine. Been a bit on edge for the last few days. I've brought him with me. He's in the car.'

'Is that safe?' What did Cris think they were doing? Were they hoping to offload him onto me here, right outside the prison?

'Probably not, but he insisted, and you know how determined he can be.'

No, I didn't know, really. Cris must've known Cain much better than I did now. Thinking about it, the few hours I'd spent with him amounted to far less than even one day. 'So what now?' I dug my hands deep into my pockets and shivered. Whatever was happening next, we needed to get away from this place, particularly if Cain was sitting waiting in the back of Cris' car. What if somebody had spotted him as we stood around blowing steam at each other?

'Well, I'll take you back to my place. I did tell him that's what we'd do, so there was really no need for him to come. Is that OK with you?' Cris stared at the ground, practised puffing out little globules of cloudy breath.

'Yeah, OK, that would be good. Thanks.'

Cris turned and set off towards a distant car park. 'You can stay as long as you like.'

I hoisted my bag onto my back and followed, legs stiff from the cold and lack of use, at least this early in the morning. Why did they need to put the car park all the way over there, when there was plenty of space right next to the imposing building? Security, I supposed – less chance of an escaped prisoner making a quick dash to a waiting car, not that I could see how you could escape from here. Or maybe it was in case someone was tempted to turn a car into a bomb, to blow a hole in the prison walls.

Cris opened the boot of a red car I didn't recognise. I decided not to comment. Why shouldn't they have bought themself a new car? If I had the money now, I'd probably go for something sleek and modern like this one, though I wouldn't have gone for red. My small bag didn't really need to go in the boot, but I guessed Cris would rather it went in there – they always did prefer things to be packed away neatly in the boot even when it was more convenient and there was plenty of space to just sling things on the back seat. So that was how I almost hit him in the face.

'Whoa! What's he doing in the boot? Er, hello, Cain. Are you OK?'

'We thought it would be safer that way.'

'And you've driven all the way down here like that?'

''Course not. It was dark. I know you're the expert on these things, but I do know something about assessing risk. No, we found a deserted patch of road a few miles from here and stopped there for him to move himself into the boot. Anyway, we should probably shut it again now, rather than staring into it like there's a person hiding in there.'

CRIS PULLED OVER into the layby. The car that had been following us zoomed on past, but we sat there for at least a minute, both holding our breath, not daring to move, just in case.

'OK, I think it's safe to let him out now,' Cris said, reaching for the door handle.

'Can I?' I opened my door and stepped out as Cris relaxed back into the driver seat with a nod. 'How does it open?' I couldn't see button or lever anywhere on the sleek rear of the car. But then there was a click and the boot door began to smoothly rise.

'We're going to find Nats now, aren't we?' Cain clambered out before the lid was fully up. 'You said we would, as soon as...'

Cain towered over me. Surely, he couldn't have grown that much in the last three months. Perhaps I'd forgotten how tall he really was, imagining him to be more similar to the son we waved goodbye to in Carlisle station, though to be fair, he had also grown taller than me by the time I last saw him on the dockside in Dover. How many times had I lain on my hard cell bed and dreamt of being on a boat in the middle of the sea with Cain, and maybe even Nats if I dared to dream big, on our way to meet Joe?

'We will, but I think we need to wait, just a couple of days. We need to be sure we're not being watched.'

Cain scanned the empty road and fields – so flat in this part of the world. You could literally see for miles in all directions. 'Nobody's watching us now.'

'Well, no, you're probably right, but...'

Cris got out of the car and came around to the back, also scanning the surrounding road and fields, with greater nervousness than Cain. 'What's going on? Let's all get back in the car and get home.'

'Only when you promise we're going to find Nats.'

'What?'

'You promised we would, and that was months ago, so we've waited too long already.' Was this really the same boy who had sat opposite me, unable or unwilling to utter a single word, in the police interview room?

'Who promised?' Cris looked from Cain to me. I didn't need to own up to it. 'Georgy, what a stupid thing to promise. How long has it been? Six, no seven months. The girl will be long gone by now. And even if she wasn't, do you really think you could find the place, based on scant instructions given to you in a hurry when you were full of emotion over seeing Joh again? It's a crazy idea.'

I could remember every detail of Joe's instructions for how to find the barn and fully trusted their accuracy. But I knew Cris wouldn't hear that and it also wouldn't help us to persuade Cain to postpone the search for another few days if he saw us disagreeing with each other.

'Then I'll go look for her on my own.' Cain backed away from the car.

'Cain, wait.' I reached out my hand towards him. 'That would be crazy. You don't even know where to start looking.'

'I know it was near Dover, and I know she was in a barn.' He didn't need to say anymore. I could read what he was saying. He'd search every barn in Kent if he had to.

I turned back to Cris. 'We are in the right part of the country, and it doesn't look like we've been followed or anything. Maybe we could just drive past on our way home.' OK, so it was in the opposite direction to our way home, but it sounded better put like that. 'It might help

Cain and I work out how best to get ourselves there when we do go for a proper look. Or tell us there's no point because it's obvious we can't find the place.'

Cris hesitated. Cain backed away a few more paces. I pleaded with my eyes for Cris to consent, even if they did it with fingers crossed behind their back to get Cain back into the car.

'OK, but I won't be stopping for you to get out when we get there.'

Chapter 56

Eva

EVA PEEKED OVER the hedge. Someone had come out of the house, but they weren't going anywhere near the barn. They strode straight over to the tatty old truck parked on the far side of the house. The engine sputtered, taking a few goes to start, but then it was off, bouncing down the track at speed. It was a good thing there were no walkers following the footpath sign down that track right now.

Tom's face peered around the barn door, looked both ways, and then, keeping low, he made a dash for it across and through the gate which they'd left off the latch. He crawled along, below the level of the hedge, until he reached Eva. 'What's happening? Was that an engine I heard?'

'A neut came out of the house and drove off in the truck. Going shopping, by the look of it – carrying some empty shopping bags.'

'So the coast should be clear for a bit then. Doesn't look like they have shops just round the corner out here.'

'Maybe, but they weren't hanging about. The speed they went down that track, I wouldn't like to count on them being away for long. And how do we know there aren't others in the house?' Why didn't Tom think of these things? He always seemed happiest to assume the simplest scenario. 'Anyway, did you find anything? You weren't in there for long.'

'Nothing, except the dog that's still in there.'

'Is it still in the same place?'

'Yeah, right behind the old tractor, and it started growling at me when I went near, so I kept my distance. But I had a good look round the rest of the barn and couldn't see any signs or messages from Nats.'

Eva rolled her eyes. How could Tom have had a good look round in the two minutes he was in there? And he hadn't even tried to look in the spot they knew was the most likely place they'd find something.

'What? Would you have just shoved the dog out of the way?'

'No, but it didn't exactly look like a vicious dog last night, and it's not very big. I'm sure we can coax it out somehow. We've got to be able to search round the back of that tractor, otherwise what was the point of staying?'

'All right, well, you go and see what you can do then.' Tom settled down on the ground and, using one of his spade-like hands, parted a bit of hedge to peer through.

Eva got to her feet, keeping in a crouch, and waddled round Tom's bulk.

'Wait!' Tom hissed. 'There's someone coming out of the house.'

Eva dropped down again, next to Tom, and squinted towards the house. She saw no-one until her eyes dropped to the bottom half of the door. A small kid, same sort of age as Charlie probably, stood in the doorway.

'Nelly! Nelly, where are you? Come here, you naughty dog!'

The child disappeared into the darkness of the house, but the door remained ajar. Eva and Tom remained frozen, eyes glued to the door. The child reappeared, this time stepping out into the yard in a pair of wellies which, Eva could see even at this distance, were clearly on the wrong feet. They called out for Nelly again and again as they meandered in the direction of the barn. Whether by luck or instinct, their path led them to the barn and they disappeared inside.

Eva realised she was still holding her breath and let it out before taking another and speaking her thoughts. 'Maybe that's our problem solved. The kid'll get the dog moved for us.'

But the kid was now back at the door and running back towards the house with no sign of the dog following. The wellies slapped on the gravelly track as they worked their way off the child's feet in protest at being the wrong way around. The child took a tumble and Eva had to stop herself from leaping up to go and help them up and rub their knees better, and that in turn made her take a stuttering breath. Her eyes blurred up. Over the last few months, she'd been so absorbed in planning for this pointless trip, she'd neglected her own kids. It had been Joe or Vicki or Dominique who'd been picking them up when they fell, wiping mud and grit off grazed knees and kissing them better. It would be her taking care of that from now on, when they got back.

The child picked themselves up, pulled the wellies back on, still on the wrong feet, and completed their dash back to the house. Eva didn't hear what they shouted as they tumbled in through the door, but they were excited about something, and there was obviously somebody else in the house. Of course there was – no neut parent would leave a kid that age on their own.

Chapter 57

Nats

THE DOOR SLAMS open as sleep is taking me, and Tris comes bursting in.

'Nats! Nats! You have to come and see!'

I groan with pain as I turn over to face them. 'Shhh! We don't want to wake the baby, remember? Not until Lori gets back with some of that special baby milk.'

'Oops, sorry.' Tris tiptoes over to the bed in a bouncy sort of way. 'You have to come and see,' they whisper with a squeak right into my ear.

I pull away and rub my ear. 'What is it? What do I *have* to come and see? Lori told you to let me rest, remember?'

'Oh, but you've rested for *ages* already and you have to come and see what I've found.'

I smile at Tris's perception of time. It's less than twenty minutes since Lori went, and for ten of those I'd been cleaning myself off in the bath. Then I'd kicked Tris out of the bedroom for a few minutes to pull on a clean T-shirt and underwear and get back into bed. Tris tugs on my arm.

'You still haven't told me what you want me to come and see.'

'It's a surprise. Just come and you'll see.' Tris giggles.

All I want to do is sleep, if the pain down below will let me. But maybe if I let Tris show me whatever it was, they'll leave me be after that. I ease myself into a sitting position.

'OK. You go over and check on the baby, but don't touch, and I'll get some trousers on.' I don't want Tris to watch as I check the wad of tissues I've shoved into my underpants. I'm glad I remembered the other girls going on about the big bleed you have after a baby, otherwise, I'd worry I was bleeding to death. How long will it go on, though, and how much blood have I got in me to lose? I already feel emptied out.

Trousers on, I hobble over to stand beside Tris and look down at the baby in what Tris proudly announced was the cot they used to sleep in. I still can't believe that little creature came out of me.

'Come on then, let's leave the baby to sleep and you can show me whatever it is. But then you're leaving me and the baby to rest. OK?'

'Joey needs to come too. I can carry them if you like.'

'Shhh. No, we'll leave the baby to sleep here. Otherwise we might wake it.'

'But Joey might want to see too.'

'I'm sure Joey...the baby, can see later and is happier sleeping for now.'

I'm wishing now I'd never told Tris or Lori that I planned to call the baby Joey. I'm not sure I still want to call them that. I don't know what I want to call them, or if I even want to call them anything at all. If I give them their name, it means they're mine, doesn't it? I hope it's OK that it's still sleeping. But what do I do when it wakes up?

'But Lori said you'd have to be looking after Joey *all the time* after they were born. So we have to take Joey with us to the barn.'

'The barn? Oh, no, Tris, I can't go all the way out to the barn. Not today. Can't you bring whatever it is here?'

Tris tugs on my arm. 'No, you have to come and see now!'

The baby wriggles and starts up a bit of a coughing whimper. Tris reaches in to touch them, but I intercept them, lifting the baby out of the cot to hold them protectively against my chest. What made me do that? The baby twitches a couple of times, kicking out a leg and an arm at the same time, just like they did so many times inside me. Then they settle, and I can feel my heartbeat pulsing against their warm body.

'Come *on*. You have to come and see what's happened to Nelly!'

'Nelly? You've found her then? What's happened to her? Is it Nelly in the barn? Go and fetch her in.'

'But I can't. She's had... You have to come and see.'

Oh, no! My mind races through possibilities now. Is Nelly lying injured in the barn? Or worse, dead? No, it can't be anything like that. Tris was full of bounce and giggles just now. I shiver at the cold breeze blowing in from downstairs. Tris must have left the front door open. But then why hasn't Nelly raced back into the house and up the stairs after Tris? I need to go and see why.

'All right then, you'd better show me.'

Tris leads us out of the door and to the top of the stairs. I hesitate. They're already at the bottom and I'm dithering dizzily at the top. I don't feel steady enough to go down these stairs, definitely not without holding on to the handrail, but that would mean letting go of the baby with at least one hand, and I can't do that either.

It was so much easier when it was inside me. I should go and put it down again. But what if it starts crying? At least it's not crying at the moment.

'Come on, Nats!' Tris calls from the bottom of the stairs and then, seeing my hesitation, they run back up and hold out a hand for me to hold.

I shake my head, which makes me dizzy. 'No, Tris, you won't be able to hold me up, and anyway, I can't let go of the baby, can I?' How am I *ever* going to manage to carry this baby down the stairs? I'll be trapped up here with it forever, unless I can sneak away and leave it here. It wriggles a bit, and for a moment, it feels part of me again. A memory flashes through my head. 'Wait there. I'll be back in a minute.'

I retrace my steps to the bedroom and find the huge, long scarf Lori got for me when I was sat shivering on the doorstep a couple of weeks ago. How do I do this without dropping the baby? I've seen Sally and Eva do it plenty of times, all while standing up, but I can't see how that's even possible without an extra pair of arms. I stop and think, then keeping a tight hold on the baby with one hand, with the other I lay the scarf out as flat as I can across the bed.

'Are you coming yet?' Tris calls out.

I don't answer but ease myself back onto the bed with the baby still clamped to my front, still sleeping. *Don't you start wriggling!* I reach around with my spare hand to find one end of the scarf and throw it over both of us. Then I swap hands and do the same with the other hand and the other end of the scarf. Keeping very still, I let go with both hands and tug at the scarf to tighten it around us both. Is it too tight? No, it's got to be tight. That's what Eva said when I told her once that she must be squeezing all the air out of poor little

Grace. I wish Eva was here to help me now...or that I was back there. I can't be a mum all on my own.

I hinge myself up and somehow manage to tie the two ends in a knot without the baby tumbling or slipping off my front. Then I pull the bottom of the scarf down round their bottom to give them something to sit on.

'Come on then!'

'OK, I'm nearly ready. I'll be there in a minute.' I ease myself back off the bed, wait for a moment until my head stops swimming and waddle towards the door, feeling suddenly more normal with the weight of a baby on my front, even though my downstairs bits scream their reminder that the baby forced its way out down there. I steady myself on the doorframe and shudder as a chill breeze pushes past me. Under the scarf, I'm only wearing a T-shirt, and it'll be even colder out in the barn. I reach for Lori's jumper, draped over their big chair and pull it on over the top of everything. It's a loose knit sort of a jumper. The baby will be fine in there, won't it? I pull on the front of the neck hole and do my best to peer down at the top of their tiny head. 'You can still breathe down there, can't you?'

With both hands on the handrail, I descend the stairs slower than an elderly crab. As soon as I've reached the bottom, Tris grabs my hand and pulls me through the front door. The icy morning breeze wriggles its way through the jumper onto my bare arms and prickles at my back. I let go of Tris and hug myself and the baby as tightly as I dare.

Tris is already at the door of the barn. I stagger over to join them. The pungent smell of raw meat hits me as soon as we step inside. I want to get back out into the fresh air before I throw up, but that smell tells me things can't be good for poor Nelly.

Tris is squatting next to my old hiding place, behind the old tractor.

'Tris, move back a bit, let me see her.'

I gasp as I sink to my knees beside Tris. Wriggling around next to an exhausted looking Nelly are five tiny black puppies.

'See, Nelly's had babies too! Except she's had one, two, three, four, five of them!'

How did that happen? Well, I guess a bit like it happened to me. But when? I'd never seen her with any other dogs, male or female. How did Lori not know that Nelly was having pups? Or did they know?

'Can I pick one up?' Tris's wide eyes beg me to say yes.

'Well, maybe just stroke them to start with and see whether Nelly minds.'

Tris leans in to pet the puppies and before I can stop them has one on their lap. Nelly seems content with it, though, and I reach out to give her a stroke as best I can without toppling forward or dislodging the big wad of paper between my legs. 'So, Smelly Nelly, we've both become mothers. You look like a natural, though, whereas I haven't a clue what I'm doing. Will you show me what to do?'

The light in the barn dims. Somebody's standing in the doorway. Lori must be back from the shop. I didn't hear the truck. I turn towards the door with a smile on my face. But it's not Lori.

Chapter 58

Eva

THE KID TOOK one look at Tom towering over them with his furry face and screamed. Tom stepped forward, ready to clap his hand over their mouth, but they were too quick for him and bolted past him, around Eva, and out of the door.

Nats got to her feet and wobbled as she turned to face them. Yes, she was in shock, but it all looked like such hard work for her. They'd already seen how pale and fragile she looked as she'd followed the kid across the yard. What had the neuts done to her? Tom reached out a hand to steady her, but maybe he gripped her arm too tight because she immediately yanked herself away and almost fell over, stumbling towards the door.

'Get off me. I need to go after Tris.'

'Leave them. We need to go now before they tell anyone we're here.'

Eva stepped into her path and held out a hand. 'Nats, we've come to take you back to France with us. Joe's there, and everyone else too.'

Nats sank to the floor. Tom tossed something to the ground and scooped a droopy Nats into his arms. Eva bent down to pick up what Tom had discarded.

'Where did you get this?' She recognised the device. It was like the thing Maggie jabbed her with when they were trying to get her into the helicopter after Sandra had... 'What did you do that for? We're supposed to be rescuing her, not kidnapping her.'

'Come on, let's go.'

Tom pushed past Eva and out into the light of the brightening day. Not stopping to see whether anyone was coming for them, he bounded off, past the house and on down the track in long strides. Eva hesitated for a moment by the barn door, then set off at a sprint after him. The kid stood alone in the doorway of the house. Maybe nobody else was home. Was Nats looking after them? Was she living with this kid and their parent? Why hadn't they turned her over to the police? Should Eva go back and make sure the kid was OK? No, no time. The parent could be back from the shops any minute. The cold air burnt Eva's throat as she forced herself on towards the road and the quads.

Chapter 59

Georgy

'OK, JUST SLOW down a bit again. I think it'll be round this next corner.'

'You've been saying that for the last two miles,' Cris moaned.

'Nonsense! We're barely more than two miles out of Dover.'

Cain kept silent on the back seat, but I sensed a growing agitation. Was it our bickering that was upsetting him, or was he just a bag of nerves? I was, as I wondered what we'd do next when we found the end of the track. We couldn't simply drive past saying *that's nice, we know where it is now,* could we? How would we know for sure until we walked down it, found the barn, and either found Nats or didn't?

'There it is! Stop!' It had to be this one. A track on the right-hand side, wide enough for a tractor to drive down, just after a bend in the road, and although I'd said to Cris we were barely two miles out of Dover, the numbers on the display read 4.6. Joe had said it was five miles from Dover. I craned my neck to see round Cris. 'Cris, stop! Back up a bit!'

Cain had taken his seat belt off to move across and peer out of the window. 'There're people on the track. They're running this way.'

'Then we'd better get out of here,' said Cris, 'Cain, put your belt back on, will you? We need to go.'

I shook my head. Cris is far too risk averse. 'No, it's probably joggers out for a run, and anyway, we're safe in the car. The doors are locked, and if there's any trouble, we can just drive off.' Then I turned to Cain. 'But Cain, probably best you get down, just in case.'

Another car came slowly around the bend. There was plenty of space to pass, but they pulled in neatly and stopped, right behind us. No chance to back up now. Cris reached down for the handbrake.

'I can't back up now. Let's get out of here.'

'No, wait, it's probably just a walker. There's a footpath down that track.' I leant forward to look in the wing mirror on Cris's side. The driver of the other car was getting out, but they weren't dressed for a walk.

'Cain! Get down!' Far from having made himself invisible, Cain's face was glued to the window.

'It's Tom!' Cain shouted, turning and lunging for the door handle.

'No, it's Jamieson, the psychologist. Stay in the car!' How had they found us? They must have tracked the car here all the way from the prison. Had they suspected we were hiding Cain all along?

'He's got Nats! He's got her!'

Indigo Jamieson had stopped, rooted to the spot, a hand reaching out to steady themself against their car bonnet. A giant of a person dressed all in black veered left out of the track, round the back of Jamieson's car and through an open gate into a field. And yes, though I only got a quick glimpse, they had been carrying something big, which could have been a person. A few seconds later, a slighter, black-clad figure raced after the one Cain claimed was Tom.

'And that's Eva!' Cain rattled at the door handle. I silently thanked Cris for thinking to engage the child locks. 'Let me out!'

Jamieson, overcoming their shock, resumed their advance towards us. *It's OK*, I think to myself, *the doors are locked and Cris still has the engine running*. But what to do next? If Cain was right about who the two runners were and thought they had Nats, we couldn't just drive off and leave them. Should we be getting out and helping them? But then what if Jamieson had called for backup?

I peeled my eyes away from the view in the wing mirror and on to Cris, whose eyes were as locked on to the mirror as mine had been.

'What are those?' said Cris in awe.

I twisted myself around to get a better look. Accelerating out of the field were two vehicles, the like of which I'd never seen before – the size of a small car but without a roof and with handlebars like a bike and their drivers, or riders, sat astride the top of them. They almost leapt out onto the road and skidded away.

'Quick! Turn around! We have to follow them!' Cain's body was almost in the front, between us.

'All right,' said Cris, already throwing the car around, 'but sit back and put your belt on.'

Chapter 60

Eva

EVA SAW THE hurried about-turn of the red car in her mirror, and that the smartly dressed neut who'd been standing between the cars had jumped back into the other one. She twisted the throttle to its maximum, closing the gap between her and Tom. But she was on his tail in seconds. *Come on, Tom, you need to go faster, can't you see we're being chased?* He was probably going steady because of Nats. Eva should have had Nats with her on her quad; she was the better rider. But then it would also have been better if Nats wasn't unconscious. Why did Tom have to do that? Why had Maggie let him have one of those things in the first place?

The red car was right up her backside now and the bluey-purple one wasn't far behind. She wove her quad back and forth across the road, determined not to give either car any chance to come up alongside them or pass them, box them in.

The car right behind her honked its horn. *You're not getting past.* It honked again, more urgently, then a long, loud blare of a horn sounded from another direction, from the road ahead. She yanked herself back in, into the narrow gap between Tom and the honking car, just in time for the approaching truck to hurtle past them all. It was the same truck she'd seen bumping off down the track this morning. In the brief glimpse she caught of the driver's face, it turned from furious curses through the closed window to a jaw dropped in disbelief.

The pulse in her neck throbbed against her tight, zipped-up jacket. What would Tom have done if she'd been mown down by that truck? At least it would have stopped the chase, given Tom a chance to get away from it all. Maybe she should be giving Tom and Nats that chance. She eased off the accelerator a little, steered back into the middle of the road, whilst keeping a keen eye ahead of her. She watched Tom's quad shrink as the distance between them opened up. She didn't want to be left behind, not actually left behind, as in caught, but maybe, if she could hold these cars back for long enough, it would give Tom time to get to the coast and out onto the water, away from their pursuers. As long as she didn't actually stop, she could get herself to the coast eventually. She looked at the clock on the console in front of her. Keep at this steady speed for another twenty minutes – that should give him enough time, as long as he didn't notice she was no longer behind him and slow down. They should have remembered to switch the comms back on before they set off. Then she could have told him her plan. But then at least neither of them had Maggie yabbering in their ears. No point getting updates on approaching cars now there were two of them right behind her. They just needed to keep going and watch the road.

Watch the road. Yes, that's what she still needed to be doing. She squeezed the brakes – a huge tractor was rolling out onto the road ahead. If it turned towards them, she couldn't see how she'd get past. If it turned up the road, they'd all be stuck behind it. At least Tom was already past that point. She slowed even more – as long as she didn't actually have to stop, she'd be OK. The tractor turned up the road and trundled on ahead of her without any sense of urgency. Eva shuffled on her seat, straightened her back a little, let the slower speed give her a chance to wriggle her stiff fingers. She needed to keep her cool.

They got to the T-junction. Ten of the twenty minutes had now passed. Tom should be nearly there, as long as he'd remembered which way to turn here. He would have, wouldn't he? Eva breathed a sigh of relief – the tractor was turning right. As soon as there was space for her to squeeze through, left wheels on the verge, she upped her speed and skidded around to the left, nudging the handlebars right a bit to straighten up as she came out of the corner. The red car held back, waiting for a bigger gap, it looked pretty new – the owner probably didn't want to risk a scratch, even in the midst of a chase. Eva grinned, feeling the rush of power coursing through her as she opened up the throttle.

The driver of the red car could afford to hold back, worrying about scratches; once onto the wide straighter road, they put their foot down and Eva watched her mirror as it sucked the car back towards her, like they were joined by a piece of elastic and the car had got caught on something for a moment before pinging forward again. She tweaked the throttle, but it was already maxed out, and by the look of it, the red car was still only cruising. The other car, the purply-blue one, whined its way towards them from the junction, struggling to catch up. If it had just been that car, Eva could have shaken them off, but not the red one.

They raced along at Eva's top speed, the red car glued to her back. Other cars and two huge lorries zoomed past them, hurrying off in the opposite direction, some honking their horns at the sight of the convoy of three that grew to at least ten, headed by the strange-looking vehicle and its even stranger-looking rider. Whenever there was a gap in the traffic on the opposite side, Eva expected the red car to pull out and rumble past, boxing her in between the red and the purple. What if others of the growing number of cars behind her had also now joined the chase? If they wanted to, they could easily surround her and force her to stop.

Up ahead was the right turn she needed to take. What should she do if there were cars in the way when she needed to turn right? She forced herself to slow a little. A line of cars was coming towards her right now, but after that white one, there was a gap. If that gap lined up with the right turn, she'd be fine.

She swerved her way through the gap; the red car swung round behind as if she was towing it. The blueypurple one hung back and was then forced to wait for the next gap. Not far now; maybe that one would never catch up.

Soon they were in amongst houses with parked cars lining either pavement – the ominous silhouettes they'd sped past last night, soon after they came off the beach. She took what she knew was her final left turn, now weaving around the parked cars on a narrowing lane, just one more right to go. She rode like the road belonged to her – ignoring the protests of drivers who had to slam on their brakes as she careened past when it was their right of way. She couldn't stop now, even if people were spotting the quad and maybe calling it in to the police. A couple more minutes and she'd be away from this land for good.

She steered around the final right turn without slowing, without looking to see if anything was coming. Nothing was, but it took a while for her to gulp her heart back to where it should be, only for it to leap back up and almost choke her as she almost hit a walker with their dog. Then, there it was – the sea – and the red car was still back at the final junction. She found a gap between the rocks and veered off the road and onto the pebbles. They wouldn't be able to follow her now, except on foot.

No sign of Tom, either on the beach or beyond. Hopefully, he was way out there by now. She rolled over the pebbles towards the beckoning waves, took one hand at a time off the handlebars to give each arm a good shake. She entered the water and stopped, her wheels still firmly on the ground. She should put the comms back on to let them know she was on her way, and Tom and Nats too, she hoped. Should she wait for confirmation somehow? Find out if Maggie had sight of them from her satellite?

'Hello, it's Eva. Can you hear me?'

'Eva, wait!'

A voice called out to her, but it was not from her earpiece. She twisted around to look. A lumbering figure was bounding down the beach towards her. She should go now, before they got to her, but how did they know her name? She squinted. *No, it can't be. It is. It's Cain!*

Cain splashed into the water and threw himself at the quad.

'Cain, how did you...? Where did you come from?'

Eva glanced back up to the road. The two cars that had been pursuing her were both parked on the road now, with doors open. There were three figures that she could see around the cars, but rather than racing down the beach towards Eva and Cain, they appeared to be getting into some sort of fight amongst themselves. Were some of them members of DiG who had rescued Cain from the police perhaps? How had they known where to find Nats? Was Joe's parent, Georgy, involved somehow? Joe said they were the only other person who knew where he'd left Nats. They'd promised to go back for Nats and bring her over to France, but Joe was certain they must have been arrested after his escape. Should she go and find out who they were, tell them that Joe was safe in France?

A line of blue flashing lights raced along the road towards the parked cars.

'Eva, we have to go now!'

'Hello, Eva? Yes, we can hear you.' Eva had never been so glad to hear Maggie's voice. 'And we can see where you both are too. Tom's already nearly at the boat, but he's not got his comms on. Did you get the girl?'

'Yes, we did. And I've got Cain too.'

Eva didn't wait for a reply before driving out onto the waves, her tired hands grasping the handlebars and Cain clinging to her middle.

Chapter 61

Georgy

'GEORGY! LEAVE THEM! Let's get out of here!'

I shook Cris off my back and marched on Jamieson, shoving them to the ground. Before they could get back up again, I leapt on top of them and pinned them down. I'd learnt to defend myself in prison, and to launch a pre-emptive attack when necessary. I was pleased to witness terror in their eyes. They may be a bully, but they'd never had to deal with physical violence against them.

'Scared of me now, are you?' I shouted in their face 'Well so you should be, you devious, lying piece of shit! I did three months in prison because of you. If you hadn't stopped me from seeing Cain, if you hadn't gone behind everyone's backs to try to get surgeons to mutilate him, if you hadn't lied about it all in court... But you've failed. Hear that? You've failed. I don't care what anyone does to me now, because Cain is free, and so is Nats, and they're both going somewhere safe where you and your surgeon friends can't touch them.'

There was a screech of tyres and the sky started flashing blue as I spat my words at Jamieson's face. Cris danced around us, still urging me to stop it, to get up and to get back in the car. But I knew there was no point now. The police were here and I was ready for another spell inside. I didn't care, because I was certain that Joe was safe.

'You go if you want to. I'll tell them this was all my idea. I'll even tell them it was me driving if you like. Go back to your comfy life in Birmingham.'

Rough hands reached down, dragged me off the psychologist and cuffed my wrists tight behind my back. As they wrestled me towards the waiting police cars, I forced myself round to look for Cris. They too were cuffed and being escorted to a police car.

'I'm sorry, Cris,' I called out to my co-parent and now co-conspirator.

I was glad we'd chosen to keep Joe, and if I could've gone back in time, I'd have still made all the same decisions again. But Cris had left all this behind them when they moved back to Birmingham. I shouldn't have dragged them back into it.

Chapter 62

Eva

Eva's weary hands held the quad steady as other, stronger hands hauled Cain up into the boat. Someone then gently prised her fingers loose, gripping her arm, encouraging her with words she still didn't understand.

With a big, heavy cape thrown over her shoulders, she was guided to a bench and seated beside Cain. Her hands were closed for her around a steaming mug of hot chocolate.

'How is she? How's Nats?'

It was Maggie's voice that replied, direct in her ear. 'Louis tells me she'll be OK, and so will the baby, but she's still out from the shot Tom gave her, which is probably for the best.'

Eva's anger at Maggie and Tom found her a new boost of energy. 'Probably for the best? We'd have got on much better without that shot. There was no need for it, and you shouldn't have even let Tom have one of those things.' She staggered to her feet. 'Where is she? I need to see her.'

Nobody on the boat was there to respond. Everyone was busy, manoeuvring her quad back onboard, pressing buttons to wind the anchor back in, readying the boat for the return to France. Eva scanned the deck, but there was no sign of Nats or Tom.

'They've got her down in the cabin. Eva, did you know about the baby?' Maggie, sitting miles away in France, seemed to be the only one listening to her right now. Did Maggie say baby?

'Baby? What baby?' Eva stumbled towards the cabin.

'Nats' baby,' came the reply. 'She had a baby strapped to her front. Tiny, less than a day old from what Louis can tell, and before you ask, it's definitely Nats' baby.'

Eva stopped, reached out for a nearby piece of railing to steady herself. Her head swam. How can Nats have a baby? Was it Joe's? Had they? Or Cain's? No, it was Nats' bleeding that led to the trouble on the train and Cain getting caught. So after that. Must be Joe's, but he'd never let on. She knew he was fond of Nats, but had they really gone that far? What other explanation could there be? Eva switched off her comms. She didn't need to hear any more from Maggie. She needed to see for herself. She carried on towards the cabin, reaching out for whatever she could hold as the boat moved off, bouncing over the waves.

Before she could enter the cabin, she was caught by Louis, bustling out with his medical bag. Dropping his bag on the floor, he grabbed Eva's arms, pressing his fingers against the inside of her wrist. He held her face for a moment and studied her before nodding, pushing her into the cabin and leaving them to it.

Nats was laid out on one of the two bunks, her face deathly white. How awful for her, to have a baby with nobody around who understood. Eva thought back to the nightmare they'd had with Kitty when they realised what was happening. She'd vowed since then to always be alert for the earliest of signs and always be ready for the birth, whether for one of the girls or for the ewes. Nats was lucky to be alive, and so was her baby. Maggie had said the baby was OK, hadn't she? What had they done with the baby now?

Tom was sitting on the other bunk. At first, Eva didn't notice the tiny scrap of life cradled in his arms. He looked up at her. 'Hi. We did it then. And even brought back an extra one.'

'An extra two.'

'What?'

'Haven't they told you? We've got Cain too.'

Tom frowned in disbelief. 'But that's impossible.'

'I know, but it's true. He's up on deck now. I guess I shouldn't really have left him there. I should go and fetch him down here. I didn't think – I just wanted to see Nats.'

'Is he OK?'

'I think so. Still not quite sure how he ended up on the back of my quad. But then I don't get how Nats has a baby either.' Eva nodded towards the little bundle. 'Have you looked at what it is yet?'

Tom nodded. 'Come and sit down.'

Eva looked back towards the door. 'I should probably go and check on Cain. But just tell me what it is. Then I can give Cain the news too.'

'It's not as simple as that.' Tom paused a moment. 'Eva, the baby's a neut.'

'What? It can't be.'

'Well, I'm no expert on these things, but even I can see it's not a boy and I don't think things look right down there for a girl either. Louis has checked too and I could see from his face that he was surprised at what he saw and was then straight on the comms with Maggie.'

Eva reached for her comms unit and switched it back on. 'Maggie? Is Tom right? Is the baby a neut?'

The only reply was an apologetic French voice. Maggie had obviously moved on to more pressing matters.

A horrible thought crossed Eva's mind. She didn't even want to entertain it, but it had to be considered, didn't it, before they got back to France and saw Joe? 'What if the baby isn't Joe's?'

'What? No, it has to be, doesn't it? Who else's would it be?'

'She was living with neuts, right?'

Tom nodded.

'But they hadn't operated.'

Tom shook his head. 'Don't think so. No, they can't have done, could they? Not if she's just had a baby.'

'What if they decided not to operate? What if they decided to experiment on her instead?'

Chapter 63

Nats

I'M AWAKE, BUT it doesn't smell right. A sharp smell tickles my nostrils. Like the smell of the stuff Lori uses to clean up after I've been sick, except without the actual smell of the sick it always goes with. My throat doesn't feel like I've thrown up recently. It's months since I last vomited – I'd almost forgotten the rough throat feeling, but that smell brings it right back.

Things don't feel right either. My bed feels higher up. How does that work – being able to tell how far off the floor you are without looking? The bed is flatter too, and the air warmer, but not a cosy warmth. It's being blown around by something noisy and persistent. What's wrong with the window?

There are other sounds. Beeps and whirrs. I had the baby, didn't I? Lots of blood. Lots of pain – like I was being peeled and turned inside out. Has Lori brought me to a hospital? They promised they wouldn't, and I was fine, wasn't I? They went shopping. Did they come back? What if they came back to find the baby was really poorly. I haven't fed it yet, and it was just sleeping – sleeping against my chest. Where is it now? Where's the baby?

I remember strapping it to my front so I could go downstairs with Tris, to see Nelly's puppies. But then Tom and Eva appeared. I must have been dreaming – I mean, Tom and Eva! Even if they somehow knew where I was, the two of them working together to come and rescue me? Don't be stupid! I love them both, but they're like worst of enemies. So if I dreamed that bit, did I also dream the puppies, and strapping the baby to my front? It's not there now. Perhaps I nearly died when I had the baby, like Kitty actually did, and then Lori *had* to take me to the hospital to save me and the baby. But if I'm in hospital, I'm done for. Sweat drips into my eyes. My armpits go cold and wet, but the rest of me is way too warm. What will they do to me? They'll take the baby away from me for sure.

'Joey? Where's Joey?'

'I'm here, Nats,' Joe's voice says, clearer than I've ever heard it in my head before – like he's really in the room here with me. But he can't be. Not unless we're both in the hospital, having our operations. Please no, if they've got me, please let Joe still be free. My downstairs bits throb. But that's just from having the baby, isn't it? My nipples are throbbing too, and my udders are so tight, I think they might burst. I need to feed my baby.

'Where's Joey? He needs feeding.'

I rub my eyes to get the dryness out of them and start to sit up. Owww! I'm so achy and sore downstairs, all over, and the brightness isn't helping. Way too bright, too noisy. What have they done to me? A blurry figure comes towards me.

'Get away from me! Don't touch me!'

'It's OK, Nats, it's Joe. You're safe now. The baby is safe too. I've fed them, with a bottle, and they're sleeping again. But I can bring them over if you like. Is Joey what you've called them?'

'Joe? What are you doing here? Where am I? Where's Tris, and Lori?'

A warm hand takes mine. Joe's hand. His thumb gently strokes the back of my hand. 'You're in France, Nats. I'm sorry, I shouldn't have left you. I should have stayed in the barn with you until your ankle was better.'

The brightness is dimming, or my eyes are getting used to it, so I let them open a bit more. It really is Joe staring back at me, stroking my hand. A tear runs down his cheek and splashes onto my wrist.

'I thought I'd never see you again.' More tears flow down his face.

'Me too.' My own eyes blur with tears.

'Can I say hello properly?'

'What?'

He leans in towards me, kisses my left cheek, leaving the wetness of his tears there, then he's kissing my right cheek as well. 'That means hello, here in France.'

'Hello, Joe,' I say. 'Is this real, or am I dreaming?'

'You're not dreaming.' He leans towards me again and this time wraps his arms around me and holds me in a big squeeze, just like he did after he thought I'd been run over by that train.

I've so missed him. My eyes fill up all over again. I'm not on my own anymore.

'Oww!'

Joe springs back. 'Sorry, did I hurt you? Where are you hurting?'

'I hurt all over Joe, but no, it's just you were squashing my udders. They're about to burst. What? It's not funny!'

He's not actually laughing, but I can see there's one in there, behind his blotchy face, still covered in tears. That face I know so well, except I feel I'm seeing it for the first time all over again.

'Sorry, no, it's just you talking about your udders as if you're a cow or a sheep. I've missed you, Nats.' And then he's crying again too.

'Well what would you call them then?'

He's embarrassed now – won't look at me.

'Where is the baby? You know they're your baby too, don't you? We're parents, Joe.'

'Yes, I know.' He doesn't say any more. Still doesn't look at me.

'Do you think we can be parents?'

'I don't know.'

I try to slow my pounding heart by taking a long breath in and then letting it out even slower. That's something Joe taught me to do, that he got from Georgy. What does he mean by *I don't know*? Is it *I don't know whether I want to be a parent with you, Nats*? Or like me, *I don't know if I can be a parent at all*?

Chapter 64

Nats

I SHOULD BE HAPPY. I've been rescued. I always knew I couldn't stay hidden with Lori and Tris forever, but I didn't really have a plan for where to go or how to get there, and now that's all been solved for me and even better, Joe and Cain are both here too, and everyone else. Almost everyone. Lori, Tris, and Nelly aren't here, and nor is Sandra. It doesn't surprise me she didn't want to leave the island, but what she did was pretty drastic, unless it really was an accident. I know others say I have no sense of danger, but I used to hate sitting up at that watch station all on my own, knowing one step too far in the dark or one gust of wind could land me down on the rocks, far below, dead. Accident or not, I don't think Sandra would have ever been happy coming here.

I want to be happy here. Joe says not all of France is like this hospital or the impossibly tall buildings that fill the view out of the window. He's told me all about Dylan and Domineek and they sound lovely, and maybe I'll be happier when we go there and I'll forget about how happy I was in the end with Lori and Tris and Nelly. What must they be thinking? Tris will be having nightmares, and Lori will be punishing themself for leaving me and Tris to go shopping. I hope they're not shouting at Tris because of it. I hope Nelly's doing okay too, with all those little puppies. I can't imagine having five babies all at the same time. I'm still not sure I want the one I've got.

The magic doors swish open, and Joe comes back in with our screaming baby. I try to smile for him.

'I think Joey's hungry again. Shall I use the bottle, or do you want to have another go? Eva's still here with the children if you want me to go and get her. You know she said she was happy to help you work out how to do it, if you want.'

I guess I should have another go. It might help me feel more like a mum. 'Okay, you can go and get Eva. But take the baby with you, please.' I feel bad saying that. 'Eva says it's best if I'm relaxed before we try it.'

Joe seems to be getting used to the idea – if the baby's not in its cot, I know that Joe will have them. My breath catches for a moment in my battered-feeling chest. Maybe if Joe's all right with this, I can be too. Soon.

Eva was convinced for a while that the neuts had done something to me to make me pregnant – like they'd put a baby inside me or something – and that's why it's a neut. But the doctors have apparently done a test on them that proves they've got something of Joe in them as well as me. Nobody can explain why they've come out neut, though. I bet all the other girls are coming up with reasons for my freak baby. What will it be like for the baby when they're older, knowing how they're different from everyone else?

'I can't do this, Eva.'

'Yes, you can, you're doing fine. It just takes a bit of getting used to.' Eva reaches out and squeezes my hand.

We got them to latch on, eventually, with me holding my breath and gritting my teeth to stop giving them a fright by shouting out at the pain. I guess it doesn't feel that bad, now we're connected up properly. Eva promises it will hurt less and be quicker when we both get used to what we're doing. But even as I feel the milk flowing out of me into the baby – into Joey – I still can't feel any love.

'No, I mean I can't be a mum. I thought it would be easier than this – that it would come more naturally, like it does for you.'

Eva doesn't say anything. She just looks at the floor. Have I said something wrong? Maybe she doesn't find it easy either. Shit, I'd forgotten about how things have changed for her so much too – losing Sandra, nearly losing Peter.

'Sorry, I didn't mean...'

She looks up at me. There's a tear in her eye. 'No, it's okay, it's just... I've not been a good mum recently. So don't try to be too much like me. Anyway, we're all different, and different is good, right?'

Epilogue

Eva

ELEVEN MICRODRONES ROSE up into the frosty December air. Little Charlie carried on smiling and waving at them, long after Eva had lost sight of the black specks. Perhaps his young eyes were keener. Everyone else had already rushed or drifted back into the warm.

Eva dug her hands deeper into her pockets and tucked her chin down into the scarf Nats had insisted she have after she said it was just like one her parents used to have. It was odd – she remembered the scarf but not which of her parents it had belonged to. If only their scarf had been visible on the satellite images, maybe she'd then have confidently picked out her parents' house, assuming they still lived there, of course. As it was, she'd concluded she couldn't be certain, so decided not to waste a microdrone on a message that would probably never get to the right people. Maggie had insisted it didn't matter; she could still send a message, even if she wasn't sure.

But there was Charlie to consider too. He was too young to remember even which part of Britain his parents might be in, let alone pick out a particular building on a particular street. He'd been very grown up and philosophical about it really, considering the whole scheme had been his idea in the first place. But Eva saw him watching from the other side of the camera as others recorded their messages. Nats had seen it too, and when it was her turn, she'd beckoned him to join her, Joe, and Joey on her video. Then, of course, Katie, Peter, and Grace had all insisted they should be in it too, so the end of the message had disintegrated into a cacophony of excited squeals and bouncing.

Charlie dropped his arm to his side. He looked around, apparently aware for the first time that he and Eva were the only ones left outside.

'Shall we go and find the others then?' Eva held out her hand towards him. 'I think there's cake and hot chocolate.'

Charlie smiled, nodded, and took her hand.

Lori

'Oi, settle down! What's all the fuss about, Nelly?'

Lori hadn't heard her bark like that in weeks – not since before the pups arrived. Lori let go of the wheelbarrow handles and ambled over to see what she was getting worked up about. The pups were in the middle of the yard, in their usual tangle of legs and tails. Sometimes Nelly would ignore them and let them get on with their play. At other times, she'd move in and give one or two of them a gentle nip, keep them in line. Today, though, she was agitated about something – circling the pups, shouting at them but not getting close, sometimes pouncing in towards them as if to try to chase them off something.

There was something. Something other than puppies in the middle of the scrum. Lori waded in and pulled them off, one by one, to see what it was. Whatever it was, it was a bit mangled. Those blummin' walkers dropped all sorts of litter on their way through the yard.

But this was no ordinary litter. This had the look of something that had somehow dropped out of the sky.

Lori strode back to the house, almost squashing several scampering, feet-nipping puppies on the way. 'Gerroff, you silly fluff balls. Whatever it is, you're not having it.'

Back in the kitchen, Lori poured out a bit more food into their bowls. It was a bit early, but it made them forget about the thing now sat in the middle of the kitchen table and their yipping soon subsided.

The thing was some sort of machine with tiny spinning parts – or at least, it looked like they would have spun freely before those puppies got hold of it. Lori turned the thing over and broke out in a grin – the first smile in weeks that wasn't forced. There, strapped to the underneath of the strange little machine, was an envelope. An envelope with their names on it – *To Lori, Tris, Nelly, and the puppies* – in *her* unmistakable, childlike scrawl. Amazing she could write at all really, given she'd never been to school.

TRIS DRAGGED ALONG behind Lori, as they had done every day recently on the way to and from the bus. Shouting at them had done no good and Lori had regretted it straight away. Tris burst into tears at the slightest incident these days, at school as well as at home, apparently. They'd been lucky not to get a visit from child protection, given how concerned the school was about the changes they'd seen in Tris. But hopefully, what was waiting for them at home would change all that.

'Come on, Tris, I've got a surprise for you!'

The weight pulling on Lori's arm suddenly lightened, as did the tone in Tris' voice. 'What is it? Have Nats and Joey come back?'

'Well, no, but...well, you'll see when we get home.'

The drag on Lori's arm returned. 'If it's not Nats and Joey then I'm not interested.'

'Oh yeah? Well, we'll see won't we.'

It took them longer than ever to trudge the short distance back to the house.

Tris stared at the thing on the table as Lori pushed the door open. 'Is that the surprise?' There was even a slight sparkle in Tris's eye as they climbed up onto a chair to take a closer look at the strange contraption littering the middle of the kitchen table. 'What is it?'

'Ah, well, I'm not quite sure, but what's more exciting is what it brought to us. Take your bag and coat off and then come and sit down here with me.'

Lori helped Tris with their bag and coat and then pulled them up onto their knee. 'Have a look at this,' they said, handing Tris the device which, apart from what it did when you opened it, was just like a greetings card but with the pictures on the inside.

Tris took the 'card' from Lori and turned it over a few times without opening it. Lori held their breath. *Why aren't they opening it?*

'Well, open it then!'

Tris gasped as the black of the tiny screen inside resolved itself into an image of Nats, sitting on a sofa.

'It's Nats!' Tris missed the wave from Nats as they turned around to quiz Lori. 'Is this from Nats? Where is she?'

'Yes, now shh, and listen.'

*Hello, Tris, hello, Lori, and make sure you
show this to Nelly and all her pups too.
I'm sorry I left before you got back from
the shops, Lori. I wouldn't have done,
but I wasn't given much choice and it all
happened so quickly. Sorry too, Tris, I hope
you haven't been having nightmares about
what happened, but I want you to know I'm
OK, and the people who came into the barn
were actually friends. They're here with
me now.*

Nats beckoned with her hand and two other people move into view, sit either side of her on the sofa, and wave. When the big hairy one appeared, Tris turned and hid in Lori's chest for a moment.

*This is Tom and Eva. I'm not surprised you
screamed when you saw them, especially
Tom, but you know what? They were actually
scared of you.*

The two strangers in the picture nodded.

*They were scared you might go and fetch
someone else from the house to stop them
from taking me with them. So that's why
they took me away with them so quickly.*

*Anyway, now I'm in a place called France,
which is across the other side of the sea.
You might have seen it. If you take a trip
out to the coast, which will be easier to
do now you haven't got to worry about me
anymore, do it on a clear day and look out*

across the sea, and you'll see some other land, far away on the other side of the sea. Of course, I've not seen it myself because we didn't really have time to stop and look when we left, but Joe tells me you can definitely see it.

Of course, I haven't told you yet that Joe's here too. That's how Tom and Eva knew where to look for me, but it was lucky really that Nelly had gone into the barn to have her pups because they wouldn't have dared to come and look for me in the house, and if anything, they hoped to find some sign or message from me in the barn, from when I was hiding in there, before you found me. They wouldn't have believed I'd actually be living with the two of you, and I wouldn't have come out of the house while they were here looking for me unless you'd dragged me out to see the puppies, Tris.

So Joe was the first to arrive here in France. He had to leave without me because... well, I can't explain all that now because I've been told I've got to keep this message short. But then the people here in France, who are more like me, Joe, Tom, and Eva than they are like you two, except they're not really that different...we're all people, aren't we? So anyway, they were able to go to my other friends and bring them here. Well, all of them except you two, because you're my friends, of course, and one other who's called Cain, but he's been

> *found too, and he came over on the same boat as me, which is all so bizarre.*

Nats looked distracted for a moment, like someone was talking to her from behind the camera. Tom and Eva got up from the sofa and stepped out of view.

> *Sorry, I haven't told you about Joey yet, have I? You must be wondering how they are, and where they are. Well, Joey's doing well.*

Nats beckoned again.

> *And here's Joey, with Joe.*

Another kid, who, like Nats also looked like they should be in school, came to sit with Nats on the sofa and in their arms was the baby – Joey. The kid nodded and smiled and then sat there gazing at Nats as she continued to prattle on. Surely, it was not natural for kids this young to be parents, was it?

> *So Joey's doing really well. We were in a hospital here at first, so the doctors could check we were both OK. That was really boring, but at least I didn't need to worry about them finding out I was a girl because that was obvious, and it doesn't matter over here. I was a bit worried about what they'd think of Joey, because most people here are like me and Joe and the others – male or female – but I've been told not everyone is, and so hopefully, Joey will grow up knowing there are others like them and*

> *that although they might be different from most people, that's OK because different is good. And I'll always remember to tell them about the two of you and how you're good too. So I hope you haven't been worrying about me too much, and now you know where I am, and that me and Joey are both fine.*

She looked up above the camera view again and nodded.

> *Anyway, I'm being told I really do need to finish this message now, but before I do, I have to introduce you to Charlie.*

She beckoned several times before a little kid stepped into shot and stood there, grinning nervously out at them.

> *It was Charlie who had the idea to send these messages, and Tris, when I first met you, you reminded me quite a lot of Charlie. Oh, and now the others want to come and say hello too. Hang on.*

The whole image wobbled.

> *So this is...*

There was so much noise from the three other kids that bounced into view, waving, that Nats' final words were lost. Then Nats was waving and the image faded to nothing.

Georgy

'THANK YOU, BOSS,' I said as I stepped once again over the raised threshold of the prison's outer door. I mustn't make a habit of this.

I half expected they might say something back this time, like *and let's not see you back here*. But no. Like last time, the door was simply slammed shut behind me and I was outside, alone in the cold. The tarmac was tinged white and the soles of my shoes, which had long ago worn down to almost nothing, threatened to slip out from under me and land me on my backside before I'd even taken a step. I stood as still as I could and looked around. Where were they? Unlike last time, they'd told me this time they were coming. Perhaps they'd had second thoughts.

I started to shuffle towards the car park, though if they're not here, I'll have to go and get a bus or something. There was no hint of red amongst the few vehicles parked there.

I was almost there and there was still no sign of them, when an old car with tyres as bald as the soles of my shoes skidded its way down the long road that led only here. The car came to a halt, straddling two parking spaces, and Cris jumped out, having to catch hold of the roof rails to avoid taking a tumble on the ice.

'Georgy, sorry, I should have been here waiting for you. You wouldn't believe how many traffic lights I had to stop at between here and the motorway. It was worse than when we went to pick up Joe, all those years ago. Do you remember that?'

'Of course I remember.' How could I forget the first time we met our son, handed over to us in a layby, like contraband?

Cris walked round the car to meet me and held out a hand to take my bag. 'This all you've got? They do give you back everything you go in with, don't they?'

'Yes, I don't own much these days. Anyway, what's this?' I nod towards the car. 'What happened to the red one?'

'Oh, nothing. I sold it, that's all. Decided it was a bit too fast for me.'

I narrowed my eyes as Cris held the passenger door open for me. 'Is this one safe?'

'Yeah. I mean, it needs a bit of work. The journey here's reminded me it probably needs new tyres, but it handles fine as long as you go gently.' They saw my raised eyebrows. 'I'll take it steady on the way back, I promise.'

Setting aside all my risk-analysis instincts, I sank down into the baggy passenger seat. By the time Cris had made it round to the driver's door and settled behind the wheel, I'd worked out why they'd really traded in their smart new red car for this old banger.

'Did you buy me a shorter sentence?'

Ever since the judge pronounced the sentence, I'd been puzzling over their leniency. I'd expected to go down for longer this time – for a second offence, committed just hours after they'd let me out. I'd been warned not to expect much sympathy, even though I was pleading guilty.

Cris didn't answer, focusing instead on scrubbing at the windscreen, which was already steaming up.

'But you loved that car!' I'd only seen them drive it the once, but that was enough to see it was their pride and joy.

'Yeah, well, people are more important than cars.' Cris eased the car around and crawled out onto the road with both hands clamped to the wheel. 'Anyway, take a look in the glovebox – I've brought something you'll want to see. I wanted to bring it when I visited last week, but I'd never have got it past security, and I didn't want to just tell you about it.'

'What is it?' I tugged on the glovebox catch but couldn't get it open.

'Oh, sorry, just give it a bash underneath. Not too hard – don't want to set the airbag off. That's it, now it should open.'

A plain white card dropped out and landed between my feet. I bent down to pick it up, tucked my thumb into the fold. It was making a noise – talking.

'What the –'

'Close it, and then open it when you can see it properly. Hang on, it's that way up.'

'You concentrate on driving!'

I opened the card and there he was – our son, with his deep voice and looking bigger and more grown up than ever, like nine years had passed, not nine months, since I'd seen him last.

> *Hi, Cris, hi, Georgy. You will make sure Georgy sees this, won't you, Cris? I hope Cain's memory is as good as he says it is, and he did pick out the right house, otherwise, there'll be some pretty shocked people somewhere out there in Birmingham, finding a strange flying object landing in their garden with this attached to it.*

So this is a message to let you know that I made it, and I'm well, and happy – particularly now Cain and Nats are here too. The people here have been really kind. We were right – they are like us, male and female. Well, mostly. And they found the island and brought everyone back from there. Or nearly everyone. Thank you for all you did for Cain. I don't know how you managed it, but you've been amazing. Both of you. I have tried to persuade Cain to do this message with me, but he's refusing to be on camera, so you'll just have to take my word for it, and the fact this message has even got to you, that Cain made it here and he's OK and was able to show us where Cris lives now.

There is someone else. Well, two people actually, that I want to introduce to you. First of all, this is Nats.

Hello, Cris, Hello, Georgy. Thank you for trying to come and...

Oi, this one's my message! Cris, I know you've already met Nats, and I'm sorry we didn't get to spend more time with you. Georgy, I know from what Cain's told me that if Tom and Eva hadn't got there first, you were about to keep your promise to find Nats and bring her over here, and Cain too. I still can't believe you all turned up to find her at the same time.

Tom and Eva were lucky to find Nats actually, because she wasn't hiding in the barn anymore. She'd been found by the owner of the farm, who's called Lori.

Well, it was really Lori's kid Tris and their dog Nelly who found me first, but when Lori found out I was there, they brought me into their house and looked after me. So I wasn't hiding in the barn all that time.

Yes, so if you wanted to meet them, Nats is sure they would welcome you, and if you thought you could, it would be good if you could show them this message. Nats has sent them one of these too, but we can never be certain that it's got to them. But seeing as you know where they live, we can ask you to go and see them.

I know that if you had made it over here with Nats or Cain, you'd have been made very welcome, and still would be, if you decided to try to make the crossing.

Joe, we still need to introduce –

Yes, I know, I'm just getting on to that.

And there's someone else I think you'd want to meet if you did come here. I'm sorry if this is a bit of a shock. It was for me. But this is Joey, and Joey is your grandchild.

THE END

Acknowledgements

The first group of people I'd like to be able to thank are all the literary agents who turned down my submission of *Joe with an E*, including those who never replied. It is thanks to these people, and nuggets of advice on social media and online writers' forums, that I got on and wrote this sequel long before *Joe with an E* was published, meaning we were able to publish it so soon after *Joe with an E*.

One piece of advice I kept on receiving was that agents and publishers don't want debut novels that absolutely require a sequel. The key phrase to use in submission letters should have been '*Joe with an E* is a standalone novel with series potential'. But I couldn't say that, because *Joe with an E* concludes with some significant loose ends. Perhaps the commercially sensible thing would have been to change the ending so that it could stand alone. But I didn't want to do that.

Another piece of advice was that most authors' debut novel isn't the first novel they actually wrote, so if you've pitched a novel and received no interest, the best thing to do is put it away in a drawer and start writing something new...though probably not a sequel to the novel for which you've not gained any traction. But that's what I decided to do, to get out of the unending loop of editing and pitching *Joe with an E* and to see whether writing the sequel might change my views on how *Joe with an E* ends. It didn't.

Thank you to my publisher, Debbie, firstly for agreeing to a timescale for *Them and Us* before we'd even got *Joe with an E* published, so that we could put a publication date in the back of *Joe with an E*. And thank you for making it happen, despite everything else you've had on your plate.

Thank you to fellow Beaten Track author Jennifer Burkinshaw, who beta-read *Joe with an E*, introduced me to her publisher, and was then also willing to beta-read *Them and Us*. It's so helpful to have someone who's happy to bat ideas back and forth. I'm afraid I stuck to my guns with keeping Joe away from the reader for so much of the book. He's just not the main character anymore.

Thank you, Nicki, for proofreading the final manuscript. I'm optimistic that this one will have as few typos in it as *Joe with an E*, if not fewer.

The observant reader will notice that the artwork for *Them and Us* is by a different artist to *Joe with an E*. Andy Thornton, who created the cover for *Joe with an E*, had too many other commissions to do *Them and Us*, so my niece, Amelia, agreed to take it on. Amelia, what you have created is stunning. You've succeeded in making the two covers look like they belong together, even though the artist is different. And sorry, Andy, I'd go as far as to say I love this cover at least as much as I do the one for *Joe with an E*.

Thank you to all the readers who have written reviews for *Joe with an E* or told me in person that you can't wait for the sequel. I hope it lives up to expectations.

Finally, thank you to my family – Jo, Martha, and Amos – for putting up with me talking about my writing and helping me to promote my books.

Content Warnings

This novel includes scenes and themes which may be upsetting to some readers, including:

- References to 'corrective surgery' to make male and female children into 'neuts'.
- Characters refusing to accept the gender identity of other characters.
- Death of a secondary character.

About the Author

Paul Rand grew up in Hampshire, UK but has now lived well over half his life in the North of England – in Yorkshire and Cumbria. After thirteen years working as an engineer, he completed teacher training and has since been working as a secondary school teacher, teaching mostly maths and business.

Paul currently teaches part-time, and when he's not teaching or writing, he's probably doing something for the Methodist church of which his wife is the minister.

Paul and his family like to holiday on small islands, both at home and abroad, referring islands that are a little off the beaten track. They have enjoyed several holidays on the Isle of Muck, which is the inspiration for the island in *Joe with an E* and *Them and Us*.

Follow Paul online at:

paulrandwriter.co.uk
facebook.com/paulrandwriter
instagram.com/paulrandwriter

Beaten Track Publishing

For more titles from Beaten Track Publishing, please visit our website:

https://www.beatentrackpublishing.com

Thanks for reading!